THE
HUGUENOT
THIEF

THE
HUGUENOT
THIEF

A NOVEL BY
L.K. CLEMENT

gatekeeper press

Published by Gatekeeper Press
3971 Hoover Rd. Suite 77
Columbus, OH 43123-2839

www.GatekeeperPress.com

ISBN Hardcover: 9780997762525
ISBN Paperback: 9780997762518
eISBN: 9780997762501

Printed in the United States of America

*This book is dedicated to my granddaughter Ava, and
my other granddaughter who knows who she is.
They are my heart.*

PROLOGUE

Charleston: July, 1969

THE PAWNSHOP HUNCHED over King Street, its cracked cantaloupe-colored stucco walls revealing ancient brick. Charles Sims stood in front of the dirty bay window that framed a mishmash of South Carolina's antebellum history. Inside the window, a tattered Confederate flag lay draped across a rough wood platform. A three-foot tall dollhouse, fashioned to resemble one of the mansions on East Bay Street, perched on the flag; a slave badge dangled from one of its miniature shutters. Finishing the display was an incongruous ESSO sign hanging from the ceiling.

Looking south, he could see no other open businesses and most of the storefronts had boards nailed across windows and doors. Like the pawnshop, the other buildings leaned over the street, each with its own variety of sad dereliction: crumbling bricks, rotten wood, fire-blackened roofs and faded stucco. He wondered if Upper King Street would ever revert to its original vibrant and bustling self.

This was the last place he would try today. Neither of the Lower King antique storeowners had taken more than a cursory glance at the item in his duffle, and on a whim, he had decided to try an Upper King pawnshop. That idea now seemed ludicrous given the obvious poverty of the area. Charles turned to walk to a phone booth visible on the next block, hoping he would find an intact yellow pages book. He would call an antique store in West Ashley. As he ambled towards the phone booth, he heard a shout behind him, "Hey, come on in. I'm open."

Charles twisted his head and saw a slight young man with an afro standing on the sidewalk. The man resembled a caramel dandelion, his black billowing hair ready to drift away with the next breeze. Charles said, "Are you talking to me?"

The man laughed. "You see anybody else out here in this heat? Come on in. We got air conditioning."

The prospect of an air-conditioned building was enough for Charles, given the unbearable heat of Charleston in July, little improvement over Saigon's weather. He trotted back to the pawnshop and pushed himself and his duffle bag through the door. A bell tinkled as the door slammed shut.

"I'm Joe," said the man, holding out his hand.

Charles shook his hand. "Charles Sims, nice to meet you." Joe was younger than Charles was, in his twenties, and his hair bobbled around him like a halo, radiating out almost to his shoulders. He also was missing two fingers from his left hand and, uncharitably, Charles wondered if the man had cut them off himself to avoid the draft.

Joe eyed Charles' army uniform. "You mean Captain Sims, don't you?"

Charles shrugged and looked around the shop. Guns hung on the wall, a few from the Civil War era. The requisite number of guitars and other musical instruments dangled from hooks on the unpainted rough brick walls—unused symbols of earnest ambitions snuffed out by lack of money, enthusiasm or talent. Towards the back of the shop was a counter, part of which lifted to allow access to a room where papers fluttered on a metal desk. Over the desk, in a rectangular hole punched into the wall was the promised air conditioner, humming and dripping condensate onto an ivy plant.

Joe walked to the counter and slapped it, saying, "Ok, whatcha got?"

"I'm not sure you'll be interested." Charles put his duffle on the antique pine floor, noticing termite tunnels, unzipped a side pocket, and then stood and put a small box in front of Joe. "My mother passed last week. I came home from Saigon to make the arrangements. She had this in a safe deposit box down at the bank."

"Sorry for your loss." Joe picked up the box and turned it around in the light. "It doesn't open?"

"Not that I can see."

Joe set the box down on the counter. It appeared to be a carved block of wood, half the size of a large brick. The corners were smooth as if rubbed by many hands. On what Charles presumed was the top was an engraved figure in a robe with its arms out. In one hand was a baby, in the other a flower. The body of the figure was composed of miniscule pieces of glass.

"This is mosaic. And this," Joe pointed to the red center of the flower with the little finger of his left hand, "could be some kind of gemstone." His voluminous hair moving gently, Joe looked up at Charles. "What do you know about this thing, Captain?"

"Please, call me Charles, not Captain."

"Ok, Charles, what do you know? Without knowing its age, or its purpose, the box isn't worth much unless that red stone is a diamond or a ruby. I don't have the right equipment to tell." Joe looked expectantly at Charles. "Your mother didn't leave any clues?"

His mother had indeed left him a letter, but Charles would not share its contents. He had never heard the family story she wrote about—that of a Huguenot girl who had stolen a reliquary from a convent and brought it to Charleston in 1685.

It was not like his mother to have kept such a story to herself, so he was skeptical, especially since she had never been religious, and, during her last five years of life, she'd had dementia. Then again, the fact that she had rented a safe deposit box just for this item made him wonder if the seemingly inconsequential object could be valuable.

After seeing the box, and reading her letter, he had left the bank, gone to the library across the street, and looked at pictures of reliquaries—beautiful gold and gem-encrusted containers that clearly were of value. Those objects were nothing like this seemingly solid piece of wood decorated with glass, with no discernable opening.

"Forget it," Charles said, grabbing the box and stuffing it back in his duffle.

Joe stepped away from Charles and reached up to touch his hair. "This shop may not look like much, but I can give you a good price for most things. You got anything else to sell?"

Charles hefted the duffle back onto his shoulder. It had been crazy for him to come to this part of town. Hospital workers were on strike, and this morning's front page was covered with a picture of visibly sweating white National Guardsmen, their guns pointed towards the mostly black shouting workers. There was another march today. A uniformed white man did not have any business loitering on streets that would be crowded with angry workers and teenage Guardsmen, their damp hands holding lethal weapons that Charles knew, from recent and nauseating experience, were easy to fire.

He'd find another way to get the money necessary to keep the farm going until he could leave the Army and come back to Charleston for good. "Maybe I'll come back later this week. I'll see what I can find in my mother's stuff," he lied.

Joe tilted his head. "Well, I won't be here, Captain. I'm headed to London tomorrow to study art. This is my uncle's store."

Charles was so astonished that he dropped his duffle bag. "London?"

Joe laughed. "I'm an artist. How else do you think I knew what a mosaic was?" He ran his hands around his hair. "This is my last day with this 'do."

Feeling his face redden, Charles stepped towards Joe and held out his hand. "Best of luck to you, Joe."

"You too, Charles. Sorry to hear about your mother. Stay safe in 'Nam."

The bell tinkled as Charles left the shop.

He stood on the sidewalk, watching the few people who were on the street move as if in slow motion, their gestures distorted by the wavy, heated air floating above the potholed blacktop. They moved as sluggishly as Neil Armstrong had when he had stepped on the moon two nights previously. Charles had watched the event, simultaneously feeling wonder and resentment; the same government that could propel men into outer space could not provide his men boots that were punji stick resistant.

He had two more days to settle everything, and then it was back to Vietnam. If the West Ashley antique store wasn't open, he'd go to Savannah. There was no strike there.

PART I

Charleston: Present Day

CHAPTER 1

A MOCKINGBIRD WOKE KATE, as it had every morning for the six months she and her husband Jack had been in this rental house. Its song was a bit louder today. Perhaps on this April morning it was calling for a mate. The bird always perched on the same branch: a branch right outside their bedroom window, a branch she had asked Jack to saw off in the hope the bird would find another location to practice its repertoire. He had reminded her that the branch was attached to an ancient live oak that couldn't be touched without prior approval from their landlord, and maybe even from the city, given the size of the tree. Their small house was in Harleston Village in downtown Charleston, a fine location to be sure, but Kate missed their former home—a cottage on the Ashley River, a house lost in the tumult of the financial downturn when they couldn't pay the mortgage. Jack's construction projects had disappeared almost overnight.

At tune number five, she sat up and pulled a strand of her hair from Jack's fist. As she slid to her side of the bed, she caught sight of her forearms, the skin puffy and red with scratches. This was the second time in the past week she had awakened to see these welts. Without telling her doctor or Jack, she had lowered the amount of lithium she took each day, attempting to find a dose that did not make her feel as if she was watching her life rather than experiencing it. This self-marking, which had occurred before in her manic episodes, meant she had lowered it too much. If Jack saw her arms, he'd demand that she return to a psychiatrist, her husband always optimistic that there would be a new psychotropic drug for Kate to try.

A fellow patient in her psychiatrist's office had once described his moods to her as a roulette wheel— mania red, depression black. He told her he never knew what color was going to come up every morning. Kate supposed a life somewhere in the middle, neither red nor black, should be her goal, but she was hoping to get a just a little of her mania, always productive, back into her life by lowering the lithium.

No matter how detailed she made the description, Jack couldn't comprehend the feeling of omnipotence a mania delivered. During the few times he had witnessed a full-fledged episode, Kate knew she must have appeared dangerous and reckless. What he observed—the endless talking, writing for days, not bathing or eating, had frightened him. From Kate's point of view, though, one of her manic episodes had helped her create her most well received work, a book on female French saints. She had been able to put herself in those women's heads, imagining their exultations and their terrors. How could she explain to anyone the intimate power of feeling that you were in the mind of someone who had been dead for centuries?

Kate showered and dressed in her daughter's bathroom. Four more days and Sara would be home for spring break. She walked over and touched her daughter's decrepit-looking teddy bear. "Little bear, she'll be home soon."

After coffee and a banana, Kate left the house and went to the small wood building in the back yard that passed for a garage. The structure held a variety of construction paraphernalia, some of which clung to her bike like spider webs. Jerking the bike free, she slammed the rickety door and heard something fall on the other side with a loud *clang*. She hoped the noise woke Jack, but not until she was gone.

Leaving early would not only avoid his questions about her arms but also serve to evade round two of an argument from the night before. He had reacted badly over her desire to attend an upcoming conference in Istanbul. The conference was a year away, and Kate was determined to go, with Jack's blessings she hoped, but without, if she had to. After the attempted coup in Turkey, and the bombings in France, he had become irrational about her traveling, and Kate was exhausted trying to explain to him how important the city of Istanbul was to a religious scholar. Besides, she had told him, the Turkish government was sponsoring the conference.

Her husband often advised her to 'get out more', believing his wife led a life too introspective, but obviously getting out more did not include going as far as Istanbul.

She was still furious, and felt spiteful and petty. Some of that was likely due to the lowered lithium, but she welcomed the anger, proof that her emotions had not been permanently sequestered by the drug.

Checking her watch, she decided to go by the French Huguenot Church on the corner of Queen and Church streets. She loved the Huguenot Church, its pink gothic spires stabbing the sky, sharp as the faith and the fear that had motivated the Huguenots to leave France. She had attended this church all her life. Most members were descendants of the original Huguenot colonists who had fled Catholic France in the late 1600s, the refugees arriving in Charleston with little more than their lives.

A half block away from the church, Kate's bike hit a cobblestone. Her forward momentum threw her into the grass along the narrow road, thankfully into a patch free of broken beer bottles and dog crap. She stood, saw the tire was flat, rejected the idea of pushing the bike all the way to the college, and pulled out her cell. She wouldn't call Jack to come get her; she'd call her boss, Adam. A car pulled up behind her.

"Dr. Strong," a voice called.

"Yes?" she said, looking up from her phone.

"Do you need some help?"

She recognized Samuel Sadat, owner of an Oriental rug store in town. "That would be lovely, thank you." He stood half out of his car, another man—his brother Imran she presumed—in the front seat. She thought the two were Russian, and seemed to remember that they had been in Charleston for two years. Samuel was plump and jovial, and was the first person customers saw when entering the rug shop. His brother, always lurking in the back of the shop when Kate visited, looked like the mask of a pharaoh, brooding and mysterious.

"We are going to the airport. May we drop you off somewhere? You are not hurt, are you?"

Kate looked at him and thought of her options. She could push the bike, wait for Adam or accept the ride. Calling Jack was still not an option. "No, I'm not hurt, and I'd very much appreciate a ride—if you don't mind putting my old bike in your beautiful car!"

She and Samuel Sadat wedged the bike in the Mercedes' trunk and she got into the back seat, chatting with Samuel about their store's newest carpet acquisitions, none of which she could afford. Imran said nothing. Five minutes later, she had thanked

Samuel and was climbing the long, wide staircase to her second floor office.

"Kate." She turned on the stairs and saw Adam Chalk—her boss, friend, and head of the history department—at the door of his office. He was not sporting his typical grin and seemed preoccupied. They had worked together for over a decade, and she knew his moods almost as well as she knew Jack's. Her research into Christian saints and relics couldn't neatly be classified by the college, so the administration had temporarily put her under Adam's bailiwick. That temporary assignment was now ten years old.

"Adam, you're in early. I thought our staff meeting was later this morning."

"No, no, you're right. I have a guest waiting to meet you."

Kate walked through his assistant's empty office to a small conference room. The College had managed to shoehorn an antique mahogany table into the space, which had a view of the oak-draped courtyard to make up for its lack of size. A man was standing by the table, looking at her with a slight smile. He was a tall, athletic, studious-looking man with a dark moustache and swept-back hair that blended into graying sideburns. He wore a dark suit and tie, an uncommon uniform in Charleston where the unofficial suit, if a man bothered to wear a suit, was of seersucker.

"Kate, I'd like to introduce you to Dr. Kamal Atay from the University of Istanbul. He has an interesting opportunity for the College."

Atay shook hands with Kate in the manner of men who never shake hands with women, his fingertips barely reaching her palm. All three stood until Adam gestured for everyone to sit down. He offered refreshments, but Atay declined. After a polite amount of time discussing Charleston, the College, and other requisite pleasantries, they turned to business.

Atay spoke fluent English with a distinct British tone. "We have an opportunity for you and the College to participate in a study that involves a Christian archaeological site." He smiled and waited for a comment. When neither of them spoke, he continued.

"During an excavation for new housing in the Cappadocia area, a new underground city was found, a city that could rival Derinkuyu. You know of this city?"

Kate said, "Why don't you give us a summary?" Adam was a renowned expert in Middle Eastern clay and stone figurines, but she wasn't sure what he knew about Turkey's underground cities.

"Of course," said Atay. "Derinkuyu is an underground city in the Cappadocia area of Turkey. The inhabitants carved the city out of the area's soft rock in the eighth century, and at one point, the city housed 20,000 people in eleven levels. There are several such structures in this area, though none so large."

Kate had seen a drawing of the city showing its underground cisterns, wine presses, stables, food cellars, and ventilation shafts. It reminded her of the ant farm she had given Sara for her fifth birthday.

"Were the residents primarily Christian?" asked Adam.

Atay seemed surprised at the question but answered readily enough. "Not at first, but yes, it did provide refuge for Christians over the centuries while the Muslims moved west from Anatolia."

Kate could see that their visitor looked a bit uncomfortable. In violent and bloody battles over several centuries, Muslim tribes had ultimately conquered the Christian Byzantines of Asia Minor, now modern day Turkey. As the Byzantine territory was overrun, its terrified Christian citizens had hidden in these elaborate underground cities in the soft rock.

Kate said, "Of course all of Cappadocia provided that type

of refuge to many, including Christians. And you say a new city has been uncovered?"

"Yes. The government kept it quiet for some time as it assessed the magnitude of the find. I am involved in one small piece of the project—studying intact codices found buried in a cruciform church. The codices refer to relics held by the Byzantines. I now have the authority to reach out to researchers. I have come to you."

Kate said nothing. Codices, or what someone not familiar with terminology would call parchment books, had often been torn apart and the parchment reused. What a find this would be if these codices turned out to have been untouched.

"Of course, the politics have been difficult, and frankly, we were stopped for a while by the former government. The new government wants to show it is a more international citizen, so the project has been funded. We found three intact codices written in Ancient Greek. The project requires an expert who can translate the Ancient Greek used by the Byzantines and, of course, someone who has a deep knowledge of Christian relics. That is why I came to you."

Kate's expertise in this language was ancillary to her primary field of study, but she was still regarded as an expert in Ancient Greek. It didn't make sense, though, why he had come to her rather than a scholar who had spent his or her entire career studying the Byzantine Empire.

"I'm still not sure why you came to me. There are many fine researchers in Europe and the Middle East who not only can translate this type of Greek, but who know the history of relics in the Byzantine Empire quite intimately."

Atay was silent for a moment, finally saying, "Dr. Strong, this is very sensitive information. What I am going to tell both of you must be kept confidential, whether the College participates or not."

Kate and Adam both nodded their agreement.

Atay took a breath. "We have had a few researchers reviewing the parchments for some months." He stopped, and rubbed his moustache with one finger. "The translations indicate that relics sent to France in the thirteenth century may not be what they were claimed to be."

What did he mean that the relics weren't what they claimed to be? The Byzantines had sent some of their most treasured items to various rulers in Europe in return for military protection, or to secure advantageous trade agreements. During most of the Empire's thousand years of existence, control of relics had been extremely important.

Helena, mother of Constantine I, the first Christian emperor of the Roman Empire, had discovered the cross Christ had been crucified on, called the True Cross, in Jerusalem around 300 AD. Over time, the cache of religious objects had grown to thousands, and Constantinople's fame and power expanded with it. Would these parchment books contain new information? Could she be the researcher to uncover new insights? It was clear Atay would share no more unless she and the College agreed to participate.

"I would be honored to be involved in any way possible."

Adam said nothing.

Atay smiled. "We would like for you, Dr. Strong, to be the lead investigator. In two days there is an important meeting in Istanbul with all the sponsors."

"Who are the sponsors?" Kate asked.

"The University, the Turkish Department of Antiquities, and the Orthodox Church."

She wondered whom else the committee had tried to enlist as lead investigator. It was likely all other candidates were male. This particular group of sponsors would not endure a woman in this role unless there had been no other choice. She visualized the faces of the sponsors when her name was suggested, and almost laughed.

"How much time before you need an answer?" asked Adam.

Dr. Atay said, "I would like for Dr. Strong to return with me this morning. We thought that because the trip is for only three days . . ."

"You need her in person? You can't be serious." Adam said. "Can't we do this via videoconference? You can email the photographs for Dr. Strong's review. Surely, you have photographs."

Atay sat up straight, apparently offended at the challenge. "I am completely serious. It has taken weeks to arrange all parties to be available. Our sponsors demand an in-person meeting."

Adam scraped his chair away from the table. "I will travel to Istanbul and have Kate participate by videoconference."

Atay continued, ignoring Adam. "Dr. Strong, I have a private jet waiting to return to Istanbul, and I would like you to be with me on the flight. After our committee's approval of your participation, which I am certain will be positive, we can proceed with a more structured plan. You will be gone for only three days."

Kate sat silent and looked down at her hands. The phrase "chance of a lifetime" popped into her head and with it, a vision of the accolades that would follow. The Vatican might invite her to study their hidden trove of relics, a request long denied. Three days meant she'd be back before spring break so she'd have plenty of time to spend with Sara. This was it! This was her chance to be the lead for a project that might be vital in the history of Christian relics. Part of her brain was telling her that this kind of opportunity never required an immediate response, but she ignored it.

Dr. Atay must also know that she was one of the few researchers in the world that had all of the right expertise to manage this project. She had knowledge of French relics and Ancient Greek, and last, though not least important, no affiliation with the Orthodox, the Vatican, or any other group that would try to steer the project in a particular direction. Both men were quiet, the clock in the conference room audibly ticking. Kate raised her head.

"I'll do it. Just give me a couple of hours to make arrangements." She tried to get a read from Adam, but he sat still, not looking at her.

"Excellent," said Atay, removing a phone from his jacket. "We can be somewhat flexible, as it is a private aircraft, but we do need to leave before lunch. Istanbul is seven hours ahead, so it will be very early tomorrow morning when we arrive. The flight itself is twelve hours. Here is a phone for you to call me when you are on the way to the airport."

Atay handed Kate the phone, and when she looked at it blankly he said, "I'm sorry, I forgot my cell phone, and I had to buy these temporary ones to use while we were here. Is that a problem?"

"No, of course not. I'll see you very shortly," said Kate, putting the phone in her pocket.

Atay stood up. Shaking hands with Adam, he nodded to Kate and quickly left the conference room. She could hear creaking from the old pine floors outside of Adam's office fading as the visitor walked towards the main staircase.

Adam began to pace, running his hand through his hair. "Kate, this isn't like you to agree to go out of town. I'll go, and you can participate via video. It's ridiculous that they want you to go all the way to Istanbul for three days."

"Don't you understand the implications of what they are describing? The existence of a Byzantine catalog of relics could be a sensational find. And the fact that some reliquaries might have been fake?" Kate grinned. "What a coup for the College it would be. Adam, be realistic. You can only do so much with videoconference, and I am the expert here. Given the sponsors they have, I'm not surprised they want to meet me."

"But you have classes to teach, and then, well, there's Jack. We also need to discuss any travel with the Dean."

"Oh, come on, you can do my classes for a couple of days until spring break starts. I'll take vacation time so the trip will be personal. We can talk with the Dean when I get back. It will be like your appraisal work, under the radar."

She said this casually, but deliberately. Months earlier, Kate had found a document on a printer in her office with Adam's name at the bottom. When she brought up the document, an appraisal of an Assyrian cylinder seal, to him, Adam explained he was merely providing an expert opinion for a South of Broad estate. Technically, everyone in the department was supposed to review any kind of outside employment with the Dean, but she knew that Adam had not done so, as it would have been discussed in a staff meeting.

Before Adam could reply, she went on, "I'll be back before Sara comes home from Clemson. As for Jack, it will be good for both of us to have me gone for a few days." Kate looked out the window and hoped Adam wouldn't argue with her. Finally, she heard a long sigh.

"I'm assuming you'll talk to Jack?"

"Of course. He's at some job site, but I can find him while you make your calls. I'll check back with you in an hour or so."

Adam was already thumbing his phone as he returned to his office. Kate headed to her own small office, walking through the reception area into the hall, mentally making a checklist to review with her graduate assistant.

CHAPTER 2

ADAM WATCHED KATE leave. When he was certain she was gone, he shut the door, and punched in a number on his cell. Someone picked up almost immediately.

"Is your meeting over, Adam?" The voice on the line was calm, and while normally this had soothed Adam's concerns about their business arrangement, the unhurried voice now made him angry.

"I thought you told me that Kate would be required only to translate, work that could be done via our teleconference set-up." Adam tried to breathe, but the next words were just as terse as the first. "You never told me she needed to travel. What in the hell is going on? You need to find somebody else."

For a moment, Adam thought the connection was lost. The reply was calm. "Dr. Chalk, you said yourself that she could do the translations very easily and that she would not ask many questions. I even had your visitor fly over to ensure her cooperation. It's too late for you to be regretful. Besides, this is a quick trip. She will be back in three days. Once she gives her expert opinion, I will send you a check."

Pacing his office, Adam could think of nothing to say. Threatening this man might be dangerous for him, and for Kate. He'd been stupid to get involved in this shady scheme. He had, of course, the oldest of motivations—the need for money.

Money he had needed when the real estate he bought during the boom went bust.

It had started innocuously at a party a year ago that a doyenne of Charleston had thrown. This woman introduced him to a man standing on the broad columned porch of her two-hundred-year-old mansion. "Adam, meet Imran Sadat. He and his brother have a wonderful oriental carpet store downtown. You must go there." She had promptly deserted them to play matchmaker for other guests.

"Nice to meet you," said Adam, shaking the man's hand, whose palm and fingers were hard with callouses. "I am a professor over at the College."

Sadat was intense, with dark eyes and eyebrows that looked painted on. His nose was straight and Roman, and with his somewhat tonsured haircut, the man resembled a medieval priest in an Italian sport coat and elegant trousers. When he finally smiled at Adam, his crooked white teeth merely increased the intensity of his presence. Adam felt like a country boy, dressed in his ubiquitous khakis.

"Yes," Sadat said, "I know. I've been anxious to meet you. I am a principal at an auction house and we are looking for experts in Middle Eastern statuary. I understand you have quite a reputation in this area."

Sadat had explained how the auction house was using modern teleconferencing technology, linking multiple locations via large screens that gave attendees the sense that everyone was at the same table. The prospective buyers, the auction house, and the appraiser could speak about an object, discuss its provenance, and its authenticity in one simple session. Adam had been flattered, and agreed to attend one of these events, held in a nondescript office building in Mount Pleasant.

Indeed, Adam had felt like he was on the bridge of the USS Enterprise, the large screen in front of the conference table showing a prospective buyer and the buyer's advisor, a retired museum curator. When Sadat asked Adam about a Zebu vase, a humpbacked bull-shaped object from twelfth century BC Iran, the two virtual heads leaned closer to hear the answer, and Adam's ego took over. He droned on about the damned vase for ten minutes. The meeting adjourned, and Sadat had smiled as he walked with Adam back to the parking lot.

A check arrived in the mail a week later with a note from Imran Sadat written in a cramped, almost illegible hand. For the last year, every other month or so, Sadat would ask him to participate in such an auction. Adam would give his opinion to the real, but not real, attendees. He reassured himself that this unorthodox way of conducting appraisals was the wave of the future. Surely, there was nothing wrong with this approach. His sanguine attitude ended when he recognized an exquisite gold chariot as the property of the Alexandria Museum, a shoebox-sized treasure from a minor pharaoh's tomb. After finishing the appraisal, Adam researched the chariot and found that the item was part of a cache stolen from Egypt the year before.

Adam had called Sadat, "I am done. Please don't call me." For six months, the man had left him alone. Then, a week ago, another call.

He had picked up the call in his office without looking at the caller ID. "Dr. Chalk here."

"Adam, how are you?" asked Sadat.

"Why are you calling me? I'm done."

"I have a one-time, very lucrative job for you. I have a client that requires that parchment books, some codices, be translated from Ancient Greek. I understand your colleague Kate Strong has such expertise. I've met her you know; she comes into our store every now and then."

This man knew Kate. How did he know she had this expertise? "Why don't you ask her yourself?"

Sadat laughed. "I could do so of course, but I thought you might want to earn a fee acting as the middleman. Of course, I will be happy to call her direct. Do you happen to have her cell number?"

If only the tax bill for his remaining rental properties had not been sitting on his desk when Sadat called, Adam might have been able to say no. The bill, arrogantly demanding an amount not commensurate with the value of the dilapidated houses, was late, and if Adam didn't pay it soon, he'd lose the properties. He was, he had to admit, a sucker for the perceived easy money. He had fallen for the lure of the "get rich via real estate" scheme, and he had fallen for the lure of the "get rich via secret appraisals."

He had agreed to arrange a meeting with Kate but never had he thought she would have to leave Charleston.

He could not let her become involved with a man like Imran Sadat, who at best did business with those in the illegal antiquities business, and at worst was directly involved in thefts from world-renowned museums.

Adam's voice was low, but still angry. "Imran, I know that last item you had me appraise—the chariot—was stolen. I want you to stop the flight to Istanbul. Never call me again, or I'll report you and your little enterprise to the FBI."

"I will stop it," Sadat said soothingly. "Let's meet, and I'll give you all the original appraisal documents you did for me. You can burn them and erase all signs of our arrangement." Sadat gave Adam an address on the Isle of Palms. "Meet me here in two hours."

Adam called Kate but only reached her voice mail. He began to leave a voice message, then reconsidered and hung up. He needed to speak with her in person. He pushed papers around on his desk, rearranged a bookshelf, and made a few phone calls, unable to sit still. Finally, he looked at his watch, strode out of the college and drove over the Ravenel Bridge to the Isle of Palms. Sadat was standing in the front of an old beach house on the quiet end of the island. Adam had to maneuver around a large blue commercial garbage truck parked on the street, but managed to pull close to Sadat. He lowered his window and made no move to get out of the car. "I will call the police if you don't cancel the flight."

Sadat remained standing with his arms closed, his hands folded across his finely woven cotton shirt. "I understand you are upset, but please do not do anything rash. I will, of course, call off the trip."

He leaned down over the driver-side window and stared at Adam, his dark eyes never leaving Adam's face. Taking a rolled up sheaf of papers out of his back pocket, he straightened. "Here are all the originals. Do what you want with them."

Adam could feel his pulse pounding. "I'll do it, I'm telling you. I'll call the police if I don't hear from Kate that the trip is off."

Sadat merely nodded.

Adam stared at the man for a long minute more, and then drove off, yearning for a muscle car with spinning wheels that would fill the man's face with sand and put holes in his beautiful cotton shirt.

CHAPTER 3

AT HOME, KATE threw clothes into a small suitcase, grabbing the toiletries she'd need for three days. She picked up her lithium to toss it into the bag, and then stopped. She'd take one full dose now, and take enough with her for half doses while she was in Turkey. Half doses would keep her a bit sharp, and make her more productive. She found an empty pill bottle, added a few of the hated tablets, and a sleeping pill to ensure she could sleep on the plane ride.

In the bathroom, she studied her face. She pulled her long curly hair back in a fuzzy chignon, smoothed her thick eyebrows with clear mascara and put on lipstick. "Well, that's better." She had never bothered much with her looks. Jack told her once that she looked like a tall, skinny Jackie Kennedy with a perm. *Good enough,* she thought.

Kate found a few websites on Cappadocia and began to download the information to her laptop as she rummaged through her desk. She finally found her passport, and flipped through the pages. All were empty, except for one page with a customs stamp from the Bahamas, a quick trip she and Jack had made when their financial situation seemed secure. She stared at the stamp for a long moment, finally tucking the passport into her purse.

Should she call Sara? It was a certainty her daughter was still asleep—the girl could and would fall asleep at every opportunity, a trait that had made her an easy child once she outgrew her colicky infant state. No, she wouldn't call now; she'd call when she landed in Istanbul.

Jack could not be avoided. Feeling guilty over the relief when she got his voice mail, Kate said, "Jack, I'm going out of town for three days. The College might be leading a huge project. It's important. Adam can tell you more. Call him when you can."

Kate paused, wondering if she should say something about their argument. No, she wouldn't. He had been a jerk. She hung up and wrote him a note with the same general message, sticking it on the refrigerator to make sure he saw it.

Her voice mail to Adam was just as brief. "Adam, I didn't talk to Jack, but I left him a message that I was going away for three days. I didn't tell him where. I'm hoping you can explain to him what the opportunity is, and why I need to go. He'll probably be upset. See you soon."

A wave of panic caused a moment of immobility, and she almost called Atay to tell him she couldn't make the trip. At the same time, she felt an excited thrumming of her thoughts, a sensation that she knew was due to the lower levels of lithium in her body.

She looked at their small living room as if for the first time, seeing the worn white slipcovered couches, and the stacks of books on a multitude of topics that provided vertical structure as well as handy surfaces to hold glasses, plates, and newspapers. Her prized painting of a Gullah woman in a rice field was the focal point of the room, and somehow looked perfectly at home with the worn Heriz geometric carpet on the floor, the faded blues and reds of the rug a perfect counterpoint to the brilliance of the same hues in the painting. *Everything is so shabby,* she thought. She needed to expand her career and make more money. This project was her ticket to recognition, financial and otherwise. Maybe it would result in a book.

She stared out of the large windows overlooking a wide front porch, part of her hoping Jack would suddenly appear. After waiting for ten minutes, she loaded her car and pulled away without looking back at the house.

Kate called Atay using the phone he had given her, and followed his instructions to leave her car in a remote parking lot at Charleston International Airport. He picked her up at the lot, and to her surprise, drove them to a small, private airport in Summerville.

"This one is far north enough for us to avoid the crowded Charleston airspace. Otherwise, we wouldn't take off for a while."

Kate walked up a ladder into the lush interior of a private jet. "Oh my, this is swanky." The plane's interior was plush with navy leather seats and gold trimmings. A bathroom and a small galley kitchen lined a short corridor leading to the cockpit.

Atay said, "I'm sorry to leave you up front here, but I have some work to finish before we land." He decamped to the back of the plane, where there were four seats and what looked like two single beds.

The co-pilot showed her how to operate the fixtures in the bath. "This is for your use. Dr. Atay has one in the back."

"Thank you," Kate sat down and opened her laptop, determined to read the two hundred pages she had downloaded about the underground cities of Cappadocia before they landed. The takeoff was exhilarating, the sleek jet climbing at an angle that made Kate grab her armrests. Once the plane leveled off, she read for a while, finally looking up at the screen in the cabin that showed their location against a world map.

The jet was already over the ocean. Kate looked down at the water, and then glanced back at Atay. He was asleep. She returned to her reading, mentally composing a conciliatory text message she would send to Jack when they landed. Uncomfortable with her racing thoughts, and beginning to feel a bit panicky again, this time about being encased in a long silver tube, she took the sleeping pill.

CHAPTER 4

ADAM DROVE A convertible Miata, a two-seater sports car that was impractical, expensive to repair, and deadly in an accident. As he returned to downtown Charleston over the Ravenel Bridge, he was oblivious of the car's faults, enjoying the April air swirling around his uncovered head. He had the windows up, mentally rehearsing what he'd tell Kate about the change in plans. She wouldn't be going to Istanbul, and they would both examine the codices via photographs.

At the apex of the bridge, he caught sight of a commercial garbage truck in his left hand mirror, barreling up in the lane beside him. Had he just seen this same truck at Sadat's house? He slowed the Miata to allow the truck to pass. He looked in the mirror again, saw nothing but the blue paint of the truck and felt adrenaline flood his body as his brain registered what was going to happen. The garbage truck rammed him in a collision so forceful that Adam's hands lifted from the steering wheel.

The driver-side window exploded, and Adam felt sharp stings on his face. The truck continued to shove him against the concrete side of the bridge, both vehicles still moving forward. He stomped on the brake, and the truck shot ahead. The car bumped to a halt, and Adam put his head down against the steering wheel, gasping. He felt glass in his mouth, and spit the pieces out, saliva covering his chin. Furiously brushing the jagged pieces off his lap with his left hand, he scrabbled in his pants pocket for his phone to call 911.

The phone skittered out of his grasp, and landed on the passenger-side floor. Hands shaking, Adam tried, without success, to release his seatbelt. He heard gears shifting, and he jerked up, horrified by what he saw in the rear view mirror.

He turned. The garbage truck was directly behind him. How had that happened? Imran Sadat was in the driver seat, hunched over the wheel, staring at him. The gaze did not break until the automated arms on the front of the truck moved down as if it were reaching for a garbage container, blocking Adam's view. Adam heard a screeching sound and the Miata left the concrete of the bridge, pinioned in the truck's lifting arms.

Adam screamed as the truck lifted his car as though to dump the car's contents in its cavernous bin. He struggled to unlock the belt, desperate to get out of the car. The truck backed up, holding the car with its nose pointed down, turned, and began to lower the arms. Adam felt and heard a massive crash as the garbage truck slammed the little convertible into the Ravenel Bridge; the car, caught between one of the supports and a light pole, canted at a downward angle like a teapot towards the Cooper River.

He felt no pain, but Adam was stunned, unable to focus, his glasses hanging precariously from one ear. He moved slightly, his chest burning from the seatbelt digging into his chest. He fumbled with the seat belt latch again, and then saw the Cooper River through the windshield.

"Help me; somebody help me!" A passing sailboat, miniscule as a toy, slammed the realization into his head that a fall would be fatal. "Oh God, somebody please help me!" He took a breath and yelled again, "I'm trapped! Help me; somebody help me."

Adam heard another crunching sound, and then felt a forward jolt, realizing that Sadat was still maneuvering the garbage truck, trying to push the car through the light pole and the bridge's support beams. He yelled again, this one an inarticulate cry.

He heard a shout. "Hey! What the hell are you doing?"

The Miata dropped two feet so quickly that Adam sucked in a breath, and then let it out in a howl. The Cooper River loomed. He windmilled his arms behind the seat, seeking to find something, anything, to hold onto if the seat belt failed.

"Help me!" Adam screamed again. He heard more shouting, and the sounds of a diesel engine revving to its full capacity. More yelling, and then the engine sound stopped.

"Are you ok?" someone bellowed. Turning his head as far as he could to the left, Adam could see a man looking at him from the rail a few feet below the car. It was a young man, and he appeared to have a rope in his hand.

"Someone tried to kill me. Call the police."

"I did," the man yelled back, his voice barely audible above the sounds of more people shouting, and now, a sound of sirens. "He was in a garbage truck. He hijacked somebody's car. Don't move, man. Stay still. I'm going to try and get you out."

Adam wanted to tell him not to do it, to wait for the police but as he opened his mouth, only a squeaking sound came out, his mouth dry. Kate, God, he had to call Kate. "Hey," Adam shouted. "You need to call somebody for me, now!"

The Miata lurched and the nose fell closer to the river. Adam felt a vibrating of the chassis beneath him, and heard the shrieking sound of the exterior scraping against the huge white girder. Adam turned his head as much as he could, "Stay there! Wait for the fire department!"

The kid yelled, "I have a rope tied to my jeep. You need to get out. Your car is falling."

Another screeching sound made Adam want to cover his ears with his hands like a child. Using his right hand to move the shoulder belt, he inched it down his left arm. In the left hand mirror, he watched the kid throw a rope, trying to get the rope to land on top of the trunk behind him. He let out the breath he was holding, and felt the rope hit his head.

The kid called out, "Ok, grab the rope and tie it around you. Unhook your seat belt. If the car falls, let it slide underneath you. The rope will hold."

Adam grabbed the rope with his left hand, and tried to tie it around his waist. With his right hand, he began to pull at the seatbelt latch again, cursing and crying as it remained jammed. Suddenly, the seatbelt released with a snapping sound, hitting him in the face, and Adam threw both hands on the rope, breathing hard.

"Ok," he heard the kid say, "The Fire Department is almost. . . ."

The last words were drowned out by a moaning sound and Adam felt the car slide beneath him. He turned his torso, his stomach on the trunk, his body stretched out along the rope as if he were Superman flying.

He saw spectators, their arms stretched towards him like supplicants, preparing to grab him when the car fell. The car jolted again, and Adam felt a pull on his right shoe. He turned his head and saw the seatbelt attached to the Velcro of his sneaker, the belt wrapped around his foot. He shook his foot wildly, crying. Too late.

With a violent jerk, the metal cocoon was expelled by the bridge, and with the car came the seatbelt and his foot, and with his foot, the rest of him. As the metal cage and its driver dropped towards the river, Adam was aware only of the pain from his rope-burned hands, and he cried, "Kate, I'm sorrysorrysorry!"

Istanbul

CHAPTER 5

WHEN THE PLANE landed, Kate turned on her phone. No service. It was 11:00 p.m. in Charleston. She supposed that Jack would have already found the note, talked to Adam, and be sitting in the kitchen at his usual work spot, fuming. Had she told him she would be on a plane? She couldn't remember, and this disturbed her until she began to think of the contents of the buried pages, visions of what she might find pushing out all other thoughts. Perhaps Adam had been able to calm Jack, and explain the importance of the opportunity for Kate and the College.

The pilot guided the passengers towards a small building where a large black SUV idled, a man in the driver's seat. "Do you know why I can't get cell service here, Dr. Atay?"

"Service in Turkey for phones from outside the country is very erratic. I'm sure service will be available soon. You did not bring much," he added, taking her small bag.

"I don't need much for three days, especially since I'm sure we'll work most of the time."

Atay looked blankly at her for a moment and then laughed. "I am used to my wife who brings her whole closet for a day at the beach."

Kate was shocked she was in Istanbul, when not twenty hours before she and Jack had argued about this very city. She took a few deep breaths. "Dr. Atay, may I use your phone to call my husband? I presume your phone is working."

The man looked at her. "I'm sorry, Dr. Strong, but remember I did not bring my own phone. Sadly, I left my temporary one in Charleston. Shall we be going?"

Kate opened her mouth to demand a phone, and then decided not to. Atay strode out of the terminal and got into the front seat of the SUV.

Kate climbed into the back, behind the driver. "Where *exactly* are we going?"

Atay turned from the front seat and said, "The government owns many old castles on the coast, most built by Christian Crusaders almost a thousand years ago. The majority of them are nothing but piles of stone, and it would cost a fortune to restore them. We are using one that the government restored for use by agencies that want to get away from Istanbul. We've added laboratory facilities that will allow us to examine the parchments in privacy."

Kate continued, without success, to get her phone to respond, and finally put it away, listening to Atay ramble about the castle. She gazed out the window while the van traveled through the dark and quiet suburbs of Istanbul, driving an hour along a coastal road before the gray massive structure appeared.

"There it is," said Atay.

She gaped at the castle, imposing even in the predawn glimmer. The edifice was made of dark stone with ramparts that hugged tall, sheer cliffs. The overall impact was triangular, much like a prehistoric arrowhead. The cliffs would have a panoramic view of the sea, the ideal site for a castle. From the three round towers—one in the middle and one on each side—the crusaders would have been able to see any ship long before it was close enough to be a danger.

When the van pulled off the main road, Kate lost sight of the castle. She sensed that the van was ascending and could see the sun beginning to rise over the sea. The van traveled for ten minutes before veering off the paved road to a dirt lane, this one more like a track than a road, quickly arriving at an open gate with a guard shack. The driver drove straight through without stopping. Kate looked back and saw two men close the gate. After passing over a pebbled driveway with massive trees drooping from each side, the vehicle stopped in front of an immense door, where a woman, presumably a servant, stood.

Dr. Atay assisted her out of the van and strode into the castle. "Dr. Strong, this way please. You will want to see the terrace at sunrise." He walked across a foyer, then through a huge dining room to three sets of double doors, one of which was open. The view of the Mediterranean Sea, with a few rays of the sun just beginning to show through the clouds was breathtaking.

When Kate gazed from the floor of the terrace to the walls behind her, she could see that what she had thought was an entire castle was merely the remains of the ramparts and walls. A modern steel infrastructure had been constructed and integrated into the natural stone and granite cliffs, clutched to the breast of the castle like a kangaroo joey. Above them was one of the three towers, a dark obelisk against the sky.

"This way, please." Atay guided her through a long corridor, up a steep flight of stone steps, stopped, and then gestured for her to enter a room. Though the red velvet drapes were closed, Kate could make out a high bed heaped with colorful pillows. Atay's eyes darted into the room, then back to her and her suitcase. He turned and pointed to a receiver hanging on the wall. "There is the house phone. You can call the castle operator and have someone bring you anything you may need."

Kate stopped him with a hand on his arm. "When is the formal meeting with the sponsors?"

"The principals?" His face relaxed. "Oh, yes, the meeting. I am not sure, but we will fly you back in three days. Do not worry."

Her head began to thrum. Turning and backing away, the man gave her a reassuring smile. "Please rest, Dr. Strong. We will speak later."

Kate plugged in her phone. She was beginning to feel panicky and regretful, and didn't know if it was the lack of medication, or concern for Jack. She took a quick shower and dressed, then lay down on the enormous bed and dozed off. A knock on the door startled her awake.

"Yes," she said from the bed.

"Are you ready, Dr. Strong?" said Atay through the door.

"Five minutes," said Kate. She tried to text Jack again. To her great relief, her text showed delivered.

Atay was waiting for her, and rather than take her down the same stairs she had climbed two hours previously, he led her farther down the corridor. Soon the granite walls of the castle gave way to a more modern material. After going through two additional doors, Atay stopped at an elevator. It opened immediately, and took them down several levels. Exiting, they walked down a short hall into a large state-of-the-art research room.

Kate entered and walked to the middle of the room. The room was equipped with a computer and high-resolution monitor. Light boxes designed for examining parchment sat on tables against the wall to the left of the door they had entered. Two rolling office chairs sat in front of the computer and the light boxes.

The wall directly across from where they had entered contained an unmarked whiteboard. A door stood in the middle of the right hand wall, with additional whiteboards on either side. The floor was of concrete, and what she thought was an antique Turkish Oushak carpet covered most of the visible floor, an incongruous addition for a laboratory. The rug was worn in the middle, as if someone had walked its length daily for a hundred years. Why would they put such a valuable rug in a laboratory?

Kate said, "Am I going to be allowed to physically examine the codices? I see that you have all the necessary equipment to do so."

"For now we have only photographs. Since time is short, do you mind taking breakfast here in the lab?" He gestured behind them to a table that held coffee and a continental breakfast.

"No, of course not. I am used to eating on the run." Kate smiled and added, "Just keep the coffee coming."

Atay walked over to the worktable, sat down and logged onto the computer. "The photographs are indexed. Here is the master file." Kate looked over his shoulder as he showed her the primary folder. "I will be back at lunch time." He gestured to the wall, "Don't forget. The receiver on the wall will link you with the castle operator if you need anything."

"Thank you," said Kate. Atay walked out and gently closed the door.

Kate walked over to the receiver and picked it up. A woman answered in accented English, "May I help you?"

"Can you make a call to the United States for me?" Kate asked. She gave Jack's cell phone number to the operator.

"Of course, I will try." Silence on the line. "I'm sorry," said the operator. "There is no answer. Shall I ring you when it goes through?"

"Yes, please."

She sat at the high-resolution monitor, and reviewed the folders Atay had showed her. The folder names were in English: site-photographs, books-in-situ, book1, book2, book3. The first folder contained pictures of the underground city and had a sketched diagram of the levels excavated. Kate studied the photographs a long time, imagining how dangerous the surface must have been for these people to build a self-contained city underground. The church itself had been built at the third level, fifty feet deep. An arrow indicated the location of the codices, behind a wall near the intersection where the cross members of the cruciform church met.

The second folder, books-in-situ, had photographs made of each codex before being removed. The remaining folders contained photographs of each page of the books, each jpeg file labeled with a four-digit number. The first number indicated which book the pages had come from, the three other numbers representing a specific page. Kate knew how tedious the job was to unearth, preserve and then prepare parchments for photographing. Whatever team had prepared these books had done a superb job.

She clicked on one image and it popped into full view. The page was in the style of illuminated manuscripts, and contained a detailed illustration of a particular relic and its container, the reliquary. The colors were bright, shielded from ultraviolet light for centuries. The exquisite text described each relic, where found and by whom. The location of the reliquary—church, monastery, convent, or castle completed the written description. The parchments were an amazing inventory of the Byzantine Empire's most precious possessions, that were, at the time, worth more than gold. Kate felt a rising excitement, and her hands began to shake. If these codices were unknown to modern historians, their existence alone was phenomenal.

Once the formal project began, the researchers would

carefully correlate the information in these parchments with other documents that described relics and their provenance. Kate calculated how many researchers the project needed for this aspect, and added to her mental list of needed resources. Some of the photographs indicated tattered pages, but Kate knew this information would be in later books. Medieval scribes spent their days copying and recopying pages—endless pages. They would have not allowed a codex parchment to decay without replicating the information.

Where in Constantinople had they kept these books? In Hagia Sophia, the great cathedral in the center of the city? When had they been moved to Cappadocia? These questions would remain unanswered until a team could form, and the complete inventory was translated. Even then, many new questions would arise.

Kate forgot about eating, quickly looking at each photograph of book1, attempting to gauge the level of difficulty of the translation. When she did the official translation, she would go slowly—letter by letter, word by word—and would ask for a minimum of three researchers to do the same. For now, she wanted a sense of what was contained in the codex.

A clatter announced someone entering the lab. Kate looked up to see Atay with food on a tray. "Thank you, I almost forgot I needed to eat breakfast."

Atay gestured to the table, the food from the morning untouched. "That is breakfast. This," he said as he lifted the tray in his hands, "is lunch." He put the tray down on the table, and drew up a rolling chair to her.

"What time is it?"

"It's after two o'clock. You've been working for almost six hours."

Kate felt a long missed pleasure in her gut, the pleasure of forgetting herself in work and losing track of time. She laughed aloud. "Dr. Atay, this is wonderful. The team that removed the codices and photographed them did an amazing job. This is years of research for a very large team."

Kate saw pain cross Atay's face. "I appreciate your kind words, Dr. Strong, but we do not have years. How many photographs have you looked at?"

Frowning, Kate turned to the table and looked at her notes. "Photographs 1 through 30 in book1."

"Ah," he said. "I would like for you to skip forward to study photographs 61 through 65 in the same book. How long will that take?"

She thought for a moment, and then said, "Another two hours or so. Is there something particular you want me to look for?"

Atay rubbed his moustache. "Those are the specific pages of parchment that concern France. I will be back in two hours." With that, Atay stood and left Kate.

Kate pulled out her phone to call Jack. Still no service, but she had a reply text from him.

Got your message. Glad you're safe. We'll talk when you get home. L, J.

She heaved a breath, immensely relieved that Jack did not seem angry. She would call him later. Head down, sipping coffee, she found herself walking the same worn path across the rug, thinking more about which experts would be perfect for the project, and how long each would be needed. No matter what Atay thought, years of work lay ahead.

She returned to the computer to look at pages 61 to 65 in book 1. Kate looked at one of the entries, and noticed the word *pseudos*, Ancient Greek for falsehood. A curious word for this type of document, and the word stood alone, almost like a label at the top of the page. She skimmed the page and saw not only the same word at the top of other descriptions but also evidence of additional writing underneath the elaborate Greek script. The palimpsest, the faint imprints of this earlier writing, would require translation too. She sat up and craned her head back. Focusing again on the pages, she began to do a cursory translation in her head. She checked the Byzantine date—1204 in the Roman calendar.

"By order of the Patriarch, I have been asked to document the wrong done to His Majesty, Louis IX, King of France. The Patriarch wishes to acknowledge the grievous insult done to the King of France and to ensure that the evil designed to be let loose in his Kingdom never comes to pass. These reliquaries should never be opened."

No, no, no, thought Kate. This couldn't be accurate; she must be off in her translation. Why would the Byzantine priest describe a reliquary as an insult? What evil could the writer possibly be referring to? She read the first few lines again. Skimming the rest of the page, she determined that the remainder of this parchment described the relics taken back to Venice after the fourth Crusade and purchased by the King of France in 1239.

The relics the king had purchased included pieces of the True Cross and the thorn crown alleged to have been on Christ while he was crucified. Baldwin II, emperor of Byzantium during the Latin Empire period, had outlawed the sale of relics but had pawned these particular items to Venice, desperately needing funds for the defense of the Empire against the Turks. When Baldwin defaulted on the loan, the Venetians offered the artifacts to King Louis IX, who paid the modern equivalent of hundreds of millions of dollars. The King commissioned Saint-Chappelle to be built in the middle of Paris as a home for these treasures. The Gothic structure, with its stained glass windows and vaulted ceiling, no longer housed the relics, which had been moved to Notre Dame Cathedral after the French Revolution, in 1802.

Kate read the lines again, then again, and finally stopped, rubbing her eyes. She could not find a mistake. The parchment clearly stated that the relics sold to King Louis IX, today reposing under massive security in Notre Dame Cathedral, viewed in reverent silence by millions of people over hundreds of years, were not only fakes, but had been seeded with disease in an attempt to begin a plague.

CHAPTER 6

ON WHAT SHE thought would be her final day in Istanbul, Kate arrived at the breakfast room, anxious to discuss next steps with Atay. The meeting with the sponsors had not occurred, a relief to her, as she was not certain how much Atay had told them about the codices' contents. The College would certainly want the project, but there was much to work out: timing, number of researchers, additional equipment for those researchers, and of course, funding for all of it.

Atay was at the dining room table when she arrived from her room, suitcase in hand. She sat and a silent servant put a continental breakfast in front of her. The room was sumptuously furnished with antiques and carpets, including one fantastic picture carpet on the wall depicting a Mughal hunting scene, complete with prancing deer, snarling tigers, and turbaned hunters on impossibly delicate horses.

"Good morning." Atay was his urbane self, impeccable as always.

"Good morning, Dr. Atay. Did you review my preliminary report? I know your own researchers found some of the *pseudos* references, or else you wouldn't have known what scrolls to ask me to study, but why didn't they stay on the project?"

Putting down his coffee, Atay gave her a serious look. "My own researchers were not entirely sure of their translations and frankly, they were nervous about the academic community. My country doesn't always produce independent thinkers." He grimaced. "You know, of course, there will be fierce arguments over your interpretations."

Atay was stating it mildly. Religious scholars all over the world would tear the translations apart. It would take very careful management and judicious "leaking" of the findings to friendly individuals to overcome what would be formidable disagreements.

"You did look at my timeline, didn't you? This project will need about thirty individuals and an initial phase will take eighteen months. I am curious as to what has happened to delay the meeting of the sponsors?"

Atay gazed at her for a long moment, and then sighed. "We have a slight problem. We need to have you stay here with us for just a little while longer."

She looked up from her plate. "I'm sorry, Dr. Atay, but that is not possible. I need to get back to Charleston and make arrangements." She smiled, but he remained stoic. She tried another approach. "Many of the researchers I've listed in my report will need to take temporary leave from their current positions, including me. That takes time to arrange."

Atay did not reply. The two of them regarded each other for a long moment. Kate returned to her plate, pushing the food on her plate back and forth, her appetite gone.

"Please," he whispered.

Kate jerked her head up and was alarmed to see the expression on Atay's face. His lips pressed together so tightly that his mouth seemed bloodless. Someone coughed behind her. She twisted in her chair and saw a man, someone new.

"I'm sorry, but who are you?"

The man walked around the table and stood next to Atay. "My name is Anton Bunin. I am in charge of the security of this site. I do not have exalted degrees in archaeology like the good doctor here." At this, he patted Atay's head. Kate was again shocked at the expression on Atay's face. He had almost flinched at the touch of the other man, and sat preternaturally still.

"Atay was sure he could persuade you to stay, but I am not prepared to wait for his gentler approach to work. You will remain at the castle until you identify all the false reliquaries sent to France, and their current locations." Bunin retrieved a cigar from his jacket and made a long production of lighting it, his sunken blue eyes not leaving her face.

He was a big man in his seventies, with close-cropped gray hair and, from his accent, she thought he was Russian. His suit was expensive, much like Atay's daily attire, but didn't hang right on his body. The cigar moved in and out of his mouth, his face red and flushed. He looked at Kate with a one-cornered smile, and at that moment seemed friendly, innocuous, like an uncle you hadn't seen in a while.

"Dr. Atay, I'm not certain that I will come back at all if this is the treatment your security people are inclined to mete out to your guests." She stood up. "I am leaving now. I'll have the operator get me a cab."

Kate walked over to the house phone on the wall and picked it up. The line was dead.

"So, Mr. Bunin, are you now scrambling all communications?" Over the last two days, she had still not been able to make a voice call but had received several texts from Jack. During her time at the castle, Atay had continued to tell her that service was sporadic, and in the thrill of the work, Kate had not pushed the issue. She made a fist and pushed it at Bunin, her voice low and hoarse. "It's outrageous that I've been able to only text my family and not speak to them."

"Dr. Strong, do you mean the three texts you have exchanged

with your husband?" Bunin pulled out a paper from his jacket and read aloud, in a rough parody of American English.

Jack, I'm sorry. I hope you got my note. I will be back in three days. Love, K.
Got your message. Glad you're safe. We'll talk when you get home. J.

Sara ok? Haven't heard from her. Love, K.
Yes, she's fine. J.

I will text when I leave. Forgive me. Love, K.
Can't wait to see you, J.

Kate stormed around the table, yanked the paper from Bunin's hand, and confirmed that the paper held a verbatim transcript of her texts to and from Jack.

"What right do you have to monitor my private texts? I cannot believe you would allow this, Dr. Atay." She stood rigid at the head of the table, her hands clenching and unclenching

Atay looked up at her from the other side of Bunin. "Please," he said again, his eyes pleading with her, his hands trembling on the table.

Bunin snorted. "Those replies from your husband? One of my very capable staff members created them. Your phone hasn't worked since you got on the plane in South Carolina. Your husband has no idea where you are."

"What?" Kate whispered this, dropping the sheet. Her right arm moved behind her to find a chair. She slumped into it. "He doesn't know where I am? Of course my husband knows where I am, and so does Dr. Chalk. What are you talking about?"

The Russian pulled another piece of paper from his jacket and tossed it on the table in front of her. It was the front page from the Charleston *Post and Courier* dated the day after she left.

Professor Dies on Ravenel Bridge

Police have no leads on the attack on Professor Adam Chalk that occurred yesterday around 11:00 am. According to witnesses, Dr. Chalk's car, a Mazda Miata, was slammed against the bridge supports by a commercial garbage truck. The truck then lifted Chalk's car in its front lifting mechanism and appeared to push it through the bridge supports. One witness, Jabos Freeman said, "I couldn't believe it. The man driving the garbage truck just lifted that little convertible and pushed it into the bridge. He ran off and hijacked somebody when I screamed at him." Witnesses attempted to rescue Dr. Chalk with a rope, but the car fell into the Cooper River before they could do so. Dr. Chalk was chair of the History Department at the College . . .

Kate gasped and looked up at Bunin in shock. Adam was dead? He had died while Atay was driving her from the Charleston airport to the private strip in Summerville. She felt sick and willed herself not to vomit. Why would anyone want to murder Adam? If Jack didn't get her texts, then Adam's death meant that no one knew where she was—unless her boss had told someone else at the college. Oh, God, why had she not left more information in her voice mail to Jack? Her head began to throb and she could not hold her hands still.

She pushed the paper aside and turned away from Bunin.

The carpet on the wall filled her view—a leopard and a fawn in a vignette so finely woven as to appear a painting, the predator in mid-pounce, the fawn forever to remain in peril as it tried to escape. She turned and in a calmer voice asked, "Who are you really, and why do you want me to remain here? Dr. Atay, please, will you explain to this man what our agreement was?"

Atay was also looking at the carpet now, his face blotchy, his jaws clenched. He did not reply.

Bunin moved his bulky body closer to the table and put his cigar down on Atay's breakfast plate. "You must find the reliquaries that are documented in the scrolls, the ones that the Byzantines call pseudos. I want to know where they all are now. Once you complete that work, we will send you back to Charleston."

"Are you crazy? Why? Dr. Atay, please tell me what is going on!" His eyes finally moved away from the carpet. In his eyes, she saw the same wide-eyed look the weaver had so skillfully manifested in the fawn, a look of terror and resignation.

"Dr. Strong, Dr. Atay cannot help you. If indeed this work will take months, you will want to begin right away."

Her last memory of that day was the smell of an acrid liquid and a hand covering her face.

ONE MONTH LATER
Istanbul

CHAPTER 7

"ANTON, EXACTLY WHAT is it that you want?" asked Dr. Zora Vulkov. She paced the dining room in the castle, waiting on the big man to answer. Anton sat eating a steak, watching her.

She had met Anton in 1981 at the newly formed and deceptively named Institute of Ultra-Pure Biochemical Preparations, located in Leningrad, the USSR's premier center for weapon-focusing biotechnology research. Zora arrived with her newly minted PhD, and the idealism of a twenty-five-year-old communist educated in state schools since the age of twelve. She and Anton were members of a team creating an aerosolized delivery device for antibiotics. Ostensibly, this was so Mother Russia could ensure her citizens received immediate treatment in the event of a biological attack by the United States.

Zora hadn't been so sure the work she did was for defensive use only, but the nagging of her conscience became subservient to her drive to be better than her peers, all of whom had grown up as the pampered children of Communist Party members. Zora, the daughter of a butcher, had pretended to be as dull as the other children that had lived in her small village, her days endless and bleak. Nevertheless, sometime after taking a nationwide test at twelve, a limousine with a dour matron in the back seat arrived at her family's wooden shack. Without ceremony, the woman announced to her parents their daughter was to be educated in a state school. This was not the traumatic separation of a sensitive child from her loving parents; it was the rescue of a curious puppy from a cage of decrepit hounds. She had never seen her family again and did not think of them, but had never thought of herself as anyone other than a peasant, albeit a lucky one.

Zora had tried to exorcise her conscience in arguments with Anton. He believed if the United States was going to study biological weapons then the USSR had to as well. She would retort that someone had to take the moral high road and stop the proliferation. Their arguments, happily witnessed by the other, more reticent member of their team, always ended in vodka shots. She reassured herself that her expertise in aerosolizing biological materials might one day actually be used for the treatment of terrible diseases such as Ebola.

Eventually, there were signs of change. Citizens marched in the streets of Poland and East Germany, wanting freedom of the press, and freedom to travel. By the time 500,000 people converged in East Berlin in November 1989 to tear down the Berlin Wall, Zora knew that the country known as the Union of Soviet Socialist Republics was no more. Zora remembered watching the fall of the wall on CNN with her colleagues, all lifelong and dedicated communists, in stunned silence, all of them aware that watching the pirated signal could land them in the gulag.

During the eighteen months that followed, as the USSR headed towards breakup, many of the lab workers, biologists, doctors, and security people simply walked away from the lab. Security became intermittent. Supplies weren't replenished. The remaining workers, including Zora, carried on as best they could. Finally, soldiers arrived and destroyed the lab records, telling those who remained that the Institute was now closed.

Zora could have stayed in Russia, as Anton had, but she decided to focus herself in a manner diametrically opposed to the clandestine work she had done for ten years. She joined Health Workers for Africa, HWA, and moved to Cameroon. Each night for a year, after dealing with ailments long conquered by the West, she had cried herself to sleep. Finally, she stopped crying, and became useful to the people she grew to love, people so like the ones in her childhood village. That they returned her affection was apparent from the number of little girls named Zora running around in the nearby villages. Until Bunin called, Zora had been living an anonymous and quiet life treating diseases the jungle spit at its human inhabitants at an unceasing pace. The promise of a donation to HWA had lured her to Istanbul.

Zora said again, "Why did you ask me to come here?"

"Patience, Zora. While I finish eating, enjoy the view," Anton waved at the terraced doors.

She watched as Anton ate his meal so slowly she became irritated. "Anton, really, please just tell me why you called me. Your request was very mysterious."

"Did you not like the plane I sent?" He grinned at her.

Zora smiled back in spite of her pique. She knew that the sleek prop plane touching down on a dirt strip near her clinic would be the talk of the surrounding villages for months.

"Sit down, Zora. I will explain." He had never been a handsome man, but for a man in his seventies, he exuded strength and power. She responded to him as though he was still her boss, and sat down, preparing a cup of coffee from the silver tray left on the table.

"Where exactly are we in Istanbul?" After the prop plane had landed, a helicopter had brought her to the castle, arriving late at night. She had seen nothing of her surroundings until this morning.

"We are an hour outside of Istanbul." After cutting another piece of steak, while he was still chewing, he said, "Do you know what I have been doing since I last saw you?"

"I don't have access to the Internet where I am, so no, I do not know what you have been doing. I presume you are rich." Zora waved her hand around the room.

"After the fall of the USSR, I was able to keep the Institute's best researchers from leaving Russia. We formed a company to see if we could make money as capitalistic researchers." He grinned. "We succeeded. My company is private, not well known outside of the Russian government. It is called New Institute of Biochemical Manufacturing. Some get the joke, most do not." He laughed, and lit a cigarette. "Do you mind?"

"I do mind." She waved the smoke away from her. "If you must smoke, let's go outside." She got up from the table and plodded to the terrace, conscious that her shabby pantsuit exhibited her poverty.

When she turned, he was watching her. "Zora, you look good. Not a day older than the last time I saw you when I took you to the airport." He walked to the railing of the terrace.

Zora snorted. She was short, with a round face and body, and stubby legs. Her years in the jungle had turned her skin leathery, and because of the interminable heat, she kept her gray wiry hair short. She looked like what she was—a Russian peasant. "Anton, please."

He puffed on his cigarette, and said, "I am richer than I

could have ever imagined. New Institute has done very well in the pharmaceutical world. We use the results of our old research—the good research, not the lethal," he said, laughing, "and apply those results to new problems, such as how to apply polio immunizations from the air. I do much work for the government." Anton spread his arms wide. "I am a powerful man," he bellowed, competing with the sounds of the ocean below them.

"Did you bring me here to brag? You promised me a donation."

"Oh, I will make a donation, as I promised you when I called, but first I need your specific expertise," he said, his arms on the railing.

Zora joined him at the railing, leaned her back on it, and looked up at the castle's three towers. "Anton, what expertise could I possibly have that would be of use to you? I patch up broken bones, stitch wounds, and deliver babies. I try to keep up with research on infectious diseases, but whatever expertise I had is obsolete now. You know that."

Anton was silent for a moment. "How many lives could you save with one hundred million dollars?"

She felt irritated now, like a dog whose owner kept the toy just out of reach. "Don't play with me, Anton."

"Zora, I am not playing. If you help me with my problem, I will donate all you need to your organization. No conditions." He pulled a piece of paper out of his jacket pocket and gave it to her.

Zora unfolded the paper. It was a check written to HWA for an amount equivalent to twenty years of their current budget. Could Anton be serious? A hundred million was a significant sum, even for someone worth billions. This donation would not be without strings, but her mind immediately filled with visions of what HWA could do with this much money. She might even be able to hire private security to protect the clinic and villagers from the roving bands of Islamic terrorists called Boko Haram. She thought how terrified the inhabitants near the clinic were, and how helpless HWA was to protect them. All she had was an old pistol and thirty bullets. If Boko Haram attacked, the soldiers would murder the clinic workers and the adults, and the girls would be taken as sexual slaves, the boys as soldiers. She shuddered.

"What do you want, Anton?"

He resumed smoking his cigarette, gazing at the ocean below. "Do you remember the targeting work we did? How to distribute a disease so it looked natural?"

"Of course I remember. Our government wanted us to target Americans. You also remember that when we told them it was impossible to give the plague to U.S. citizens without eventually infecting our citizens, they didn't believe us."

That idea had been only one of many the politicians brought to the Institute. The rest of the scientists let Zora take the role of chief educator, as she dumbed down the scientific details such that the politicians understood the impossibility of their requests. Sometimes she was successful in dissuading them, sometimes not.

"My company has been studying various ancient diseases."

She looked at him, Bunin silent while he lit another cigarette. "Why? Russia is out of the bioterrorism business, isn't it?"

He suddenly blurted, "If we can create a disease that will result in a thirty-five percent reduction in population in the Middle East, the Russian government will pay my company ten billion dollars. That is, if we make it look entirely natural."

Zora laughed. "Another impossible demand by ignorant politicians. Not much has changed, has it? Anyway, why would Russia do this?"

She watched Anton try to control himself. She knew the

clench of his jaw and hunching of his back presaged a tantrum. She had seen it many times in the laboratory. To her surprise, he spoke calmly.

"Russia has been trying to influence the Middle East for years. It has been a farce. First, we went into Afghanistan, now we are trying to control Syria. The government is tired of living next to a mass of people that hate anyone who isn't a certain kind of Muslim."

Anton stepped back from the railing, spread his hands and then clenched his right fist, the cigarette sticking out like a weapon, pointing it at her. "At the end of WWI, Russia had Constantinople in its hand, and the traitorous British yanked it away. We would have tamed that region. Now, the countries the English imbeciles created by drawing outlines on a map are going to destroy the rest of the world. Pakistan has nukes, and others will too, no matter that so-called treaty with Iran."

He leaned his face closer to her. "When thirty-five percent of the Middle East population is dead, Russia will march in. We will control the oil. We will make the Middle East Christian again. We will save this area from the barbarians who live there now." He stepped back from her a few steps and shot the cuffs of his jacket. "And the rest of the world will thank us."

Zora leaned back against the railing, her hands gripping the rail, the hard metal pressing against her back. Anton's words assaulted her, and even though he was now ten feet away, she felt that the force of his controlled anger might fling her over the metal barrier to the crashing surf below. Was he serious?

Anton crushed his cigarette with his foot on the stone terrace. "Zora, I apologize for my explosion. I am frustrated. Russia has been working in the Middle East for years, trying to support leaders that will provide stability." He paused.

"We have failed. The area is corrupt, ruled by despots who

hoard resources, and control by fear and intimidation. Terrorist groups are killing those who will not convert to Islam, and the governments of that area do nothing to stop them. The bombing of a Russian jet by the Islamists has finally spurred our government to act."

Zora waited for Anton's breathing to slow, her own mind racing, thinking of how Boko Haram extremists were threatening Africa. She walked past him and returned inside, putting her head in her hands. She heard him come in and sit down opposite her.

Zora lifted her head. "It's not possible to do this without the world knowing it was Russia."

"The USSR and the United States have studied potential bioweapons for years. We know the lab each strain came from. Finding an unknown microbe is the answer. My researchers have been looking at various sources for an unknown microbe, like frozen mummies from Siberia. We didn't find anything. Then I received a copy of a document found in a monastery in Russia. It's a confession of a sort. The letter was from a Greek Orthodox monk who described how he had inserted diseased material into reliquaries after the Fourth Crusade."

"What? When Christians attacked Constantinople?"

"Yes. After the crusaders sacked the city in 1203, they gathered all the reliquaries and took them to the Monastery of Pantocrator. Apparently, this monk poisoned many reliquaries right under the nose of the Crusaders, not only with blood, but also with skin from a dead cow, and scabs from what he called a pox victim."

That sounded like smallpox. Zora felt a tremor in her body.

"I asked my scientists if reviving a microbe sealed into a reliquary, not exposed to the elements for eight hundred years, was even feasible. They initially said it was not, but we obtained a sealed reliquary from a Russian church, opened it in our secure lab, and one of the lab technicians found an intact piece of DNA."

"Why would you want to replicate a germ that old? If you want to commit genocide, you know there are better candidates." In spite of herself, Zora began to feel engaged, as if she were back at the Biopreparat, debating the best way to annihilate the United States with germs.

"I need something that will look entirely natural, like anthrax. We will stage the germ in an area where the Islamists have destroyed ancient remains and graves, and the resulting epidemic will be blamed on them. Spreading whatever we find, if we find something, is the problem. That is why I need you."

This story might be believed, she knew. Anthrax had lived in the open ground for at least fifty years. How long could it last in a sealed container?

He said, "I believe I am close to finding the reliquaries the monk referenced in his letter. Two years ago, archaeologists found codices in an underground city in eastern Turkey. They describe Christian relics the Byzantines used in their diplomatic efforts. Dr. Kemal Atay of the Istanbul Museum was leading the project. When his people were too slow in completing the translations of the parchments, he went to his uncle to seek help, a Russian Orthodox Patriarch who happens to be a friend of mine. Atay thought his uncle would have access to better experts in Ancient Greek."

He lit another cigarette and put the match in the silver sugar bowl.

"Atay's uncle sent me photographs of the parchment with the translations. He meant it as a joke, to show me that even a thousand years ago the idea of biological warfare was around. From the translations that Atay's people did, the codices describe exactly which reliquaries the priest poisoned, and provide more details on the disease agent he put in each reliquary."

Anton began to play with the cream container on the table.

"I discussed this potential opportunity with certain Russian representatives. That is when they made the offer. The government is serious. They want this cesspool of an area decimated, but it must look natural, not engineered."

Zora said, "Anton, Russia will be vilified for hundreds of years."

"I'm telling you, no one will know it was us. Reliquaries have the perfect contents to facilitate this research—blood, teeth, bone marrow, and saliva. We will culture whatever we find. The contagion will appear perfectly natural, an ancient scourge unearthed by the indiscriminate looting of archeological sites by terrorists."

"But the Byzantines had thousands of reliquaries. How will you find the ones you want?"

"For almost a month, an American religious expert has been working to answer that question. She had to be persuaded to cooperate."

"What do you mean, *persuaded*?" asked Zora.

"We showed her pictures of her family, implying that they will be harmed if she does not cooperate. Dr. Kate Strong is the only expert in French reliquaries and Ancient Greek that we could find who could disappear for a while, and be motivated to do the work we need done in a short amount of time. Dr. Strong is bipolar, so I have been giving her doses of amphetamines. She has done a remarkable amount of work in a short period of time."

He paused, and then added, "She is in the basement of this castle."

Zora felt an icy wave cascade down her body. He was talking about this woman as if she was a lab rat. She jumped up and pushed away from her chair. "Anton, you kidnapped a United States citizen? You are out of your mind."

"I am not a murderer, Zora. When she has finished here, I will send her back to America, drugged and amnesic. No one will know where she has been. She will be alive."

"Not a murderer? You are talking about the annihilation of millions of people." Zora cackled. "I suppose kidnapping is nothing compared to that. Why me, Anton?"

"If we are to seed a large area with a microbe, we need to find an undetectable way to keep it alive for a few days, and make it look entirely natural. No one else has been able to replicate your experiment, where anthrax lived in the air of a laboratory for three days. You do remember that accomplishment, don't you?"

Of course she did. The problem of keeping a bacterium or a virus alive long enough to distribute it had caused her colleagues at the Institute to reject most of the agents they investigated. At the very end of her time at the Institute, days before the soldiers closed the facility; Zora had found the right formula—a combination of ingredients that would suspend bacteria in the air for three days without the microbe losing its infectious ability. She had never published a paper and never disclosed her exact techniques.

"Anton, do not ask me to help you. It's monstrous." Zora slumped back into her chair, and tried to pour a cup of coffee, spilling it all over the tray.

He looked at her thoughtfully and leaned over, not shouting, which made his words more frightening. "As monstrous as destroying ancient cities like Nimrud? As monstrous as cutting off people's heads and videoing the act? As monstrous as forcing ten-year-old girls to be given to licentious old men as sexual slaves? Please, Zora. World leaders tear their hair out trying to appease the Middle East. The area is a cauldron of megalomaniacs, religious lunatics, and obscenely wealthy despots. Do you really believe that Russia has not whispered this plan to Washington, to London, to Paris?"

Zora tried to take a sip of her coffee, but her hands were shaking too badly. She put the cup down. "Washington would not sanction the destruction of Israel. It's one of the United States' closest allies. If something like this happened, the world will blame the Jews."

Anton laughed. "For once, the Jews will not be blamed. They too will have horrific losses. I am not heartless, Zora. My company will distribute antibiotics to stop the epidemic."

Finally, she said, "And if I don't help you?"

Drumming his fingers on the table, he said, "Then you will be found to have abused the children treated at your clinic. You will be a pariah."

She gasped and stared at him. He stared back at her, implacable.

Zora felt a welling of rage at Anton that he would manipulate her in this way. Her organization would never support Zora working with children once allegations surfaced, and if Anton were determined to use her, he would manufacture "irrefutable" proof.

She recognized the certainty of the zealot. She had seen it in the communist bureaucrats that had come to the Institute. She saw it in the faces of the petty functionaries in Africa, newly rich and replete with absolute authority. She had even seen it in the faces of well-meaning American philanthropists who were certain that with the right education her adopted country could evolve from a confederation of tribes to a single country. In one generation, no less.

Zealots did not respond to logic. If she appeared compliant, she might be able to slow his project. She had an expertise he didn't have. She could claim she needed time to catch up on the research, to learn new equipment, anything to delay his plan. Would she be able to call someone? Zora stared at her former colleague and remained silent. He needed to believe the prospect of money motivated her. Immensely rich people believed that money could incent the vilest of behaviors. They were usually right.

"I want half the money now," Zora said calmly. "And I want to understand Dr. Strong's research."

Anton smiled. "Excellent," he said. "Let me make arrangements." Anton stood gracefully, belying his size, buttoned his jacket, and went to the hall. Zora could hear him ordering someone to clear the table and bring more coffee. Now. She needed to do it now. Zora hefted her squat body out of the chair, and hurried to the terrace.

CHAPTER 8

TWO STORIES BENEATH Zora, Kate looked in the mirror, and picked at the frizzy strands of her hair, remembering a March day when she and Sara had gone to the salon together. Kate's hair had been highlighted and coaxed into cascading ringlets. It had lasted for an entire three hours before puffing back to its usual frizzy unruliness. Jack had called her Rapunzel and danced her around the living room, making her feel dainty and graceful, not a familiar emotion for a woman who was almost six feet tall. An overwhelming feeling of fear made her eyes tear.

Kate knew she was on the precipice of a depressive episode. She had awakened a few hours before, cowering in the corner of the workroom, dirty and disoriented, realizing that the manic frenzy had abated. Kate had found it an enormous effort to lift herself from the floor and go into the bathroom. From the looks of her grown out hair, it had been four weeks since Bunin put the chloroform rag on her face in the castle dining room.

After Bunin had drugged her, she had awakened in the same workroom. The door on the right hand side had been open. She had walked through it down a short hall and found a bathroom on the left and a room with a double bed on the right. The bedroom had a small chair and a nightstand without a lamp. There were toiletries in the bathroom; and the few pieces of clothing she had brought with her were hanging on hooks. None of the rooms had any windows. The ceiling in her three-room prison was fourteen feet above her with ceiling vents and speakers, both mounted too high for her to reach.

Kate had gone to the workroom and stood in the middle of it. "What do you want, Bunin? I know you're listening. If you let me talk to my family so they know I'm ok, I'll do some more work on the documents. You have to tell me exactly what you're looking for. I'm not a mind reader." No response. Kate returned to the bedroom, looked under the bed and in the nightstand and found her backpack. She checked the contents. Her keys, phone, and nail file were gone, but her iPod Nano, wallet and passport were still there. She had no more lithium.

The last dose would have been twelve to fifteen hours previously. She had returned to the research room, and pounded on the door again, this time noticing that it didn't have a normal doorknob, just a handle. She felt no give in the door when she jerked back and forth on the handle, but suddenly, and very unexpectedly, when she pulled, it opened.

Atay came in, and Kate rushed past him, intent on escaping, only to be stopped by two young uniformed men, who shoved her back into the room. The door slammed shut.

"Let me out," she screamed. "I've been kidnapped!" When she heard nothing, she turned to Atay, who stood in the middle of the room.

He said, "Dr. Strong, we need your help. After you identify the items Bunin wants, you can go home. I promise you."

He motioned her to the table, where they both sat. When Kate looked in Atay's face, she almost felt sorry for the disheveled, unshaven man. Gone was his sartorial perfection; his shirt was stained and suit wrinkled. No doubt, she looked as unkempt as he did.

"Dr. Strong, I am sorry you are in this situation." He looked away.

"What happened? How long have I been here?"

"You were out for about six hours. No one harmed you."

"Are you kidding me? You kidnapped me. You know that, don't you?"

Atay rubbed his moustache. "Dr. Strong, Bunin will not let you leave. *I* cannot leave." Atay looked away, and then, astonishingly, he began weeping and pushed an envelope across the table to Kate. She stared at it.

"Open it," he whispered.

Kate took the envelope, her fingers fumbling on the envelope. She took out four photographs. They were 8 x 10 pictures of Jack and Sara.

Kate touched each of the pictures before laying it aside. The top picture showed Jack and Sara at Leo's Restaurant with Amarintha Sims, mother of Sara's best friend, Ava. Another was of the two in the kitchen, another, meeting with a police officer in their living room. In all the shots, they looked devastated and lost. When Kate looked at Atay, he stopped crying and wiped his eyes with handkerchief.

"Bunin has pictures of my family as well. He filmed a visit his ruffians made to my house." Atay clenched his teeth. "One of Bunin's men threatened to rape my daughter."

Kate felt a rush of sympathy for Atay. "How do you know he won't kill us both?" she asked. She felt unexpected calmness; her own fury held at bay by Atay's fear and her tenuous sanity.

"All he wants is to find the reliquaries marked 'pseudos' in the parchments. I don't know why. Can't you do that?"

Pseudos. False. He wanted to find the false reliquaries, the reliquaries without real relics. Could she find where these items were today? What could he do with this knowledge?

"Who is Bunin? Why is he doing this?"

Atay looked up at a small camera in the corner of the room. He turned around so that his back was to it, and said in an almost inaudible rush. "Bunin has a company called New Institute. They took over the project."

What could he possibly want with these artifacts? What was the alternative? If she said no, would Bunin kill her?

Atay looked away from her. She saw the fear in his face. Did she have a choice? "Yes, I will do it."

The look on Atay's face was childlike in its gratitude.

"Hold on a minute." Kate made a list of books and websites she needed and gave it to Atay. "Take this, and leave me alone." He backed out of the room.

Hours later, Atay brought her stacks of printouts from the websites. Kate began to read.

Within a day of Kate's promise to find the false reliquaries, Atay once again became the urbane host—though now a slight tremor in his hands and circles under his eyes revealed his situation. To work as quickly and intensely as possible, she asked him to leave her alone. The uniformed men, visible whenever Atay entered killed any thoughts of trying to escape.

Kate had stared at parchment images, and then had begun to create diagrams on the whiteboard. She slept just a few hours per night, if at all, and bathed resentfully. Atay brought food to her, and more often than not, took it away uneaten. Her fear and a pounding energy kept her working to collapse. On more than one awakening, she found herself in one of the corners, clutching the pictures of Jack and Sara. Rational Kate knew she was in a manic episode. Frenetic Kate kept working.

Finally she had collapsed and slept what she believed was twenty hours, an extended unconsciousness portending the advent of a depressive episode, a dark hole that might clasp her as tight as a straightjacket.

Now, four weeks since Bunin had chloroformed her, standing

in the bathroom, feeling the depressive apathy take over, she vowed to remember whatever Bunin told her from here on so that at some future opportunity she could demolish him. She walked into the workroom, and stared at the whiteboards covered with her writing, and wondered if what she had uncovered would be enough to let her go.

Charleston

CHAPTER 9

THOMPSON DENTON SAT on the porch with his laptop, completed his notes and hit "send." With the death of Dr. Adam Chalk, Thompson was certain Interpol would call him home to headquarters in Lyon, France, where he would begin another case. Not for the first time, he asked himself whether he was up to another assignment that led, as almost all of them did, to a dead end. The Works of Art Investigation Team at Interpol could claim few successes, having fewer investigators than a Charleston book club.

Adam Chalk's murder on the bridge four weeks earlier was still making the occasional news story, but Charleston Police had not arrested anyone for the horrific homicide. He had been Thompson's most promising target, an American academic creating phony provenance documents for Alternative Auctions, a company connected to a Russian oligarch named Anton Bunin.

Alternative Auctions bought looted antiquities, paid academics like Chalk to create phony provenances, and then sold the items to Western buyers and museums. Bunin then distributed the proceeds to the terrorist organizations that the Russian government thought might emerge as a winner from the chaos of the Middle East.

A year ago, Interpol and the FBI had agreed to a joint operation to shut down Alternative Auctions. Interpol created Thompson's cover as an interior designer, inserted him into Charleston, and waited. The mission was to turn Chalk into a cooperating witness, to identify the other US-based members of the ring, and have the FBI make simultaneous arrests.

For the past months, Thompson and his FBI colleagues had built a compelling case against Chalk and an owner of a local carpet store. All that had remained was turning Chalk, which all agreed would be the easiest part of the investigation. The professor would fold easily when presented with evidence of who was benefiting from the sale of these priceless items. Now Chalk was dead, and so was Thompson's case.

Thompson had learned of Chalk's death from a local television announcer while working at home. He immediately went to the Charleston Police Department to find whoever was assigned to the case and offer his help. Thompson was almost certain that Chalk's death was connected to the smuggling ring. After waiting for an hour, a tall black man had come out to the lobby, scowled at his badge, and motioned for Thompson to follow him into a small meeting room.

"I'm Detective Frank Edson. I'm investigating the murder of Dr. Chalk. Why didn't I know about you?" asked the detective.

Thompson sat and spread his arms on the table. "I don't know. I've been working with the FBI on an antiquities smuggling ring that involved Chalk, and figured they'd tell you what was going on."

Frank sat, scowled even more, and said, "They don't share. Tell me all of it."

Detective Edson was clearly offended that an agent

from an international law enforcement agency was in town investigating one of his citizens without his knowledge. After an hour of listening to Thompson and learning Chalk's role in the smuggling ring, the detective's scowl had turned into a thoughtful frown.

"Do you think this group might have killed Chalk?" asked Frank.

"Grabbing a man's car and throwing it off a bridge is not a typical way to commit murder. The Russians are dramatic sons of bitches; so yes, I do believe they executed him. I don't have much that will help you, but I'll cooperate anyway I can."

Thompson had made a copy of all the phone, bank and email records he had on Chalk and sent them to the detective. For the past four weeks, he had frequently met with Frank, answering questions about Anton Bunin and Chalk's role in the smuggling ring.

Now, four weeks later, he had finished his report and conveyed all he knew to Detective Edson. It was time to leave Charleston.

Thompson's cell rang. He left the porch and went inside, recognizing his boss's number. "Hello, Sergei," he said.

"I received your report. Nice work wrapping up the case."

Molotov's wording annoyed Thompson. "Wrapping up the case" would have meant an arrest. He supposed that his boss, who spoke excellent English, though with a very heavy accent, did not know the exact meaning of the phrase. Had he even had time to read the report?

"I can be ready to leave Charleston in a few days. Where are you sending me now?"

"Actually, I have new information that needs to be looked into." Thompson could hear Sergei take a deep draw on his ever-present cigarette.

"What new information?"

"You investigated all of Dr. Chalk's colleagues, didn't you? How deeply did you look into Dr. Kate Strong?"

Thompson certainly had investigated all of the man's co-workers, including the missing Dr. Kate Strong, who had disappeared the day Chalk died. Before Strong's disappearance, Thompson had cleared her of any involvement with Chalk's illegal auction activity. He found no extra money, and no emails to or from suspicious people—nothing remotely incriminating.

The day after Chalk died, and Thompson's meeting with the detective, Frank had called him. "We're trying to find a Dr. Kate Strong who worked for Chalk. Was she involved in any way with this syndicate?"

"Not that I've found."

The detective was silent, and then finally said, "The woman left a voice mail for her husband that she was going out of town, and told him to call Chalk. By the time the husband got the message, Chalk was dead. Her cell phone signal ended in Summerville, and there hasn't been a peep from it since. We want to talk to her. Can you come in?"

After hours of reviewing every piece of information Thompson had gathered, the two investigators agreed that Kate Strong was not involved in Chalk's illegal activity. She was just gone. Her disappearance was a local police matter.

"Sergei, you know I did all the background work myself. We have no evidence that Kate Strong knew anything about the phony provenances, much less that she was involved with Alternative Auctions."

"The office in Istanbul has received an anonymous call that a Dr. Kate Strong is being held as a prisoner by a man named Anton Bunin. There cannot be many Dr. Kate Strongs in the world. What do you think of that?"

Thompson didn't reply.

Sergei lowered his voice. "Don't you think it suspicious that

Dr. Kate Strong's expertise is in Christian relics? Perhaps she is not a captive but a willing participant in the scheme."

"I found absolutely no evidence that she is involved. Does the Istanbul office know anything about the anonymous caller?"

"The tip came in on a phone line, in English, and a woman only said that Kate Strong was being held prisoner. The call ended suddenly, so we have no name or location. We are analyzing the voice and the words used—that sort of thing. Istanbul will send the tape to the FBI."

"The Charleston Police Department has a copy of my case file on Chalk, and on everyone who worked for Chalk, including Strong. I'll make sure the FBI has all of it too. The FBI already is aware of Alternative Auctions."

"Tell me a little more about this group."

"Did you read my report?"

"Tell me anyway, Thompson. I have the time."

Sergei was maddening. That today's terrorists trafficked in art was incomprehensible to Sergei, or so he pretended. "Anton Bunin funds Alternative Auctions. He also is the CEO of a legitimate pharmaceutical group called New Institute of Biochemical Manufacturing. It's a play off the name of his old employer, Institute of Ultra-Pure Biochemical Preparations. That was the Russian government division that handled the USSR's research into biological warfare, also called the Biopreparat."

When Sergei did not respond, Thompson continued. "Bunin hasn't kept it a secret that he funds and supports Alternative Auctions. In an interview with a French newspaper, he says he founded the auction house in order to protect humanity's treasures in the Middle East, by buying anything that the Islamists steal. Supposedly, he is going to safeguard these items until legitimate governments can return order to places like Iraq and Syria. In reality, he's been using the millions he gets from selling the stolen items as leverage over the Islamists. He's acting as a proxy to Russia's government supporting groups that Russia's government believes can create a single empire, much like the Ottoman Empire. Russia wants a more unified Middle East under Russia's control. They've had that goal for over a hundred years."

"What do you mean?" said Sergei.

"Remember, the Soviet Union, or the USSR—Union of Soviet Socialist Republics—whatever you want to call them, did not exist before 1922. Russia came into WWI supporting the Allies. In return for this support, the Brits promised that they would get control over Istanbul and other Middle Eastern territories. The Allies reneged on the deal, and the Soviet Union got nothing. US intelligence analysts believe that Russia is maneuvering to get the Middle East under its control, to right what they see as a hundred-year-old betrayal. And, of course, for the oil. Russia's support of Syria is part of the objective and Bunin is helping the government by funding certain terrorist groups that allegedly further that goal."

"How did you even get involved in the political aspect of this case? You were supposed to be helping the Americans get evidence to arrest people."

"Sergei, I'm on a team with FBI agents. The Americans always want to understand motivation. They believe it helps their investigations."

Sergei snorted, but said nothing.

Thompson said, "Bunin has also made some startling statements about the rights of Christians to worship at Hagia Sophia, the museum in Istanbul that was initially built as a cathedral."

The first time Thompson had seen Hagia Sophia, he had stood motionless, rooted to the Roman-era square spanning the width of the building, imagining the immense golden-domed structure a thousand years before. The minarets wouldn't have been there, of course, but pilgrims to Constantinople must have been struck dumb on seeing it for the first time. Thompson later read that, in the tenth century, a group from Russia had reported, "We knew not whether we were in Heaven or earth. For on earth there is no such splendor and beauty." Thompson had felt a similar wave of awe standing in the square, motivated to move on only because one of the omnipresent rug sellers would not leave him alone.

"So Alternative Auctions is helping fund certain terrorist groups by buying their stolen goods, getting experts to create phony provenances, and then auctioning the items to raise money. Sounds like small potatoes," said Sergei.

Thompson took a deep breath, trying to control his temper. "The Islamists beheaded Palmyra's museum director after they blew up most of the city. He refused to reveal the location of the archeological treasures of Palmyra. Alternative Auctions is fueling this type of barbaric activity by acting as the primary buyer of what the Islamists steal. I'm sorry you don't think it's worthy of your time." He wanted to slam the phone down. If his own organization didn't support his efforts, where could he go? Who would do the work? The Americans had several organizations that tried to stop the flow of stolen antiquities; maybe he could work for one of them.

Sergei spoke soothingly, "Thompson, I don't mean that. I will read your report and send it to the proper recipients. Until we know more about the situation of Dr. Strong, you will stay in Charleston. Our headquarters has notified the FBI of this anonymous call."

Thompson could hear Sergei take a drag from his cigarette. "Interpol Istanbul almost gave the tip to the U.S. Embassy in Istanbul, rather than the FBI. Let the local Americans chase their tails around the bazaar looking for a wayward wife." At this, Sergei laughed so loud that Thompson moved the phone from his ear.

"Thompson, are you listening to me?"

"Sorry, the connection was bad for a minute. Please repeat."

"I have another case that I'd like you to begin working. It's even more of a wild goose chase than finding Kate Strong in Istanbul. Someone at the Vatican called our boss."

"What? The Vatican called Director Petit?"

"Yes, yes, the Vatican. You know how difficult the Vatican can be to work with, my friend. They start where the buck stops, as the Americans like to say. They told Petit that a reliquary from the Convent of Corbie in France has gone missing, and they want us to get it back."

Again, Sergei laughed, but this laugh sounded tubercular. Thompson moved his phone away again in an unconscious attempt to avoid infection. "An old French convent is being restored, and the altar was brought back to the Vatican for repair. The reliquary is somewhere in the altar, I suppose, or in this case, it is not."

"Why would you want me to stay here when the items were stolen from a French convent?"

Sergei took another drag before responding. "Because the Vatican told Director Petit that the missing item had been taken to Charleston. Make sure you keep me updated."

Thompson was barely listening to Sergei. Kate Strong kidnapped by Anton Bunin. Why?

CHAPTER 10

AMARINTHA SIMS STARED at the empty lot, trying to imagine a future in which she wasn't dead. The brain tumor she had was slow growing, so her oncologist said, but so was an alligator. Both would kill you once they got to the right size. As a biologist, on leave from the Medical University because of the cancer, she knew too much about her situation to have false hope.

The property had been in her family since 1975, when her father, Charles Sims, had bought it from a Charleston estate. Her parents never had enough money to build a house, but they did pay the taxes on the lot, and the three of them had made many trips downtown from their farm in Summerville to check on their little piece of South of Broad property. Her father would spread a blanket, her mother Fannie would unpack a picnic lunch, and the three of them would talk about the Charleston single house they would build one day. Her father had even put a rope swing on the large live oak that had stood guardian for over two hundred years on the northern corner. His death, when she was ten, in 1986, ended that dream for her mother, but Amarintha had never lost her desire to build a house one day on this little piece of property.

She had saved for twenty years, and the day after the bank approved her construction loan, her doctor showed her an MRI with an innocuous-looking dark spot in the back of her head. In the weeks since learning of her diagnosis, she had not had time to do anything but drag herself to radiation and chemotherapy. Both were finished now, thank God. How could she get this house completed before her steadily progressing tumor took her sight, her movement, and finally, her life?

Out of habit, she brushed her hair behind her ear, remembered there was no hair on her head, and turned the gesture into a scarf adjustment instead. She slid out of the car and made her way over to the woman and two men talking in front of the empty lot. The woman, Nudie Boyer-Henry, was the representative from the Board of Architectural Review, known as the BAR. She and Thompson Denton, an interior designer, were looking at blueprints; the third man, who she did not know, pointed to something on the page.

Nudie had referred Amarintha to Thompson, claiming that he was writing a book about building modern houses in historical areas, and suggesting that he would act as Amarintha's representative to the BAR if she allowed him to document the entire building process for his book. Amarintha decided to attend a BAR meeting to see for herself how it operated. The meeting had occurred in Charleston's City Hall under a life-size painting of George Washington standing on the shores of Mount Pleasant, the steeple of St. Phillip and the rest of the Charleston skyline faintly visible in the distant.

This particular session included a debate on the virtues of the "shadow line" of 5/8 inch Hardiplank versus the "shadow line" of 3/8 inch Hardiplank. Amarintha had raised her hand and asked why it mattered, at which point a lecture had commenced on the virtues of dimensional cement as an exterior siding that looked like wood, but wasn't. Since it was Charleston, a quintessential Southern city, the lecture had not been directed at her alone, so the speaker educated all attendees for fifteen minutes on the topic, some of them directing exasperated looks at her.

As the ten-foot tall George Washington looked down on the assembled group sitting in small antique cane chairs that appeared to be moments away from collapsing, Amarintha thought that George likely felt as embarrassed as she did. The faint white horse painted behind him, added after the painting had been approved by the city, had its tail up, seemingly ready to drop manure on the City of Charleston skyline, just visible under its rump. Perhaps the city, in 1792, had failed to pay what the artist viewed as an acceptable fee. Why someone had not painted over the horse in the intervening years she did not know.

Escaping the meeting, she had called Thompson and agreed with his proposal to represent her project at future BAR meetings. Amarintha was positive that Mrs. Henry would be relieved to have someone to confer with who appreciated the difference in the shadow line between 5/8 and 3/8 inch cement siding.

Her house would be a traditional Charleston single: three stories stacked on each other, with the requisite side porches, outside shutters, and standing seam metal roof. It would look as old as the neighboring homes, albeit with insulated windows and modern baths. Based on what she understood of the specified stucco thickness and depth of concrete foundation, it would survive another Hurricane Hugo and then some. If Ava and Fannie didn't want to live in the house, they could sell it. Real estate agents had many buyers who wanted to live in a house in the historical district that did not cost eight-hundred dollars a month to keep cool.

As she walked over, the three people standing in front of her small patch of ground turned to greet her.

"Hello, Amarintha. How are you today?" said Nudie.

Nudie Henry had her ebony hair coiled into a twist and stood holding a hat that likely cost more than Amarintha's entire outfit. Amarintha wanted to brush the yellow pine pollen off Ms. Henry's hair, but decided that it added a colorful touch otherwise missing from the woman's funereal ensemble—black linen dress, black hat, and black sandals.

Thompson Denton, in contrast, was dressed like a safari guide in khakis that had an astonishing number of pockets. With his wavy chestnut hair and tanned skin, he was a much handsomer version of Humphrey Bogart in *The African Queen*, a look accentuated by his military-looking sunglasses.

"Hey there, Amarintha. I've been talking to Ms. Henry and Jack Strong here about your house." Thompson grinned at her and gestured to the third member of the group.

Once Amarintha had agreed on the phone to Thompson's involvement, they had spent a few hours in a local restaurant reviewing the plans so that Thompson could create specifications that the prospective builders could use for their bids. Although the results were satisfactory, Amarintha did not believe interior designer was his first profession, although he gave her no information to the contrary. He was strangely, and unexpectedly, attractive to her. She did not date, ever, and it had been a long time since she had been tempted to do so.

Amarintha held out her hand to the second man. "Hello, I'm Amarintha Sims. I'm assuming you are Jack Strong. You come highly recommended."

The man shook her hand, nodded, and said, "Yes, I'm working with Thompson on another project, and of course, all the builders know Nudie. She wants to make sure the integrity of the house is solid."

Amarintha turned her head to the BAR woman, who continued to tap her expensive sandal. "Integrity? I assume that is another word for whether the neighbors will like it or not."

Nudie's expression was severe, and even though Amarintha was still smiling, she took offense. Fortunately, the woman's phone rang, "Please excuse me," she said, and moved away from them to answer.

"So, Mr. Strong, have you built on the peninsula before?" He was bald, but by choice, not nature, with a worker's tan and sea green eyes. He was very tall, probably six and a half feet. He wore a wedding ring, and she assumed the rugged, worn Ford truck parked twenty feet away belonged to the builder. She had met a few other builders, all of whom drove fancy vehicles. This old paint-splattered truck lifted her spirits. Perhaps, she could work with this one.

"Yes, but please call me Jack."

"Ok, Jack." A sudden image of the Farmer's Market a few months ago came to her. "Hey, wait a minute. I just figured out who you are. You're Sara's father. It's nice to meet you again. I'm Ava's mother."

The builder looked at her blankly. He finally spoke. "Oh, right."

The two of them shuffled for a few moments, with Strong looking away, and Amarintha remembered his personal circumstances. The death of his wife's boss had been front-page news a month before. Ava then told her mother that Kate Strong had disappeared the exact same day, and no one knew where she was. The Strong's daughter Sara was a close friend of Ava's, and Amarintha had not even called the girl after learning about Kate. A wave of shame went through her. A month of cancer treatments definitely had burned out pieces of her memory as well as her normal solicitude.

"Jack, please, I look very different from when we met." Amarintha tried to laugh, not wanting him to be uncomfortable. "What a nice coincidence. I never knew what business you were in."

Clearly embarrassed, Strong scratched his head. He handed her a binder. "Here is a complete portfolio on what I've done. It has references you can call."

"Did Thompson or Nudie tell you I have only four months to build this home?" asked Amarintha.

Nudie put her hand over her phone and shouted from where she still stood, "I have told Amarintha that time frame is simply impossible." Mrs. Henry was indignant now, striding back over to the other three, her faux accent cracking. "The BAR needs to be involved every step of the way, and we just cannot see how this house, with the restrictions on parking, materials, and everything else, could be finished in that time."

"I've worked with tight time frames before, and, if you give me the job, I can finish it in four months," said Jack. "One question though: Do we need to follow the approved plans and dig out piers as deep as what is on the plans? That's pretty unusual for Charleston, and if we could avoid it, that would save some time."

The BAR lady squeezed a sound from her throat that could have indicated derision or laughter. "You would have to resubmit to the Board if you change anything on these plans."

"How long would that take?"

"A month or more."

"That's impossible. I can't wait." Amarintha turned to Jack. "When could you start?"

The builder rubbed his head, looked at Mrs. Henry, and said, "Five days."

Five days. Amarintha looked at him, and said, "Send me the final estimate tomorrow, and I'll let you know by the end of the day."

Thompson had been studying the surrounding houses with baffling intensity. He finally spoke. "I've got some color samples for us to review." He whisked out a fan of paint chips from a gigantic leather bag. Dressed in his safari get-up, holding the paint samples, and cradling the big bag, Thompson looked like a jungle guide-turned-magician, trying to distract his clients from an anaconda on the trail.

Amarintha put her hand to her temple, again forgetting she had no hair. This time she adjusted her sunglasses. "Thompson, I want the stucco to be beige, the trim white, and the shutters black. Do you need anything else from me today?"

Nudie murmured a goodbye, as did Thompson and Jack Strong. Amarintha walked back to the car, determined to exude energy and confidence. Mrs. Henry had already brought two couples to the job site "because of—well, my dear, because of your situation."

Amarintha floored the accelerator, or at least as much as you could floor a VW bug engine. She had to finish this house. Fannie would make sure Ava had food, shelter, and clothing. She would also pester Ava until her granddaughter found a husband and produced a great-grandchild. They would be ok.

CHAPTER 11

JACK ARRIVED HOME with the blueprints for Amarintha's house, planning to finish the estimate that night. He needed the business. He'd have to do some of the detail work himself on the house, but that was ok—anything to keep him from dwelling on Kate.

The idea that his wife had been missing for four weeks was still intolerable. What had happened to her? The morning she had disappeared, Kate had been gone when he woke up, and he figured she was still angry with him over the argument the night before.

He had gone to a jobsite on James Island where he was building a boat dock. At lunchtime, while eating a sandwich in his truck, he received a call from Adam Chalk's assistant. Sobbing, she told him that Adam had died on the Ravenel Bridge, and then asked Jack if he knew where Kate was. The College needed her to come in immediately. Jack had pulled out his phone to call his wife, and then saw that she left him a voice mail. Expecting to hear a message about Adam's death, Jack was astonished to hear:

"Jack, I'm sorry we can't talk, but I've got to go away for three days. The College might be leading a project. It's important. Adam can tell you more; call him when you can. I'll be back in three days."

In bewilderment, he listened to the message twice more, and then hurried to the College. Chalk's hysterical assistant yielded no other useful information other than the fact that there had been an early morning meeting. Adam had been at work, but rushed out around 10:00 a.m.

Jack raced home and scoured the house for a note he was certain existed somewhere in the messiness of their home and finally found a Post-it note on the floor in front of the refrigerator.

Jack, I tried to reach you, but couldn't. I have an opportunity to be the lead investigator on a project that could change the course of the history around French relics. Call Adam and he'll tell you about it. I'll be gone for three days. The break will be good for us. Kate

Change the course of the history of relics? Where had she gone? He frantically looked for any other evidence of where Kate had gone, and found her passport missing, as well as her computer and some clothes. When he found the bottle of lithium still in the bathroom, fear added to his anger and confusion. Why had she left the lithium?

Jack logged on to their credit card account. There were no charges for a plane ticket. He called Chalk's assistant, and asked her if she would see if the college had issued any plane tickets for Kate. She promised she would, right after she arranged for substitutes for Dr. Chalk's classes. *That would take a while,* he thought.

The doorbell had rung, and when Jack opened the door, a tall black man was holding a Charleston Police Department badge up for him to read.

"I'm Detective Frank Edson; may I come in?"

Jack motioned the man inside, mute with fear that something had happened to Kate.

The two men stood in the small foyer. "I'm actually here to see your wife, Dr. Strong. We're investigating the death of her boss, Adam Chalk. You heard about that, a couple of hours ago?"

"Yes, I did, but my wife isn't here; she's out of town."

"We need to speak to her, Mr. Strong.

Jack put his hand on the door. "I'll tell Kate to call you when she gets home."

"Exactly where is your wife, Mr. Strong?" asked the detective, who took a fractional step towards Jack.

Jack stepped back and leaned against the wall, not looking at the detective. "I don't know. It's something with work. She left me a voice mail and a note that Adam would tell me where she was going, and I got the messages too late to talk to Adam."

"Let's sit down," said the detective.

Jack led the police officer to the small living room and motioned him to sit. They sat facing each other over a mahogany coffee table. Jack cleared a space and put his phone down, looking at the detective. "Detective Edson, my wife left me a voice mail about ten this morning. I'll play it for you." Jack fumbled with his phone and played the message for the detective, his phone speaker barely audible.

Detective Edson brought out a small notebook, and after the voice mail finished asked, "Anything missing from the house?"

Jack swallowed, and managed to say, "Her passport, purse, computer, and some clothes."

The detective made a note. "And you have no idea of where she might be?"

Jack rubbed his head, and said, "No, I don't. I thought I might ride around the airport and find out if her car is there.

There isn't a charge for an airline ticket on our credit card, but I called the college. They'll check to see if a ticket was issued."

Detective Edson made a few more notes, then said, "Mr. Strong, you do know that Adam Chalk's death is being treated as deliberate, a murder to be exact."

Jack looked past the detective at a trophy on the wall Sara had received for soccer in high school. "A murder," he said slowly, turning his head back to look at the detective. "I thought his car went off the bridge in an accident."

"No, his car was actually picked up by a commercial garbage truck and shoved into the girders of the bridge. It fell into the river before Chalk could get out."

Jack bolted up, remembering Adam's convertible. He had always warned Kate not to ride with the man in what Jack thought of as a death trap. "Are you sure my wife wasn't in the car?"

"No, she wasn't. We're sure."

"How do you know?"

"There were many witnesses on the bridge. Chalk was alone."

"Who would murder Adam?" said Jack. "He's a college professor."

The detective stood and closed his notebook. "That's what I'm trying to find out. The last person who saw Adam Chalk was his assistant, and before that your wife. We need to talk to her." He handed Jack a business card and they both walked to the front door.

Jack watched the detective turn to leave, and before he could stop himself, he put his hand on the doorjamb. "Wait," said Jack. "My wife is missing, and only Adam knew where she was. Now he's dead. You've got to help me find her," he added, his arm now blocking the front door.

Jack remembered Detective Edson's face when the two men's eyes met; it had been kind and non-judgmental. "Mr. Strong, we will be trying to locate your wife, and I'll let you know what I find out."

After the detective left, Jack had driven to the airport and spent two hours driving through every single parking lot. He finally found her car, opened it with the extra key on his ring, and sat in the driver's seat. He opened the glove box and the trunk and found nothing. Nothing but what he always bugged her to carry: a flashlight, jumper cables, a first-aid kit, and last year's Christmas present to her, a small tool kit. With his head on the steering wheel, he had wept.

The next morning, he went to see Detective Edson and filed a missing person report. He told the detective about finding Kate's car at the airport. He also told the detective about Kate being under treatment for bipolar disorder. The detective had been quiet, listening, and assured Jack that if his wife were still missing forty-eight hours after her expected return home, he would add her to the missing person's database. This database, the detective said, was regularly reviewed by hospitals when an unidentified person was admitted, an unspoken acknowledgement of Kate's medical condition.

The meeting ended with Detective Edson walking Jack to the lobby and saying, "Mr. Strong, our department will continue to look for her because we need to talk to her. I'll call you when we learn anything new. In the meantime, I suggest you call your family; perhaps they can help."

Nothing had helped. Kate seemed to have been teleported from the airport parking lot to a space ship. Now, four weeks later, their daughter Sara clung to the life raft that Jack had given her—that Kate was in a hospital, unidentified, and eventually would be identified.

Jack and his daughter didn't talk much about Kate's disappearance, both of them determined to be optimistic when in the other's presence. Kate was the force that held the three of them together. Without her, he and Sara floundered, pretending to each other that nothing was wrong, that Kate would be home soon.

"Dad," Sara said. Jack looked up from the blueprints to see his daughter standing in the doorway of the kitchen. She moved to the table. "Dad, I need your advice about something."

"Shoot," he said.

"I have a friend whose mother has cancer. She tells my friend that everything is fine; the house is going to be finished, and she needs to finish—"

"Wait, cancer—you said her mother has cancer and is building a house?"

"Yeah, some kind of cancer of the liver or something."

"Brain."

"Huh?"

"Her cancer is in her brain. Unless you're not talking about Ava's mother, Amarintha."

His daughter now looked directly at him with her cobalt eyes. "Dad, how do you know about Ava's mom's cancer? Oh, is it their house you're working on?" She gestured to the blueprints on the kitchen table.

"Yes. She had to remind me that we had met at the Farmer's Market. When I met her today, I didn't recognize her at all. She looks—well, she looks sick."

Sara sat down at the table with her head down. She eked out, "Dad, I miss Mom. I want to tell Ava to come back home. You never know what's going to happen." She began to cry.

Jack looked at his calloused and cut hands. He wanted to hold his daughter; he should hold his daughter. The sobbing continued, and she made the decision for him, moving her chair next to his. She put her head on her father's shoulder. He rested his lips against Sara's forehead and kissed her. "It's ok, kiddo. I miss her too. The police are still looking for her. They will find her. Her car wouldn't have been at the airport if anything bad had happened to her."

Sara lifted her head. Her eyes looked like wet sapphires. For the hundredth time she said, "Dad, I just don't understand why Mom hasn't called, or texted—not even a letter to let us know where she is."

"Honey, we talked about this before. I think she's in a manic episode, like the one she had after you were born. I don't know why it happened now, especially since she's been taking her meds. We will find her, I promise." Jack said this forcefully and confidently, a confidence he did not feel.

Kate could be mercurial, oblivious sometimes when working on a project, but never thoughtless. For Kate not to call Sara meant the worst. How and when was he to tell his daughter that Kate was likely dead?

Sniveling, Sara wiped her eyes. "What should I tell Ava? She's super brainy, but if she comes home, she won't be able to study. She'd become her mother's nurse. I know her."

The return to the question of whether Ava should come home jolted Jack.

"Dad, what would you do?"

Jack was silent, wondering what Kate would say. Finally, he said, "Let's go downtown and get something to eat. We'll figure this out."

Sara said, "Let me get my phone." She walked back to her bedroom. Jack could hear running water.

Jack rolled up the blueprints and washed his own hands. When Sara returned, they hugged, Jack holding onto his daughter for a long moment. Both were silent as he drove his old pick-up truck, windows open, down King Street. Spotting an open parking space, they wedged the old truck into it and fed the meter.

Sara wanted to go to Leo's, a small diner, now open only

Monday through Friday because Leo had gotten tired of explaining to the weekend tourists what grits were. Locals filled the restaurant. As they walked in, a couple of people nodded. Jack knew they would leave it at that. Unlike a death, no one knew what to say to a disappearance.

She picked up the menu even though she never ordered anything but a BLT. Leo caught Jack's eye and mouthed "the usual" with a raised eyebrow. Jack nodded.

When the bell on the front door rang behind them, Jack saw Sara staring at whoever had entered. He turned around to see Amarintha Sims standing in the doorway looking for a table. He studied her under the guise of looking for their waiter. She seemed even smaller than she had this morning—slight and fragile. She was wearing an old loose tunic and jeans and another crazy scarf on her head under a straw hat. Her glance finally found him. She smiled slightly and waved. Finding nowhere to sit, she turned to go. Jack got up suddenly and motioned her over.

"Amarintha, please—sit with us."

"Oh, no, that's all right."

"I insist. Sara wants to see you," he said and walked over to take her arm. It was like a twig.

Jack led her over and seated her next to Sara.

"Hello, Sara, it's nice to see you. Usually you and Ava show up in Charleston about the same time," Amarintha said, picking up the menu.

"Hi, Ms. Sims, I didn't go back for spring semester—you know, because of Mom." Sara looked at her sideways, trying not to stare.

Jack squirmed a bit in his seat. "I'm sorry I didn't remember meeting you in the market."

"Please don't pretend I resemble that woman you met. I do not, and everyone knows it. Besides, I didn't recognize you either. The bald head is new." Amarintha looked directly into Jack's eyes. Now he could see that the smiling woman from the market was still there. At the home site today, he hadn't noticed that she had eyes of two different colors. One was green, and one brown, and the vibrancy of the green eye against her pale skin was somewhat eerie.

She looked at Sara again and took her hand. "How are you really, sweetie? I know you must really miss your mom."

Well, here is one person who isn't afraid to tackle the issue head on, Jack thought. He briefly wondered whether she had ever met Kate. He interrupted. "We had the surveyor over after you left. Now I'm ready to bring the subcontractors in to dig the piers. Why are you building now?"

Amarintha did not seem perturbed at his comments. "My father bought the property years ago, and it's taken me this long to save the money."

"I know you have to finish it within four months, but no one said why."

"That's about all the quality time I have left," she said. "I've had chemo. I've had radiation. That's about all medical science can do."

Jack looked at Amarintha. This woman seemed happy in spite of what was happening to her body and he felt radiating warmth from her. An image of chickens under the Piggly Wiggly heat lamp popped into his head. He flinched, realizing that the radiation and chemotherapy treatments had indeed been cooking her body.

Amarintha leaned over, held Sara's hands in hers, and looked directly at her. "Sara, I'm so happy you and Ava are friends. She has trouble being social."

"I know. I actually have to force her to go out with me, you know, just to eat and stuff. She is worried about you and misses. . . ."

Sara put her head down to keep from crying. All three were silent.

Amarintha put the menu down, stared into space, took one gulping breath, and began to cough. The pallor of her face moved from translucent to cherry as she put her fist to her mouth. One hand tightened on the table, as though to thrust the cough away and still she could not stop. She put the napkin to her mouth, shoved herself away from the table, leaned over, and gasped. All the diners were now staring.

Wavering a bit, Amarintha stood. "I need to go," she said, barely breathing. She stumbled to the door. Before Jack could help her, she fell to one knee, pushed herself up, and grabbed the knob as if exiting the diner would solve everything.

Jack followed her outside. Amarintha insisted she was all right, but he ignored her protests and helped her to her car. He opened the door and eased the now marble pale woman into her seat. Amarintha lifted her hand in an attempt to wave, and Jack shut the car door. He turned, and saw Sara watching both of them through the diner's picture window. Jack stepped aside and watched the VW bug drive off.

He returned to the diner and stood by the table without speaking. When he leaned down to retrieve Amarintha's napkin, he noticed the red flecks on it, and left it there. Sitting down, he pressed his thumb and index finger on his eyelids. When he opened his eyes, he saw Sara staring at him with tears in her eyes. Jack shifted, looked away, and finally said, "I think you should call Ava and tell her to come home."

CHAPTER 12

Amarintha had accepted Jack's quote without any questions and sent him a deposit. The two of them now met at the site every day, and each time he saw her, she looked more diminished than she had at the restaurant. Amarintha reviewed decisions with him in a manner that suggested she was committing to memory the entire unbuilt house, questioning him closely about the view from each window and wanting to know how the sun would light each room. No one ever came with her to the site, and Jack didn't know whether Sara had talked to Ava about coming home or not. Neither of them mentioned what happened at Leo's Restaurant.

Jack rose each day at 5:00 a.m. to study the missing persons sites that Detective Edson had shown him. By 7:00 a.m., he felt depressed and tired, knowing he had ten hours of work ahead of him. The hours he dreaded most were the meetings that served as social events for their attendees, dragging out discussions that could have been resolved with a five-minute phone call.

Yesterday, the BAR had wanted to interview the owners on either side of Amarintha's property to ensure that they would not object to her modest Charleston single. Richard Anderson, the neighbor closest to Amarintha's lot, hadn't had any objections, but Jack wasn't so lucky with the owner on the other side: a Mr.

Jameson Whitcomb, a hedge fund billionaire who lived in New York.

His huge antebellum home dwarfed Richard's small brick Georgian-style cottage. The billionaire sent an underling in a black limo from the airport, flown in from where Jack didn't know and didn't ask. The young man carried two smart phones that did not stop ringing, buzzing, or pinging the entire time he pretended to inspect the job site. Of course, there was nothing to inspect yet, and Jack suspected the employee would make a few more unscheduled visits to make sure nothing marred the perfection of the house his employer never visited. With Amarintha's house between Richard's home and the billionaire's, both in size and in location, the three houses would resemble the baby bear, momma bear and papa bear of Charleston dwellings.

Today Richard was sitting on his porch steps with the *New York Times* waiting near a big thermos of coffee, a ritual the man had started on Jack's first day on the job site. Jack would walk up the steps and sit. Richard would hand the paper carefully to Jack, a paper he seldom had the time to look at, along with a Styrofoam cup of coffee, and then comment about the top stories in the paper, stories that had little bearing on Jack's life in Charleston. This time, Richard waved Jack over after he had parked his truck. Jack ambled over, took the cup of coffee, and sat down on the front porch steps.

"Well, sure is a fine day for breaking ground," mused Richard.

"Yes, sir. I'm hoping for a few more weeks of this weather so we can get the house dried in." Jack sipped his coffee, knowing that there would be many days where he would have no time to sit and talk to this genteel man.

Richard looked up and down the street at all the other homes. "I'm surprised this lot didn't get built when all those financial types were buying up everything. It has to be the only empty lot left around here." He took a long draw of his coffee, smacked his lips as old men do, and then continued.

"You know, I always wondered why that lady professor didn't buy this lot. I saw her over here last fall more than a few times. I wonder whether anybody ever found out what happened to her." The old man sipped his own coffee and scratched the little bit of chin whiskers he had.

Jack went still, not certain he had heard correctly. "What do you mean—*the lady professor*? What lady professor?" His words came out harshly, and Richard turned and looked at him, his face showing hurt at the tone in Jack's voice, an inflection Jack knew he had never used with the man.

"Don't you know what I'm talking about? She worked for the professor that was murdered on the bridge by that crazy driver in the garbage truck. Never caught the guy."

"I'm sorry, Richard. I guess you don't know, but it's my wife that is missing." Jack dropped his head. Tugging the brim of his cap, he rubbed his eyes.

"Oh my, I'm sorry." Jack looked up to see in Richard's face both sympathy and unabashed curiosity.

"She . . . she just went to work and never came back. Nobody saw her after an early morning meeting with her boss. It's been four weeks, and I have no idea what happened."

Richard took another sip of his coffee.

"Son, I'm real sorry. I didn't know that was your wife. When her picture was on the news, I called the police and told them I had seen her walking around Queen Street a couple of times, but I guess the detective I talked to didn't think it meant anything." Richard stopped talking and stared down the road where a Mercedes sedan idled at the corner of Queen and Church streets.

Jack was silent, remembering how he had badgered Detective Edson to put Kate's picture on the television, something he wished he had not done. A rash of crank calls to both the police station and their house had not offered any new information, and some of the calls had been frightening, the callers claiming to have Kate and offering to return her for money. "Wait a minute, Jack, the day she, you know, the day she—"

"Disappeared?" Jack asked flatly.

"Yes, what day was that?"

"April 10."

Richard stared at the Mercedes idling at the stop sign. "Excuse me, son. I need to look for something."

Jack watched Richard open his screen door and heard him opening desk drawers and rummaging through them. Just then, the subcontractor responsible for the foundation drove up, pulling a huge auger on a trailer.

"How are you, Buck?"

"Well, not too bad. Glad to see business picking up." Buck was a middle-aged man with the permanently reddened look of someone who has worked outside for decades. Jack had worked with him on many jobs. He knew Buck was reliable, good, and fast—though not cheap. Not with this exotic equipment. The auger, which looked like a giant flathead screwdriver, was going to make it possible to drill holes for the foundation piers anchoring the house.

A young man stepped out of the truck and asked, "Well, we ready?" He was pale and skinny with a shaved head and a blond soul patch that looked like dirt. He started backing the trailer into the location of the piers, beginning with the rearmost one. The auger used a loud diesel engine, and Jack knew they'd have complaints about the noise. Jack walked over to the stakes the surveyor had hammered into the ground.

"Ok," he shouted. "Here is the foundation marked out. You're scheduled for three hours, right?" Buck spit and nodded. The kid got out of the truck and carefully lowered the big auger into place. Buck would pile the dirt on the lot, and Jack would offer it free to another builder. On the peninsula, with ever-present flooding, contractors always needed dirt to shore up the ground's constant migration to the sea.

The big engine roared, the drill came down, and the drilling commenced. The din did not push Kate from Jack's mind, but it did silence the needling, ever-present belief that Kate was in danger and he was helpless to save her.

Istanbul

CHAPTER 13

"**I**'M FINISHED, YOU bastard," Kate said towards the speaker in the workroom. She slumped in the chair, her eyes on the walls of her prison. She swiveled listlessly in the office chair, proud of her achievement, yet overwhelmed with fatigue and depression.

Ten feet from the whiteboard, she could see innumerable hairline horizontal lines, black against the white background. Standing two feet from the walls, a visitor would see organized rectangles with names, dates, locations, and nationalities. The south wall began with the oldest, dating to 300 AD, with the lineage lines moving counterclockwise to the last contemporary units. The images showed an enormous family tree of relics.

A closer look showed, superimposed on these trees, odd icons of faces, body parts, and non-living objects. These icons formed their own lineage charts, showing the original whole relic, say a body, and the many ways it had been broken apart. And, broken apart they had been.

The dry academic record of what had happened to a dead saint's remains belied the true horror of the event—fistfights over body parts, theft of the same, and accusations among devout believers, all scrambling to hit the holy relic jackpot. The entire room resembled a marble wall, a visual record of the reliquaries stored in the Monastery of the Pantocrator during the Crusader sack of Constantinople.

The breakthrough was her analysis of the palimpsest, the remnants of earlier writing on a few of the parchment pages. The scribes had scraped the parchment and reused it, a common practice before the widespread use of paper, as parchment was time-consuming to make. In ancient times, this would have been all but impossible to decipher, but using the special photographic analysis program on the computer, Kate was able to decipher the previous notations. She knew that other researchers would have seen the palimpsest as well, but the almost hidden writing was in a code, a code using the ancient Roman, not the Byzantine, calendar as its key. Initially Kate ignored the writing, believing it to be unrelated, but she persevered and found the story hidden in the parchments, a story almost too incredible to be true.

Twelve reliquaries had been deliberately seeded with disease.

In 1204, Crusader knights had sacked Constantinople, ripping reliquaries from churches and piling them in a monastery until the loot could be divided. While in the Pantocrator Monastery, a Byzantine monk had opened the reliquaries and inserted scabs from a pox victim, skin from a cow that had died of what the monk called murrain, a word Kate did not know, and blood from a plague victim.

Five of the twelve, now at the Vatican, contained bones of St. Paul and other apostles, and presumably, each one had one of these toxic materials. Another five reliquaries, purchased by King Louis in 1239, were in Notre Dame Cathedral in Paris, and were purported to contain pieces of the Crown of Thorns and the Robe of Christ. The last two of the twelve artifacts were sent to an insignificant convent in France. One of them did not have disease material inserted into it. In coded language, the priest identified this reliquary as unholy. The coded text indicated that this particular object had caused healing in a Mussulman, a word used for Muslims at the time and therefore was "of Satan, and Satan hath no better agent on Earth than the treacherous Franks."

The codex was clear about the motive of such medieval treachery—revenge on France for Frankish Christians looting and destroying Constantinople in the Fourth Crusade.

These twelve reliquaries were the ones Bunin wanted, and given his willingness to kidnap an American citizen as well as blackmail a Turkish professor, Kate was certain he wanted them for a malicious purpose. Did he want to deepen the existing schism between the Catholic and Orthodox Churches by announcing that reliquaries held by the Vatican were contaminated? Was there a group in Russia that believed that exposing this secret could provide ammunition for whatever unconventional catechism they espoused? Even if Bunin made the information public, Kate wondered whether anyone would believe it. It was impossible to imagine that the Vatican, or whoever had legal ownership of the reliquaries, would allow an examination. She was deep into her thoughts, attempting to divine what Bunin wanted, when the door opened.

Bunin. This was the first time she had seen him in almost two weeks.

"Dr. Strong, how are you?" He was wearing, of all things, a yellow leisure suit. He looked like a toxic banana.

"I have finished. Let me go home." Kate couldn't stand; she felt too weak. "I have identified the fakes, the ones you wanted. Kate gestured to the boards. "There they are."

Bunin nodded his head and left. She unexpectedly felt disappointed, as he left without even a look at the intensive detective work she had completed, immediately followed by scorching shame that she even desired praise from her captor.

An hour later, he returned with Atay in tow. The two of them talked in low voices as they studied Kate's intricate charts. Atay took out a professional Nikon camera and took pictures of the walls. Kate did not know how long the two men stayed. She did know that she was in the bipolar roulette wheel described so long ago to her: red/black, red/black, red/black. Throb. Throb. Throb. Frightened and exhausted, she dragged herself to her bed and fell asleep.

Charleston

CHAPTER 14

THOMPSON GROANED AND stretched his back. God, the work was tedious—and maddening given that from his porch he could see several blocks of King Street's restaurants, bars, and art galleries, none of which he had time to enjoy. He had sent copies of what covered his desk to Detective Edson the day after Adam Chalk's death, but his case file was now going to the FBI, and Thompson wanted to review it once more. The file contained hundreds of pieces of paper: bank statements, cell phone records, office phone records, printouts of URLs Kate Strong had visited, and emails from her personal and work accounts. Even her PhD thesis was somewhere on the table, although what that would tell him, he didn't know.

Had he missed something? Logging onto his computer, he sent a message asking the technology team in France to pull the emails between Strong and her boss one more time and run an analysis on the contents. Maybe that would reveal some reason for her alleged kidnapping. He gathered the papers from the table and locked them in his briefcase. Time to head to the FBI and listen to the tape from the Istanbul office, the recording where the caller claimed Strong had been kidnapped. What help he could give the FBI and Charleston Police, Thompson couldn't imagine, but he found himself wanting to stay in Charleston, a city he had grown to appreciate.

Thompson's stay in the city this time was a magnitude calmer than his first. Over twenty years ago, friends had dragged Thompson to a weekend football game in Charleston. After the game, in the euphoria of postgame celebration, Thompson and his best friend had flashed the money they won in betting on the game. They had promptly been robbed on the street. The other buddies left town without the unlucky two. Lacking any other acceptable options, Thompson and his friend slunk to the local sperm bank that paid for contributions.

He laughed at the memory of the scruffy visit and wondered whether today's students were ever that desperate for money. Not likely. The number of expensive cars on the streets near the College indicated that today's college slackers didn't need to resort to desperate measures to get funds. Any donation of bodily fluids was strictly for pleasure and completely voluntary.

Charleston had been a good base for him. He'd befriended a few builders, including Jack Strong, and once Kate was cleared, Thompson had recommended Jack for a few projects, including the job for Amarintha Sims.

Amarintha intrigued him in spite of her illness, a proverbial axe always hovering. He thought she was beautiful, even with a naked head, and knew she was brilliant, based on the little bit of research he had done about her work at the medical university. Most intriguing was how calm and funny she was in the face of circumstances that would cause many people to gulp tranquilizers.

He especially enjoyed the days when he, Amarintha, and Richard sat on her soon-to-be next-door neighbor's porch trading stories about Charleston. Richard, who had lived in Charleston for fifty years, had a huge repertoire of tales, including experiences connected to losing the Navy Yard, surviving Hurricane Hugo, and, now, the resurgent popularity of the city. Richard had educated Thompson on the many interpretations of "bless your heart," and Amarintha had laughed at his surprise that the term wasn't always used benevolently. Thompson and Richard hooted as she described the donors' lab visits, her graduate assistants having mastered the art of describing the potential benefits of Dr. Sims' research into organ regeneration. Bye, bye, Viagra.

His cell rang. "Thompson Denton."

"It's Sergei. Have you met with the FBI yet?"

"I'm leaving shortly. I've been reviewing the case notes one more time."

"Actually, I'm glad that you have not yet spoken to them. The situation has changed. The FBI has asked for more of our assistance, and we are always ready to help Uncle Sam."

"What kind of assistance do they need from me?" Thompson tried to sound reluctant, but he felt an unexpected pleasure at the thought of sticking around a while longer. An image of Amarintha came to him. Perhaps he could stay until her house was finished. After he did whatever the FBI wanted, he could take some leave; he certainly had it to spare, and Amarintha might need help in the coming weeks.

"The FBI is trying to consolidate all of its investigations into Anton Bunin into one large Task Force. Until we can definitely say Kate Strong is or isn't involved, the Special Agent in Charge wants you to stay on the case."

Thompson said, "I know her. Brook Reynolds is decent and doesn't seem to have as big an ego as some SACs I've met. Is she in Charleston? The field office is in the capital, Columbia."

"She's in Charleston at a satellite office. She's waiting on you before she calls the agent in Istanbul that got the tip about Kate Strong."

CHAPTER 15

STANDING IN THE lobby of a nondescript 1980s brick office building, Thompson wondered why the FBI leased space right in the middle of Charleston's historical district. Although he had walked to the building, he knew parking had to be an ongoing problem given the congestion in this part of the city. He rode an elevator to the fifth floor, swiped a key card, and entered an unmarked door into a large expanse of office space divided by chest-high cubicles, with conference rooms around the perimeter. The space had a transient feel, the dreary, ash-colored cubicles undecorated with pictures, books, plants, or food—ubiquitous office décor around the world. Most of the cubicles were empty. A receptionist sat at a tall counter.

"Good morning, Agent Denton," she said. "Haven't seen you in a while."

Sally Heath had been trying to get Thompson's interest for the entire time he had been working with the FBI, and although he wasn't interested in her, he inwardly applauded her persistence.

"I need to wand your attaché," Sally said with a grin, pulling out an electronic wand from a drawer. She waved it at him in a vaguely sexual gesture.

He gave Sally his slim leather case, and said, "Please tell Special Agent Reynolds I'm here when you're finished." The receptionist ran the electronic device over his case, handed it back to him with a frown, and then disappeared down the hall.

She returned with Brook who said, "Come with me, Thompson. Detective Edson is already here." Thompson followed the SAC to one of the secure conference rooms. The room was windowless, and had equipment to defeat listening devices.

A young woman worked with an elaborate speakerphone on the small table. "Agent Reynolds, you're good to go." She scampered out.

Detective Frank Edson and two junior FBI agents who Thompson had been working with on the Adam Chalk case were already seated.

"Good morning, Thompson," said Frank.

"Good morning, Frank. Hello, Gerry and Amanda." Thompson and Brook sat.

Brook said, "Agent Denton, the FBI has made a formal request to Interpol for your case records relating to Drs. Strong and Chalk. We believe that since Dr. Strong may have been kidnapped by Anton Bunin, your investigation into her boss's activities related to antiquities theft and money laundering should be folded into the FBI." She nodded at Frank, and added, "The criminal investigation to identify and arrest Adam Chalk's murderer remains with Charleston Police Department."

Thompson looked at the FBI agents, Gerry, Amanda and Brook. They looked like a Brooks Brothers ad. He said, "I wore a tie just for you FBI guys." When the agents just looked at him, he loosened his tie and said, "Agent Reynolds, I understand. Your guys will swarm into Istanbul, and by your overwhelming presence you'll frighten the bad guys so much they'll return Strong."

Brook nodded, "Well, that is part of it. We can mobilize

great numbers of resources. Recovering kidnapped American citizens is part of our mission."

Brook straightened her file folder, and put her hand on the conference line.

Thompson said, "Before we listen to the tape of the call, I have a question." He paused. "I assume you already have a file on Anton Bunin's associates in the area. Like Imran Sadat? He's the person who actually runs Alternative Auctions here in the States."

Brook opened a file and showed Thompson and Frank a picture of a young bald man taken from a surveillance camera. "We do. We've been watching him for a while. He's hip deep in the money services business here in South Carolina. His brother, Samuel, seems to be uninvolved. They present themselves as Egyptian, but they are actually from the Chechen Republic. There are quite a few Hispanic gangs that move money for Sadat, but since they technically aren't doing anything illegal, at least by South Carolina laws, all we can do is watch."

Frank added, "We've heard rumors on the street that Sadat— Imran, not Samuel—will pay top dollar for stolen antiques. Charleston Police doesn't have anything we can arrest him on either."

Thompson pulled two folders from his attaché. "Here are my personal case notes about Adam Chalk and Kate Strong. I've sent all of you the electronic case file via email. I hope it helps."

"The FBI is very grateful for your help," said Brook.

Thompson was surprised. She sounded as if she actually meant it.

"Let's speak with the agent in Istanbul." Brook leaned over the phone and punched in some numbers. The line rang with the odd sounding European tones.

"Agent Phillippe Baras here," said a deep voice in an indeterminable accent. "Who else is on the line?"

"FBI Special Agent in Charge, Brook Reynolds, in Charleston, SC. With me is Detective Frank Edson from the Charleston Police, Agent Thompson Denton of INTERPOL, and FBI Agents Gerry Davis and Amanda Travis."

"How do you want to begin?"

"How about your position there in Istanbul, and a little about the tip line," said Brook.

"Not much to tell. We have a toll-free tip line, like every other law enforcement agency. Also like everybody else, we get calls from drunks, pissed spouses, and crooks ratting each other out. My mother is American, my father Turkish, so I get to listen to any calls that are in English. My normal assignment is liaising with any English-speaking law enforcement agency outside of Turkey. That's how you got me." He paused. "I'm real busy."

"Agent Baras, any clue as to where the call came from?" Frank asked.

"No. The call came in on that open line. Anyone in the public can get the number. Why don't you hold your questions until you listen to it?"

There was a pause, and then a woman's voice came over the intercom. Thompson heard what he believed were crashing waves in the background.

"Dr. Kate Strong, from South Carolina, in America, is being held near Istanbul, Turkey by a man named Anton Bunin. I am afraid she will be killed if you do not rescue her. I cannot give you my name, or I will be in trouble as well. The location is an hour from the city, in an old castle. . . ."

The call ended.

Thompson blurted, "That's it?"

Baras said, "Yes, that's all we have. We've put the recording through a voice analysis program and as a result have some information that might help. The call came in on our tip line at 12:00 p.m. yesterday. The voice shows signs of distress, but not deception. We heard sounds of two separate waves in the background, and based on the wave pattern, our analysts believe the call was made somewhere on the Mediterranean, not the Black Sea. There are six of what could be called old castles within an hour of Istanbul. Three are museums owned by the government, one is owned by a local politician, one is abandoned, and one of them has a complicated ownership that we haven't been able to trace. The woman's accent indicates that she is Russian and has spent time with Americans."

Thompson was startled at the amount of information the Istanbul office had gleaned from a ten-second call. "How do you know she spent time with Americans?" he asked. "And 12:00 p.m. would have been 6:00 a.m. here on the East Coast of the U.S., right?" He looked over at Frank, who was taking copious notes.

"Yes, that's right. She used the words 'in trouble,' an American expression. I don't suppose there is any doubt about who Dr. Kate Strong is. And I assume the FBI knows of Anton Bunin?"

"No doubt at all," Brook said, trying to sound confident. "There are no other Dr. Kate Strongs in South Carolina, and no other women with the name are missing from the United States. Yes, we are familiar with Bunin. What is he involved in on your end?"

Baras barked a laugh. "Anything involving the theft, movement, and sale of antiquities. He claims to be saving priceless art from ISIS, but that's bullshit. They're stealing these things and making money selling them to your people."

Thompson saw Brook frown. "It isn't just Americans that buy stolen goods, Agent Baras."

"You're right," said Baras, sarcastically. "What do you want us to do next here in Istanbul?"

Agent Reynolds tapped on the table. The other two agents watched her, waiting, as did Frank and Thompson.

"Agent Baras, is your office continuing to trace the ownership of all the castles? Can you do that without alerting everyone in your office? And, how many people know about this call?"

Agent Baras didn't reply for a moment, and when he did, his tone was less friendly. "Agent Reynolds, we have compartmentalized procedures just as you do. The person who logged the call heard it; I heard it, and my boss heard it. We notified Interpol headquarters of the information but did not provide a transcript or recording. I will, of course, send both to you since I'm assuming you will want your own FBI technicians to analyze it."

Brook said, "I apologize for asking. Please continue your investigation into the ownership of that last castle you mentioned and secure warrants to search the castles, if you can do it in an unobtrusive way. Is there any indication of where the call came from or how it ended?"

"We're still trying to trace its location, but Turkey doesn't have the same capabilities to trace calls like in Europe or the U.S. As for why it ended, let's hope it was a dropped call and not harm to the caller."

She said, "Agent Denton will be briefing the FBI team on everything he knows about Dr. Kate Strong. I have your information and will share contact details of our team shortly. I need to brief Washington before I can send agents to Istanbul. Do you have facilities we can use? We will need your help and the help of local authorities."

"I understand, Agent Reynolds, but by the time the FBI plane lands and your team gets to our office, every informant in Istanbul will know you're here. You don't want that, do you?"

"No, we don't. We'll be sure to coordinate with you. It will take 24-36 hours to arrange."

She looked at Thompson and Frank. "Agent Denton, Detective Edson, do you have any questions?"

Thompson sighed and shook his head. Frank shrugged and said, "Agent Baras, thank you for your time. I know how difficult tip lines can be. I've had that duty before."

Agent Baras said, "Why thank you, Detective. Let me know if you need anything else from us. I'll stand by on the resources here in Istanbul."

CHAPTER 16

Amarintha arrived at the lot and went to her usual perch on Richard's porch swing. On the first day she had come to the job site Richard had walked to the pile of concrete blocks where she had been sitting and insisted that she not only enjoy his swing, but also his bathroom. She had graciously accepted both offers, and now she usually went straight to the swing on Richard's porch where Jack or any other contractor could easily find her.

She pushed herself on the swing and considered how to break the news from her oncologist to Ava and Fannie. There had been no surprises. The scan, taken a week after the last treatment, had been on one screen, the prior scan on the other. She saw no appreciable difference in the size of the growth, although the doctor had optimistically pointed out 2-3 millimeters of shrinkage. If her doctor was correct, the cost of the infinitesimal shrinkage was dear: all her hair, thirty-five pounds, and who knew how many thousands of dollars.

The doctor had finished his monologue by thrusting papers into her hands and saying something about the "next approach we'd like to try," as if her body was a recalcitrant oven that just needed the right recipe to produce a good cake.

Stumbling out of his office, she had gone straight to the job site, where distractions were plentiful.

At times, she forgot she was sick. The chemo and radiation treatments had been so debilitating that their cessation gave her an illusory sense of health, at least until the inevitable mirror presented itself. The disease had stripped whatever curves she had possessed. With her new uniform—a scarf, ball cap, jeans, and t-shirt—from behind, passersby likely thought she was Jack's skinny teenage son, at least until they saw her face.

Amarintha and Richard now met every morning on his porch, each of them benefitting from the camaraderie. It was Thompson, though, who she most enjoyed. He hovered about the site most days and had stopped showing her anything in coral, periwinkle, or any other pastel. He was smart, funny, solicitous and thoroughly heterosexual after all. She was annoyed with herself that she had jumped to the conclusion that he was gay, based on his profession, when there was evidence to the contrary. She had watched him deal with a variety of women that came to the job site—the kitchen cabinet person, the tile lady, and the window saleswoman. Once she had even caught him checking out one of these women head to toe.

He had blushed when he had met her eyes but had not turned away, staring back at her with a grin that she could not help returning. This parade of women continued, their presence premature given there was no foundation yet. Clearly, Thompson was the attraction.

Amarintha was pleased not just with Thompson but with Jack as well. He was even-tempered, detailed, and excellent at his job. In spite of his positive demeanor, there always seemed to be an air of sorrow gathered round him that reminded her of the almost invisible flying gnats, no-see-ums, which stung locals as well as visitors in an equal opportunity torment. This sadness was due to his wife's disappearance, she knew. How did he deal with it? If Ava disappeared, Amarintha did not think she would be able to hold herself together for even a day, much less a month. The rumor was that Dr. Kate Strong had just run off, but Amarintha couldn't imagine a woman who would not contact her child, even if she had left the child's father for another man.

Watching Jack work with the men who would be digging the piers, the vision of the finished house came to her, along with that familiar piercing realization that she might not be there to see the finished product.

Amarintha put her feet down, stopping the swing, and pressed both hands to her eyes. *Ava needed to come home now. Fannie would sort it out.*

She waved at Jack, who had parked his truck across the street. He walked over and put one foot on the step of Richard's porch, waiting for her to speak. "I found out today I don't have much time left to make good decisions."

Jack jerked his head. "But you might—"

"Jack, you and I have become friends. Let's not ignore the obvious. I'm bringing Ava home from Clemson, and my mother will make sure you get what you need to finish this house, if I'm not able to."

Jack nodded and rubbed his head, a gesture she had seen more than once when he had to receive or give bad news.

Just then, Richard came out of his house, letting the door bang. "I finally found it," he yelled, holding up a piece of paper.

A second later, the subcontractor yelled, "Jack, I've been looking for you."

Buck hollered again, pointing to something in the ground. "We found something."

Jack looked from the old man to Buck to Amarintha. She made the decision.

"Let's go see what they found." She pushed herself off the swing. "Richard, you coming?"

"No ma'am, but I'll wait right here for y'all."

CHAPTER 17

THOMPSON LEANED AGAINST the wall in the FBI conference room, looking out a window at Meeting Street. Gerry and Amanda were flitting around the room trying to lower a screen that was hanging two feet down from the ceiling like a wet sheet, too high for the projector. The two debated in low voices, ignoring the buzzing noise coming from the ceiling motor. These two FBI agents could handcuff a bad guy blindfolded, but were clearly flummoxed by the audiovisual screen.

An hour previously, Sally Heath had called, telling Thompson that he needed to attend a meeting at the FBI office, "right away." She had brought him to a conference room, where he now waited. At least the FBI had provided coffee, and Thompson nursed a cup, watching a horse carriage leisurely making its way down the street.

Detective Frank Edson sauntered into the room. "Hello, Thompson." They shook hands, and Frank walked over to the break table. "You know what this meeting is about?"

"Something to do with Kate Strong and Adam Chalk, or so said Sally Heath. She said to get here right away."

"Same as me." Frank poured a cup of coffee and claimed a chair at the conference table. "What's your gut feeling on the call in Istanbul being legitimate? Could your Russian crime boys really be holding Kate Strong captive?" He sipped his coffee. "You know, everything we found points to her leaving Charleston voluntarily. There were calls to her husband, a call to her boss. She sure wasn't driving the truck that threw her boss off the bridge, and she wasn't in Chalk's car."

"I don't know, Frank. I can't figure out why Alternative Auctions would kidnap anybody. So far they've been able to find plenty of experts who would do the appraisals without coercion."

At that moment, the projector screen dropped the remaining six feet to its proper location, and a muted cheer broke out at the front of the room.

Frank laughed. "Looks like this show is about to start."

Brook Reynolds walked into the room, followed by several other people. Three were in uniform.

The SAC remained standing and waited for everyone else to sit. When the room quieted, she said, "Thank you all for coming so quickly. I've convened this meeting to discuss some recent developments regarding the reported kidnapping of Dr. Kate Strong."

Frank looked at Thompson and raised his eyebrows. Thompson shrugged and wondered who the other attendees were.

"All of you know me, of course. Would the rest of you identify yourselves?"

She looked at Thompson, and he said, "I'm Thompson Denton, from Interpol's Art and Antiquities Investigation Team. I've been in Charleston looking into a smuggling ring that is operating out of South Carolina."

Frank spoke next. "I'm Detective Frank Edson, from the Charleston Police Department. I'm investigating the death of Dr. Adam Chalk, one of the individuals Agent Denton was investigating. He was also Dr. Kate Strong's boss at the College."

A tall man stood. He was wearing what Thompson thought looked like a Royal Canadian Mounted Police uniform. He was ramrod straight, his arms bulging out of the sleeves of his shirt. "I'm Major Victor Munez. I lead the South Carolina Information Security Team. It's part of SLED, the South Carolina Law Enforcement Division."

He did not introduce the two other uniformed men, who sat against the wall, but he did gesture to a young woman sitting at the table with him. "This young lady, Tiffany Gray, is our resident computer analyst. She holds degrees in physics and statistics from North Carolina State University." He paused. "Most of the time I don't understand a single word Tiffany is saying." Major Munez sat down.

Fleetingly, Thompson wondered why a computer analyst had been included in a meeting to discuss the possible kidnapping of Kate Strong.

Brook gestured to a harried-looking, disheveled man with a mullet haircut. "I'm Dr. Kevin Umstead. I lead the infectious disease group at South Carolina's DHEC. That's the Department of Health and Environmental Control."

Munez said, "Agent Reynolds, your office told me you needed SLED here to discuss a development concerning Kate Strong, but why did you ask me to bring Ms. Gray?"

She tapped on the table with her finger. "Bear with me, Major. I assume that both you and Dr. Umstead have listened to the transcript of the anonymous call and read the summary report about Agent Denton's investigation?"

The two men nodded.

"Interpol in Istanbul sent us the recording of the call. Forensic agents in D.C. analyzed the voice, and this morning they found a match. That is the primary reason you are all here."

Thompson realized he was holding his breath. He let it out as Brook said, "The voice is Zora Vulkov, former senior researcher at the Biopreparat in Russia, and protégé of Anton Bunin."

Dr. Umstead groaned.

Frank said, "What is the significance of that? What is Biopreparat?"

"Biopreparat conducted most of the bioterrorism research in the old USSR. Anton Bunin led a team that spent years attempting to aerosolize bubonic plague as well as anthrax," said Brook. "Vulkov has apparently been in Cameroon working as a medical doctor for the last thirty years. We do not know why she has surfaced now."

Umstead ran his hands along the long grayish hair at his neck, and said, "I assume the government had recordings of Zora Vulkov's voice?"

Brook said, "Yes, we did."

Thompson's stomach flipped again and he realized that the U.S. government had squirreled away millions of voice files, likely including his own. He said, "Agent Reynolds, does the FBI have any idea of a motive for Bunin to have kidnapped Dr. Strong, or why Zora Vulkov would be involved?"

Before Brook could respond, a young man, slightly built, with big glasses and a short-sleeved white shirt came into the room and sat behind her.

"The information in an email I'm about to show you makes the possible kidnapping of Dr. Strong, and the apparent involvement of Zora Vulkov, a more threatening development." Brook touched her laptop, and an email came up on the screen. "This is from the Centers for Disease Control. They received a blood sample a week ago from a hospital in Rome, taken from one of three priests who were admitted to the hospital about ten days ago. The patients presented with high fever, coughing, and other symptoms that indicated an infection. The hospital put them in isolation."

Thompson looked at the email. It was from the Office of Infectious Disease at the CDC to a long distribution list that included recipients in multiple government groups.

He skipped to the bottom and read:

This bacterium sample is Bacillus anthracis, but it is not a known modern variant. The researchers were working with a reliquary from an altar in France, allegedly not opened in 350 years. Our analysis of the bacteria indicates that it is the same variant that caused an outbreak at the Charleston Navy Base in 1986. We recommend that the FBI in SC, along with South Carolina's Law Enforcement Division, and South Carolina Department of Health and Environmental Control, take the lead in investigating a possible link between the 1986 event and the cases of anthrax in Rome.

It took only a few minutes for all the attendees to finish reading, and when they did so, the room erupted in noise.

CHAPTER 18

AMARINTHA AND JACK picked their way over to the hole in the ground, thirty feet from Richard's front porch. The kid with the soul patch was squatting, his face covered in dirt, and wearing a grin. He was happy to have an audience.

"There's something down here that sounded like metal, so I stopped digging to look at it." The big auger that was part of this task sat to the side with its diesel motor turned off. He climbed out of the hole easily, brushing dirt off his pants. "I run this thing all the time, and I'm telling y'all, I've never heard a noise like that around here. The last time something like this happened, it turned out to be a big chest of silver."

Amarintha touched the young man on the arm. "What's your name? I'm Amarintha."

He went to shake her hand, but instead rubbed his hand on his pants and nodded. "I'm Jimmy, ma'am."

"Let's take a look. Help me down."

Jack started to object, but then reached over and helped Amarintha down to Jimmy, who had jumped back into the hole. The kid stooped down, brushed away some dirt, and showed them what looked like six square inches of cast iron. *Could just be an old frying pan,* thought Jack, but he didn't say this aloud.

"Jimmy, I'll pay you extra for digging this out by hand. Can you do that for me?" She grinned at them, and Buck and Jimmy nodded.

Jack helped her out of the hole and said, "Let's go back over to Richard's porch to see what he wants to show us. It will take a while to uncover whatever is buried down there. This is a good time for some of his lemonade."

As they walked back over to the porch, Richard stood up. "What did you find?" he asked.

Amarintha laughed. "It looks like a frying pan. How about you? What did you want to show Jack?"

Sitting on the steps, Jack said, "Here, Amarintha, you take the swing." She walked over to the swing and sat down, moving it with her tiptoes.

Richard was holding a standard 3 x 3 photograph printed on a laser printer. "A month ago my granddaughter gave me a new camera. I was trying to see whether that super zoom thing worked and took a bunch of random pictures. I remembered that one of them might be important. I gave the camera to my granddaughter yesterday and asked her to print the pictures."

"Look at this." Richard thrust the picture towards Jack, who sat down next to him, expectant. "Is this your wife?"

The picture showed a red Mercedes at the stop sign on Church Street and his wife. His wife? The woman was only visible from the back, but he recognized Kate. It was the hair and the silhouette he knew so well. She was getting into the car's back seat from the right-hand side. At the driver's door, Jack saw a man standing, looking to the left. Another man was in the back seat. The license tag on the car was in the middle of the picture, with the people and the car slightly less in focus.

"What day was this? Do you know who the man is?" Jack knew his tone was harsh, and he willed himself to calm down.

"The 10th of April, a month ago. That man and his brother own the rug store downtown."

Stunned, Jack erupted. "Why didn't you tell the police? How did you just now find this picture?"

"I took this picture on that Monday morning at about 7:00 a.m., which I know for sure, since I got the camera the night before on my birthday. I didn't remember I had taken the pictures until the other day when I saw a car just like this one. Then I gave the camera to my granddaughter, so she could print out the picture."

"Are you absolutely sure this was Monday, April 10th?"

"I am." Richard seemed irritated that Jack was questioning him. "And if I'd remembered the darn picture before yesterday, I would've taken it to the police."

Amarintha had stopped her swinging, and held her hand out for the picture. Instead of handing it to her, Jack stood stock still for five seconds, turned, and ran to his truck.

As he opened the truck door, Jack heard Buck yell, "Hey, Jack, where you going? We almost got it!"

CHAPTER 19

THOMPSON WASN'T A biologist, and had no idea how a bacterium could survive in a reliquary for 350 years. He watched Dr. Umstead furiously making notes as the email on the screen stayed visible.

The Major said, "That email is from two days ago. Why have you been sitting on it?" He turned to Umstead and added, "What is this outbreak of anthrax in 1986?"

"I don't know," said the doctor. "This is the first I'm hearing about it."

Brook said, "I have a team looking into the 1986 situation. We should have an update later today. This email also went to the FBI's Field Information Group, what we call FIG. The FIG is testing an advanced software program, and has analyzed the information in this email as well as other data we have related to Bunin."

Brook looked down at the table for a moment. "We missed 9/11. There were clues buried in the data the government received, but we only saw the pattern after the attack. The FIG group has created a program using advanced mathematics that can link billions of pieces of information, to see relationships a human wouldn't be able to detect. We aren't the only ones analyzing this information, so don't think the fate of the United States rests on your shoulders."

She gave a wan smile, then added, "I'm going to let Chad Jackson, from the FIG team, explain to you how the program works." She typed on the laptop a minute more, and a faint chart came up on the screen.

The slight young man who had been sitting behind Brook stood up, and in a disarming southern accent said, "I'm going to try and explain something that took a dozen PhDs in statistics to create, so bear with me. Take a look at this." He pointed to the screen, which was barely visible, walked over to the drapes, and closed them. A bulleted list popped into view:

- Dr. Adam Chalk is killed on April 10 of this year.

- Dr. Adam Chalk, Kate Strong's boss at the College, performed appraisals on stolen antiquities for Alternative Auctions, funded by Anton Bunin.

- Dr. Kate Strong, expert in Christian reliquaries, disappears April 10.

- On May 10, Dr. Zora Vulkov, former member of Soviet bioterrorism agency, Biopreparat, reports that Anton Bunin has kidnapped Dr. Kate Strong.

- Anton Bunin is the former top researcher for Biopreparat and colleague of Vulkov.

- On May 1, Vatican researchers fall ill from strain of anthrax known to have occurred in South Carolina in 1986.

- Outbreak is reported to the FBI by the CDC on May 12th

Chad said, "The software looks at all events we feed it, but only examines those that are potentially dangerous. The probability of an event is calculated statistically. This is the software's conclusion." He hit a button on the laptop and a written paragraph appeared on the screen:

It is more than a 34% probability that Anton Bunin is seeking to locate new biological organisms unknown to scientists, either inaccessible due to climate, as in permafrost that has now melted, or inaccessible due to religious custom such as material in sealed reliquaries in the Hindu, Buddhist and Christian faiths. This is likely related to his desire to discover new drug compounds, or possibly to create a biological weapon available for sale.

"Mother of God," said Dr. Umstead.

The attendees stared at the screen. Finally, Thompson asked, "Is the FBI considering this actionable information? And if you are, why?"

Chad looked to Brook, then back at Thompson. "We ran a simulation to see if the FIG's program could really predict a catastrophic event."

"What does that mean?" said Major Munez

Chad rubbed his hands together. "We input all the information that was available in August 2001, like the report that Middle Eastern students wanted to learn how to take off, but not how to land an airplane. There was a good bit of data that various law enforcement groups had."

No one said anything. Chad looked at Brook again. This time she spoke. "The FIG software said it was a 70 percent likelihood that terrorists were planning to crash planes into New York or Washington, D.C. Had the program been operational at that time, it would have made this prediction ten days before the events of 9/11. So we are going to take this prediction seriously. We cannot afford not to."

CHAPTER 20

AMARINTHA SAT WITH her head in her hands and felt Richard touch her shoulder. She looked up at him and asked, "Do you really think this picture means anything? I wonder why the owners of the rug store didn't go the police once they saw Kate on the television. I certainly remember seeing it."

"Maybe they did. I feel like a fool for not remembering. I probably should have taken the camera to the police first rather than get Jack's hopes up." His voice was quavering.

"Could she be alive?"

Richard sniffed and was quiet for a long time. "People have disappeared before for a lot longer and then showed back up. You just don't know. Maybe she sent Jack a letter he never got."

"My daughter knows Jack's daughter. They are best friends, and I'm sure Sara's mother has never contacted her."

Finally, Richard stood up. "I think we're past the lemonade stage for today. How about a whiskey?"

Amarintha nodded and walked with Richard through the front door. She hadn't been past the front room or the small bathroom right off the foyer, and looked around with great interest.

The dark blue walls held a few paintings and many small shelves with figurines on them. The furniture was old, not quite antique, but solid 1920s walnut and mahogany. There were small rugs all over the floors, not just classic Persians but some styles she recognized from Morocco, China, and Egypt. None of them was room-sized, which seemed strange, and the effect was similar to walking through her daughter's bedroom, where Ava's clothes were always strewn across the floor.

Richard took her through the small kitchen to a covered porch that overlooked a small garden, furnished with a brick patio and gurgling fountain. A six-foot matching brick wall covered with creeping fig, Lady Banks roses, and ruby azaleas enclosed the entire garden. Camellias decorated three of the backyard's walls, making the entire yard an old-fashioned garland. There were several beautiful and unusual weeping Japanese Maples in strategic locations. It was a perfect, small garden,

"Oh, this is so beautiful, Richard!" Amarintha smiled and spread her hands wide. "It is just what a garden should be."

He gestured to a set of comfortable chairs around a tea table on the patio. She fell into the chair and put her feet up on the matching ottoman.

"Now, how about that whiskey?" he asked, still standing.

"You were serious? I need to drive out to Summerville later today, so no thanks."

Before Richard could leave for the kitchen, they heard, "Hello, are you in there?" from the front door. They both walked back through the house to see Buck and his young helper on the front porch.

"I'm sorry to interrupt, Ms. Sims, but we've uncovered this thing. I'm glad you're still here." Although the tone of his voice was calm, Buck rocked back and forth on his boots, and Jimmy was grinning and almost jumping for joy.

"We found a treasure chest!" Jimmy announced.

"Now hold on, Jimmy," said Buck. "Ma'am, I don't think it's a treasure chest, but it sure isn't a frying pan. That's what I thought it'd be, but no, it's some sort of trunk or box for sure."

Amarintha and Richard opened the screen door and followed
Jimmy and Buck next door. She walked over to the hole and
saw a rectangular box made of what looked like dark wood. The
box was about two by three feet, and Jimmy had tied a rope
around it.

"My goodness, is it heavy? It looks small enough to lift
without a rope."

Jimmy danced excitedly. "I can't lift it. I had to dig all the way
around it and had a heck of a time getting the rope around it.
That's why we need the truck. It's real heavy, so it's got to have
gold or something like that in it."

"I've told him that it just as likely could have rocks in it,"
said Buck, but his face was lit with excitement like his young
helper's. "Go on then, Jimmy, run the winch."

Jimmy went back to the truck and started the winch. The
rope moved, and the small trunk began to lift out of its nest of
dirt and small rock. When the trunk was almost at ground level,
Jimmy and Buck moved the rectangular object by hand to lower
it on the ground.

"Hey, this looks like somebody's idea of a joke. That lock's
not that old," said Jimmy.

Buck said, "As heavy as this thing is, it's probably lead for
bullets or something."

Richard said, "That's exactly what I think. This is an
ammunition case from the Civil War. There must be ready-
made bullets inside for it to be so heavy, and we probably need
to have a specialist open it."

"Darn." Jimmy's shoulders became still. "I thought it'd be
treasure, but it's just some Confederate stuff."

Buck put his arm on Jimmy's shoulder and said, "Come on son,
let's go get some coffee and leave these people to figure it out."

Jimmy cranked the wire cable back in place and the truck
pulled out into the street.

"Well, my dear, you may have something very interesting here," said Richard, kneeling down to look at the trunk.

"I thought you said this was a Confederate item with bullets or something. I wondered how you would know that just looking at it," said Amarintha.

"That was for your interested observers on the street in that regrettable horse-drawn carriage that went by while Jimmy was yelling about treasure. Knowing the tour operator, the story of the box we found may already be part of his repertoire."

"So, what do you think?"

Richard looked at the box and lifted his eyebrows. "Well, we could open it. I have some bolt cutters."

Amarintha nodded. "Let's do it."

He disappeared into his small garage and returned with the needed tool. "You ready to do this?"

"I am," said Amarintha. After a few tries, the lock fell apart and Amarintha and Richard knelt to lift the lid. A small leather bag lay nestled in small pebbles, which filled the trunk. "We know why it was so heavy."

She opened the bag and brought out a wooden rectangle about half the size of a small brick, small pieces of glass on the top outlining a scene. A figure in a flowing robe stood, holding both hands out; in one hand was a baby and in the other what appeared to be a flower. The flower had a huge red stone in the middle of the petals.

Amarintha turned the rectangle round and round in her hands. "Let's take this and the bag to your back yard. When Buck and Jimmy come back, I'll show them the trunk and the pebbles. We'll time it so that the next carriage driver has a full view. No one will know it had something inside it."

"Good idea," said Richard, and he followed Amarintha to his back yard.

CHAPTER 21

"**W**HY IS THIS not being investigated by Homeland Security?" asked Frank.

Brook looked up at the ceiling for a moment. "The program was coded by Chad's team here in Charleston. Homeland believes the mathematicians at the CIA, the NSA, and the DOD should analyze the program. I have quite a few emails telling the FBI why the FIG program is flawed."

Tiffany, who had sat perfectly still during the entire meeting said, "The people at those agencies believe that anyone without a mathematics degree from MIT or Stanford is an idiot." Major Munez turned in astonishment to his young protégée, who just shrugged and added, "I'm just saying."

Thompson mused that Western Civilization would collapse due to bureaucratic infighting, truly the fiddling of Rome while civilization burned; only this time the participants would be sending emails to each other during the fire. He said, "I assume that the FBI disagrees with Homeland?"

"My command chain wants us to validate the facts and the program's conclusions. Thompson, let's start with the Interpol investigation."

Thompson looked at the other attendees, and said, "I've been on assignment in Charleston for almost a year, investigating a large antiquities theft ring with connections to Charleston.

The local FBI office has been aware of my assignment and has provided assistance. The key individual I was investigating was Dr. Adam Chalk.

"Dr. Chalk is alleged to have been a key participant in an auction scheme. A terrorist group steals an antiquity and notifies Alternative Auctions what they have. Alternative Auctions contacts one of their paid experts, telling the expert that an antiquity has just come to market from an estate, or some other plausible story. The expert attends an auction and states to the potential buyers that the item is authentic, creating the all-important provenance of the item. The final buyer, happy to have a previously unknown antique, pays top dollar. Alternative Auction funnels the money back to the terrorists, using money service companies in South Carolina to disguise who the recipients are." Thompson paused. "The terrorists don't have checking accounts."

Someone laughed.

Dr. Umstead furrowed his brow. "Why hasn't law enforcement closed down the money transfers?" Thompson saw the major and Frank look at each other.

Frank said, "We can't. Until South Carolina decides to regulate the money services companies, every crook between Florida and New York is going to launder their cash here." Major Munez looked thunderously angry, as though discussing this issue violated some unspoken rule.

South Carolina was the only state that didn't require the money services companies and funds wiring companies like Western Union to gather the most rudimentary information about their transactions. Anyone could walk into one of these establishments, hand over thousands of dollars, and for an exorbitant fee, wire money to Mexico, Egypt, and France— literally anywhere in the world that had an Internet connection. There were hundreds of these places near I-95, and millions of dollars were illegally transferred every month. He knew, as did everyone else in this room, that hundreds of individuals in SC did nothing but tote illegal cash from place to place, all day long.

Brook Reynolds stood up. "Bunin, with the tacit support of Russia's government, has been funneling funds from the auctions to certain terrorists in order to gain influence in the area. Bunin's public statement is that he is saving Christian antiquities. We estimate that Alternative Auctions is responsible for the theft and resale of over three hundred million dollars of antiquities from the Middle East, primarily Iraq and Syria."

She waited, and when no questions came, looked at her watch and pointed to the list still on the projector. "I know we're going out of order of the events on the screen, but bear with me. The CDC doctor is waiting for our call."

Brook leaned over the table and pushed a few buttons on the conference phone. "Do we have the CDC on the line? This is Agent Brook Reynolds, FBI Special Agent in Charge for South Carolina."

"Dr. Clifford Gilstrom of the CDC is here," said a voice.

"Dr. Gilstrom, I understand you have limited time. I have a roomful of people here. Rather than introducing everyone, I'll send you the names with the transcript of this meeting. Please tell us your findings so far on the Vatican situation."

The speakerphone squealed, and Brook adjusted the volume.

Gilstrom said, "The bacterial agent cultured from the three patients in Rome is a strain of anthrax that is a precursor of strains that exist today. The three researchers were likely exposed when an altar from a convent called Corbie was opened." Dr. Gilstrom sounded quite energetic. "They were working in one of the Vatican's controlled environment rooms, thank goodness, and are now under quarantine."

Gilstrom continued. "As I said in my email, the strain

cultured from the patients in Rome matches the bacteria that caused the Charleston outbreak in 1986."

The doctor from DHEC put his hands over his face.

Frank asked, "Did the CDC have a sample of what caused the Charleston outbreak?"

"Yes. In 1986, someone sent us a sample that was scanned into our DNA catalog and then forgotten."

The name of the convent, Corbie, registered in Thompson's brain. "Wait a minute; you said the altar was from a convent called Corbie, in France?"

"I did."

"The Vatican called Interpol two weeks ago to report that a reliquary was missing from the Convent of Corbie." Thompson looked around at the others. "The Vatican told our director that the missing reliquary is in Charleston. It's from the same altar as the one that caused the anthrax."

CHAPTER 22

J ACK SAT IN his truck, the engine idling, looking at the rug store, debating what to do. The place was dark. He should go to the police station and show Detective Edson the picture, even though he doubted this information would motivate CPD to reopen the case.

He put the truck in gear. Glancing back at the rug store, he saw a shadowy figure securing a sign inside of the store's door. Backing the truck up, he read, "Will reopen at the end of June. Please call Misty Lauren if you need assistance during that time." The phone number was a local Charleston one.

Jack abruptly parked again, left the truck, and strode toward the entrance. He banged on the glass so hard the figure started.

"We are closed," the man yelled through the glass, gesturing to the sign.

"I need to speak to you now. It's important," Jack shouted, simultaneously slapping the picture on the glass of the door. The man squinted at it, turned to speak to someone, and unlocked the door.

"Come in, please, sit down. I'm Samuel Sadat, and this is my brother Imran." He gestured to the second man who was sitting at a banker's desk a few feet away. Imran looked up, scowled and then began to shuffle papers around on the top of the desk. Against three walls were rugs: rugs rolled, hung, and laid flat on stacks according to their dimensions. They were all different, and all seemed faded.

"How can I help you?" asked Samuel, still standing. Turning on a small lamp on the wall, he looked at Jack, expectant.

Jack held the small picture on the wall in the light of the lamp. "This is a picture of my wife getting into a car; this is your car, and this is the two of you, isn't it?"

Samuel took the photo to the desk where his brother sat, pulled glasses out of his coat pocket, and studied it closely. He handed it to Imran who glanced at the picture but made no comment.

He came back to where Jack waited by the door. "Yes, this is our car, and this is my brother and me. You say this is your wife. We know Dr. Strong, of course. She is a frequent visitor."

Samuel and Imran glanced at each other briefly, and then Imran said, "I'm sorry, but I did not get your name."

"I'm Jack Strong. My wife disappeared the day this picture was taken, April 10th, a month ago." It occurred to Jack, too late, that confronting these two men alone was one of the most boneheaded things he had ever done. Why, why, why had he not gone directly to the police station?

"I'm so sorry, Mr. Strong. Yes, we did give Dr. Strong a ride to the College that morning. We put her bicycle in the trunk of the car, and then we drove her to the College. She got out, and we lifted her bike out of the trunk and secured it to one of the bike racks. But, I must ask you, who took this picture, and are you sure it was the same day your wife disappeared?"

"A man who lives on Church Street took it, and, yes, it was the same day. And you had no idea that this woman was the one whose picture was all over the news for weeks after this date?" Jack could not keep the suspicion from his voice.

"Mr. Strong," said Samuel, "we were in our car that day heading to the airport for a trip to New York. We saw her at the stop sign, and we gave her a ride. Nothing more. And you say no one has seen her since that day?"

Jack stared at these men at a loss for words. Their explanation of why the police had never spoken to them seemed logical and genuine. What could he say? The fact that they were leaving again so soon after their trip just a few weeks ago seemed strange, but he knew nothing of the rug industry.

He rubbed his eyes and finally asked slowly, "Did she seem upset or worried?"

Samuel spoke gently. "Mr. Strong, she was a woman dealing with a broken bike. We put our windows down and asked her if she needed help. She said if we didn't mind putting her old bike in the trunk of our beautiful car then, yes, we could give her a ride."

Jack knew that Kate would put it like that . . . her "old bike." He rubbed his head. "I'm sorry to have bothered you. I'll have to tell the police about this. They'll probably want to ask you the same questions."

"Of course. Please let them know we will be happy to speak with them, but we are leaving tomorrow for an extended trip, so they should call us today. I am so sorry for your trouble, and I hope that the police can gather some useful information from us. Dr. Strong was in our shop quite often, and we will pray she is found safe and returned home to you." Samuel handed Jack a card, and gently herded him to the door. Jack stumbled into a beautiful spring morning in Charleston and wondered what in the world he was going to do next.

He pulled out his cell to call Detective Frank Edson. Jack knew the detective would speak to the Sadats. What good it would do, he didn't know. What kind of motive would these brothers even have? It didn't seem that anyone had a reason for harming Kate. Kate's colleagues, her students, and her family loved her.

However, she had vanished before.

Sara had been three months old and colicky. Without a word, Kate had run off, leaving him alone with a screaming baby. His only memory of those two lonely, loud days were his efforts to comfort Sara, his tears flowing over his wailing daughter's face, mixing with hers.

What had made her leave this time? What had happened to her? As the days passed without a word from Kate, and absolutely no information as to why, the decision he faced each morning was whether to let Sara spend another day with some sliver of hope, or to tell her Kate was likely dead.

He put his truck in gear and drove towards the police station. Even if Detective Edson wasn't there, Jack could at least fill out some paperwork detailing his conversation with the rug owners. Jack did not see Samuel Sadat watching him out of the window of the store.

After Jack Strong drove off, Samuel turned to Imran, his normal jovial face contorted with rage. "What have you done, Imran? Have you gotten Dr. Strong involved in your activities?"

His brother looked up from the desk. "If you had not stayed in Egypt for the last three weeks buying more damned rugs, you would have known that," said Imran. His own voice was calm and low. "She will be returned after the job."

Samuel walked over to the desk and slumped in a chair. "This game you are playing with your auctions will not end well."

Imran Sadat lifted one shoulder and smirked. He pointed to a stack of rugs that lay on the floor in disarray. "Big brother, stop worrying. Go play with your carpets."

CHAPTER 23

EVERYONE WAS LOOKING at Thompson. He said, "Dr. Gilstrom, are you sure that the strain you have on file as occurring in Charleston and the strain from Rome are the same?"

There was a long silence on the phone.

The CDC doctor cleared his throat. "Yes. Our investigators in Rome are sending the reliquary to Atlanta. We will conduct more analysis when it arrives. But if the Vatican believes that the second reliquary is in Charleston, we should assume it is contaminated until we rule out both artifacts as the source for the anthrax."

Dr. Gilstrom spoke a few more minutes, speaking English, Thompson was sure, but the words were in scientific jargon. There were no questions from the audience. Only Dr. Umstead seemed to understand everything that Gilstrom said, and his face became paler as the CDC doctor went on.

Gilstrom finally took a breath and said, "None of the patients in Rome will be released from isolation. I will send field epidemiologists to work with Dr. Umstead."

"How serious would an outbreak be?" asked Thompson.

"This strain of anthrax is showing resistance to our antibiotics. If Anton Bunin is indeed attempting to create a biological weapon, a strain of antibiotic-resistant anthrax is the perfect weapon, assuming he figures out how to disperse it over a large area."

There was no sound other than the scribbling of Dr. Umstead.

"Thank you, Dr. Gilstrom," said Brook. "We'll sign off now." She pushed a button and stood up. "Let's take a break. I've had some agents working on the Charleston Naval Base angle since I first got this email. I need to check in with that team."

For ten minutes, the attendees crowded around a table in the back of the room heaped with pastries. Thompson mused that not even the prospect of an ancient disease could diminish the bureaucratic appetite for sugar. He took a cheese Danish and sat down in the back of the room.

Frank made his way over to Thompson. "I can't believe that not a single person in this room knew about the anthrax outbreak in 1986."

Thompson took a bite, and shrugged. "Why would they know? That was over thirty years ago. Maybe some sailor brought it back from a foreign country. The navy base was open in 1986, right?"

Brook bolted into the room. She knocked on the table and raised her voice over the conversation. "People, please, sit back down. I have information."

Everyone shuffled back to their seats, juggling their pastries and coffee. Brook said, "In 1986, forty percent of a fifteen-person research group died, six in all. From the records the FBI just got from Department of Defense, it appears that the outbreak was contained on base and that DOD told family members it was radiation poisoning. I have no explanation for why DOD didn't call it anthrax. The FBI is attempting to track down the individuals that were in the group."

"Did you find out if health officials in South Carolina knew about this? If so, I might be able to find records in Columbia," said Dr. Umstead.

Brook shook her head. "DOD shared the information with no one. The FBI had a difficult time finding anything ourselves. The only thing we know at this point is that they are the same bacteria."

"Agent Reynolds, what is it that you expect Charleston Police to do? None of this information is actionable by law enforcement." Frank was clearly frustrated. "The only indisputable facts we have are that Adam Chalk was murdered, and Kate Strong is missing. I can start rounding up all the chumps that move money for the auction company, but is it likely that they would know anything at all about a biological weapon?"

"I agree," said Major Munez.

Brook ignored the comment. "Dr. Umstead, we need a detailed plan of action if anthrax appears again in South Carolina. Make sure your team knows as much about this bacteria as the CDC team in Atlanta."

"Major Munez, I would like your team to work with Chad and tear apart all the parameters of the FIG assumptions." He started to protest, but Brook continued, "This isn't just a computer issue. We need real, solid human intelligence. Make sure Chad and Tiffany know the assumptions the program used and validate that they are real world." The major looked gratified that the computer geeks would have supervision by law enforcement.

Brook left the room without any further commentary.

The following hour was a slog, with brief arguments about jurisdiction and ownership, but in the end, a preliminary plan was in place. The primary burden was on the SC Department of Health. DHEC would alert hospitals as to a heightened risk for anthrax patients, as well as mobilize quick response teams, equipped and ready to create isolation units.

The SAC returned to the meeting after an hour absence and again knocked on the table to get everyone's attention. Her report was brisk and short. She had found little else on the event in 1986. The deaths of six researchers were kept from the public and local authorities. No cause or vector was ever found, and the file was closed and forgotten.

The meeting had all but ended when the SC DHEC contingent protested about why, thirty years prior, the United States Government had not bothered to inform the State of SC that anthrax was in the state. Of course, no one knew the answer, and the other team members let the SC Department of Health folks vent their frustration without comment.

The sun was low in the sky when Frank and Thompson left the FBI meeting. Both were exhausted and had calls with their perspective bosses they needed to make. As they were walking out, Brook said, "Thompson, one more thing.

"Interpol received a picture from the Vatican of the missing reliquary. Sergei sent it to both of us, and I took the liberty of asking Chad to run it through our image recognition program."

"Thanks, Agent Reynolds. I appreciate it, although I doubt anything will come out of it."

"The program will take a couple of hours. I'll call you if we get anything," she said and headed to the parking lot.

"Come on Frank," said Thompson. "Do you have a car? I walked over here and need to go by my condo to pick up Strong's case file. I've got a hundred pages on Kate Strong that your office is going to want."

CHAPTER 24

J ACK HAD BEEN to the Charleston Police Department only once, to file a missing person report. At the sight of the building, Jack experienced a wave of fear so unnerving that he turned the truck, ready to go back home.

A car with city tags swerved in front of him and parked. Jack halted, recognizing the driver, and got out of his truck. "Hey, Detective Edson. It's me, Jack Strong." Edson was half out of his car, and seeing Jack, said something to his passenger, who was also getting out.

The other passenger was Thompson Denton.

"Thompson, what are you doing here?" Jack looked at the two men, standing by the car. "Is he under arrest? He's not that bad a designer." Jack laughed, and after a beat, both of them did too.

Thompson walked over to Jack. "I had a theft at my condo, so I came here to fill out the reports." He pulled out a couple of sheets from his briefcase and waved them in the air.

"Yeah, you know, reports," added Frank. As Frank turned to gesture to the building, he bumped into Thompson, and the sheets came loose and fluttered to the blacktop. Jack reached down to pick up one, and heard an intake of breath from Thompson, just as he brought one of the pages up to his face. It was titled:

Conclusions on the role of Dr. Kate Strong:

Jack stared at the sheet, not fully comprehending the words, as Detective Edson and Thompson scrambled to pick up the rest of the fallen papers. Backing away from the two men, Jack felt a rushing sound in his ears and read the next few lines.

Interpol has received a reliable tip that Anton Bunin, a Russian individual involved in stolen antiquities, is holding Dr. Kate Strong in Istanbul, Turkey. Dr. Strong may be involved with the illegal . . .

Thompson jerked the page away. Jack stared at his hands, looking for the words he had just read. He lifted his head, made a growling sound, and launched himself at Thompson, propelling them both to the ground. Jack heard shouting above him and saw multiple feet in shiny, black shoes, scuffling around him. He felt a sharp burning pain, and his hands came loose from Thompson's neck.

CHAPTER 25

RICHARD AND AMARINTHA brought the wooden artifact to the back garden and placed it on the small table by the fountain. Richard put on his reading glasses and examined the entire surface of the little rectangle.

"I can't see a way to open it. It might be valuable, but that red stone could be glass for all I know."

Amarintha said, "Burying something in the ground is strange, especially if you wanted to preserve it. It's almost as if whoever buried this didn't want it to survive, but then why protect the box with a leather bag, and pebbles? I still think Thompson might be the best person to look at it. Surely an interior designer knows more about this type of thing than we do." She laughed and realized she missed Thompson.

At that moment, Amarintha's phone vibrated. She looked at her phone and said, "I need to go. My daughter is on her way to my mother's house. Will you hold onto this and ask Thompson what he thinks? It's kind of late, I know, but he was supposed to come by the job site this afternoon."

Richard said, "I'm thinking that maybe you should put it in your car. It is your property."

Amarintha went to pick up the box, but her hand collided with Richard's as he put his hand on the table to stand up. The box fell, and split into two.

"That's one way of getting it open." Amarintha reached down, carefully picked up the pieces, and put both on the table. The box had come apart unevenly at what had looked like a natural irregular variation in the wood. Inside were small rounded objects the size of small pearls. She touched one with her finger. "What could these be?"

"Amarintha, this could be a reliquary—a container that the Catholic Church would put relics in. Those things could be teeth. Given how the box was hidden, it might have been stolen. I can call somebody over at the FBI if you want me to. I retired from the Charleston FBI a few years ago and still know people over there."

"What? I never knew that you had been an FBI agent."

He grinned. "Well, I was just a librarian, but don't tell anybody." Richard leaned over the table and studied the two pieces of the box. "Why don't we put it back in the leather bag?"

"Can you take some pictures first?"

"Sure." Richard used his cell phone to take pictures of the box and the inside contents. Amarintha placed the top and bottom together, then nestled it back in the bag.

"Richard, please let me leave this here. If Thompson comes by, you can show it to him."

"Ok, you got it. Have fun with your daughter."

CHAPTER 26

THOMPSON SAT OUTSIDE the cell in the holding area at Charleston's Police Department, waiting for Jack to wake up. He and Frank were in an area typically used for juveniles. It had one cell, a few chairs, and was out of the way of the normal bustle of the department. Jack Strong lay on a cot inside the cell, breathing, but still out of it. The red spot on Jack's neck where the rookie cop tased him seemed to be glowing.

Frank had been almost incoherent in his anger, yelling at the rookie after the young officer tased Jack. The detective had run into the building as a crowd gathered, leaving Thompson sitting on the pavement, cradling Jack's head. Discovering that the police department had a defibrillator, epi-pens, enough gauze to wrap a hundred mummies, but no stretcher to carry an actual patient, Frank resorted to calling the fire department.

Thompson and Frank had watched as the EMT checked Jack's vitals. The firefighters wanted to transport the fallen man to the hospital, but the detective overruled them and directed the stretcher to the cell. He wondered if Jack would even remember seeing the papers. Maybe the tasing had zapped his short-term memory.

Jack was groaning now.

"We need to move him out of the cell." Frank's phone rang. "Detective Edson." He listened for a minute. "Ok, what's the number you want me to call you on? Got it."

He walked over to Thompson. "Come on. The FBI has something to show us right away. I need to use one of the computers to do a video conference."

Thompson looked over at Jack, still moaning, lying on the bunk in the cell. "What about him?"

"We're just going over to one of the conference rooms. We'll hear him if he wakes up."

The two of them walked across the hall from the holding cell. Frank used his badge to enter a room that was equipped with a computer and a large monitor, and propped the door open with a chair. He turned the equipment on, waited, and then entered a phone number. After a few seconds of electronic buzzing, the same conference room they had been in earlier in the day appeared on the screen. Brook Reynolds and Chad, the FBI computer support person, entered and sat down in front of the video camera.

Frank said, "What is it you've got to show us? We have a little situation here."

Brook raised her eyebrows, and Thompson hoped that Frank didn't choose this time to share that a civilian had seen confidential documents. Eventually, they'd have to tell her, but not yet.

"We got lucky, guys. Very lucky. You remember the picture of the missing reliquary that the Vatican sent? Brook was clearly excited. "Chad, show them the picture."

Chad moved a piece of paper closer to the video camera. A picture of a small rectangular box, the top a mosaic depicting a saintly figure with its hands outstretched, appeared. In one hand the figure held a baby, and in the other a flower. The flower had a red stone in its center. In spite of the stone, the box was somewhat unadorned compared to most reliquaries Thompson had examined.

"This is a photocopy of a painting of the missing reliquary."

Chad leaned towards the camera. He face loomed in the screen, and Thompson instinctively reared back. "The description that Interpol received from the Vatican estimates that the stone, which is a diamond, is about 100 carats, which means the diamond alone could be worth millions. That doesn't even include the value of what's supposed to be in it. The contents themselves might be worth even more to a collector."

"Jesus, are you kidding me?" said Frank. "No wonder the Vatican wants it back. What's supposed to be in the thing? "

Chad said, "The documentation found in the altar states that one reliquary, the one that has tested positive for anthrax, contains bones from a saint."

"That's pretty typical," said Thompson. "Reliquaries can have thorns, nails and cloth from the resurrection of Jesus, blood and sweat from apostles, bones from saints, and so on."

When Frank snorted and started to speak, Thompson held up his hand. "Whether you believe that the items inside are truly what believers claim them to be is not the point. The point is that many people believe that a reliquary and its contents are sacred and would pay big bucks for either the contents or the container—some Catholics that is."

"It wouldn't be a Baptist, that's for sure," scoffed Frank.

Brook said, "Gentlemen, you can argue about that later. I told you, we got lucky. The FBI has the ability to scan an image into our computers, and then compare the image to every single picture on every worldwide webpage to find a match." She paused, and then added. "We got a hit. The picture that the Vatican sent us of the missing reliquary matches a picture taken in Charleston, in 1986."

Thompson said, "You've got to be kidding me."

Brook smiled. "I called the Vatican. They are sending an envoy to take possession of it when we find it."

"Didn't they tell Interpol the reliquary was in Charleston? How'd they know that?" asked Frank.

Thompson said, "I forgot to ask my boss that. Still, even though we know it was in Charleston in 1986, aren't the chances of finding it pretty slim?"

"Not really. Anybody who once saw it would remember it, especially since the picture is from a newspaper article," said Brook.

The FBI SAC picked up another picture from the table. She held it up to the camera for Thompson and Frank to see. "What is it?" asked Thompson.

"It's a picture that was found on a dead site," said Chad.

"Dead site?" asked Frank.

"Yes, an Internet site that isn't currently active. It's a photograph. Can you see it?"

"Move it a little," said Thompson. The picture came into view. "Now hold it there."

The picture was in color and showed a smiling man standing in front of a long table. Various objects sat on the table: a locket, an old bottle, an ancient shoe, and a small box.

"Look at the bottom of the picture. It's the very reliquary we are looking for," said Brook.

"Jesus," said Frank again.

Thompson asked, "What is this, and who's the man?"

"It's an article from the Post and Courier. The man's name is Charles Sims," said Brook. "He apparently worked at the DOD site in 1986. He was there when anthrax broke out."

CHAPTER 27

THOMPSON AND FRANK left the conference room and returned to the cell across the hall. "You bastard. You hit me." Thompson whipped around to see Jack sitting on the cot, glaring at him. "Detective, why in the hell am I in jail?" Jack moved to the bars and began pounding on them, his voice rising. "Where is she? Where the hell is Kate?"

The detective moved to the cell, motioning for Thompson to step back. "Nobody hit you. A rookie cop saw you and Thompson on the ground, and tased you. Thompson is one of the good guys, just like me. If you calm down, I'll let you out."

"Is she alive? What's in those papers? You need to let me see them." Jack collapsed onto the cot. He took a breath. "I want to call a lawyer."

Thompson spoke from behind Frank. "We'll tell you what's going on, but not if you call your lawyer. If you do that, I can't help you."

"I don't need your help. Frank, tell me, is my wife alive?" Jack was now at the bars, holding them, his voice cracking. "Please."

"Yes, Jack, we think Kate is alive."

Jack began to weep. "Oh my God, she's alive. She's alive."

Frank opened the cell's door. Jack stood straight and brushed his eyes with his sleeves. "Frank, what's going on? Please, tell me."

"Come on out, Jack; let's sit down and talk. Here, read this." Reaching into his attaché, Thompson handed a couple of papers to Jack. "I can't give you the rest of the report, not without approval from the FBI, but at least you can read the rest of what you saw outside."

Jack sat down and quickly read the summary pages of the case report. He looked up, his expression quizzical. "I don't get it. Why would you be investigating my wife?"

Relieved that Jack was willing to look him in the face, Thompson said, "I've been in Charleston for a year investigating your wife's boss, Adam Chalk. He was involved in an antiquities theft scam as an appraiser, dealing with items from the Middle East." Thompson rubbed his eyes. "I won't lie to you; Adam Chalk was involved with some bad guys. For some reason, he was able to persuade your wife to go to Istanbul. We think she's there being held by the same crime ring that was running the theft ring—"

"Hold it, Thompson. We can't say anymore until we talk with the FBI. I'll call the SAC to see whether she can give you an update now."

"The 'sack'?"

"The FBI's Special Agent in Charge, Brook Reynolds."

"Am I free to leave? Maybe I don't want to go to the FBI."

Thompson spread his arms. "Don't be stupid. If you leave here and call your lawyer, the FBI and Interpol won't share any information with you. Come on, man."

Jack ignored him and turned to the detective. "Will you help me? Are you sure she's alive?"

"If she is, our department will do whatever we can to get her back. I give you my word on that."

Istanbul

CHAPTER 28

THE SINGLE DOOR into Kate's prison opened and Atay came into the room. "Good morning, Dr. Strong. I hope you are well today."

With him was a woman she had not seen before. The woman had her hair covered with a loose scarf, but otherwise was in Western dress. She was close to sixty—twenty years or so older than Kate, short and stout, with a leathery tan face

"Dr. Strong, I'd like to introduce you to Professor Zora Vulkov. Dr. Vulkov has been studying some of the work you have done and has some questions. Please, let us sit."

It had been two days since Atay and Bunin had studied the walls. Kate had barely been able to get herself out of the bed, and had forced herself to get dressed. She now sat in one of the rolling office chairs, lethargically pushing herself back and forth. Frenetic Red Kate was gone. Depressed Black Kate was in charge.

"Dr. Atay, has your guest been told I am being held here without my consent? That I wish to speak to the Embassy? That I have a family in the United States that likely believes I am dead?" Listless, Kate spoke without raising her voice. "I demand to be allowed to call my family. What else could you possibly want from me?"

He pointed to the walls. "Dr. Vulkov needs to validate your work. We will take you home soon."

Kate looked at him. "I don't believe you."

Atay motioned for Dr. Vulkov to go to the other side of the room. Kate watched the woman study the writing that covered three walls of the room. Atay leaned down, his face close to hers, his words surprisingly kind. "I assure you, we are going to send you home. If you talk about your stay here, it will be regarded as somewhat unbelievable given your medical history."

Kate glared at Atay. "I suppose I will have to add theft of personal information to the long list of crimes you and Bunin have committed."

Atay leaned further to whisper to her. "Dr. Strong, when you arrive in Charleston, you will unfortunately be quite ill. You will recover, with little memory of the last weeks. The supposed abduction will be explained by the fact that you went off your lithium. Listen to me. This plan will save your life."

He stood up and very briefly touched her hand. Kate couldn't take her eyes off his face.

If Atay were telling the truth, then she would be drugged in Istanbul, taken back to the U.S. on a private jet, and dumped somewhere. She would not be able to tell Jack or anyone else what exactly had happened. Jack would believe she had had a manic episode, similar to one early in their marriage. She felt a tremor run through her at this memory, a longing for the manic Kate, a Kate that might be able to muster enough energy to fight her way out of this room.

Kate's eyes filled with tears; she let them fall in full view, hoping that Atay would leave the woman with her.

Atay stood up and said to his female companion, "Perhaps

you can speak to Dr. Strong and impress upon her our urgent need to complete the project."

With that, he left the room.

Dr. Vulkov waited for the door to close, then leaned over, and whispered, "I would like to help you. How can we communicate more freely?"

Dumbstruck, Kate considered the woman for a long time. She had hoped that she could persuade the woman to help her, but the thought that Vulkov might be an ally cracked through her like static electricity. *Think. Think. Think.* She couldn't let herself trust this woman, but might at least get information from her. Kate finally walked over to the computer, motioned the woman over, and typed:

```
This will make the people watching us believe
we are working. What day is it? How long have
I been here? Who are you? Why would you help
me?
```

The woman sat and said aloud, "Dr. Strong, please let me tell you more about myself. I am an expert in Byzantine civilization."

Kate typed:

```
I am being held against my will. You must
contact the U.S. Embassy at once. Please.
```

"That is very interesting, Dr. Strong. I can see how you documented this one relic. Let me list the others we are interested in." Kate moved aside, and Dr. Vulkov began to furiously type:

```
You have been here for four weeks. I am not
an expert in the Byzantines. I used to work
with Anton Bunin when we both were in Russia.
I understand that you are afraid. You will
need to trust me.
```

Kate's hands gripped the sides of the chair.

```
You must pretend that we have been collabo-
rating. I will come every day.
```

With great effort, Kate said. "I understand what you are showing me. I will look at your suggestions."

Zora stood up and began to walk away from the terminal towards the door. As she passed Kate, she handed her a tissue and spoke firmly to the silent Kate, now standing.

"I understand that you miss your family and are ready to leave Istanbul. You will be home soon. The next time we work together, it will be far easier for you if you can contain your emotions."

Zora walked to the door and knocked. One of the guards cautiously looked in, opened the door wider for her to pass, and shut it just as quickly. Kate clutched the tissue, felt something stiff inside, and walked to the bathroom, the only place she was not under surveillance. Weeks ago, she had spotted the cameras in the workroom and the bedroom. She had meticulously searched the entire bathroom, but had found no cameras in the little tile room. Closing the door, she opened the tissue and saw a piece of stiff paper. Careful not to create a sound, Kate read what Zora wrote.

Bunin has been drugging you through the air vents with a stimulant. He wanted you for this project not only because of your expertise, but because he believed that given your medical history, you could disappear and then reappear without it being traced back to him. When Atay discovered that the Byzantines seeded disease in the reliquaries sent to France, Bunin took over the project. Bunin wants to know exactly where those reliquaries are now. He is keeping you here until you can locate them.

So she had been chosen for this project not just for her intellect or training but because she was the most controllable candidate. She left the bathroom and stumbled into the workroom. Kate grabbed an eraser and began to erase the writing on the white boards, laughing hysterically. The laughing turned into sobbing and she leaned against the walls, covering her face, finally sliding down the wall to the floor.

CHAPTER 29

ZORA'S VISIT WITH Kate Strong earlier in the day had shaken her. Before the meeting, she had read Strong's curriculum vitae. The woman's academic accomplishments were impressive. Her picture showed a square face, dark eyebrows and eyes, and long dark hair pulled back from her face. She looked confident, reliable and true to her name—strong. The Kate Strong Zora had seen in person was a caricature of the woman in the picture.

She stared down at the rolled piece of paper in her hand. It had taken her many drafts to write the fewest, most informative words possible. Was Strong stable enough to comprehend what Zora wanted to tell her? Certainly, Dr. Atay was not able to assist Zora.

Anton had introduced her to Dr. Atay as an archeologist. Atay believed it, and had droned on and on about how the team found and conserved the parchments. Atay had been obsequious, and it was clear that he feared Bunin. Consumed with making a plan to stop Anton, she had barely listened. She was certain that Atay did not know of Bunin's true motives. He seemed to think that Bunin was looking for a sacred relic of Christianity that he could steal from the Catholics to give to the Russian president. If only something so benign were the motive.

She went to her purse, rummaged through her cosmetic case,

and found an old lipstick tube. After she flicked the pigment stick down the toilet, she carefully inserted the miniature scroll into the mirrored tube, replacing the top.

Taking a deep breath, she put the little tube in her pocket, straightened her jacket, and prepared to meet with Anton.

Charleston

CHAPTER 30

J ACK SAT IN the squad car, hands on his legs, his booted feet banging the floorboard. His head felt too big for his body. His neck hurt where the cop had tased him, and he got out of the car quickly, not waiting for Frank or Thompson.

They were on Meeting Street in front of an office building that Jack had passed a hundred times without knowing that the FBI occupied an entire floor. The three men rode the elevator to the top floor, and Thompson opened an anonymous looking door with a key card. A receptionist, whose nametag said "Sally," nodded at Thompson and guided the three of them to a conference room where another woman stood.

"I'm Brook Reynolds, Mr. Strong. Please sit down." She turned. "Sally, will you bring us some coffee, please."

Jack chose a chair across from the woman. He could feel his heart beating, the blood pulsing on the side of his neck where the officer had tased him. It felt as if the blood was leaking out of his neck and he put his hand to the spot, surprised when he felt no moisture. He was aware of Frank sitting beside him. Thompson went to stand in a corner, his head down.

"I understand that you found out that Interpol received a tip that your wife is being held in Istanbul," said Brook.

"I did, and I want to know why this information was kept from me," Jack retorted.

Brook handed him a legal-sized document across the table. "Please read this, and sign it if you would."

As Jack read the document, his anger grew. The document threatened him not only with detention, but also with a variety of other penalties, most of them dire. He looked up in disbelief.

"This is bullshit. I'm calling my lawyer." Jack threw the document across the desk and looked angrily at Brook.

"Mr. Strong, if you had not seen that report, you would have been completely ignorant of Thompson's true identity, wouldn't you?"

"That's right, but I did find out. I demand to know what you know about my wife." He heard the detective groan.

Brook was silent, holding Jack's eyes for a long time. "Do you know exactly what the Patriot Act is, Mr. Strong?"

"I guess so. I read your document."

"The Patriot Act allows the United States government to act very quickly when threats appear against the United States. That law is a direct consequence of 9/11. To put it in non-legal terms: I have the ability to march you out of this room directly into custody of the FBI. I can withhold legal counsel; I can confiscate your bank accounts; I can tap your phones," she airily waved a hand, "and, the only question I will be asked is whether you pose a threat to the security of the United States. Do you understand?" The woman had not stopped looking at him.

Jack wanted to look away. He could feel his face flushing and looked over at Thompson, certain he would see glee in the man's face. He did not. Thompson was biting his lip and looking at Jack. Then the so-called interior designer nodded at him, and

Jack realized that he was beginning to think of Thompson as an ally. "I understand."

"The FBI has no obligation to tell you anything about an active investigation. If you go to your lawyer, I will invoke the Patriot Act. Your attorney will turn tail and run back to his peeling paint, real estate-closing, ticket-fixing, navy blazer-suited office." Brook stood, her hands on the table, leaning towards him. "Do you understand?"

Jack's eyes tracked upward as she rose, like a cobra in a basket.

Frank coughed. "Come on, the guy just found out his wife is alive. Do we really have to go through all this?"

"Mr. Strong needs to know that anything he learns here is a gift. We are not obligated to tell him anything." Agent Reynolds put her fingers to her lips, looking at Jack. "We have a complicated situation. Turkey is a sovereign country and we cannot drop commandos from ropes and rescue your wife. It does not work that way in real life. We do not have a location for her. At this point we are only investigating a tip. Are we clear?"

Jack nodded.

"What have you been told?"

Jack looked at Thompson. "I only know he is an Interpol agent, and I met Detective Edson when my wife first disappeared."

"Agent Denton, why don't you tell Mr. Strong about your case?"

Thompson sat on the edge of the table. "Adam Chalk was approached two years ago about being an expert appraiser on some artifacts from the Middle East. The approach was made by a group called Alternative Auctions, a front for a Russian named Anton Bunin."

Jack asked, "How did you find this out? Where did this information come from?"

"Emails. Looking at correspondence was part of the process. I looked at anything electronic. The auction house and Chalk were communicating for many months via an email account Chalk set up in another name. We found it because he used his own credit card to pay for the service."

Thompson motioned to Frank. "Detective, tell him what we believe happened."

"We think Chalk got cold feet and tried to back out, or he might have threatened to expose the scheme, but it's a certainty that he was murdered. We don't believe that Kate knew anything at all about his murder, and left Charleston on her own. Who persuaded her to go, and their connection to Alternative Auctions, we don't know."

Jack said nothing. The evidence supported the assumption that Kate went willingly: her car at the airport, the missing passport, and a cash withdrawal she had made the morning of her disappearance.

Thompson said, "I had to probe the backgrounds of everyone in Chalk's department, but I cleared your wife weeks ago. The agent paused, took a breath, and added, "Then she disappeared."

Jack looked at Frank. "Did you know that Thompson was investigating my wife the day you came to interview her?"

Frank didn't look away. "Not until later that day."

Jack dropped his head to his chest, waiting for all the words to line up in his head. "Do you know who killed Adam?"

Frank said, "No, we don't. We don't have any good leads either. The garbage truck was stolen that morning from Isle of Palms. The perpetrator left it on the bridge and hijacked another motorist's car. Any witnesses were busy trying to save Chalk's life."

Images of Adam came to Jack's head. Adam, the jovial runner. Adam, his and Kate's friend for years. *Had he set Kate up? Why?*

As if Frank was reading his mind, the detective said, "Chalk was in serious financial trouble. He had about fifteen real estate properties, and all of them were worth less than he owed. He had involved several others in a real estate trust, and his partners were going to lose everything as well. We believe that's the motive for his involvement with this illegal group. Using the payments from Alternative Auctions, Chalk had been able to keep from going bankrupt."

Jack remembered Adam driving him and Kate to a dilapidated South of Broad house that was defying gravity and still standing, trying to get them to invest with him. He and Kate had been appalled that Adam, with absolutely no background in real estate, had bought the mansion with the intention of remodeling it, then flipping it.

Jack said, "Do both Interpol and the FBI believe this tip? That this man Bunin is holding my wife. Do you know why?"

He watched Agent Reynolds and Thompson glance at each other briefly.

Thompson answered. "Jack, we do believe it to be true. Because of her knowledge of reliquaries, we don't think her life is in danger. This group needs her specialized expertise."

"Reliquaries? You mean because she can appraise them, and they can sell them?" Had Chalk, or this ring, asked Kate to study previously unknown relics, and poof, she decided to go? He had to admit it was possible. And, her note had said the trip was about French relics.

When Sara was about six months old, Jack had come home to find Kate twirling around the house, ecstatic, singing something. When he got her to sit down and speak, out of her mouth had tumbled this belief that she was the reincarnated Joan of Arc. That was the final manic episode before her bipolar diagnosis and her relationship with lithium began. Another thought leapt into his head.

He scrambled to his feet, almost turning over his chair. "You said Adam was murdered. She might already be dead while we sit here talking." Jack was close to vomiting, sick with fear in the realization that a gang that murdered Adam was holding Kate. He paced the room, his hand to his mouth. He could feel the others looking at him.

Frank said, "This criminal ring buys antiquities, gets them appraised, then sells them. We believe there might be one in particular they are looking for. This reliquary has a diamond on its top, and the diamond could be worth ten million dollars. That's what they want. Kate should be safe until they find it, and they won't find it because the FBI will find it first."

Jack was certain that this was a partial truth, and he was just as certain that if he protested, he would learn nothing else. "So who takes the lead on getting Kate back? The FBI? Interpol? Who is looking for this diamond? Will you use it to bargain with this group?"

"Our department will be working under the direction of the FBI. The State Department and the Turkish authorities will also be involved. We haven't figured all this out yet, Jack. Be patient."

Brook added, "You should know that without a ransom demand or any group claiming responsibility, it's going to take some persuasion for the Turkish government to give us approval to investigate inside their country."

Jack's eyes began to sting, but he could see in Brook's face that she would wait for him to speak. He swallowed. "So, I need to wait while the FBI, the State Department and the Turkish authorities agree on what to do? Are you still investigating this group for other reasons?"

Neither Thompson nor Brook looked at him. These two behemoth organizations would pursue this criminal ring for their own reasons and would not lift a finger to get his wife back if doing so would jeopardize their cases. His rage and helplessness were close to overwhelming him. His body wanted action—now—but knew that he could lose any chance of these organizations cooperating with him if he lost control. He let his breath out very slowly.

"When you get her back, she won't be arrested, will she?"

"I haven't found any evidence that has done anything illegal," said Thompson.

"So, are we done then, Frank?" Jack was ready to get out of here and figure out with the detective's help what the next steps were.

"Yes," said Frank. "We're done."

CHAPTER 31

FROM THE WINDOW in the conference room, Thompson watched Jack and Frank leave the FBI building. He knew that Brook had not left the room and turned to see her watching them as well.

"Do you think I scared him enough so that he won't call his lawyer?" she asked.

Thompson shook his head. "No way to know. Frank understands. He'll keep Jack in line. I'm worried that when Strong starts to think about our story, he'll see the holes. An appraisal is a one-time event. He'll figure out that Bunin wouldn't need Kate after she does the appraisal, and when he does—well, Jack is a smart man."

Brook put her hand on Thompson's arm. "We cannot tell him about the researchers at the Vatican or that the FBI is investigating the possibility that Bunin is looking for lethal germs in reliquaries."

"I know," Thompson said. He looked back out the window. "What's the latest with the patients in Rome? Has your team found anything about the reliquary and the man in the picture, Charles Sims?"

"Charles Sims died in 1986 in a car wreck. His wife, and a daughter, Amarintha Sims, are living in the area today. I've told the team to scour electronic sources first to see if we can find any other reference, or any reason Sims would have brought a religious object to his work, then we'll start interviewing his family. In a perfect world, we'd find one of his descendants sitting in his living room with the artifact sitting on a shelf behind them."

Thompson wanted to groan. *Amarintha was Charles Sims' daughter.* He knew that the FBI would want to interrogate Amarintha and her mother, and they would never share with the women why they were asking questions. Amarintha would now have the stress of the FBI on top of her illness and trying to finish her house before she died.

"The FBI is fighting with the Department of Defense about who should lead the search for this religious item. The DOD believes it should be their operation because Sims worked for them on a project whose scope they won't describe."

"What did he do?" asked Thompson.

"DOD won't say."

"Why would a biologist be working for the Department of Defense in 1986? Didn't the United States agree to cease biological research in 1975?" asked Thompson.

"Yes, we did. Maybe there will be a clue in the two hundred emails I haven't read yet from all kinds of folks in DC."

"Does the Task Force have that much visibility in Washington?"

"Well, let's see here. We have a secret project conducted by DOD where people died of anthrax, Vatican priests in quarantine from exposure to the exact same microbe, and a computer program that says a Russian who once ran the USSR's bioweapons program is seeking a biological weapon."

She put her hands on her head, rubbing her temples. "Add that this same Russian may have kidnapped an American citizen who just happens to be an expert in Christian relics. Yes, Thompson, this has visibility in Washington, especially since the computer has now bumped up the probability of a biological attack on the United States to fifty percent."

"Why?" Thompson asked.

"Chad added what we found out about Charles Sims, that he owned the reliquary in 1986." The phone in her pocket chirped and she said, "Agent Denton, be prepared for an army of people coming to Charleston. The Vatican has sent an envoy. They want to share the missing reliquary's history in person, and of course take possession of it when we find it, assuming it isn't contaminated with anthrax.

"Chad is the one member on my team that is smiling, and that is only when he thinks I'm not looking. He's been on the phone for hours with Homeland explaining the FIG program to their computer scientists."

She walked with Thompson out the front door. "Be back at 5:00 p.m., please. An entire contingent of FBI agents from Washington arrives around then. One more thing: The Vatican wants the word 'reliquary' removed from all of our conversations and our written notes. They do not want the Catholic religion to be associated with a government investigation."

"That's nuts. If some crazy group is stealing the Vatican's reliquaries because they believe there is some ancient bug contained in one, then the Vatican ought to want to find them." He looked at Brook. Fluorescent light wasn't flattering to anyone, and she looked exhausted. "Am I free to leave? I have reports to write."

"Of course. Let's take the stairs. I need the exercise." She led him to a door in the hall, opened it with her key card and guided him down the five flights to a private exit. He pushed the door open to leave.

"Wait, Agent Denton." Thompson turned, halfway out into the parking lot. He could hear people laughing from the street.

"Do you believe this? That we may have some sort of ancient anthrax hiding in that missing reliquary?"

He shrugged. "Doesn't matter. If a terrorist group believes it, we're in trouble either way. If they don't find a bug in a reliquary, these people will move to something else. There's a long list of stuff that can kill thousands."

"You're very knowledgeable of weapons for someone with a PhD in art history." Agent Reynolds attempted to smile.

Thompson's face was flat. "Since we picked up the first rock, humans have slaughtered each other and celebrated their victories. The winners memorialize themselves in fantastic architecture, sculptures, and paintings. War is second only to religion in its ability to stimulate creativity." Thompson looked at her. "To understand art, you must understand war."

CHAPTER 32

THE SLIGHT PRIEST in dark robes left the plane at the Charleston airport, carrying nothing but a small overnight bag and a locked aluminum briefcase. He had thought that a dark-skinned priest in a city like Charleston would be a somewhat unusual sight, and he prepared to receive sidelong looks, but his fellow travelers had done nothing but smile or nod at him.

The year before, he had followed the story of the murders of nine parishioners at Mother Emmanuel AME Church with a feeling of sick anticipation, waiting for protesters to fill the streets in a lava flow of rage. It didn't happen. Several days later, when the families of the victims offered forgiveness to the perpetrator, a pale young man with a bowl haircut, he had gone to the Sistine Chapel and given thanks that the city of his birth had not devolved into violence.

Monsignor Giuseppe Ogier was an anomaly at the Vatican— an American with an Italian first name, French last name, and dark skin. After almost forty years in Rome, he was no longer the only African-American wandering the grounds of Vatican City, but since he was from the southern part of the United States, he was frequently consulted on the latest ethnic crisis in the world, his peers believing his upbringing gave him secret knowledge of racism. He had learned there was no secret knowledge relating to racism. Some born to this world were just evil, and he had long given up attempting to find any logical reason for their existence.

The secret knowledge he did have was about reliquaries, and he was elated at the thought of putting his hands on the one missing from the Convent of Corbie since 1685.

CHAPTER 33

"THOMPSON, ARE YOU coming over here this morning? Amarintha and I missed you yesterday afternoon." Richard sounded querulous on the phone, quite different from his normal voice. Thompson had almost not answered the call. He was standing in front of an FBI conference room, preparing to go in and explain, again, to the FBI how Bunin's auction scheme worked. He had no energy to deal with Richard. Kate Strong, Bunin, anthrax in Charleston in 1986, and an FBI computer program predicting Armageddon were all fighting for his mental attention, attention he did not have.

"I had planned to, but something else has come up. Is something wrong at the site or with Amarintha?"

The night—and early morning—had been exhausting. After the meeting with Jack Strong, he had left the FBI building, gone home and changed clothes, and then returned. By that time, around 6:00 p.m., there had been several new faces, presumably FBI agents, ensconced in the previously empty cubicles. The night was a blur of meetings and updates with these new agents, repeating what he knew about Kate Strong, Anton Bunin and the world of antiquities smuggling. The fact that Thompson was, through his cover as a designer, involved with the husband of the kidnapped Kate Strong, as well as working for the daughter of the man who had owned the missing reliquary, seemed to be of utmost interest to the new agents.

Monsignor Ogier, the Vatican's emissary, had arrived from the airport in the early evening. Sally brought him to a conference room where Frank and Thompson had been working. The monsignor, a slight coffee-skinned man in his sixties, smoothed his robes and put his hands on the table, a model of composure and dignity. "I appreciate you allowing me to come. I sincerely hope I can help you find the missing reliquary, and more importantly, when we do find it, I pray it is not contaminated."

"How are your priests?" Thompson asked.

Monsignor Ogier looked at him a long while before he spoke, his fingertips together on the table. "They are recovering, but slowly. Many are praying for them."

Frank shifted in his seat, rubbed his eyes and said, "Can you tell us a bit more about both reliquaries? How old they are, how one could have been stolen, anything that might help us locate the other one?"

"I have reviewed all known accounts and references to both reliquaries," said Monsignor Ogier, "and I am certain that the missing one was stolen from the convent in 1685, by a Huguenot woman who later came to Charleston. If you are interested, I have a report that details the complete story."

Later, Thompson wondered why it had taken over three hundred years for the Vatican to report the stolen item to Interpol's Art team; at the time, he had been too dumbfounded to ask.

"The missing item isn't one of our most notable reliquaries, and it took me some time to track down the proper records. Both reliquaries date from the 1200s, and were given to the convent by King Louis IX after he purchased ten artifacts from the

Byzantines. We cannot know when the altar was contaminated with anthrax, but I'm assuming your health authorities are operating under the assumption the missing item is also contaminated. Here is a dossier you may find interesting." Monsignor Ogier had handed them all a spiral-bound document that Thompson had not had a chance to read, then left for his hotel.

He realized Richard was saying his name again.

"Thompson, Thompson, can you hear me?"

"Yes, sorry, what is it that you need?" Thompson was barely listening to Richard.

"Those two guys digging the foundation piers yesterday found a trunk buried on Amarintha's lot. We opened it and it had a little box in it.

"Amarintha wants you to look at it. It could be valuable, unless the top is completely costume jewelry stuff, which I guess it could be, but I looked at it with my magnifying glass and the stone on the lid sure looks like a ruby or a big diamond. We figured you might know something about this type of decoration, since you know art. I can keep it here until you show up tomorrow. Amarintha's not here anyway."

Thompson's comprehension was about two seconds behind Richard's words. He stopped walking. "Wait, you found *what*?"

"A small decorated box. It's quite unusual, with a figure on the top. It was in a leather bag—"

"Richard, do you know how to take a picture with your phone and text it to someone?"

"I do."

"Richard, please listen very carefully to me. In my job, I sometimes see notifications of stolen art. What you have sounds familiar. Can you text me a picture right now?"

"Well, sure, Amarintha put it all back together, but we took pictures first. You want me to open it again?"

"*No!* No, just text me a picture. We'll have to hang up for you to do that."

"I'm on my land line, so I'll get my cell phone and send it to you."

He heard rustling, banging, a chair scraping, silence, and then a click.

"You got it?" Thompson asked.

"Sending it to you now."

Thompson pulled the phone away from his ear, shaded the screen away from the sunlight, and waited. He heard the single note of his text notification, and a picture appeared.

"Oh my God," whispered Thompson. It was Charles Sims' reliquary. Taking a deep breath, Thompson said more calmly, "Richard, what you have there may be dangerous. Has anyone touched it?"

"What do you mean dangerous?"

"Has anyone touched it?"

"Amarintha touched what was inside the box. You want me to take a picture of what's inside?"

Thompson was already walking to the room where the FBI agents were waiting for him. He covered the phone, and whispered, "Get Agent Reynolds. *Now.*" One agent nodded and hurried away.

"No, Richard. You need to leave it alone. I know this is confusing, but there is a risk that what you have is contaminated with—" Thompson thought quickly, "—contaminated with mercury used to glue the gems on the top."

Richard was silent. Brook Reynolds came rushing down the hall. Looking carefully at his face, she led him to an empty room.

"Hold on, Richard," he said. Thompson put the phone on speaker, muted it and wrote on the whiteboard.

The artifact is at Amarintha Sims's home site on Church Street. Her next-door neighbor has it.

Brook rushed out of the room, and Thompson leaned against the wall. Amarintha's father must have buried the reliquary. Why? The only connection was what happened at the Base in 1986.

Thompson could see others in the hallway outside talking to Brook. She came back in and sat down.

"I think we need to tell Amarintha. It's her property," said Richard, his voice surprisingly loud given the small speaker of the cellphone.

"I'll call her, Richard. In the meantime, some people are going to come to your house and pick up what you found. They will take the item with them." Thompson looked over at Brook, his eyes raised. She nodded.

Richard gave a snort. "You know, I worked for the FBI for a long time. I wasn't a field agent, but I know spin when I hear it. What's really going on?"

Brook Reynolds was typing furiously on a terminal in the conference room. She turned the screen around and showed Thompson a screen with a picture of Richard Anderson with the status of 'retired.' She mouthed, "I know him." Thompson pushed his phone over to her.

"Mr. Anderson, this is Brook Reynolds. You and I met right before you retired."

"I remember. You're the SAC now. Special Agent Reynolds, perhaps you can tell me what is going on."

"The small box you are holding is a reliquary, a box that holds relics. A man named Charles Sims, who worked on the North Charleston Naval Base owned it, and is likely the person who put it into the ground. We're not sure why. I will be sending people from the FBI to secure the item. If you can agree to a voluntary quarantine, you can stay at your house until we determine whether the reliquary is dangerous."

Thompson and Brook looked at each other waiting for Richard's reply.

Richard expelled his breath, a long, old man sound conveying agreement as well as resignation. "Did you say Charles Sims? That's Amarintha's father. He's dead now. I knew him, and his wife Fannie."

Brook said, "He also worked at DOD, and that box may have been contaminated at the base."

Thompson gave her thumbs up. Brook had given Richard a much better reason to secure the box than his lame story concerning gem paste.

"I understand. Of course, I'll cooperate, but I'm worried about Amarintha. She is the one who touched what's in that box and then went to her mother's house. Go find her, Thompson."

CHAPTER 34

MARINTHA WOKE UP in her old bed at Fannie's with that same feeling she had had every morning when she was a kid before her father died—that she could conquer the world. Charles Sims had been Amarintha's hero. The two of them had tromped through the farm multiple times per week; always looking for evidence of life—scat from a deer, a raccoon skeleton, or perhaps a squirrel's nest. After one of these walks, she had wanted to know how lizards could lose their tails and then grow them back. Her father told her to become a biologist and discover the answer for herself. Had Amarintha known how much education it would take just to begin to answer that question, she might have found an easier way to make a living.

At ten, he died in a car accident. Amarintha could not remember anything from that year except for the memorial service, when several people came up to Fannie, with Amarintha white-faced and mute at her mother's side, and described how Charles Sims had changed their lives.

Rolex's barking brought her back to the present, and she heard her daughter and mother laughing outside. Her mother had taught that fool dog not to bark at the birds in the back yard, but in the front yard, he still barked at and attacked the sprinklers. He would do it for hours if allowed. What danger a dog thought sprinklers presented no human would ever know.

The evening before, her illness had not been the primary topic of conversation. She had told her mother and daughter about the trunk the contractors found, and the little box inside it.

"Too bad we didn't find something like that years ago. Your father and I could have built the house if the thing on top is really a ruby," Fannie grumbled. "I would have pried that stone off and sold it in a second."

"Mama, we can still do that, as long as it's not stolen," Amarintha laughed.

"Finders, keepers," Ava had trilled.

Amarintha heard the two women and the dog tromp back into the house up the side porch that led to the kitchen. She pulled on a robe and walked down the stairs to the kitchen. Ava and Fannie were sitting at the table, all eyes on the paper, so she padded towards the coffee pot. The dog barked and Amarintha turned and said, "Good morning."

The women looked up from their respective sections of the paper. Ava made a little screeching noise, and dropped her coffee cup, creating a waterfall of hot coffee that Rolex began to sniff.

"My goodness! You're a fumble fingers this morning," laughed Amarintha, as she knelt down and picked up the cup. She grabbed paper towels, competing with the dog to clean up the mess. Amarintha looked up from her kneeling position. Her mother and Ava were staring at her. "What are you two looking at?"

Amarintha stood. "I mean it. What is wrong?" Her mother and daughter rose simultaneously from their chairs and pulled Amarintha to the bathroom in the hall.

In the mirror were three faces: Ava, with her long bangs and those unmistakable eyes, just like her mothers, tear-streaked and smiling; Fannie, her lined face offset by the thick white braid;

and, in the middle, Amarintha, with ever so faint eyelashes and eyebrows. She had been without both for so long that her eyes looked framed with a black marker. The face itself was no longer ghost pale but pink, and surrounded by a barely visible halo of hair, some of it back to its original, copper-penny color. Amarintha stared into the mirror, running her hands over her face, pulling her eyelashes, touching her hair, turning, hugging her mother and her daughter, all of them beginning to speak at once.

"Oh my, oh my. I just can't believe you look so much better than you did yesterday." This was all Fannie could say. Amarintha rubbed the mirror as though her reflection was an illusion. It didn't change. She looked at herself again and realized that Ava and Fannie were just as they had been yesterday, but she was undeniably not.

The three women hurried back to the kitchen and sat at the table.

"Ok, now guys, let's not get too excited." Amarintha tried to dampen the mood, attempting to put her scientific brain in control.

"Mom. You looked so awful yesterday. I'm sorry, but you did. You look so much better today. You have eyebrows and lashes coming back."

"Hair grows back differently once you've had chemo. This could be nothing but a momentary glow, you know, from seeing you for the first time in a month." Amarintha kissed her daughter.

"Don't you think it might be a good idea to go to your doctor as soon as you can?" asked Fannie.

Could the terrible treatments actually have had an effect? "You're right. After Dick sees me, we'll go to the Angel Tree."

The three of them quickly dressed, packed a lunch and piled into Amarintha's car to make the trek to downtown Charleston.

The visit with her doctor was brief. He said he saw no difference in her appearance, but agreed to have her blood checked. When he left to get the phlebotomist, Amarintha gazed at herself in the mirror on the back of the examination door. She saw only a thin, haggard woman looking back at her, no different from the dozen cancer patients Dick had likely examined before her.

Amarintha shrugged when she saw her mother and daughter's anxious faces in the waiting room. "He'll have some results from my bloodwork in an hour or so. Let's go."

Once under the boughs of the oldest living organism east of the Mississippi, most visitors to the magnificent tree were awed into silence. Not so two little girls that Amarintha watched as they ran around the tree, attempting to circumvent their parents and climb onto the thick grey limbs that touched the ground. The tree shaded 17,000 square feet of ground and the trunk was more than twenty-five feet in circumference. No thinking person could ever stand and gaze upon this tree without a feeling of insignificance. Amarintha, Fannie, and Ava brought out their sandwiches, ate—and then took another walk around the tree's trunk.

When Amarintha's phone vibrated, she moved away from the tree next to an old wooden bench. She saw her doctor's number and answered, her breath squeezed in her chest. "What did you find out?" At first, she couldn't hear anything and then Dick coughed. She plopped down on the bench, her knees knocking together.

"We ran your blood, but it might have been contaminated. Can you come back downtown? I'd like to ask my partner to see you too."

She groaned, and he heard it. "Ok, I know you don't exactly like the guy, but he is the president of the National Oncologists

Association. If we need some specialized equipment or attention from the National Institutes of Health, he can get us that."

"Why would NIH be interested in me, Dick? What are you not telling me?"

"If your blood results are accurate, it appears that your body is creating antibodies against the cancer, and has done so since your last tests. If the last round of chemo had this kind of effect, well, that could change the prognosis for similar patients."

She was silent. Worrying about every other brain cancer patient out there was very low on her to-do list.

"Ok, I'll come in tomorrow afternoon."

CHAPTER 35

"THOMPSON, ARE YOU telling me that your client Amarintha Sims just happened to dig up what we are all looking for? That is too convenient."

Thompson was with Brook Reynolds in the same conference room as the day before, pungent with the smell of old coffee and pizza. Brook had sent one FBI agent with two Centers for Disease Control field investigators to Richard's house. The CDC investigators carried locked metal boxes—one for the reliquary and the other for samples. She had opted for plain clothes, knowing that white-suited men stepping out of an ambulance would cause quite a stir in the neighborhood—not what the she needed right now. The CDC's job was to get samples from the reliquary, Richard himself, and anywhere in the house that the reliquary had touched. The FBI agent's job was to make sure Richard Anderson stayed put.

"Mr. Molotov," Brook said.

"Please, call me Sergei. I insist." Thompson wanted to groan.

"Ok, Sergei. The reliquary is at a local hospital that has a lab trained to deal with pathogens—the same team that was trained a few years ago when Ebola showed up in the U.S. We have a representative from the Vatican, who arrived last night, and he will keep Rome informed of the results of the tests on the reliquary."

"Sure, sure." Sergei was not interested in the safe handling of the bacteria. He was thousands of miles away from any danger. "What I am wondering about is the fact that the person who somehow had the reliquary in 1985, over three hundred years after being stolen, is apparently related to the owner of the property where the reliquary was found. This Amarintha Sims, Thompson's client? Tell me, Agent Reynolds, does Thompson look like a designer to you?"

Brook looked sympathetically at Thompson. "Sergei," she said. "Sims did indeed have a daughter and that daughter is Amarintha Sims. Her father, Charles Sims, bought the property in the 1970s. The picture of him with the artifact was taken late in 1985 during a gathering to highlight new radiocarbon equipment at the North Charleston Naval Base. The employees were asked to bring in their oldest possessions, and the science team showed off their new equipment for dating the items. It was a public relations gimmick. We still do not know exactly what this team was doing. A month after the picture was taken, anthrax broke out."

"Where did Sims get the artifact? Does anyone know? And who outside of your team knows about the reliquary?" Sergei asked.

"We don't know where he got it," replied Thompson.

Brook said, "Amarintha Sims and Richard Anderson, the neighbor who lives next to the property, were the only ones who handled it. He is under voluntary quarantine. Two workers actually dug up the trunk, but they were not present when Amarintha opened it. The CDC has told us that based on the sequence of events only Amarintha Sims and Richard Anderson might have been exposed."

Sergei laughed. "You believe that, Agent Reynolds? A nasty bug that has been alive for almost 350 years surely has some tricks up its sleeve."

Sergei had a point. Two reliquaries had once shared an altar in a French convent. One had caused anthrax in Rome. The other, stolen in 1685, had popped up over three hundred years later and likely had caused an outbreak of anthrax in Charleston.

Neither of them replied. Brook said, "Amarintha Sims was at her mother's last night. As soon as Thompson received the picture from Richard, we sent agents there but Amarintha, her mother, and Amarintha's daughter, Ava, were not there."

"Not there? How curious," said Sergei. "What have you told Jack Strong about his wife? I'm assuming you are proceeding as though the tip from Istanbul is valid. I read in Thompson's report that Kate Strong is an expert in Christian artifacts. Do you believe this missing reliquary has anything to do with her disappearance?"

"We have told Mr. Strong that Interpol received a credible tip that his wife was kidnapped. Mr. Strong is being looked after by the Charleston Police Department." Thompson noted that Brook did not share the details of the computer's prediction; that Bunin was stealing artifacts, including reliquaries, in order to find viable germs.

Sergei made no reply. Thompson added, "Strong does know that we're looking for one reliquary, but he thinks it's because of its value. Detective Edson will get the State Department involved. They will help manage the family."

Thompson heard the click of a lighter, and a deep inhalation from Sergei before he spoke. "Ok. I have another question. Is there any possibility that Amarintha Sims or her family could be involved with Alternative Auctions?"

Thompson thought of Amarintha: her brave face, her hairless head, her smile, and the tone of her voice when she talked about Ava, or Fannie—he hadn't met either of them, but felt he knew them both. He remembered blundering through Richard's garden and spying her, watching her grab her stomach, lean over and vomit, and then fall to the ground sobbing. He had backed away before she saw him. When she did see him ten minutes later, there had been no sign of what had happened, and she had grinned at him.

"No, no chance at all," he said.

Brook ended the call with Sergei. Thompson stood up, and she waved him back into his chair. She said, "Thompson, there are members of the respective teams who are asking that you be dismissed from the briefings."

"Suits me. I'll go home today," he laughed. Then he saw her expression, and said, "You're serious?"

"Yes, unfortunately, I am."

Thompson felt a flare of intense anger and a childish desire to bolt from the room and slam the door. "Who exactly is concerned and why?"

Brook looked at him steadily. "Too many coincidences and my bosses hate coincidences. You working for Amarintha Sims. You recommending Strong to Amarintha. Jack Strong's wife working for Adam Chalk. You spend a good bit of time with Ms. Sims and Mr. Strong, don't you?"

Thompson took a breath. "Yes, I do spend time with them, but working under my cover, both of these relationships are understandable. I was introduced to Amarintha by a woman from the Board of Architectural Review and to Jack Strong by a clerk at Morris Sokol Furniture. Do your superiors suspect the BAR and the furniture store as well?"

Brook Reynolds chewed her lip. "I want you to know that I believe that these events are just coincidences, no matter what anyone else believes. One of the Washington agents believes we should hold you indefinitely until we resolve whether or not Bunin is trying to make a biological weapon." She added, "Detective Edson threatened to quit if you were released from the Task Force. He says we would know a lot less if it weren't for you."

Thompson felt strangely gratified that Frank had stuck up for him. "It's not even 9:00 a.m. and I've already found the reliquary. You've got twenty other people trying to figure out if the damned thing is dangerous and what Bunin's motive might be to kidnap Kate Strong, and you want to sideline me?" He was angry now. "So what do you want me to do?"

Brook stood up. "For now, go home. Think of this as an unofficial temporary hiatus. I'm sure we will clear this up, and you'll be back with us soon, Agent Denton." Brook touched his shoulder, and walked out.

Sally Heath came into the room, and gestured for Thompson to follow her. She led him down the stairs, with more hip movement than was necessary, to the entrance foyer. "May I have your key card, Agent Denton?" Sally said, and held out her hand, a smug, self-satisfied smile on her face.

Istanbul

CHAPTER 36

K ATE WAS SLOUCHED on one of the rolling chairs, lethargic and barely awake, her depression acting as a weight on her body that prevented her from moving. Zora Vulkov entered the room holding a tray, and suggested that Kate might want to put on some lipstick, tossing a tube in her lap. The idea struck Kate as so ludicrous that for a moment she thought about throwing the tube back at the woman. The look in the older woman's eyes stopped her. After Vulkov left, Kate went into the bathroom, and opened the lipstick case. She carefully removed the roll of paper, and smoothed it against her knee. It looked to be a piece of paper from an adding machine, torn in a long strip. Vulkov had printed a message:

Bunin has a pharmaceutical company in Russia. He has guaranteed Russia's government that he can create a bacteria that will target only the people of the Middle East. You must not tell him which of the reliquaries may contain any ancient biological material, as he will have his people steal them. I knew Bunin many years ago in the old USSR. We both worked in a government division that studied biological warfare capabilities. I was able to leave a short message at Interpol's office in Istanbul. I believe they will investigate and hope that by now your family knows you are being kept here as a prisoner. The safest course of action is to tell Bunin that the reliquary he wants is in the Vatican. Even Bunin will have a difficult time stealing something from inside those walls. In the meantime, I am pretending to work with him. Do not lose hope.

Another piece of the puzzle had just fallen into place. Kate read the paper again and then, turning on the sink to cover the sound, shredded the paper into the toilet. Bunin thought he would find viable bacteria in the false reliquaries. Russia's government wanted to let loose a biological weapon in the Middle East? It was crazy. She sat in the bathroom, holding her head and moving it forward and backward trying to understand Vulkov's note.

When that didn't help her think, Kate went to the bedroom to lie down. Images of medieval Europe, its cities deserted and the dead stacked like wood, ran through her head. Entire towns had been stricken with the bubonic plague, the survivors stumbling down deserted streets, their livestock rotting, dead from neglect, their wells contaminated, and no one to work the fields. Those who did not die from the plague, their lymph nodes bursting inside of them, died from starvation. During the 1300s, some estimated that 100 million out of the world population of 450 million had died in Europe. It took four hundred years for the world to recover to pre-plague population numbers.

The bacteria had fundamentally changed the world and plunged Europe into a decline that lasted centuries. Relics and reliquaries held center stage as the populace surrounded cathedrals begging the priests to bring out the sacred objects so that the people could plead with the dead saints to intercede in their behalf. Processions, with reliquaries held high, weaved their way through the filthy streets, led by priests in their finest vestments, the people stumbling behind, begging God to save them. Even as the dying collapsed, their orifices spilling dark clotted blood, the people believed God could provide a cure. The cult of relics gained power as miraculous cures and deliverances were attributed to one saint or another.

Bunin wants to let loose something like this?

Kate knew that, in many ways, little had changed in the past one thousand years. She pictured the evangelist who asked his viewers to place their ailing parts against the television to receive a miraculous cure—a cure that would work only if you called an 800 number and provided your credit card number first.

Bunin was trying to fulfill the mission of those long-dead Byzantine priests who seeded the reliquaries with plague, smallpox, and whatever else plagued Constantinople at the time, seeking to avenge the Byzantine Empire's rape by its fellow Christians in the Fourth Crusade. This time the target was not the French but the people who lived in the old Byzantine Empire: the Jews and Arabs. In the depths of her depression, Kate wondered if this wasn't what the world deserved.

Charleston

CHAPTER 37

S ALLY DIDN'T NOTICE that Thompson was gripping the
report from Monsignor Ogier as she escorted him out the
door. Neither Brook nor Frank had bothered to pick up
copies. He understood. The reliquary's history wasn't relevant
to the FBI, at least not at the moment.

As he walked back to his condominium, Thompson
wondered what value Kate Strong could provide Anton Bunin.
Maybe reliquaries hid new pathogens; blood from a saint that
had been dripped into a glass bottle and never opened; teeth
whose pulp could be crushed and analyzed; bones whose
marrow might harbor unknown microbes.

What would Frank do with Jack Strong? Thompson
doubted the man would wait submissively while the FBI, police
department and the State Department came up with a plan to
rescue Kate. He had worked with Jack long enough to know that
patience was not one of his virtues.

Thompson trudged up the stairs to his condominium,
opened the door, tossed the Vatican's report on his desk and
began to brew some coffee. *Should he call Sergei?* No, the FBI

SAC certainly would have called him right after dismissing Thompson.

When confronted with inexplicable events, humans tended to blame the outsider. The individuals that had been working so enthusiastically less than twelve hours before, treating Thompson as one of their own, now just as mindlessly agreed with their superiors that now the agent bore watching. *Would they just watch him?* He wondered whether he was really in danger of arrest and thought about calling Jack. Maybe they could get the same lawyer.

What should he do about Amarintha? Did the FBI believe he could be involved? He understood why the FBI needed to test her for exposure to anthrax. Would that be the end of it? He realized that of all problems he was mulling over, ensuring Amarintha's welfare was the most important.

Thompson picked up his phone to call her.

"It's Thompson. I need you to call me when you get this message. Richard told me about the box that you found at your lot, and there may be a problem. Call me."

Glancing over at the Vatican briefing document, he decided to look at the summary on page one. It appeared to be new, the report typed on bright white paper.

To: Brook Reynolds, Federal Bureau of Investigation Special Agent in Charge of South Carolina

From: Monseigneur Giuseppe Ogier

Attached is the full report on the reliquary. The item was stolen in 1685 and brought to Charleston by a Huguenot woman named Marin Postel. The events leading up to the theft are documented in the attached report, first written in 1885. The first three pages that describe the item in detail are likely the only pages your agents will need to become familiar with as they conduct their search.

Thompson reviewed the next three pages, which also were printed on new paper. The pages described the artifact in detail, including the red gemstone. The last sentence stated that the red diamond in the middle of the flower could be worth $10-15 million.

The following pages were marked as copies of originals. Based on the typeface, the document appeared to have been created on an early typewriter.

Property of the Vatican Archives

Commissioned by Cardinal Pierre Manigault

From reports on the Trial of Abbess Marie Postel in 1686 for the crime of heresy

This report respectfully compiled in 1890 by Monsignor Jean Lavelle, Curator of Documents at the Apostolic Palace, 1885-1910.

Transcribed and edited, from the original report

This report was created based on statements from eyewitnesses, each of whom were present at all or part of the events this report will describe. The eyewitnesses were Sister Simone, portress, Sister Theresa, infirmarian, and Sister Anne, sacristan, all resident at

the Convent of Corbie in the year of our
Lord, 1685. Madame Pepin from Dieppe, former
Huguenot, also bore witness to these events.
This report was commissioned by Cardinal
Manigault, in 1890, who wished to understand
the circumstances leading to the only known
persecution of an abbess for the grave crime
of heresy.

Thompson was hooked now. Monsignor Lavelle had been asked to report on an event that had occurred almost two hundred years prior to the request by Bishop Manigault. It was a story of a Huguenot woman, a thief, who he suspected would be found to be an ancestor to Charles Sims and therefore to Amarintha. When this was all over, maybe he would show this report to her.

PART II

Outside Paris: 1685

CHAPTER 38

SISTER MARIE, PRIORESS of the Convent of Corbie, heard a faint rattle and looked up from where she knelt in her private chambers. The portress, Sister Simone, stood quietly, clutching the convent master keys that were her responsibility to secure.

"The wagon is almost here. We can hear it on the road," said the portress.

The prioress pushed up from the cold stone floor. "Thank you, Sister Simone. Are the rooms ready? The travelers will be tired and hungry." She put her hand on Sister Simone's shoulder, and the two women moved out of the chamber into one of four long stone-covered walkways that outlined a square herb garden. As they walked, a shaft of the setting sun illuminated the columns lining the corridor. The crouching lions, monkeys, and demons carved into the granite tops of the columns were a constant reminder to the nuns that the world outside held unknown dangers. Sister Marie often wanted to smile when she saw them, the figures reminding her not of monsters, but of the carnival she had seen once as a child.

The prioress could hear slow hoof beats, a creak of leather and the rattle of wheels. Reaching an arched door at the end of the north corridor, Sister Simone pulled out a large key. This door was one of two that led to outer corridors that formed the primary walls of the convent. The chapel, meeting house, treasury, kitchen, infirmary, and parlor formed the connecting rooms housed in the north, east, and west corridors. The rooms in the south corridor, built to house noblewomen who visited the convent from time to time, were now a prison.

The two nuns walked through the door and down a small hall past the parlor, reaching another door more massive than the first and locked with three different mechanisms. This was the receiving door, and the prioress, sub-prioress, and portress were the only nuns in possession of keys to unlock it. This door led to the outside courtyard, the last barrier between the convent and the outside world. Sister Simone methodically fitted the keys into the three locks, never fumbling for the right one, and pushed the large door open, not an easy task because the door was heavy. It was meant to keep visitors out, not to welcome them.

As Sister Marie walked through to the courtyard, the wind that constantly blew on the hill where the convent stood chilled her. She stood with her back to the door, looking through a wide iron gate set into twelve-foot tall stonewalls. A wagon crept up the ascending lane to the convent, pulled by farm horses, their heads down. Two soldiers sat beside the driver. The driver was dressed in the dull, dirty clothes of his station, while the soldiers wore yellow livery, in the form of elaborate embroidered jackets and tall black boots. The curly wigs of the soldiers bobbed beneath wide velvet hats that held exotic feathers waving in the breeze. One of the soldiers turned and said something to a traveler behind him in the wagon.

The prioress heard crying, and a woman giving an angry retort to the soldiers. The two men laughed, and jumped down as the scowling driver waited for the nuns to open the gate.

The first soldier bowed to her as he walked to the gate and took off his hat. "My good woman, our horses are lame. Do you have someone who can attend to them?" Sister Marie saw two magnificent horses behind the wagon, one favoring a leg. The young soldier was handsome. His companion stood on the ground, holding his musket, while the driver, not a military man, remained at his post, dour and clearly unhappy.

Sister Marie nodded, and the portress unlocked the iron gates. Sister Simone waited for the soldiers to push open the heavy iron of the opening, but neither of them moved. Finally, the soldier at the gate shrugged, and shoved it open with ease. The driver clicked and the two horses pulled the wagon into the courtyard.

The prioress could see that the wagon contained ten or so women of all ages and half a dozen or so small children. The women were clothed in rough gray wool with dirty white cloth covering their hair, but she could see that two of the women wore finer cloth, their hair covered with embroidered caps. In the fading light, she also saw eyes turned to her, waiting for her instructions.

She had seen a bear baiting once in her childhood village, and remembered the eyes of the bear, sentient and pleading, as the dogs tore him to pieces. These eyes looked the same.

Addressing the men, she said, "My good sir, do you not have your business to conduct with me before we attend to your horses? I believe you and your passengers have been on the road for some time. Let us attend to them first."

One of the soldiers grimaced and swept his arm towards the

wagon. "These heretics? These are just Huguenot whores. They are not harmed, and while they are putting up a fair stink, there is no urgency to their care. I insist that you tend to our horses to so that we might return to Paris."

Sister Marie said, "What is your name, my son?"

"I'm Henri de Lefort, son of the Duke of Bifou."

"Well, Henri de Lefort, since I presume you are a good Catholic, I will tell you that if you attempt to deter me from my duty to these women, I will send a letter to your father, informing him that his son did not behave in a way fitting to a Christian and a son of a duke. Now, I insist that you and your companion leave this courtyard immediately and go to the stable just there." She pointed to a building a little distance away outside the gate. "First I need the papers."

The convent, something she thought was common knowledge, disallowed men, other than bishops and priests from passing through the iron gates. She wondered whether he was insolent or simply ignorant as he lingered in the courtyard.

He sullenly handed her a sheaf of papers, and said in a sly tone, "Are you able to read these, good Sister, with only one eye?"

Sister Marie touched the eyepatch over her left eye, and said, "Perfectly well, young man." She began to read. This wagon of Huguenots was from Dieppe. *Dieppe?* Sister Marie had spent the first sixteen years of her life in a village outside of that town, so some of the names were familiar. A few of the women appeared to be from notable families. She blinked hard and sniffed, handing the document to the portress.

"Come, come," she said to Sister Simone. "Let us get these poor unfortunates to their quarters."

The soldiers untied their horses from the wagon and walked back outside towards the stables. Henri de Lefort stared at the prioress over his shoulder, but he did not utter another word.

The prioress walked to the wagon and looked up at the driver. He finally unlatched the wagon postern and stepped down. "Well," she said, "please help your passengers down."

He spat. "I'll not put my hands on such as these." He walked to the front of the wagon and began to adjust the bridles.

The head of the convent looked at him and decided she would not argue. She spoke to the oldest woman in the front. "Are you able to climb down on your own? What is your name?"

"I'm Mistress Pepin, from Dieppe." The woman climbed out of the wagon, turned, and began helping the others. Most of them were crying.

One of the smaller girls uttered anguished gulping cries. "Papa, papa!" Her mother, or perhaps her sister, tried to comfort her.

The prioress led the sad, bedraggled group into the convent, through the red door that demarked the courtyard from the convent proper, occasionally saying in a soft voice, "Come this way, please." These Huguenot women would be made to bathe, their hair inspected for lice, and what meager belongings they had would be taken from them. They would be fed and then locked into the south corridor prison. The choir nuns knew their duty, as this was not the first group of Huguenot women the bishop had sent to be imprisoned. How the prioress was to obtain the funds to keep her flock from starving she did not know.

Sister Marie turned and watched the wagon move slowly out of the courtyard, the driver taking it to the stables where the soldiers were. After it cleared the heavy iron gates, the portress pushed them closed herself, the hinges screeching from their lack of use, locked them, crossed the courtyard and relocked the receiving door behind her.

"Sister Marie, I will take care of this group of Huguenots.

Please rest. We will need to talk to the bursar tomorrow about funds."

Yes, thought Sister Marie. The nun who held the purse strings would certainly have some words to say. The prioress nodded and moved slowly away from the courtyard towards her apartment to continue the letters she had begun earlier that day, and to pray, always to pray, for direction.

A sound came behind her. She and the portress turned and saw a young woman in the corner behind the door.

"Child, come forward, please. What is your name?" Sister Marie held out her hand. The young woman shook her head and began to shout, holding her arms out to her side.

"My father told me that papists were wicked because you wanted all of us dead. What are you going to do with all of us? Are you going to sell us to the Turks?"

The prioress was shocked to her core—not about the girl's accusation that the papists wished the Huguenots dead, which held some truth to it, but about the Turks. She stepped back. "Where did you hear such a wicked idea? Of course we are not going to sell you to the Turks. What a thing for you to say!"

"My brothers were sent to the galleys. If they become sick, they will be sold to the Turks."

Sister Marie walked quickly over to her, holding her arms out to the girl. "I am Sister Marie, the prioress of this convent. If you return to the true faith, you will be allowed to return home."

At that, the girl gave a cry and ran into the cloister towards the other women from Dieppe. The prioress put her hand on the cool stone of the walls and turned towards her rooms. What was she to do with these Huguenots? She did not want to become harsh as her bishop advised. He had often insisted that only physical mistreatment could show these Huguenots the error of their ways. According to the bishop, one of the convents had gagged their Huguenots, an example he was eager for her to follow here at the Convent of Corbie, for he said that after their gagging all of the women had recanted their Protestant faith.

If the girl's brothers were in fact in the galleys, they would not be given any opportunity to recant, much less escape. If one of them did become ill, he was doomed. The King's ships gave no succor to the galley slaves. Sick men would be thrown overboard or sold at the nearest port. She shuddered at the thought of any Frenchman, even a heretic, being sold to the Turks, and made the sign of the cross.

CHAPTER 39

A T DAWN, THE prioress led prayers in the chapel, hearing several of her young novices whispering to themselves about the latest group of children and women delivered to the convent. This was the fourth group of Huguenots to come to their sanctuary. The first group had been kept in the meetinghouse, a room where the convent's inhabitants met to conduct business, but this had not been satisfactory due to the location of the privy, which required the Huguenots to pass by the chapel. Some of the women would shout blasphemies at the nuns in prayer. After attempting to manage the situation for a month, the prioress had finally requested help. The bishop moved the first group of Huguenots, to where she did not know, and gave the prioress funds to convert the rooms in the south corridor to a self-contained prison with its own privy.

Before retiring the night before, the prioress had read the official letters condemning each of the Huguenot women to her convent prison. All of them had refused to adjure. Most of the women presumably had male relatives, and the prioress knew that if these women's husbands, sons, and fathers had also refused to recant, the men would indeed have been sent to row ships for His Majesty's navy.

How long she was to house the women she did not know. She would have to ask the bishop on his next visit. He and his retinue visited from time to time, with pomp and fanfare, bringing nobles and clergy from all over Europe who wanted to see the relics her convent housed in its altar.

All of this ran through her mind as she prayed, realizing with a start that her robes were cold and wet, and the nuns behind her in the chapel were silent. Two young nuns came over silently and helped her up.

A novice, whose name she couldn't remember, stood to the side. "Excuse me, Sister Marie, but there is a messenger here from the bishop. He is most anxious to see you privately. The portress said he is in the parlor."

She looked at this young woman, saw entirely too much animation, and thought the messenger must be the bishops' young nephew, a comely young man who had recently taken the orders. As a priest, he would be waiting inside the cloistered halls in the parlor, visible to any of the nuns who happened to walk by. He had been here once before and had brought much unwelcome attention to himself, although she had to admit, he did not seem to be aware of his good looks.

Entering the room, she saw her surmise was accurate. The young man stood quickly, bowed, and kissed the ring on her outstretched hand.

"Please sit down. I believe you are Edward?"

"Yes, I am, but now I go by Pastor. The bishop sends his regards and hopes you are well. He has sent me on a mission to this convent and five others with news. You must prepare for more heretics. His Majesty ordered dragooning in your district, and while the bishop expects this act to move more heretics to return to our faith, there will certainly be those who will not."

The prioress was stunned. To place armed soldiers in the homes of the Huguenots would ignite the flames of religious hatred, simmering now, into a boil. Dragooning, as the occupation of homes by soldiers was called, was the most feared weapon of the king. She had heard that entire villages of Huguenots had recanted in advance of the arrival of the dragoons. These soldiers were allowed to do anything they wished, short of murder. The king had bowed to pressure from the pope and was going to plunge his country into chaos, if not another civil war. She dropped her head to her chest, feeling tears in her eyes.

"Sister Marie, shall I ring for someone?" asked the young priest in a solicitous tone. "We gave thanks this morning that all of France would return to its rightful religion to receive the blessings of our Lord. His Majesty has received a message from God and has acted on it." The young man's face was shining with devotion and certainty.

The prioress stood. "Thank you. I will take you to the kitchen so you may be refreshed for your ride to the next convent." She walked with him slowly through the corridor to the kitchen, certain there were many watching eyes. Far better for her to pretend she didn't notice.

"Please give my sincere regards and prayers for the bishop's health to your uncle." She bowed and turned to leave the kitchen.

"Oh, there is one more item. I have a letter for you." At this, she stopped and turned to face the young man. He produced a letter from his robe and handed it to her with a sly smile. "I don't believe you have many letters other than from the bishop. He is most curious as to its author."

Sister Marie stood stock still, recognizing the handwriting. She looked at the wax seal, praying it had not been opened. "Please tell the bishop that this is from a remote relation of mine who promised to write when her daughter was of age. I expect that this letter will confirm the dowry we will receive when she takes her vows."

She knew that avarice, which surely had been passed down to the nephew from the bishop would divert the young priest, and from the expression on his face, she was right. Funds from dowries provided a great deal of income for the bishop. Looking at him, the prioress thought that he would probably be a very successful man of the church.

CHAPTER 40

SISTER MARIE WALKED back to her rooms, closed the door to her quarters, and sat down at her small desk. With shaking hands, she unsealed the letter and smoothed it open. The author was her father.

Dearest Marie,

I remember with shame the time of our last meeting. How I devoutly wish the words that passed from me to you had never been uttered. I pray for your forgiveness, which I know you will freely offer, given your kind and gentle nature that I am too late to admire.

By the time you read this, I will be dead. I am in prison and have the same fever that killed your brother's wife. Your brother and his sons have been sent to the galleys. The only one of your family that is left is Marin, my granddaughter and your niece. She has been sent to your convent with a group from Dieppe, a feat that has been accomplished with our Lord's blessing and help from a devoted friend, a friend who also smuggled this letter out of my cell.

Sister Marie stopped reading and recited a prayer for her father. Over thirty years ago, she had rejected the Protestant religion of her parents and refused to marry the man of their choice. That she would become a nun in order to escape marriage had enraged her father, and the rest of the family had been forbidden to acknowledge her existence after he ordered her to leave. The last family members she had seen were her brother and mother, still as the suits of armor in Dieppe's castle, staring at the wagon that took her to this convent. Some years ago, she had received a letter from a remote relation about her mother's death, and she knew her brother had married and had children, but nothing else until this.

I beg of you to be kind to her, to love her as your own, and to protect her as best you can. She has your eyes, one brown and one green. She tries to hide this as some have said it is a sign of witchcraft, but you know well that this is a monstrous lie. She does not know you are her relation, and I leave it to you and God if she should be told.

The nun put her hand to the patch that covered her left eye. On the road to the convent thirty years ago, she had adopted this patch, and none had seen her without it since. She read on:

Oh, how I was mistaken in believing the Comte's character was of a good man. The one you refused so many years ago is indeed a man of few scruples, no honor, and much greed. He is the reason for what has befallen our family. He created terrible tales about how our family desecrated the Holy Bible and took them to the local bishop. Our property has been seized and will be given to him.

I remain faithful to God and know I will be reunited in heaven with my entire family, papist or not. It has never been you, dear daughter that I despised, but those that perverted the Lord's teachings for their own earthly desires. I am, and always will be,

Your loving father
Jean Postel

The prioress let the tears flow now, weeping for her father, her brothers, and the nephews she had never met. She knelt to pray for guidance but could not stop the memory of that horrific day so long ago. She had burst into her father's study. She could still see him now, turning to her as she spoke.

"Father, I will not and cannot marry that despicable man." Her father's face turned hard. He spoke harshly.

"Enough of this, Marie. He is a good match and will make a fine husband."

"You are wrong, Father. I have just seen him beat his dog to death for not coming to him quickly enough. I watched it from my window. He is a vile human being and will mistreat me, I am sure. Is that what you want for your only daughter?"

Her father stood and he yelled, "Go to your room and do not leave it until you come to your senses."

Neither she nor her father relented. For three weeks she remained in her room, where she heard arguments between her parents, some frightening loud. Her mother begged her to relent, to marry this man chosen by her father, but still Marie refused, the cries of the beaten dog still in her head. Desperate, she managed to send a note to the local priest by way of the cook, Rebecca, asking to be rescued and taken to a convent.

The story of the Huguenot girl who had forsaken her faith and taken orders in the Catholic Church had humiliated her father. She doubted that in the thirty years since, the story had been forgotten by anyone in Dieppe or the small villages surrounding it.

The prioress remained on her knees for a long time, patiently waiting for God to reveal his will. Finally, she felt a sense of peace come over her, and she stood, hurrying to complete the day's duties. She would find her niece this evening, after prayers.

CHAPTER 41

THE PRIORESS TUGGED the heavy wooden door open and stepped into the south corridor, into the prison rooms. Each room had been fitted with a thick oak door with a grille at face height. Faces began to appear as the inhabitants of the rooms heard footsteps. A variety of expressions showed in those faces: defiance, despair, hope, and desperation. How was she to find the one she wanted to find? Finally, she cleared her throat.

"I am the prioress of this convent, Sister Marie."

She heard nothing, and continued. "I understand you are afraid and worried for the safety of your other loved ones. We will allow some correspondence to be given to you, and weekly you will be allowed to write letters after service on Sunday." One of the women started to speak but was hushed.

"I wish to speak to Mistress Pepin, of Dieppe," the prioress said.

"Here." The voice came from the small room behind her, and the prioress turned to the sound. "Here." The prioress walked to the grille and recognized the older woman she had spoken to last night by the wagon. The woman's eyes were swollen with weeping, and her hands on the bars had ragged, ripped nails, white at the knuckles that gripped around the iron.

"I am Mistress Pepin, of Dieppe, where the others are from

as well. What do you want of us? What further misery will you now bring upon us? I have lost my husband, my sons, and the dragoons have shamed me. What more do you papists want?"

How could she possibly single out one of these women, assuming of course that her niece was in the group? The prioress put her hands on the woman's fingers and felt them loosen just a little.

"I have come to hear your stories." At this, she could hear murmurs from the others who had heard the exchange. Looking beyond the woman in front of her, she could see a few other women, their expressions hard. Suddenly realizing that that it might be dangerous for her to enter the rooms alone, she stepped back from the door.

"Tomorrow we will speak about your situation. Tonight I will pray for each of you." At that, more sounds of disbelief came from the cells, but she chose to ignore them. "Good night and may God have mercy on you."

She turned and began her long slow walk back to her rooms, her mind already at work on a plan to have the youngest girls brought to her one by one over the next few days.

CHAPTER 42

SEVERAL DAYS PASSED before Sister Marie identified her niece. At first, she planned just to interview the young women, but had changed her mind and decided she would hear all of the Huguenot stories. She had endured hours of weeping, cursing, singing and recitation of the Bible from the Huguenot women. A few of them had indeed told their entire stories, from happy times when they were allowed to worship in peace, to the dragoons coming to Dieppe to destroy what the king believed was a revolution against his country and himself. The tales of the dragoons horrified the prioress. One woman's husband had had his feet plunged in boiling water. Another had been held by two soldiers, screaming, made to watch her daughter's rape.

She was listening to the lamentations of an old Huguenot woman who had lost her husband and five sons to the galleys when she heard a light knock on the door.

"Sister Marie," said a young nun as she opened the door. "There remain only two Huguenot women that you have not yet spoken to. We can bring them to you tomorrow."

"No, I will see one more this evening." She patted the shoulder of the old woman whom the nun was now leading back to the prison rooms.

The prioress could hear the nun outside her door and another voice she did not recognize. "I don't want to meet the old papist. I don't care that she is the prioress." At that, the door was pushed open and a girl was shoved in, promptly falling at the prioress's feet.

Standing up, the girl looked straight at the prioress, and before she could toss her hair, Sister Marie saw the brown eye on the left and the green eye on the right. This was her niece! She was tall and willowy, with a graceful bearing, good teeth, and beautiful features. Indeed, she looked much as she, herself, had looked at the same age.

"My dear, won't you sit down?" The prioress gestured to a small chair by the fireplace, sitting down opposite. The girl glared back, the brown eye now covered by a wave of hair.

"Your name is Marin, is it not?" The prioress could see the surprise in the face, but the girl nodded and sat down slowly just on the edge of the wooden seat, her bearing much like a rabbit ready to bolt to the deep woods. "I wish to hear the story of how you came to be here."

"Why? You know the story. The king hates the Huguenots and wants our lands and property to give to his papist friends."

Sister Marie leaned over. "His Majesty only wants you to return to the true and proper faith. It is your souls that he is most worried about."

With this, the girl raised her head and looked up incredulously. The prioress recognized her younger self in the narrow face with the large nose, full mouth, and dark eyebrows. Marin was a beauty, she thought, just as she had once been.

"How old are you, Marin?"

"I am sixteen." She did not lower her gaze and watched as Sister Marie rose and walked to her small writing desk across from the fireplace. After fumbling with the lock to her desk, the prioress removed the letter from her father and walked back to the two chairs. She sat and returned Marin's look, holding the letter and her breath.

"What about your family?"

The girl began to weep, holding her hands to her face. "My close relations are all gone," she said, her voice muffled. She raised her head, and wiped her eyes with her palms. "My grandfather is in prison. My mother is dead, and my two brothers and father were sent to the galleys. I have no one."

The girl began to cry again, and Sister Marie thrust the letter towards her. "I am putting myself in your hands, for if this letter were to be read by some, I would lose my place and you your protection."

The girl started at that, but then spoke harshly. "I don't need protection. I need to be released to find my mother's relations in England."

Sister Marie handed Marin the letter. The girl took it and looked down in bewilderment until she saw the broken seal. One hand flew to her mouth.

"He is alive? He has sent me a letter?"

The prioress immediately realized her error. She quickly said, "No, this is not to you. The letter is addressed to me. Can you read?"

The girl's defiance returned. "Of course I can read." The girl flung off the prioress's hand, stood, then crouched by the fire to read the letter.

The prioress watched Marin's face as she read. She expected many reactions save the one she got. Marin began to laugh. "So you are my rebellious auntie! Do you know that I have longed to meet you my entire life? They never told me you had become a prioress, only that you were in a convent. I learned the entire story from Rebecca, our cook."

Astonished, the priories asked, "Rebecca is alive?"

Marin did not answer the question. "She told me the story of how you refused to marry and went to a convent." Marin was silent a long time, picking at her homespun dress, tapping one foot. Finally, she looked up and spoke. There were unshed tears in her eyes.

"My grandfather's friend, the one who helped him, told Grandfather that I should marry the Comte, the same man you rejected. If I had, perhaps we would all still be together at home." Her voice trailed off, and she lowered her head again.

Sister Marie sat frozen. The idea that this man, this horrible man, had never stopped lusting after her father's property pierced her like an arrow. She took a deep breath and said, "Tell me the whole story, please."

Marin confirmed that the Comte had never stopped trying to buy the Postel lands. Over the years, he had garnered all the lands except theirs, and had made multiple offers to the elder Postel. Marie's father rejected them all, including an offer by the Comte to marry Marin.

A man humiliated twice by the same family was indeed dangerous, and the Comte finally concocted a story that the Postel family was practicing their false religion at home, and had been seen desecrating the Bible. Soldiers arrested her father and brothers, leaving only Marin, her grandfather, her mother, and Rebeca.

"Mother died a few days after the arrest," Marin was crying again. "Rebecca and I tried to take care of the farm. My grandfather's friend came to warn us that soldiers would be dragooned in our home. Grandfather didn't believe it. He was writing letters to the king and was sure we would be left alone. His friend told him I should marry the Comte because then we would be safe. I should have told Grandfather I would do it. I should have married him."

Marin wiped her eyes with her hands. "A week after we buried Mother, the Comte came to our house with soldiers, and they took Grandfather away. The soldiers locked me in the cellar."

Marin stood up and began to walk. "The Comte came to the cellar alone. I tried to hide in the corner, but he started to quote scripture while he unbuttoned his britches. He said he would marry me but wanted to sample the wares first." The girl stopped and began to laugh, though with a note of hysteria.

"The only thing that stopped him was that his men came looking for him. One of them was my grandfather's friend, who told the Comte that I needed to be cleaned up to be made worthy of a nobleman's attentions and took me away."

Sister Marie was silent for a moment and then asked, "How did you get here?"

"Grandfather's friend, Monsieur Larue, hid me in a closet. I heard him tell the Comte that I had run away into the fields. While the soldiers were looking for me, M. Larue took me to town and put me in the wagon that was coming here. My name isn't on the papers, is it?"

"No," the prioress said. "That should provide protection to you—if you are sure that M. Larue is reliable."

Both women were silent for a long time. The Comte had ruined her family in a final and horrible manner. If he actually married Marin, the final heir, possession of the lands would be unquestionably legal. The Comte could not be allowed to find Marin.

"Our relationship must not be discovered, and you must not try to leave." She could see that Marin was surprised. It was the prioress's turn to laugh.

"Do you think I do not know what is in your head? Ways to escape unnoticed? You must not. The Comte will find you. Promise me you will not leave."

Marin sat down again, her head in her hands. "I cannot promise that, but knowing that you are my relation has given me much to think about. May I leave now?"

"Very well." The prioress nodded and called for the nun. The two women stood, looking at each other. The prioress badly wanted to reach out and embrace the girl, but she could see in Marin's face that the gesture would be rejected. So be it for now.

CHAPTER 43

OVER THE NEXT two weeks, the prioress, under the pretext of counseling Marin, contrived to have the young woman brought to her on multiple occasions. The prioress managed to send a discreet inquiry to the mayor in Dieppe. After a week, the mayor confirmed that the three men were indeed in the King's navy, rowing in the galleys. Marin sobbed, begging her aunt to do something. The prioress saw an opportunity to safeguard Marin and agreed to continue to make inquiries if Marin would not try to escape. Sister Marie also prayed that Marin would reject her Protestant faith and recant. Only then would the girl be truly safe.

All the Huguenot prisoners above the age of five were required to attend daily religious instruction, and most simply endured the instruction of the nuns in silence. One morning, Marin arrived at her aunt's quarters flushed and angry from attending a religious session that discussed the importance of holy relics. She paced in her aunt's small quarters as she raged.

"Jean Calvin said that if you added up all the pieces of wood that are supposed to be from Christ's cross, you'd have enough to build a fleet." This was only one of Calvin's writings that the girl knew by heart. "Indulgences are wicked, against God's word. There is nothing in the Bible about them."

Sister Marie sat calmly by the fire, listening. The convent was

L. K. Clement

named for the patron saint of sick children, Colette of Corbin. The prioress believed in the miracles attributed to the relics held in their small convent. Sister Anne, their sacristan had witnessed a child's healing. Perhaps Marin would listen to the story and her heart would change.

"Marin, please sit down," said the prioress. The girl did so and put her hands in her lap. "I understand Calvin's teachings in this regard, but he is wrong that relics are false." Marin began to speak, but the prioress gave her no opportunity to do so. "Our sacristan, Sister Anne, witnessed a healing in our chapel. Will you listen to her story?"

Marin looked down at her hands. "What is a sacristan?" she asked.

"She is responsible for decorating the altar, maintaining the sacred vessels, and opening the church on feast days. She ensures that our small chapel is fit for worship any time of the day or night," said the prioress, picking up a bell from a small table and ringing it.

A novice came in and stood silent. "Please ask Sister Anne to join me here." The novice left and soon returned with an older woman. The novice gently closed the door, leaving the three women in Sister Marie's room.

The prioress arranged her robes and said, "Sister Anne, this is Marin Postel. She is one of the Huguenot women staying here in the convent." Marin made a noise that her aunt knew was one of amusement.

"Yes, Sister Marie," said the sacristan. "I know this girl." The prioress realized that of course this nun would have been responsible for instructing the Huguenots on the subject of holy relics.

The sacristan was a heavy woman, immaculate in her robes, her dark eyes framed by gray brows. She sat down on a bench facing the fire and turned to her superior, her expression calm.

The prioress said, "I would like for you to tell Marin the story of the miracle you witnessed for yourself some years ago." Both the sisters made the sign of the cross. "First, would you explain how our holy relics found their way to our convent?"

Sister Anne gave a grim smile. "I will be happy to do so, as this particular Huguenot left my instruction this morning before I could share the details."

Whatever thoughts Marin held behind those remarkable eyes were hers alone for she sat with her head down and did not make a sound. The prioress wondered just how disruptive Marin had been in the morning session with Sister Anne.

The sacristan cleared her throat and said, "King Louis IX made many trips to the Holy Land to further his faith in the Lord and locate the remains of our Savior and saints. Many times he gazed upon the remnants of the Passion held in Constantinople. He was able to obtain remnants of the True Cross and other important relics of our Blessed Savior and bring them to France to bless our lands." At this, both Sister Anne and the prioress crossed themselves again, while Marin sat, her head still bowed.

"Most of these precious relics are at Sainte-Chappelle in Paris, but the king, in his benevolence, shared many relics with the important cathedrals of France. Our modest church has had possession of two reliquaries with relics from a martyred saint for over three hundred years. Very few have ever been able to gaze upon them." Sister Anne stopped.

When Marin finally did look at her aunt, the prioress realized that the girl was ready to laugh. Marin said, "Sister Marie, isn't it true that King Louis bought the relics from the Venetians, because King Baldwin of Byzantium had to pawn these items to fund his palace? For all we know, the reliquary could hold chicken bones."

Sister Anne's hand flew to her mouth as she stared at Marin, then at the prioress.

The prioress was shocked herself. "Marin, these are false teachings that you must renounce! I beg of you, child, repent of your wicked thoughts." The prioress was truly distressed now and realized that none of her instructions to Marin had worked to turn the girl's heart. With horror, she became aware that she was weeping, and, at this, Marin came to her.

"Dear Aunt, please, do not distress yourself. I am but trying to lighten the moment." She pulled away and held the prioress's hands.

"Aunt?" They both turned at this word, still holding hands, realizing that Sister Anne had heard them. The nun walked backwards towards the door, wide-eyed with alarm. The prioress recovered.

"Dearest Sister Anne, Marin and I are from the same town. It is but an affection." The sacristan continued to back away and hurried out the door.

The prioress and Marin stared at each other. Finally, Sister Marie said, "You must apologize to her, Marin."

The girl nodded and scurried to follow Sister Anne.

CHAPTER 44

TWO DAYS PASSED before Marin was brought to her again. Her niece entered the room and sat down by the fire. "How are you, my dear?" Sister Marie looked anxiously at her niece as she spoke, seeing exhaustion and worry. "Have you spoken to Sister Anne?"

"Yes, I apologized for leaving her class. She sat with me in the garden for a while. She believed me when I told her we were from the same village." The girl looked up. "She told me of what she witnessed, a child cured of his lameness." Marin scratched the fabric of her dress with a fingernail. "I cannot believe that she would lie, yet all my life I have been told that relics cannot effect such a miracle."

Sister Marie looked at her niece and said nothing. She knew well the difficulty of questioning childhood teachings. After her arrival at the convent, it took a full year to put her Huguenot teachings aside and another three years before the bishop allowed her to become a nun. "Is this all that troubles you?"

"Three of the young children are very ill. One is close to death. The sisters have been helping us tend to them, but it is very grave."

The prioress had been told of the illnesses, but a report from the infirmarian, Sister Therese, had indicated the children were on the mend. "Have these children become worse quite suddenly?"

"Yes." Marin sounded exhausted.

"Take me to them."

Marin looked at her and whispered, "It might be the plague."

Sister Marie closed her eyes and said a fervent prayer that it would not be so. "Come. Let us see what we have before us."

Marin and the prioress hurried to the south corridor, stopping at the now open, arched doorway leading to the Huguenot rooms. The prioress could see Sister Therese leaning against the stonewalls. All the doors to the rooms stood open.

"Sister Therese, is it the plague?" asked the prioress.

The infirmarian leaned close and whispered, "Yes, Mother. You must not come closer. We believed the children were getting well, but all of them have black swellings under their arms now. I have requested the priest, in the event that these heathens will allow the last rites. We have put all the sick children in the last room."

"Let me see them," said the prioress.

"Please, Sister Marie, you must not." Sister Therese moved to block the way and held out both hands beseechingly to her superior.

"Sister Therese, take me to these sick children." The prioress did not raise her voice, but her tone was implacable and the other nun relented. Marin stood by, silently. When her aunt moved into the gloomy corridor, she followed.

The smell of urine, vomit, blood, and unwashed bodies became stronger as the prioress walked towards the cell where the Huguenot children were kept. A Huguenot woman stood by the doorway and glared at Sister Marie. "Yer not going to say those papist words over my boy. He doesn't need praying from some dried up old nun to get to heaven."

The prioress stopped and gazed from this angry, heartsick woman and realized that what had appeared to be a bundle of cloth the woman held was actually a very small child, covered with a shawl.

"What is yer religion going to do with this one, ey? What can yer God do that mine cannot?" With this, the woman quickly parted the shawl, thrusting the bundle in the nun's face. Sister Marie reeled back from the smell and from the horror in front of her. The child was not two years old and was covered in weeping, red sores. His hair had been shorn, and his body was so thin that it resembled an old man rather than a healthy child. He was preternaturally still now, his eyes closed, his small chest barely moving. The woman holding him, presumably his mother, moved the shawl back over his face, causing an outcry of pain from the boy that pierced her heart. Without thinking, the prioress made the sign of the cross.

She felt herself being pulled backward out of the room, and the blow the distraught mother had attempted fell short. She turned, finding Marin and not Sister Therese had kept the strike from falling. Another Huguenot woman stepped in from the sick room and pulled the child and his mother, now wailing, further into the gloom of the sick room.

Sister Therese stepped up to her superior and began to speak very softly. "Please, prioress, you cannot help here. These women believe that God is punishing them for not attempting to escape. I am tolerated only because I have some sleeping draft for the children who are suffering. All will die, it is certain, perhaps even me. You must leave here now. And this one," she said, pointing to Marin, "should stay here and provide the help I require. She is one of the strong ones. I beg you, prioress, return to your rooms."

The prioress stood a moment longer, then nodded, and turned to make the long walk back, this time alone.

CHAPTER 45

ONLY THE SICK children and their mothers were allowed in the last cell of the south corridor, but Marin could hear murmurs from the other rooms and knew the other Huguenots were praying. She helped Sister Therese bathe the children, singing lullabies to soothe them.

The infirmarian removed a flask she kept tied to her robe and administered small amounts of a liquid to the children and their mothers. "They all should sleep for a while," said Sister Therese. "We have a long time before dawn. I do not believe all of these souls will still be with us then."

Marin felt a momentary anger at the resigned attitude of Sister Therese. Why was she not seeking the healing power of the convent's relics? With light from a candle, Marin covered each of the children with a ragged blanket. She stood up and said, "Sister Therese, Sister Anne told me that she witnessed a child healed by the relics kept in the chapel. Why do you not bring the objects here?"

The nun looked up, but Marin could not see her face clearly in the dark. "The bishop must decide."

Marin turned away. She tried again, "In our village, the relics were shown only to those that had money for indulgences. Why can't you go to the chapel and get the reliquary?"

The old woman sagged against the floor and remained silent,

finally saying, "Go to your room and sleep. I will call you if you are needed."

Marin went to one of the empty rooms and lay down, careful to put her candle on the dirt floor away from the straw. Her back and knees ached from the hours she had spent on the floor. Sleep hovered, waiting for her to relax, but thoughts of the reliquary would not leave her head. Wouldn't God forgive her if she prayed for intercession using the reliquary? These children would die.

What if Calvin was wrong in this matter? Wouldn't God see her heart—that her only desire was for the children to be cured? She sat up, looking outside the square window high in the wall. At that moment, she heard a dove in the rafters make a cooing noise. The bird flew down to the straw on the dirt floor and cooed again, cocking his head at her. When the bird flew out the tiny window, Marin saw the moon. She bolted upright, her decision made.

Picking up her candle, the girl crept down the corridor to the sick room, where she saw Sister Therese stretched out on the straw, her hand on the chest of one of the suffering children. In the light from the candle, Marin saw that everyone was asleep. She turned and made her way towards the end of the corridor. The infirmarian had not locked the arched door that separated the prison cell's corridor from the rest of the convent, and Marin's stealthy passage to the sanctuary of the church was unseen.

Marin placed her candle on the stone floor and removed the velvet cloth covering the altar. She traced the carvings on the top and tried to still her shaking hands. Grasping the top of the marble enclosure, she pushed it to the side. The scrape of the stone top echoed into the sanctuary. She stopped, her heart thumping. After a few moments of stillness, Marin reached in and felt a leather cloth covering a small box. She pulled the box and its leather covering out of the altar and put it in her apron, shoved the stone top back into place, and scurried back towards the Huguenot quarters.

Stopping in an alcove, Marin slid down to the stone floor and placed her candle to the side. Removing the box from the leather, she moved it closer to the candle. The box was small, and plainer than Marin thought it would be. A figure was carved on the top, its two hands outstretched, one holding a baby, one a flower. Surely, the baby was a sign that she was doing God's will. She closed her eyes, said a prayer, took a breath and removed the lid. In the dim light, what looked like seeds of corn lay in the bottom of the gold box. She pushed these with her fingers, uncertain as to how these small items, with their undistinguished appearance, could possibly be from a saint.

Marin quickly put the top back on the box, shoved it into her apron and hurried back to the sick room. Holding the candle up to see the children, Marin gasped at the sight of the small bodies on the straw. Many of them had thrown off the blankets, and the pustules covering their shrunken bodies were readily visible. All the children were awake, the candle reflecting in their sunken eyes. One of the children, a girl, made soundless cries, her mouth opening and closing. She appeared to have grapes clustered under her arms.

She leaned over, choking back her grief. A few short months ago, all of these small children were happily playing at the Maypole in Dieppe on May Day. Now all of them resembled shrunken, bald, old men.

One of the women woke up, looked at the child lying next to her, and said, "Marin, what are you doing here? Nothing can be done for us. We are damned by God, and he is punishing us by taking our children first."

"Mistress Pepin, I only want to provide a bit of comfort." The woman watched her, too exhausted to protest. Marin ladled water from a clean bucket. One by one, she held each child's head and brought refreshment to their dry mouths. Each one managed a sip. None of the other mothers or Sister Therese awoke.

Marin could not bring out the reliquary in front of Mistress Pepin, so she dawdled with her task, waiting until the watcher and the children went back to sleep.

CHAPTER 46

T HE PRIORESS WOKE suddenly from a nightmare, waking just as the Comte she had rejected reached for her. She heard shouts and dressed quickly. Outside of her rooms, she determined that the source of the noise was the Huguenot quarters and hurried towards the south corridor. Sister Therese was bending down and standing up, then moving a bit to the side, and bending and standing again. The prioress realized that each time she did so, Sister Anne was examining one of the sick children. Two Huguenot women were actually smiling and two others knelt, audibly praying.

"What's this, Sister Therese?" asked the prioress.

The infirmarian turned to face her Mother Superior. "The children are better this morning," she said.

The small patients were still prone, but one small boy was laughing, his arms held out to his mother to be picked up.

One of the women, standing to the side, harrumphed. It was Mistress Pepin. She was scowling at the group. "Mistress Pepin, why are you not sharing in the joy of this moment? Is something troubling you?" asked the prioress.

The woman shook her head and stepped back from the group.

At that moment, Marin rushed into the room. "Get away, get away, you witch!" screamed Mistress Pepin.

Marin shrank behind her aunt. "What is going on here? I demand that you tell me," said the prioress.

Mistress Pepin crept closer to the prioress, who could feel Marin pulling closer to her.

"This one, this one here. She is the reason these children are not dead. She did something to them last night, something against nature. She has made a pact with the devil, and these children now are damned. They are no longer of God's world, but the devil's!"

The other women now grasped their children. Some began to check their small, sad bodies for signs of the devil, looking in their mouths and under their arms. Sister Therese crossed herself. The prioress felt a cold dread coming up from her very stomach, rising into her face and chest. She restrained herself from genuflecting, certain that the gesture would not been seen as comforting to anyone, even herself.

In a calm tone, she spoke again. "Mistress Pepin, we should all be rejoicing that these children are better. This is God's will, not the devil's. You are tired and are not yourself. Please let me provide you some wine and bread so you can rest." Sister Marie could hear the mothers murmuring their agreement as they looked at Mistress Pepin, who still stood staring at Marin.

"God's will be damned. Examine the girl, prioress. She has a magic box in her apron and has always had the witch's eyes." At that, the woman grabbed Marin, and pulled her into the middle of the room, holding the girl's face between her dirty hands, turning it one way, then the other, so all the others could see the two different color eyes.

One of the other women said, "Stop this talk. We have always known that Marin had eyes of different colors. Others in her family had it too. You know the Postels. They were always a faithful, God-fearing people."

"Yes, I did know her family. I believe the prioress knows

them as well." The Huguenot woman looked strangely at the prioress as she said this, and with horror, Marie realized her secret was no longer.

Sister Marie felt her knees begin to weaken, and she put her hand to her eye patch without thinking. At that moment, the Pepin woman rushed over, still holding Marin, and seized the prioress. She thrust them both down to the filthy straw, put a knee on each woman's back, and pulled the eyepatch away from the prioress's face. The Huguenot woman reached over, and pulled the reliquary from Marin's apron. She stood, and held it high, turning in a circle to show the other women, many of who also began to weep. Marin and the prioress remained on the ground, their heads bowed.

"You foolish women thought that this prioress would be different. You thought that you might be able to appease God by doing what this evil papist wanted you to do. Look at their eyes. Look at them!"

This last utterance was screamed, and at this, Sister Therese finally moved. She shouted, "Get away from her, you heretic; get away I say!" The infirmarian moved over and pushed the Pepin woman aside as two of the other Huguenot women restrained her. Mistress Pepin began to pray, continuing to mumble that Marin was a witch and the Huguenot children were damned.

Sister Therese leaned down and helped the prioress get up, retrieving the eye patch. She stared at the reliquary, which had also been dropped to the ground, but finally leaned over and grabbed it, pushing the box into her superior's hand. The infirmarian pushed Marin and the prioress through the door of the sick room, whispering, "Hurry, leave here, and lock the door to the south corridor behind you."

Sister Marie pulled Marin and they both rushed down the corridor. The prioress locked the arched door, grabbed Marin by the shoulders, and said, "I do not know all that has happened, and you will yet tell me, but you must be strong. For your safety, I will lock you in a cell by yourself. We will need all of our wits to keep you from the pyre, especially since it appears you have not only been accused of witchcraft but have stolen a reliquary from the sanctuary. Come, be quick." With wide, frightened eyes, Marin nodded.

CHAPTER 47

THE PRIORESS REMAINED in her rooms, praying. She had returned the reliquary to its leather bag, but she could not return it to the altar without a consecration ceremony. The bag sat on her desk, innocuous and small. Marin was locked in a room away from the Huguenot corridor, and the prioress dared not attempt to visit her.

Late in the day, Sister Simone, the portress, came into the prioress's rooms and sat down. She put a parchment on the table and sat down by the fire as the prioress stood.

"How are the children?" asked Sister Marie.

"They are continuing to recover." The portress sat with her hands folded in her lap, attempting not to stare at her superior's eye patch.

The prioress gestured to the parchment. "Is this Mistress Pepin's statement?"

The portress nodded. "Sister Marie, I have been to the quarters three times. Not only has Mistress Pepin not wavered in her accusations, but also two more women who are weak willed and did not observe any of these events, now support her. Papist or Protestant, who can deny that supernatural events have occurred?"

The prioress picked up the parchment and read,

I saw the girl, Marin, spit into a box and mix water from the pail with her spit, which she poured into the pail. She then gave a sip to each of the children, speaking words that were not French. She touched each child and made a sign on each one's head. I was unable to move due to the spell that the witch had cast upon me. I saw the moonlight gleam in her green eye, which moved in a different direction than the brown eye. The children began to speak in a different language.

The Prioress spoke softly. "And what do you believe, Sister Simone?"

Moving slightly, the Sister was silent a long time before she spoke.

"Prioress, I know the girl Marin is your kin. Sister Anne told me. I believe that the girl stole the reliquary from the altar in a true attempt to help the children. What troubles me is that the children are healed in a way that should not be possible, given they are heretic. I have been praying for God's guidance, for Him to send a sign that the healings are a miracle sent by God and not the other."

"Do you not believe that our God could work through a Huguenot girl to heal these children?" asked the prioress, sitting opposite her portress.

Sister Simone stood. "Can you imagine what will happen if the bishop agreed this miracle occurred? I cannot see that outcome, for it would only give the Huguenot evidence that they are not lost to God and would make the king look foolish. You are well aware of this. I beg you to prepare yourself. The girl will be judged a witch and you will lose your position."

The two nuns looked a long time at each other. Marie knew that Sister Simone was speaking the truth.

Finally, Sister Simone said, "I don't believe that your relation to the girl will be of interest to the bishop." The nun said this as she looked away, and the prioress let out her breath, knowing that Sister Anne and Sister Simone would not reveal her secret. This woman, her friend, had gone as far as she could.

"Sister Simone?"

"Yes, Mother?"

"Would you please wait until tomorrow before you send this confession to the bishop? You can inform him that we wanted to be quite certain that the plague was gone from the convent."

"Yes, of course." With a slight bow, Sister Simone left the prioress to her tumbled thoughts and prayers.

CHAPTER 48

THREE DAYS AFTER Sister Simone sent the Huguenot's statement to the bishop via the stable master, a messenger arrived. The bishop would be arriving soon. The prioress had not left her quarters in those three days, but now asked Sister Simone to take her to the cell where Marin was, a room normally used to store donated items from the townspeople. Other than the south corridor, it was the only area with a lock.

Sister Marie stood while the portress unlocked the door. Marin was on the floor, her head to her knees. She looked up and said, "What is to happen to me? No one will say."

The prioress put her hand on her niece's head. "Marin, you must recant. Tell the bishop you want to take vows. That will save your life. I beg you to do so."

The girl stood up, and the two embraced for a long time, both weeping.

"I will consider it," said Marin, stepping back.

Sister Simone, standing by the door said, "Sister Marie, you must go now. No one should see that you visited this Huguenot."

"Very well," said the prioress. She pulled Marin's face to hers and kissed the girl's forehead. "I believe you experienced God's grace when the children were cured. You must repay it by dedicating your life to His Will."

Sister Marie turned and went back to her rooms, hearing

Sister Simone lock the cell to Marin's dreary prison. She removed the reliquary from its bag, kneeled by the fire, and kissed the top. Noise erupted in the hall, and the prioress turned. The door opened; it was not the bishop, but another man, seemingly a nobleman. The wide-eyed novice behind him had not been able to announce him first.

"What, what is the meaning of this?" Sister Marie felt indignant, yet that outrage quickly turned to fear as she recognized the man. She fell back upon her knees, her bowels threatening to disgrace her. *That face. No, no, it cannot be.* The prioress was biting her hand, her back teeth clenched and her tongue far back in her mouth, a self-strangulation she prayed to accomplish.

"So, you do recognize me."

The Comte had changed for the worse, not the inevitable changes that middle age brought—thinning hair and a growing middle—but a graying of both his face and hair, missing teeth, and red scaly spots on his face that made him appear more like a gargoyle of Notre Dame than a man. Likely, none remarked on this, silenced by the obvious signs of wealth on his person. White fur edged the sleeves of his coat, but this only served to highlight his dirty hands curled like talons. Without waiting for an invitation, he sat in her chair by the fire as she slowly stood, with difficulty, from her kneeling position.

The prioress cleared her throat. "Why are you here?" She sat down trembling, in the only other chair, too close to the man, but she feared she would fall if she did not sit. Her question created an expression on his face so palpably violent that she stood quickly again and moved behind the chair, wanting a barrier between them.

"Do not use the familiar with me, woman. You are fortunate that the bishop was wise enough to involve me in this wretched situation. He sought my counsel, because I am, as you well know, very familiar with the heretics of Dieppe. I have presented him with a solution that he has accepted. I am here to tell you your fate and the fate of your niece, not because you can affect any change in what is going to happen, but because I want to see your face when you hear what I have to say."

The prioress could scarcely control her trembling, and she could feel her legs begin to fold under her. She vowed to herself and prayed to God that she would not faint. "What is, exactly, the solution you have proposed? I cannot believe the bishop would seek your advice without consulting me."

The Comte snorted. "You and she are going to escape the pyre. I will marry your niece, break her, and get a son from her. After that, she is free to die for her religion. You will be confined to a convent for the rest of your life, but not this one, and not as a prioress. You will be treated as a prisoner." He stood up and pushed his face a few inches from hers. "Your family has humiliated me for the last time."

The nun looked at the madness in his eyes and felt the spittle from his words on her face. She said nothing.

The Comte stepped back and pulled the waistcoat down over his fat middle. He smoothed the few strands of graying hair back over his head, never looking away from her. He deliberately licked his lips, a leering approximation of a lizard.

"She looks just like you did at that age, Marie. I expect that she will be resistant and difficult to bed, but I know how to treat a girl like that. I will give her the benefit of the experience I have had since you spurned me. The doctors tell me I might have the pox but that I should be able to father a child."

At this, the image of this hideous man on top of Marin—thrusting himself on her, dripping pus from his boils onto her face, bruising her everywhere—gained hold and she fell. Her last thought was regret that she had not married this man thirty years before.

CHAPTER 49

THE CONVENT WAS quiet. The Huguenot women remained, but many of the nuns had chosen to remove themselves to another convent, one without plague, heretics, witches or a disgraced prioress. Sister Anne told the prioress that the bishop had left guards just outside the gate. Marie was determined to complete one last task before her imprisonment—to get her niece Marin out of France. She had asked Sister Anne, the sacristan, to deliver a letter to the old cook Rebecca, in Dieppe, and prayed that her childhood confidante could help.

In the few days since the children's cure, King Louis had revoked the Edict of Nantes, which in 1598 had given the Protestants the right to worship as they pleased. The revocation energized the persecutions of the Huguenots. Sister Anne brought troubling news of hangings, torture and murder. Thousands of her countrymen were seeking refuge in Protestant countries: England, Germany, Switzerland, and, she had heard, the English colonies.

Sister Anne continued to share her uneasiness that a Huguenot girl had effected a miracle with the reliquary. No one missed the object, so the prioress had hidden it in her robes, rubbing the corners frequently as she prayed. Marie had become convinced that God had used Marin to cure the children, marking her niece in some yet-to-be-disclosed way, for some future purpose.

She paced her small rooms, praying that Rebecca was still alive.

CHAPTER 50

THE PRIORESS HELD Rebecca's worn hands as they both sat by the fire. "Thank you for coming." The guards had not objected to this ancient woman seeking an audience with the prioress of the convent. Marie marveled that Rebecca's hair and eyes were the same, and the mouth still smiled, but she noted that mouth was now without most of its teeth.

Rebecca nodded and said, "There's only one choice, and that is to send her to the colonies. She'll be safe there, and even the Comte will leave her alone if she is across the ocean. Read this, Marie." Rebecca took a small folded paper from her pocket.

Marie did not correct her childhood companion as to the proper way to address a prioress. She would not have that honorific much longer, so what did it matter?

The small handbill was from England and had the seal of the English king. She read:

The chief of the Privileges are as follows:

- *First, There is full and free Liberty of Conscience granted to all, so that no man is to be molested or called in question for matters of Religious Concern; but everyone is to be obedient to the Civil Government, worshipping God after their own way.*

- *Secondly, There is freedom from Custom, for all Wine, Silk, Raisins, Currance, Oil, Olives, and Almonds, that shall be raised in the Province for 7 years, after 4 Ton of any of those commodities shall be imported in one Bottom.*

- *Thirdly, Every Free-man and Free-woman that transport themselves and Servants by the 25 of March next, shall have for Himself, Wife, Children, and Men-servants, for each 100 Acres of Land for him and his Heirs forever, and for every Woman-servant and Slave 50 Acres, paying at most 1/2d. per acre, per annum, in lieu of all demands, to the Lords Proprietors*

Marie was shocked that the English were willing to give so much away for colonists to go to Carolina. She had heard it was full of savages and hot as hell itself. No wonder the King of England had to pay people to colonize this faraway place.

Rebecca was looking at her when she looked up. The woman was surely seventy now, her hands crooked and red, her face lined like an old saddle. "Rebecca, can you truly spirit Marin away from here?"

"I can do it because of that fool Comte who has decided to send a few casks of his wine to the bishop. My son, who works at the winery, will make sure one is empty. He'll bring the casks, but take one away from the convent, and tell the guards it was spoiled. She'll be in that cask. I have someone who will take her to the coast in a wagon." Rebecca pointed to the small handbill. "As long as she agrees to go to Carolina, she'll get on the ship."

Carolina—home of crocodilian beasts, huge flying insects, and heat that could not be born. What of the natives? Were they violent? What choice was there? The bishop would dress in his finest robes and conduct a trial that would be replete with the ceremonial pomp only the Catholic Church could display. The girl would be sentenced to die as a witch. If by some miracle she were found innocent, she still would not be safe. In the frenzy of the Revocation, mobs were dragging Huguenots out of their homes and burning them alive. The mob would kill her if the bishop did not.

Rebecca snorted. "That crone Mistress Pepin has become a papist. Her testimony will doom the girl. There is no other way."

The old cook was right. Nothing other than an escape or a recantation would save Marin's life. Let the child leave France and live as her true self, a freedom Marie had never enjoyed.

The prioress nodded. "I have something for Marin. I am not allowed to see her myself, but the guard will let you into her cell." She reached into a pocket of her robe, removed a leather bag, and handed it to Rebecca. "This will allow her to buy property when she arrives in Carolina, and provide a dowry. Will someone travel with her?"

"I will travel with her. My family will be on the same ship. All of us are leaving this godforsaken place to start a new life. I pray that I survive the journey."

The prioress removed a ring from her finger, kissed it, and placed it in Rebecca's lap. "This is for you and your family." Rebecca put the leather bag and the ring into a small purse tied at her waist.

"Will you sing with me, Rebecca? Even though I am an old papist?"

"I will."

The two women, one old, the other older still, stood and embraced. Both were weeping. They knelt before the fire and Rebecca began to sing Psalms in a breathy and low voice. At first, the words would not come to Marie, but then the memories of her childhood in the Protestant temple flooded her mind. The two of them sang the forbidden songs, their voices raising and echoing through the stone of the room. Marie felt a lifting of her heart, and did not care that all in the convent, perhaps all in the town itself, could hear them.

PART III

Charleston: Present Day

CHAPTER 51

H AD ANYONE ELSE read this? How did the girl get to Charleston? Thompson looked down at the questions he had jotted while reading the account of the abbess.

Was there any evidence that the children were cured of the plague?

Is there any evidence that Marin Postel told her descendants this story or of her experience at the convent?

He thought of another and added it:

Does the Vatican believe that a miracle occurred at the convent?

Perhaps this third question could be easily answered. Thompson pawed through his leather attaché, found the priest's card, and punched the number into his phone.

"Yes," said a voice.

"Monsignor Ogier?" asked Thompson. "This is Agent Denton from Interpol. We met last night. Is this a good time for me to ask you some questions?"

Thompson heard rustling, and the priest said, "Of course."

"I have some questions about the document you handed out last night," said Thompson.

"You read it? I did not believe anyone was interested."

"I did. It's quite a remarkable story."

"What do you have questions about?"

"I have two questions. Were the children actually cured, and did the Vatican investigators conclude that a miracle occurred at that convent?"

There was a long pause, and Thompson heard more rustling. Was the priest in bed?

"Agent Denton, these events occurred during a difficult time for the Church and for France. The Huguenots were poorly treated. Though their treatment was a political decision enforced by the French King, not the Vatican, the Church was complicit because at the time we did not embrace those who believed the Church needed reform."

Thompson thought that was the understatement of the millennium; no, make that the understatement of two millennia, but he remained professional and said, "I understand, but surely even then, a conclusion was reached about the children's recovery."

"At that time, the more pressing issue for the convent was the actions of the abbess. She not only kept her relationship with her niece, a Protestant, secret but also she allowed sacred items to be taken by a nonbeliever. That is why we had an official trial. Abbess Postel was found guilty and imprisoned until her death."

"Would you be willing to find out the answers to my questions?" said Thompson.

"Agent Denton, I am here in Charleston to take possession of the reliquary once it is found. I am confident it will not be infected, and will take it back to Rome. We will then begin the debate as to when it will, if ever, be returned to the convent."

"Why are you so sure no anthrax bacteria will be found? The Lavelle report says that both reliquaries were installed in the altar in 1245. If one item in that altar is infectious, surely the other will be," said Thompson.

The priest ignored the question. "Now I have a question for you. Can you arrange for me to speak to Amarintha Sims? I understand she found the reliquary and handled the contents. The Vatican would like to hear her story in person."

Why would the Vatican want to speak to Amarintha at all? In person or not, the request so astonished Thompson that he literally could not reply.

"Agent Denton, I can certainly call Director Larue if you'd like."

This was beyond strange, Thompson thought. Very carefully, he said, "Monsignor, Amarintha Sims is a United States citizen. Interpol has no authority to make her speak to you, in Rome or in Charleston. Surely you know this."

Monsignor Ogier forced a laugh. "Of course. I am just so interested in her impressions. Now, I really must go. Good-bye."

Thompson was left holding his phone, wondering why the monsignor had ended the call so abruptly. What else did the priest know? He punched in another number.

"Gilstrom here."

"Dr. Gilstrom, I'm Agent Denton from Interpol. We met during a conference call two days ago."

"Yes, Agent Denton. Am I late for a briefing? I'm finding myself constantly behind these days."

"I'm calling to get a status on the testing in Rome."

"Did you not read the report I sent?"

Thompson thought quickly. "My laptop is acting up. Do you mind giving me the highlights?"

After some keyboard sounds, Dr. Gilstrom said, "Well, the anthrax bacteria came from pulverized bovine material that was in the reliquary. Skins most likely, which are notorious for harboring anthrax spores. We did find vestiges of human DNA, and a few plant seeds that we're analyzing now."

"Can you tell how old the material is?"

"Working on that now. We haven't found anthrax in the lab the priests were working in, or inside the altar itself. We consider the outbreak in Rome contained, and the first reliquary is being sanitized under the direction of the Italians. It will be given back to the Vatican. Right now we're intrigued with the test results from one of the priests."

Thompson needed to act as if he'd seen this report. "Very interesting, wasn't it?"

Gilstrom's tone became warmer. "To say the least. We have finally found an antibiotic that is effective against this strain, but the third priest, frankly, should be dead. He was the first to open the reliquary and apparently had dust fly up into his face. The pneumatic version of anthrax is invariably fatal, even with antibiotic treatment, yet he shows no signs of the disease now, and he recovered before we administered the antibiotic. He's an interesting patient. Has a bad case of vitiligo."

"Vitiligo?"

"It's a disorder where large patches of the skin are without any pigmentation. Not deadly, but can be very distressing. This particular priest was participating in a clinical trial for a treatment for vitiligo, so we had access to an old DNA profile. The results are fascinating. Genes relating to inflammation and skin color, the MC1R and related genes to be exact, have begun to express themselves. We think this is how his body defeated the anthrax."

"Does Monsignor Ogier know this?"

"I assume so."

"Thank you, Dr. Gilstrom."

Thompson hit "end" on his phone. He lifted his laptop, and googled Monsignor Giuseppe Ogier. The first few entries were generic, from the Vatican's press release office, discussing Monsignor Ogier's participation in art restoration at the Vatican Museum.

On the second page was a newspaper article in Italian. He could pick out the monsignor's name, but little else. Thompson opened Google Translate, cut the first paragraph, and pasted it into the text box. The translation read:

Monsignor Giuseppe Ogier of the Vatican Museum is a trained art restorer, and in that role has seen enormous improvements in the tools and techniques available to the restorer. He told this reporter that he believes it is time for the Vatican to embrace modern analysis techniques and allow scientists to examine relics that purport to be from the time of Christ's crucifixion. "The Vatican needs to move beyond the fiasco of the Turin shroud and work with researchers that have the proper experience," said the monsignor. Requests from this reporter for a follow-up interview with the monsignor have been denied.

CHAPTER 52

DETECTIVE EDSON SAT in an unmarked Charleston Police vehicle, two blocks from Amarintha's property, watching moving dots on a display on the dash. Blue was Jack Strong, the red Thompson Denton, and a green dot represented Amarintha Sims. The Task Force had received warrants to track their phones, and based on the moving dots, Amarintha was headed to her property. Frank was supposed to explain to her that the box found on her property might be contaminated, and she needed to be tested. An FBI agent was listening to every word Frank said, and, if his polite entreaty to Amarintha didn't work, he supposed the FBI would send in the troops.

It was noon, and the April sun was shining into Frank's eyes. He was hungry, pissed about Thompson's dismissal from the team, and exhausted from working almost all night. On his way home to get some sleep, Frank had found Jack Strong sleeping in the lobby of the FBI building and taken the man home, rashly promising an update at 10:00 a.m. After dropping Jack off, he had had only a few hours of sleep, and then had returned to the conference room at the FBI before eight.

Frank had sat in the conference room listening to the Department of Health, SC Law Enforcement Division and the FBI, while they outlined their plans of action if the reliquary was contaminated, as well as discussing what they would tell the public. Even if the lab found no sign of active microbes, the FBI and SLED would remain on high alert. Brook Reynolds was running her Task Force as if there was indeed an active plot centered in Charleston to find and plant a biological weapon.

At one point during the meeting, Homeland had their own statistician on the line who argued with Chad about the predictions of the program. Terms such as Markov chains, Monte Carlo distributions, Bayesian algorithms and a host of other words were tossed back and forth between the two, and when they finally stopped talking, there were no comments. Frank understood little of the exchange and all he could think of was Mark Twain's comment— "There are lies, damned lies, and statistics."

A small FBI team was attempting to locate the Department of Defense's AAR, the after action report, from the 1986 outbreak. There surely would have been one, and the FBI was relentless when they wanted something from another government agency. Everyone who had been on Charles Sims' team had died in the intervening thirty years, and interviewing the surviving family members would take weeks. Finding the report was considered critical in understanding the link, if there was one, between the events in 1986 and the eruption of the same bacteria in Rome.

Frank could not wrap his head around the fact that in only twenty-four hours, a huge team had been spun up simply because a computer program had woven seemingly unrelated threads of information into a tangible threat, although he knew that Zora Vulkov's involvement in Kate Strong's kidnapping made the prediction more concrete. He pulled out the report and looked at the list again.

- Dr. Adam Chalk is killed on April 10 of this year.
- Dr. Adam Chalk, Kate Strong's boss at the College,

performed appraisals on stolen antiquities for Alternative Auctions, funded by Anton Bunin.

- Dr. Kate Strong, expert in Christian reliquaries, disappears April 10.

- On May 10, Dr. Zora Vulkov, former member of Soviet bioterrorism agency, Biopreparat, reports that Anton Bunin has kidnapped Dr. Kate Strong.

- Anton Bunin is the former top researcher for Biopreparat and former colleague of Vulkov.

- On May 1, Vatican researchers fall ill from strain of previously unidentified anthrax known to have occurred in South Carolina in 1986.

- Outbreak is reported to the FBI by the CDC on May 12.

- It is more than a 34% probability that Anton Bunin is seeking to locate new biological organisms previously unknown to scientists, either inaccessible due to climate, as in permafrost that has now melted, or inaccessible due to religious custom such as material in sealed reliquaries in the Hindu, Buddhist and Christian faiths. This is likely related to his desire to discover new drug compounds, or possibly to create a biological weapon available for sale.

He knew enough about statistics to respect that there were techniques to determine whether disparate events were related or correlated. He also knew that correlation did not mean causation. Was this program biased towards linking events together? What about motive? To a cop, nothing was more important than motive. What was the motive for some Russian rich guy to spread anthrax in the United States? The United States was the best market for Bunin's stolen antiquities. You didn't kill your best customers.

The team needed Thompson Denton's insight into this group. Instead of being grateful for the agent's involvement and knowledge, the FBI higher-ups had become suspicious of him. Frank had no doubt that this was partly due to Thompson's being a member of a foreign law enforcement agency. Frank had argued, as politely and sincerely as he could, against Thompson's dismissal from the Task Force, and when met only with silence, had left the room. Brook followed, and he told her he would quit if Thompson was forced out.

She had merely said, "Stay with me Frank. I need you."

When one of the paranoid weenies from FBI headquarters wanted Thompson and Jack Strong monitored, and Amarintha Sims found, Frank volunteered for the job. At least he would be out of the FBI building. Even he, a former Marine, was finding the level of testosterone way too high at the FBI office.

He was wearing not only a body camera that would film and record everything he saw but also an earpiece, allowing the FBI team sitting in a car a few blocks away to give him direction. Brook Reynolds, who was at FBI headquarters, could also hear what was going on. Both she and the agents in the car could see the moving dots on their own displays.

Frank's cell rang. He recognized Thompson's number, pushed the stop button on the camera and turned off the transmitter in his earpiece. No one would hear this conversation.

"Detective Edson."

"Frank, it's Thompson. I imagine you heard about my temporary hiatus?"

"Yeah, I did. It's a raw deal. I'm sorry it happened, and I hope won't last long. Those Washington guys need to get their heads on straight."

"Can you tell me what's happened with Richard and Amarintha? Are they in quarantine?"

Frank certainly wasn't going to share with Thompson that his cell phone was being tracked, but this question he could answer. "Not yet. I think the CDC will likely want to quarantine her until they can determine whether she was exposed. I haven't heard whether test results are back on Richard. The reliquary is at MUSC's special lab they set up last year."

The year before, when a nurse became ill with Ebola at a Texas hospital, even after following the detailed instructions on dealing with patients, designated hospitals in each state invested in state of the art isolation wards. The CDC had determined that MUSC's isolation lab was the perfect location for a preliminary test of the reliquary.

"Richard didn't touch the contents. Is that why he was allowed to stay home?"

"That's about it." Frank cleared his throat. "Have you spoken to Amarintha?"

"No, I haven't. I thought I'd go over to the jobsite and see her. No one told me I couldn't do that." Frank heard the slight hostility in Thompson's voice, and he didn't blame him. The situation was unfair. "Who is going to tell her about her father having the reliquary in 1986?" Thompson asked.

"What would we tell her? DOD still hasn't told us anything about what he was doing or why anthrax broke out. The FBI is only inferring that the reliquary is what caused the outbreak in 1986. Charles Sims died a few months later, and the rest of his team is dead, or the FBI can't find them. No one knows who buried the reliquary."

Frank knew that the FBI would put Amarintha into custody, at least temporarily, not only to determine whether she had been exposed, but also to question her about her father. Amarintha's mother would be questioned as well. Thompson

L. K. Clement

would eventually figure this out. *What would the agent do?* Based on Thompson's and Amarintha's locations, he'd have to move fast to reach the woman before Thompson did.

"Frank, did you read what the priest handed out last night?"

"No, did you?"

"I did. A Huguenot woman stole a reliquary from a convent in France in 1685. During her time there, she handled the reliquary, and several children were cured from the plague. They were *cured*—not made sick by it. Don't you think that's odd?"

Frank, a Southern Baptist, wanted to say that anything connected to a reliquary was odd to him, but he didn't. "I don't know," said Frank.

"Dr. Gilstrom also told me that the third priest doesn't have anthrax anymore. His body's DNA is changing."

Frank was silent for a moment. *DNA changes?* "Thompson, why don't you put your thoughts in an email, and I'll make sure Brook gets it. I also think that the FBI will come to its senses and bring you back."

Thompson said, "Can you tell me anything else?"

Frank could hear the FBI agent in his ear asking why the camera wasn't recording. He ignored it and said, "The FBI is still working with the State Department to get approvals to go to Istanbul. The office there hasn't had any more contact with the anonymous caller, and it turns out there are over thirty of what the locals call 'castles' within an hour of Istanbul. I have to tell you, nobody is optimistic we can find Kate Strong."

"Has anyone told Jack that?"

Frank blew out a breath and said, "Not yet."

CHAPTER 53

Jack's head woke him up with a vibrating that rivaled the big auger at the job site. After Frank found him sleeping at the FBI building, the detective had driven him home and said, "Jack, I'll call you at 10:00 am with an update. Get some sleep if you can." He was surprised that he had been able to sleep at all given his alternating fear and elation over the news from Istanbul.

He looked over at the clock, saw it was after 11 a.m., sat up and pulled over a legal pad, and started jotting down everything he had been told at the FBI office. He wanted to be prepared to call his lawyer if Frank didn't come through with a plan. Waving the Patriot Act in his face had worked for a while, but Jack knew that the FBI would do most anything to avoid a media stink about a kidnapped professor.

He padded over to the kitchen to where his laptop sat, and began reading news stories about American citizens kidnapped overseas. Jack could discern no clear pattern of what actions would and would not result in a return of a hostage. At least Turkey was still ostensibly an ally to the US. That would help. One thing that did seem to make a difference was getting the right spokesperson, someone who could manage the media and the government.

Jack slapped his laptop down. If Detective Edson didn't call him soon, he'd call his lawyer and ask for help in setting up a press conference. He wouldn't share anything that could get him jailed, but might get leads, and he would definitely get attention.

His phone pinged, and he looked at a text from Amarintha. She wanted him to meet her at the jobsite. He started to reply that he couldn't make it, but thought better of it. He quickly texted one of his reliable subcontractors that he had to go away, and would need the sub to keep the project going. He'd meet Amarintha and explain.

After leaving the kitchen, Jack went to the safe in his office, and removed his passport. He aimlessly packed enough clothes for two weeks, paying little attention to what was going in his suitcase. He also began to think of some reason for his absence that would sound legitimate to Sara. He wasn't going to share what he knew with her, but just as quickly, he began to question that decision. He trudged back to his office, reopened the safe, and added Sara's passport to his bag. One way or another, he— no, he and Sara—were going to Istanbul.

CHAPTER 54

"DETECTIVE EDSON, DETECTIVE Edson, are you there?" Frank heard the agent in his ear again and restarted his electronics.

"Yes. I'm here. Amarintha Sims is almost at her house," said Frank, watching the moving green dot.

Brook Reynolds' voice sounded in his ear. "Detective, we're seeing what you see on our displays, and it would appear that Jack Strong and Thompson Denton are headed to the jobsite as well. Why do you suppose that is?"

Frank shook his head. From what he understood from Thompson, Jack and Thompson had been at Amarintha's jobsite most days, lollygagging on Richard Anderson's porch in between working with contractors.

"Agent Reynolds, I think that's pretty typical, but I do believe Ms. Sims will arrive at the jobsite before Thompson. I'm guessing Jack is just doing what he does every day—checking on his projects. I don't want to call him until you guys have a plan to get his wife."

Brook didn't reply.

Frank saw a VW bug turn onto Church. "I have visual on Amarintha Sims." The car pulled into a parking space, and three women got out of the car. "She has an older woman and a younger woman with her, her mother and daughter, I'm assuming. Do you still want me to approach?"

"Wait. Let me check with Dr. Gilstrom on whether all three need to be tested," said Brook.

From his location down the street, Frank watched Amarintha and the other two women walk down the sidewalk to Richard's house. Out of the corner of his eye, something moved. When he turned, he saw Thompson striding down Church on the opposite side of the street, also towards Richard's house. The agent had not seen Frank sitting in one of CPD's unmarked cars.

"I have an update. Thompson Denton, Amarintha Sims, and the two other women are all converging on Richard's house. Is your agent still with Richard?" said Frank.

Frank heard nothing but static in his ear for a moment. Brook said, "Detective, Richard Anderson's test results came back negative. No results yet on the reliquary itself. Thirty minutes ago, I dismissed the agent that was at Anderson's house. Richard Anderson is alone in his house and is under orders not to discuss the situation with anyone. Monsignor Ogier is pressuring the CDC to treat Amarintha Sims just as the priests in Rome have been treated, in other words, a quarantine. Bring her in and we'll sort it out later."

The detective opened his car door. At that moment, Jack Strong's truck came down Church, and the builder pulled directly onto Amarintha's lot.

"Agent Reynolds, Jack Strong has just arrived at Richard Anderson's house," said Frank. "I'm not sure this is a good time for me to approach Ms. Sims."

"We know. We see the display. Sit tight for a minute."

CHAPTER 55

PARKING DIRECTLY ONTO the lot and blocking the sidewalk, Jack knew he'd get a ticket but didn't care. His plan was to talk to Amarintha, tell her what was happening, and explain that one of his subcontractors would manage the construction while he was gone. Jack knew Amarintha would understand his situation, and the sub he would put in charge would work well with her.

Amarintha and Richard stood on the old man's front porch having a conversation. Sara's friend, Ava, was moving back and forth on the porch swing with an older woman, who he thought must be Ava's grandmother. Jack started up the oyster shell sidewalk from the street, and waited at the bottom of the porch stairs, looking up. It occurred to him that he probably looked awful—a thought confirmed in the multiple faces that frowned when they saw him. Amarintha walked down the four steps.

"Jack," she said, "you know Ava, and this is my mother, Fannie Sims." He walked up the steps to shake hands with Fannie.

"Hey, Mr. Strong." She smiled at him from the swing. "Where's Sara today?"

"She's at work. Does she know you're back in town?"

"Not yet."

Amarintha touched his arm. "I've got some good news. My cancer has been knocked back a bit."

Jack looked at her and stepped back. Amarintha was still thin, very thin, but her face was pink, and she was moving in a way that didn't look like a dying praying mantis. "What happened to you? I mean, you look good. Not that you didn't look good before, I mean . . ."

"I know what you mean," Amarintha laughed. "My blood tests indicate that I'm making antibodies against my cancer, and I feel stronger. I don't know if it's permanent, but today at least is a very good day." She smiled at Jack, and then turned to Ava and Fannie, both still on the swing.

Richard said, "Come on in the house, Jack. I was just going to make some more coffee."

"Good morning," said a voice behind Jack.

Jack wheeled around and saw Thompson striding down the sidewalk. He regretted his anger towards the man and was anxious to understand how Chalk had seemingly manipulated Kate. Kate's boss had been a good friend to Kate, making it easy for her not to travel because of him. What had really happened? Thompson reached the bottom of the porch steps and looked at Jack, who held out his hand and said, "How are you, Thompson?" The agent held Jack's grip for a long time, nodding.

Jack saw Thompson look at Amarintha, his eyes widening, a huge grin appearing on his face, holding his hands out to her. She took two steps towards him.

As Thompson touched Amarintha's hands, a concussive *roar* boomed and Richard's porch shook. A second later, the group was hit by a whoosh of air, its unexpected presence, rather than its force, causing Amarintha to topple forward onto Thompson. Jack stumbled, and fell on his hands and knees to the sidewalk, the rough surface scraping his palms. Through the ringing in his ears, he heard the shrieking of car alarms and screaming from the porch. Still on his knees, Jack raised his head and looked northwest in the direction of the blast of air and saw a dark cloud rising, undulating, and spreading against the otherwise cloudless blue sky.

He crawled to the porch steps and grabbed the rail. Richard had tumbled against the chains holding the swing to the porch ceiling. Underneath Richard, Jack could see Ava and Fannie struggling. Jack yelled to them, "Are you all right?" Richard nodded, pushed himself off the swing, and pulled Fannie and Ava into him. Looking behind him, Jack saw Thompson and Amarintha fumbling against each other on the ground, trying to stand.

"Are you two ok? What . . ."

A second *boom* extinguished his words. Jack looked in the direction of the second sound and watched in horror as the steeple on the Huguenot Church pancaked into the sanctuary below it. A wave of dust galloped towards them as if propelled by an invisible herd of horses. Car alarms continued their screeching. Through the continued ringing in his ears, Jack heard Fannie yelling, "What happened? Was that an earthquake?"

Residents from every house rushed out onto the street. As Jack plunged into the crowd, he saw a cloud of smoke rising from the Huguenot Church, and another black plume rose higher from the west where the hospital was.

"What the hell was that?" yelled Richard as he rushed down the stairs. Thompson was pulling Amarintha off the ground.

"An earthquake!" Amarintha cried. Jack saw Thompson glance at Amarintha and then rush down the sidewalk to the street to join him. The two men grimly looked towards the hospital, a huge plume of smoke continuing to spread, a burning smell now reaching them.

"That was no earthquake," Jack yelled to Thompson.

"No, those were explosions," Thompson shouted back. The agent stopped in the street and turned back to look at Amarintha as Jack made his way towards his truck.

Jack turned, cupped his hands, and bellowed to Richard, who still stood on the porch. "I'm going to find Sara. All of you get into the house and wait. Turn on CNN." Jack jerked open the door of his truck and sat still for a moment thinking of how to get through the mass of pedestrians to the lawyer's office where Sara worked. The route came to him and he sped away.

CHAPTER 56

F RANK OPENED HIS eyes, feeling a trickle down his face. He touched his scalp, and brought his fingers to his face. Blood. Floppy white material covered his steering wheel. The airbag had deployed, and there was a buzz of voices in his ear.

Static and then a voice, not Brook's, but one of the agents in the car a few blocks away, said, "Detective Edson, what is your condition? Were you near one of the explosions?"

"I'm ok, but something hit my car. What happened?"

Static again and then the same voice. "A bomb has exploded at the Medical University and possibly one at the Huguenot Church. No information on casualties. Can you drive? We're leaving to go to the scene."

"Give me a minute. I'll radio you back." Frank pulled himself out of the car, looked towards the rear of the vehicle and realized his sedan had been rear-ended by a small Toyota truck. He could see a driver slumped over the steering wheel, and a similar white cloth covering the truck's dash. The detective rushed over to the other vehicle, opened the door, and put his fingers on the driver's neck. The man was dead.

He smelled burning tires in the air, and when he looked up, Frank saw two rising plumes of smoke being pushed northwest by the prevailing ocean winds. The undulating columns were converging in the sky, hundreds of feet overhead, creating a canopy of darkness that resembled tornadic thunderheads. Frank recognized the sirens of police and fire and briefly wondered how Charleston Fire and Police could cover both scenes.

He stood motionless, and only a frenzied cyclist almost running into him motivated him to move off the street. He pulled up the body camera and asked, "Do you know what happened?"

"Detective Edson, are you still near the Sims property?" The voice was Brook Reynolds' and was rushed and high pitched. "Detective, I need you to bring the Sims family into protective custody."

"What? Why?" asked Frank. "My car was rear-ended. The driver behind me is DOA. Can you call it in?"

"I will," Brook said, "but nobody will come, not for a long while. All units are at the scenes. You can imagine what is going on. I need you to get the Sims and take them to police headquarters."

Frank looked at the traffic on Church Street and a block beyond towards Broad. Not a single car in the two streets was moving. "I got gridlock here. What's the urgency on the Sims? Surely testing them can wait."

Brook's voice became very emphatic. "Before the explosion, two men went to the lab and knocked out the two FBI agents guarding the lab. One of the technicians had just called 911 when the explosion occurred in the street. Two hospital employees were injured. The reliquary is gone. Do you hear me? It was taken."

"How the hell did anyone find out where it was?" asked Frank.

"I don't know. Just get the Sims and bring them in," Brook said.

Frank strode towards Richard's house, pushing through the people that were now thronging the street. "You're sure the reliquary is gone?" he yelled.

"Yes," Brook said; her voice uneven as if she was running.

Frank kept moving. "I'll call you when I have the Sims."

CHAPTER 57

TORN BETWEEN STAYING with Amarintha and running towards the Huguenot Church to assist, Thompson stood frozen in the street. Only minutes had passed since the explosion at the Church and already fire trucks were pulling in front of the sanctuary.

Richard had rushed inside his house, and Thompson heard high-pitched, excited voices from the television in the living room. A new sound made its way into the continued jumble of noise and he looked up to see a news helicopter hovering overhead. Thompson began to push his way through the crowd, now milling in the street, towards Richard's house. *Where had all these people come from?*

Dozens of people were yelling, their efforts to communicate amidst the noise fruitless. The scene was surreal. Faces were angled down towards the electronics in their hands as the onlookers stumbled about, bumping into each other. Children were either part of the zombie-like crowd with their own electronic tethering devices, or were glued to adults' legs and screaming like animals.

Richard flung open the screen door. "Get in here. A bomb exploded in front of MUSC. The Huguenot Church was bombed too."

Thompson rushed through Richard's front door. Ava, Fannie,

and Amarintha sat huddled on the couch. Richard stood to the side. They all stared at the television.

Amarintha's appearance was still startling. Just moments before the explosion he had been shocked when he saw her. Now that she was still, he had the chance to study her. "Amarintha," said Thompson, grabbing her arm. "Let's get you home. Richard, do you have a car?"

Richard started to say something, but then looked at Thompson's face and nodded, "This way." He led Thompson out the back door to his small garage and moved a trashcan out of the way, as Thompson pulled up the garage door. Richard squeezed his way through the garage, and brought out a golf cart. "This is all I have. My car is in the shop."

Thompson went to the street to see whether they could make it through the crowd. The onlookers seemed to be either going back inside or getting their own cars out of their small garages. Everyone was on the move.

"Thompson," someone yelled from the street.

He turned to see Frank Edson running towards him, a wound on his scalp dripping blood.

"What happened, Frank?" Thompson cried. "Are you ok?"

The detective stopped and put his hands on his knees and took a few breaths before he replied. "I need to take Amarintha and her family to the police station. Agent Reynolds wants them in protective custody. The reliquary was stolen from the hospital during the explosion." Frank wiped his sleeve on his head, smearing more blood on his face.

Thompson gaped at Frank. "Someone stole the reliquary?"

Richard got out of the cart. "Why would you take them? My tests came back ok. Are you with the CDC?" Richard asked.

"I'm Detective Frank Edson, CPD, and I was asked to bring the Sims family into custody. They aren't being arrested. This is for their protection, and the protection of the citizens of Charleston. The Vatican wants to talk to Amarintha."

The reliquary stolen—Amarintha perhaps affected by the contents of the reliquary—this was too much. He had to get her away from Charleston. Thompson moved close to Frank and hissed, "Taking them to the FBI could put them in danger. Don't you realize that there has been a leak? Nobody outside the group knew about the reliquary. I don't even know if Richard has told Amarintha that the CDC took it."

The detective shook his head and walked past Thompson towards the house.

Thompson followed him, stopping only to whisper to Richard, "You have a boat right?"

Richard nodded.

"Get the Sims women off this peninsula. Take the three of them to Georgetown. If I can't go with you now, I'll meet you at the B&B that's downtown."

Richard whispered back, "Are you sure?"

Thompson nodded. "Somebody wants that reliquary, and when they find out you two are the only ones outside of the investigators at MUSC who touched it, they may want both of you."

"Mr. Anderson, what's wrong? Who is this?" asked a voice. Thompson turned to see Ava on the porch steps. Her grandmother Fannie stood with her. The two of them stood still, and he could hear Amarintha behind them in the house. Frank had reached the porch.

"This is Detective Edson," Thompson said, looking at Ava.

The girl's hands were shaking as she pulled her hair out of her face. She said again, "What's wrong?" Ava turned her head to the right, her widow's peak coming into view as she pulled her hair into an elastic band, the cleft in her chin pointed towards him.

"He needs to . . ." Thompson stopped speaking, his throat closing. "I, uh, I . . ." A memory of his own mother flooded him—her widow's peak, her cleft chin, and her head always turning to the right when she asked him an uncomfortable question. He stood still, gaping at the now empty space as Ava and Fannie marched past him to stand by the golf cart.

"Thompson, are you all right?" Amarintha asked. He heard her clatter down the stairs. She put her hand on his arm and shook him. Thompson started, looked at Amarintha, but said nothing.

Frank had to yell over the continuing cacophony of sirens, yelling and the helicopter. "Ms. Sims, I'm Detective Edson with the Charleston Police. I need to take you, your daughter, and mother to the police station. We want to test you for pathogens." Frank held out his badge to her, his head still oozing blood.

Richard, standing by the cart with Ava and Fannie, yelled at Frank, "For God's sake, I haven't even had a chance to tell her about the damned reliquary."

"What are you talking about? Thompson, what's happening?" Amarintha cried, her voice barely heard above the din.

"Please Amarintha, you, Fannie and Ava get in the golf cart." Thompson saw Frank put his hand on his handcuffs.

"Thompson, I've got to take them in." Frank pulled his camera to his mouth, presumably to ensure that whoever was listening could hear him over the noise. "I'm sorry."

Rushing to Frank, Thompson grabbed the handcuffs, shoved one of the bracelets on the startled detective's wrist, and slammed the other shut on a thick porch rail. "I'm sorry too," yelled Thompson, as he leaped into the golf cart and said, "Drive, Richard."

CHAPTER 58

J ACK DROVE THE truck for only three blocks before it became impossible to move any farther. He veered into an alley, got out, and pushed against the crowd towards the hospital on the west end of the peninsula. Sara's office was only two blocks from there.

He ran for five minutes before seeing the fire. Jack shoved his way through an agitated line of people held back by the police, watching the firefighters from the Cannon Street Station pour water on the flames. Volunteer firefighters wearing James Island Fire Department uniforms rushed into the hospital, Scott packs on their backs. The noise was incredibly loud, a mixture of screaming, sirens, and alarms

Hospital workers in scrubs of various colors stood crying, some trying to go back in the buildings, restrained by their co-workers. One woman, not in scrubs, but in a dark pantsuit, stood resolute with arms folded, scanning the crowd. It was Brook Reynolds, the FBI woman from the meeting.

She saw Jack and pushed her way over to him. "What do you know about this?" she shouted at him, shaking his arm.

"Nothing. I'm trying to get to Bee Street. I came to find my daughter," Jack yelled back, not looking at her, as he paced back and forth attempting to see over the heads of the alarmed and frightened people. Could he get through to the lawyer's office where Sara was, or would he have to make a multi-block detour?

"Mr. Strong, you can help by getting over to the main police station, so you can be interviewed." She waved her other arm to an officer, not letting go of Jack.

Jack pushed her away. "Listen, I'm just a citizen who wants to find his daughter and then find my wife. Yesterday was the first time I met you, and until Thompson dropped his files at my feet, all I knew was that my wife was missing."

"This bombing is connected to your wife's disappearance!" She was almost shouting, and then said in a calmer voice, "I need you to cooperate, Mr. Strong. I promise we'll get your wife back." A policeman saw Brook and was moving toward her, reaching for his radio.

Jack looked at the flames and the billowing smoke and calculated how long it would be before Brook Reynolds' attention would turn from a bombing to a missing wife. Not soon enough. He shoved her away and stumbled into several people, making his way south away from the scene. He finally disappeared into the crowd, running back towards his truck.

Leaping over a low gate into a walled garden, Jack crouched behind a porch. He was breathing in halting gulps, his heart racing. Where was his daughter? He pulled his phone from his back pocket to call Sara and saw a text from her.

U there?

He replied quickly: *Yes. Where u?*

I wasn't downtown, was out on MP.

Jack thought quickly. She was in Mount Pleasant, ten miles or so from Awendaw. He typed, *Get to Awendaw and wait for me at the old store we used to go to.*

RU ok, Daddy?

Yes, I'm fine.

Daddy, I'm scared. I heard there were explosions downtown. One was at Mom's church.

I know, we'll be ok, I'll see you soon.

CHAPTER 59

THOMPSON PUSHED FANNIE into the front seat beside Richard, jumped up into the back of the small cart, and held onto the grab bar as he pulled Ava and Amarintha into the back.

"Why did you do that?" Amarintha asked pointing to Frank, as Richard backed out. "Who is he if he's not a detective?"

"Oh, he's a detective all right, but you cannot be taken in for testing," said Thompson.

"Testing for what, for God's sakes?" Amarintha was holding onto Ava, trying not to fall into Thompson's lap as Richard moved through the remaining people on the street.

"We're headed to the marina. I'll explain once we get there," said Thompson.

"The marina? Why?"

Richard started driving towards the marina as fast as the cart was capable of moving. Ava was on the other side of Amarintha, so she leaned towards Thompson to hear, giving him another jolt of recognition.

"Amarintha, your reliquary was taken to the hospital. Someone stole it from there," yelled Thompson.

"Who took it to the hospital? Why? Richard, did you take it?" she yelled back.

Richard paid no attention to the passengers behind him,

intent on dodging bicycles, pedestrians, and, in the middle of the chaos, a horse-drawn carriage, stopped dead in the middle of Queen Street.

Fannie screamed and covered her eyes as Richard's driving careened his passengers from side to side, barely avoiding the carriage. Amarintha stared at Thompson and leaned over to yell in his ear, "Who the hell are you, Thompson Denton?"

"Later, please," he yelled back. "We need to survive this ride first."

Richard kept moving and turned right onto Broad Street. The road was clogged with cars, so he darted off the pavement onto the sidewalk, dodging the palmetto trees that lined Broad Street like an entrance to a Palm Springs golf course. The large blue stone blocks rattled the little cart, each one tooth jarring. Soon Broad Street turned more residential, but Richard continued to steer through the streets and the yards as fast as he could, until the cart was stopped dead by a flowerbed of chest-high delphiniums.

An elderly woman holding shears and a basket straightened up behind the flowers. The old woman removed earplugs. Stunned, she said, "Is that you, Richard Anderson?" Before he responded, she looked outside her front yard and noticed dozens of pedestrians on the street.

"Mildred, get inside and turn on the TV. You might need to evacuate," yelled Richard.

"Richard, you know I don't own a TV. What in tarnation is going on? What in the world are all these people doing here? It's not the Spring Tour of Homes, is it?"

Richard backed up, and pulled onto the road. Thompson looked behind him to see her still standing, holding her shears.

Handling the little cart like a man possessed, Richard continued veering onto sidewalks and, when necessary, driving through people's yards. When they sailed by Colonial Lake,

Thompson motioned to Richard to pull over into a driveway belonging to a half-built house.

The noise in the streets elicited Thompson's memories of 9/11. Suddenly he was there again, standing in front of the Twin Towers. He had been ready to go into the building when the first plane hit. Frozen in the street, he had stood looking at paper drifting from the top of one of the World Trade buildings, only to realize, in horror, that the papers were human bodies, either propelled out of the building by the airplane's crash, or people jumping, an unthinkable decision made to avoid being burned to death. After 9/11, his ears had vibrated in a pulsing pain that had not subsided for weeks. A memory of this pain reverberated even now, brought back by the noise, and Thompson realized that the fear he felt for Amarintha was affecting him physically in the same way that 9/11 had.

Ava and Fannie stood to the side, murmuring to each other. Amarintha walked over to them, and all three hugged. The group was too close to MUSC for Thompson's comfort. The police would shut down all egress from the city, and law enforcement would eventually show up at the marina, just a few blocks away from the hospital.

"Amarintha," urged Thompson. "We need to get to Richard's boat. Let's leave the cart here and get over to the marina. You sure your boat is fueled, Richard?" asked Thompson.

"Yes."

Thompson turned to the three women. "I will explain everything, I promise, but right now, we need to get Amarintha and Richard out of Charleston. The two of them touched what was dug up in Amarintha's yard."

Fannie turned to Amarintha and said, "We probably can't get out of town any other way than by boat right now. Let's just go."

"Where are we going?" asked Ava.

"A B&B in Georgetown," Thompson replied.

Amarintha nodded and grabbed Ava's hand. Ava tilted her head to the right. Thompson shut his eyes, and for the first time in many years, said a silent prayer, asking whoever was listening to watch over them.

CHAPTER 60

"HEY, *HEY*, SOMEBODY reading me?" yelled Frank. He pivoted around the post rail trying to reach the handcuff keys and hoped the body camera hadn't filmed Thompson latching him to the porch. "Hey!" he yelled again. The street in front of Richard's house was almost deserted now, everyone apparently gawking at the fallen church steeple a block away, or going back inside to hang on every word of CNN.

"Detective Edson, do you read?" said one of FBI agents who had been in the car.

"I do, I do read. Can you get somebody to Richard Anderson's house on Church Street? I'm handcuffed to a porch rail."

Frank looked at his watch; realizing only fifteen minutes had passed since the explosions. He was lucky to get anyone's attention. He debated about whether to tell the FBI just who had slapped the cuffs on him, and quickly decided not to. The fact that Thompson, a smaller and older man, had been able to pull him over to the railing and fasten the cuffs was humiliating. Added to that, the statement Thompson made about the Task Force having a leak, repeated in his ear like the refrain to an unwanted song: *There's a leak, there's a leak, there's a leak.*

"Did you say you're handcuffed to a porch railing?" asked the agent.

"Yes, you heard right. Do you have someone you can spare? The handcuff keys are in my back pocket but I can't reach them. Tell Agent Reynolds that the Sims family is not in custody. They have left the scene, and I don't know where they are."

He could take the FBI's kidding, but it looked like he'd have to be rescued by someone at CPD. He'd never hear the end of the story about how the great Detective Frank Edson had to be unlocked from his own handcuffs.

The regular officers already treated Frank differently, because he was from Ohio, and because he had received a degree in Criminal Justice before joining the force. The patrol officers called him "Brainiac." A new moniker would result from this fiasco.

Frank gritted his teeth and said, "Call somebody at the CPD main station. They should have a clerk or someone who can come down."

"I'll call over there as soon as I can, Detective, but as you can imagine, we're pretty busy."

Frank sat down on the steps, lowering the cuffs down the post with him. Mentally, he tallied the number of people who had known that the reliquary had been sent to MUSC, and possible motives for leaking its location.

The FBI: No way there was a leak there.
Charleston Police: The same.
The Vatican: Impossible.
CDC, Homeland, SLED, DHEC. Not them either.
Not Thompson.

That left Thompson's boss Sergei something and the agent in Istanbul who had received the tip about Kate Strong's kidnapping. Frank didn't want to be xenophobic, but he had worked with everyone else on the Task Force, all from U.S. agencies, and didn't think any of them could be the leak. In any event, every single agent on the team knew exactly where the reliquary had been taken. If the exact location of the reliquary had been leaked, why bomb the church?

A voice in his ear said, "We've called your headquarters. They will be sending somebody."

"Wait. I have a question about the bombings. Does the FBI have surveillance tapes from the hospital yet?"

The agent replied, "We've just received the first footage. Two men entered MUSC, and one man went into the Huguenot Church's sanctuary. We are getting ready to run the video against our facial recognition systems."

"Where have you set up Incident Command? I'll be there as soon as I can."

"We're at the Francis Marion Hotel. Get here when you can."

Frank had no doubt that Bunin, through Alternative Auctions, had criminal contacts in the area that could easily make and place a bomb within a few hours. Thompson had validated that Richard had the artifact at approximately 8:00 a.m., and before 9:00 a.m., the FBI had taken it to the special lab at MUSC. It was now 12:15. In three hours, the perpetrator had identified where the reliquary might be, made and planted the bombs.

Frank yelled into his body camera again, "You got an ETA on somebody to cut me loose?"

No one answered him, and at that moment, he heard a rumble. A police officer on a motorcycle rounded the corner and stopped in the front yard of Richard Anderson's house. The officer parked the bike and took off his helmet. Frank groaned. "You?"

The rookie who had used the Taser on Jack Strong looked at

him like a puppy dog. "I figure I'd do you a favor, so you'll go easy on me in your report," the young rookie said earnestly.

"Yeah, yeah, ok," said Frank. "Just get me out of these things. I need to get to the Francis Marion Hotel."

CHAPTER 61

T HOMPSON CHECKED HIS watch. Twenty minutes since the explosion. He envisioned scores of firefighters, police, and FBI agents working the scenes. The FBI would certainly be in charge and have already established an Incident Command, a central location for all activities related to the bombings. The police would not allow any more vehicles downtown, and the interstate would be a parking lot of cars, trucks, delivery vans, and airport shuttles, all holding their drivers hostage.

As the five of them approached the marina, Thompson noticed a large group of people standing on the restaurant porch, looking towards the explosions, but no one paid attention to the group as they walked down the pier. Richard reached his slip and untied the lines, motioning everyone to board. Thompson watched Amarintha hop into the boat, an effortless movement that telegraphed her improving condition more than her appearance. Ava and Fannie followed, with only Fannie needing a hand. The three women went immediately below deck.

Although Amarintha would not believe him, he was certain that handling the reliquary had something to do with the dramatic change in her health. What about the priest with vitiligo? He too seemed to have experienced something—a cure, a remission? Had these two modern people experienced the same type of miracle that children in 1685 had experienced?

Thompson had not been able to find any other articles about Monsignor Ogier and his profile on the Vatican Museum's website was brief. The man was a trained art restorer, and was American. He had been in Rome for almost thirty years. Why would he want Amarintha? The reliquary, yes, he got that, but Amarintha?

He was certain that the monsignor knew more about the missing reliquaries than he had shared. Why had someone leaked the location of the reliquary? For the diamond? The value of the stone was enough to tempt the most honest cop. The motivation might be as simple as money. The only reason Bunin was the suspect was because of the FIG computer prediction and Zora Vulkov's voice on the recording that reported an alleged kidnapping of Kate Strong. What if all of them had the motive for the theft of the artifact completely, utterly wrong?

Richard eased the boat out of its berth and brought it around to navigate Charleston Harbor towards the Cooper River, where he would turn northeast to Georgetown. The boat was about thirty feet long; a comfortable cabin cruiser with what Thompson presumed was a bedroom, small galley, and head below. He did not know whether to be relieved or worried that all he could see on the Ashley River was a lone sailboat. Thompson turned and looked towards Charleston, watching the two plumes of smoke, their tops billowing into one. The day was warm for April—80 degrees, so no one was wearing coats, but the weather could change quickly this time of year, and Thompson thought he might rue his decision to get Amarintha and her family out of town with nothing other than the clothes on their backs.

What about Frank? As soon as he got loose from the cuffs,

he'd name Thompson as the culprit. Abruptly, he said to Richard, "Give me your cell phone." He stuck his head below deck, repeated the request and then began to remove the batteries from Richard's phone.

"Why? Are we being tracked?" Ava was looking up at Thompson, her question sincere, and with the sight of her face, he felt another jolt, a sense that his life had tilted.

He had suppressed his feelings for Amarintha because of his work and her illness. No, his burgeoning affection for a grown woman had not been the only motivation for the spontaneous, headlong flight from Richard's house. It had been the sight of Ava standing in the grass that had driven him into action.

The girl looked just like his mother. What were the chances that a teenage girl living in Charleston, South Carolina was the doppelganger of a sixty-five-year-old woman living in Lyon, France? That Ava Sims could be the result of Thompson's long ago ejaculation into a cup for gas money, while he had slouched in a bathroom, made him want to throw up.

Looking away from Ava, he said, "Yes or at least I might be."

Amarintha handed him three phones. "You need to tell me what's going on" She sat down on one of the benches that hugged both sides of the boat.

"I know. I'm sorry for dragging all of you into a situation you didn't have a chance to understand. Give me a minute." Thompson went below and yelled up, "Richard, you want a beer?"

"Yep, I do." Smoke was still rising above the city. The Battery, the most southern part of the Charleston peninsula, was now full of people, some of whom were waving at the boat.

The waves were choppy, and Thompson felt salt spray on his face. "Don't go over there, Richard."

"I won't. I guess they have the roads north blocked, and folks are desperate to get off this piece of land. This is like 9/11. I never thought I'd see Charleston like this. Who do you suppose did it?"

Fannie and Ava came up on deck and sat beside Amarintha. The women stared at the Battery, and its frightened mass of people. Fannie said, "I've heard a lot about you, Thompson Denton, but I'm damned if I believe you're an interior decorator."

At this, Thompson laughed until tears came from his eyes. He pulled at the label on his beer bottle and sat opposite the women. "First of all, Mrs. Sims, you are right. I am not an interior designer. I'm an agent with Interpol." He had expected some sort of reaction, but not the one he got.

Amarintha snorted. "Well, thank God. I kept thinking that you couldn't be a designer, but figured the cancer and chemo made the reasonable seem ridiculous. An agent from Interpol. That certainly never came up on my list of your potential professions."

Thompson shook his head. "What did you think I was?"

She shrugged. "Well, the story you told me about writing a book was obviously not true. You never wrote anything down. So then I thought you might be a scout looking to do a real estate show about Charleston." She looked down. "I hoped whatever the reason you were here might keep you around for a while."

Fannie looked hard at Thompson, but said nothing.

Amarintha gazed out at the water. "We have a while before we get to Georgetown. Start talking." She went below, grabbed a beer from the refrigerator, and gave Ava and Fannie bottles of water.

Ava rolled her eyes. "Really, Mama. I could use a beer too."

Thompson wiped his mouth and said, "First, if Detective Edson reports that I handcuffed him, Charleston's finest may want to arrest me. Richard can stop in Mt. Pleasant and I'll get off the boat. You all can go on to Georgetown. He was silent for a moment.

"I want to know why the detective wanted to take me in first. You're not getting off this boat until you explain that," said Amarintha. Ava and Fannie nodded their agreement.

Where to begin, he thought, *and how much to tell them?* "What you found is a reliquary, one missing from France. No one knew that until the Vatican brought the contents of a convent church's altar to Rome. When the researchers checked the Vatican's records, they discovered that one item was missing from the altar, your reliquary. Three Vatican researchers became ill from handling the other contents of the altar. That's when the Vatican notified Interpol that an item was missing and that it might be contaminated. I happened to be in Charleston working a case focused on a professor at the College named Adam Chalk."

"That's the one that was murdered on the Cooper River Bridge!" Fannie put her hand to her mouth, all eyes.

"Right. Kate Strong worked for him, and she went missing the same day."

Ava gave a gasp, her eyes as big as Fannie's. "Is that why she left town?"

Thompson took a deep breath. "The truth is she was likely kidnapped." He put his hand up as he saw Amarintha open her mouth. "Yes, Jack knows. There is a lead on her whereabouts, and he's in contact with the FBI."

Amarintha studied his face. "How does this tie into my reliquary?"

"Your reliquary is very valuable. The FBI believes that Kate Strong's kidnapper, a Russian named Anton Bunin, was pressuring her to find it, and perhaps other relics."

He looked over at the Battery again. "What exactly did the reliquary have in it, and did you touch the contents?"

Amarintha drank the rest of her beer in gulping swallows. "Seeds. I think they were some type of seeds. Yes, I touched them."

He certainly had not expected this. Based on his knowledge of what typically was in reliquaries, he was expecting cloth, pieces of wood, or bones. Seeds? That was odd.

"What are the researchers sick with? I assume that is what I need to be tested for," said Amarintha.

"The researchers are sick with anthrax, a strain no one has come across in modern times." Thompson watched Amarintha.

He thought she would protest and say it was impossible. Instead, she said, "Some biologists have been afraid that one day archeologists would find an unknown microbe in an object or in a body that had been buried, or mummified."

Thompson looked at her, astonished. This woman continued to surprise him. "So, it isn't out of the question that bacteria could live that long?"

She shrugged, "Anthrax can form spores. Live anthrax still hides along the Old West's cattle trails, so we know it can live in the ground for at least a hundred years. I'm guessing that when the researchers were found to have an unknown variant that the CDC was called?"

Thompson gave silent thanks for Amarintha's scientific training, and nodded.

"But why would anyone believe the reliquary was somewhere in Charleston?" asked Ava.

"The Vatican sent the FBI a picture of it. An FBI image recognition program matched the Vatican's picture to one of your father and the reliquary, taken in 1986."

"My *father*?" replied Amarintha. "Where was this picture taken? Do you know if he's the one who buried it?"

"The picture is from his workplace. It seems likely he's the one who buried the thing, but we don't know why," said Thompson.

Fannie turned to Amarintha and said, "You know your daddy studied germs for the Department of Defense, which back in the '80s was experimenting with bacteria and viruses. He was very troubled by the work they were asking him to do."

Thompson gaped at Fannie. He wondered how many FBI agents were still trying to uncover the information that she had just nonchalantly shared.

"Mrs. Sims, do you remember seeing anything like what Amarintha found? She did tell you what it looked like, didn't she?"

"She sure did, and believe me, I'd remember if I'd ever seen a box with a giant red stone on it. He was always looking for antiques that had sealed tops, like old bottles. We used to rummage through estate sales for stuff like that. His group wanted to analyze air that hadn't been exposed to modern contaminants. I found it all quite interesting to listen to, even though I didn't understand everything he told me. How did this reliquary end up in Charles' hands?"

One corner of Thompson's mouth turned up. "It may have been an ancestor of your husband. The Vatican gave me an old report to read, and it states that a Huguenot girl stole the reliquary in 1685 from the convent, and brought it to Charleston. Her name was Marin Postel."

Fannie and Amarintha looked at each other, but said nothing.

Richard said, "So, when I called you yesterday, you realized we had dug up this missing thing, and then those people showed up to test me. Scared the bejesus out of me too."

"Wait a minute." Amarintha threw her hands out. "The explosion was at MUSC. That's where you said the reliquary was. What are you not telling us, Thompson?"

He thought for a long moment and looked at Amarintha. "The explosions are connected. The reliquary is gone, taken from MUSC."

There was no reaction to Thompson's statement. The boat rocked gently as Richard stopped at a marker separating the harbor from the Cooper River. The five of them watched a giant container ship move ponderously towards the port a few miles upstream, all of the passengers silent. Thompson was surprised that the freighter would be allowed to dock, but such was the power of capitalism. The people of America needed their stuff.

Finally, Ava said, "Agent Denton. I don't understand why you wouldn't let the detective take us to be tested. If the reliquary might be infected, couldn't Mama have been exposed? Why wouldn't you want her to be treated?" She gazed at him, and he knew her head would soon begin to tilt a little to the right.

Istanbul

CHAPTER 62

ZORA SAT IN the small office that Anton had given her, reviewing the horde of scholarly publications on anthrax. Although Anton had not told her she was a prisoner, he had not given her access to the Internet, and the last time her phone had worked was when she called Interpol from the terrace. She had smiled throughout a long evening dinner with him, and her boss did not question that Zora was now on board with his reprehensible project. Given their joint history, why would he?

For ten years, Zora had attended meetings and dispassionately discussed mortality figures, expected death rates, modes of transmission, and a variety of factors that had detailed how to kill Soviet enemies in the most cost effective way. She worked for months trying to create a biological weapon from cobra venom and influenza, months of her life that Zora suppressed as a nightmare, because what kind of twisted mind thought of that combination? Had that mind really been hers?

She had not questioned using biological research to change

the course of history. Anton still did not question it. For him, nothing had changed. Russia was his homeland, and if his homeland wanted him to decimate an entire region of the world, and was willing to pay billions of dollars for him to do so, he would. The billions from the Russian government to create an apocalyptic biological weapon was a long overdue reward for the years he spent essentially doing the same work, for the same employer, for a pittance and a free apartment.

Zora pushed the research paper away from her and leaned back in the chair. Anton had concocted a brilliant plan. The sources of the anthrax would be the ruins of Palmyra, and similar sites that the Islamists had destroyed. The mortar used by the ancients had sometimes contained ground up animal bones, so blaming the spread of the bacteria on these cities' destruction might appear feasible. Anton talked about this plan with no reservations, no suspicion that she was anything but his brilliant, subservient colleague. She had never defied him, never even questioned him in the days he had been her boss. He had ignored the fact that she had spent twice as many years trying to cure people as she had trying to exterminate them, and seemed blind to the woman Zora had become.

In 1991, a part of Zora had known that to stay in Russia would be giving legitimacy to a government that, with its demise, exposed the objective of the Institute to be as lethal as the diseases they had studied. Her utopian idea of communism had begun to die when she stepped off an ancient Boeing prop plane into a steaming jungle. By the end of the four-day jeep ride to the clinic, she had shed her idealism, her Caucasian sense of superiority, and her certainty of how life should be lived, as easily as she shed the useless paraphernalia—she had brought a hair dryer of all things—she thought indispensable for jungle life. Communism and capitalism were feeble ideas in a region of the world where it took four hours to retrieve water that was drinkable.

At the most basic level, the people in the small villages were no different from those anywhere else. They wanted their children to be healthy, their crops to flourish, and their loved ones to live a long life. Any form of government other than a council where grievances were taken was considered ludicrous and unnecessary. Their lives were beset with woes, but unless Lenin managed to return from the dead with a foolproof method to eradicate mosquitoes, communism could not ameliorate these woes. Her years in the jungle had honed Zora's sensibilities away from destruction, towards a singlemindedness that tried to save one baby, one toddler, one child at a time.

"Well, Zora, I see you have been studying."

Zora turned to see Anton, wearing an enormous grin, standing in her doorway. "I have news for you. One of my associates has found one of the twelve poisoned artifacts in the United States. I will not have to storm the Vatican or Notre Dame."

He took a cigarette and pointed it to her. "My source in Interpol told me that two Vatican researchers have an unknown form of anthrax. The priests got it from a reliquary that was in an old French convent's altar. The altar was in Rome for repair, and it was supposed to contain two reliquaries. Only one was there, and that one was infectious."

Zora gave a slight shudder. "Are you sure the priests have anthrax?"

"Yes. My Interpol friend sent me the results of the CDC's testing of the priests, as well as a copy of a picture of the missing reliquary found in the U.S. It's quite ordinary." Anton took a heavy folded sheet out of his pocket and handed it to her. The reliquary was wooden with a mosaic top. A human figure stood with its arms outstretched, one hand holding a daisy-like flower, the center of it appearing to be an enormous red gemstone.

"The FBI plugged this picture into their image library, and like magic, the reliquary was traced to a place called Charleston, a city on the eastern coast of the United States."

He leaned forward and touched the picture. "This box was found buried in a garden. Just think of it. The germ has been sitting in a box for over three hundred years and might still be viable. What do you think of that?"

"How did you get it?"

"Zora, you do not want to know the details. Suffice to say that I have contacts everywhere and was able to hire people in Charleston to steal the reliquary right from under the nose of the FBI." Anton boomed with laughter.

He stood up and put his hands on the back of the chair. "I no longer need Dr. Strong. I do need you, dear Zora. We still need to figure out a way to ensure distribution of this little present."

She put her hand on his. "Anton, will you let Dr. Strong go? You said you would drug her and dump her at the U.S. Embassy. Will you still do that?" Zora paused and then asked, "What will you do with Dr. Atay?"

"Atay? I will let him go back to his parchments. He cannot stop me. As for Dr. Strong, I think you are right. No one will believe her. Have tea with her. I will give you something hallucinogenic to put in her drink, and drop her off on our way to the airport. The good doctor might even be able to dress herself again one day." Anton walked out, snickering.

Zora took a deep breath. *Hang on, Dr. Strong,* she thought, and then wondered how she would save herself.

Charleston

CHAPTER 63

THE SIRENS DID not stop their wails during the ten minutes Jack rested under an ancient twenty-foot-tall camellia. Each time he moved his arms, a cascade of pink petals silently fell on his shoulders. The longer he stayed hidden, the more likely the police would cordon off the entire peninsula. He needed to get out of town.

Jack stood up, surveyed the area and realized he was on the corner of Ashley and Wentworth Streets, west of King Street and south of the hospital. His truck was parked near the hospital, many blocks away from where he stood. That area would be swarming with law enforcement. Assuming he could even get to the truck, driving it off the peninsula was out, as was a taxi. No way were the police going to allow any vehicles to leave downtown without a thorough search of each one, and given Agent Reynold's reaction to seeing him, law enforcement might be looking for him.

His anxiety was reaching a level that approached the first days after Kate's disappearance, and now that he had a sliver of hope that she was alive, he was determined to get out of Charleston and to Istanbul by any means.

A way out presented itself when he saw the truck from Jackman's Lumber creeping slowly down Ashley Street with what looked like the trusses for Amarintha's house. The project plan had called for the roof trusses to be delivered today. Normally, no delivery ever actually occurred on the day it was scheduled, and Jack took it as a sign that events were finally happening in his favor.

The police had been pushing the crowd towards Lockwood, which ran north to south on the west side of the Charleston peninsula. Presumably, the police would corral people there, and then determine whether to let them leave. Reversing course, Jack ran down Wentworth towards the east side of the city. He'd go to the cruise ship area, as far away from the hospital as possible. Perhaps he would find a way north from there.

Jack ran east on Wentworth, detoured to East Bay Street, then slowed and walked a few blocks to the Maritime Center, where throngs of people aimlessly milled about. A massive white cruise ship loomed at the dock, lines of passengers at every rail watching and pointing to the smoke. Every passenger was holding a cell phone or camera, narrating the visible events for videos, some that would end up on YouTube if they weren't there already.

At the end of the dock were several employees from the cruise line arguing with a police officer. Several huge buses idled, their diesel engines adding to the noise of the sirens and alarms. Jack busied himself inspecting the tires on the buses, watching the police officer, and trying to listen to the conversation.

"I've got five hundred people expecting to tour Charleston in those buses," said an anxious woman, who kept gazing down to her clipboard and then looking up, as if the scene would surely have changed in the meantime.

"Ma'am, we've had two explosions in this city. Nobody is getting off that ship. The tour is cancelled. I have two thousand tourists already downtown and I don't want any more from your ship. I've a good mind to confiscate those buses to help with the evacuation," said the officer. He walked a few feet away and spoke into his radio.

"I've got five buses by the docks and each one can take out about a hundred people at a time. After you check people for injuries, get their IDs and fingerprints and then send them to the Maritime Center. I'll load the buses and send them to the North Charleston Convention Center where we can do formal interviews."

Jack could not hear the garbled reply. He walked closer, thinking that he might be able to meld into the crowd the cop was talking about and slip into one of the buses.

The cruise woman leaned forward and shouted, "You can't do that!"

"Ma'am, yes I can," the officer said. "Hey you!" He yelled to Jack, "Get that bus ready to board."

Jack froze, thought quickly, and said, "I'm not the driver. I'm a tourist."

"Get on the bus," said the officer.

Jack turned and saw an escorted column of people three blocks away, mostly older men, women, and children, moving towards the busses. Jack quickly boarded, found a Veteran of Desert Storm ball cap on an empty seat, and sat down. He took his jacket off, and pulled the cap low over his eyes, pretending to be asleep. Jack sincerely hoped no one would ask him any questions about Kuwait or Iraq, but if they did, he would claim amnesia due to exposure to something toxic.

The first passengers scrambled on board, and after five minutes, a man got into the driver's seat. Once the bus was full, the driver headed toward North Charleston. Looking out the back window, Jack saw a crowd of people, gesturing, crying, some on their cell phones, all looking shocked and angry. More than a few seemed to be arguing with whoever in uniform that was nearest to them, a mixture of volunteers, police officers, and firefighters. The cruise ship was receding from the shoreline.

Jack yawned, rubbed his eyes, and asked the nearest person. "What's going on?"

An elderly man across from Jack said, "You slept through that? My poor wife and I were on a carriage tour on Rutledge Street, and the building on the next block just blew up. It was horrible."

A babble of excited voices erupted. From what Jack could glean, the bomb at the hospital had created a twenty-foot fireball, causing devastation to an area about forty-feet wide.

"Then that other explosion happened, and I swear, I thought Charleston was under attack," said another elderly man with 'WWII Veteran' on his own ball cap.

A younger man, looking at his cell phone said, "The other one at the Huguenot church wasn't as big as the one at hospital." He held his phone up, and Jack could hear the tinny voice of a well-known CNN anchor.

At a stoplight on East Bay, the driver turned around and shouted, "You people just relax back there. I'm supposed to take everybody to the North Charleston Coliseum."

By the time Jack had heard four or five versions of the story, the bus was at the northern end of the peninsula, idling at a barricade across I-26 West. An officer boarded the bus and gave a cursory look to the passengers. "Thank y'all for your cooperation. We're almost at the coliseum."

When the officer left the bus, Jack let out his breath. He could see barricades on the westbound side of I-26, holding back an ever-growing line of cars originally heading south into the city. Law enforcement was attempting to reroute traffic out of downtown, but given the interstate was elevated and dead-ended at downtown Charleston, providing a way for the eastbound traffic to go west, away from Charleston, would be a nightmare. Jack thought it likely that eventually a nincompoop would leave his car and try to climb down the enormous concrete pillars supporting the interstate, thus snarling traffic even further.

Jack called his daughter.

"Daddy, where are you?"

"Where are you, baby?" he asked simultaneously.

"I got a ride to Georgetown. Ava texted me. They're on a boat going to the B&B. Where are you?"

"I'm on my way out of Charleston. I'll meet you in Georgetown," said Jack.

"Daddy, Ava told me about the picture of mom. When were you going to tell me?" Sara asked this in a resigned way, too upset and distracted to badger him.

"I'll tell you everything later, including what I've found out since Richard showed me that picture and what we need to do."

"Yes, but, why? Why won't you tell me what is going on?" She was beginning to cry now.

"I will, I promise. Just not over a cell phone. Get going."

Silence. "Ok. Come get me, Dad, please."

"I love you, and I'm on my way. I'm about an hour behind you."

CHAPTER 64

FANNIE SQUINTED AT Thompson. "Ava asks a very good question. Why wouldn't you want Amarintha to be tested?"

At that moment, the freighter let out a long blast of its horn, a deafening noise that gave Thompson a few moments to think. He sat with his hands hanging between his knees, the three suspicious, impatient women sitting opposite him, waiting for his answer.

When the noise stopped, he continued. "Do you remember there were three researchers at the Vatican?" They nodded. "The third priest recovered from the inhalation form of anthrax."

Amarintha started. "That's almost never heard of."

Thompson kept his eye contact with her. "The priest was in a drug trial, and the CDC tested his current DNA profile against an old one. Genes related to inflammation, the MC1R genes, have caused his body to heal itself. You're not infected with anthrax. Something else has happened to you. "

Amarintha stood and moved her hand to push her nonexistent hair behind her ear; a gesture Thompson had seen her do dozens of times. She finally said, "Those particular genes have been linked to how people age, and influence how the body handles inflammation. There are also relationships between cancer and bacterium that could explain what happened to the priest."

"And what happened to you, Mama."

Amarintha went into teacher mode, her tone flat. "Bacterium can release toxins that disrupt cell growth, which can affect cancer. Over a hundred years ago, a bone surgeon named William Coley noticed that when patients had virulent bacterial infections, their tumors shrank."

She glanced behind the boat as Richard steered it away from Charleston, then turned to look at Thompson, her eyes narrowing. "You still haven't explained why you'd handcuff a Charleston detective to keep him from taking me to MUSC to be tested. Any tests that MUSC can't do, we'll get the CDC to do. I need to get back to Charleston."

"I kept the detective from taking you in because I'm afraid there is a leak at the FBI or at CPD. No one could have learned about the reliquary except through a leak, so the fact that you handled the item could now be known by whoever orchestrated the theft. I'm assuming it's Bunin."

The three women gawked at him. Wanting them to understand the magnitude of the potential danger Amarintha was in, he went on, "Amarintha, you are at risk, especially if it's discovered you were exposed to the material in the reliquary and are now recovering from cancer. Can you imagine if the reliquary contains something that can provide a cure for cancer, and a criminal gang is the only one who has it? Everyone wants to talk to you. The Vatican is asking that you be quarantined, and I suspect the U.S. government would want to have access to you as well."

"Access? What does that mean?" Amarintha put her hands on her head, swaying as a wave rocked the boat. They were all waiting, Richard too, for some reassurance that "access" did not mean being locked up, poked with medical instruments, or held in isolation. Their faces showed an expectation that their rising agitation would be relieved, that he could make the entire situation bearable. He couldn't do it. He couldn't lie.

"Nothing good," Thompson said.

The boat rocked as it crossed the wake from a massive freighter.

Fannie huffed, "Surely you've figured it out by now, Mr. Secret Agent." She flipped her white braid over her shoulder as she went below. She said, "Whoever planted the bombs and stole that thing is doing the same thing my husband was doing in 1986—looking in old containers for something that can cause a lot of trouble. If a superbug is found that we have no treatment for, that's worth more to a criminal than any diamond."

CHAPTER 65

FRANK EDSON SAT at a long banquet table in one of the ballrooms of the Francis Marion Hotel, the white tableclothed surface now covered with his fellow officer's gear. Scenes he had witnessed from his motorcycle ride from Richard Anderson's house to the hotel would not leave him.

A dead horse, still connected to its overturned carriage, had been lying prone on Calhoun Street behind yellow tape. Two motionless lumps lay close to the carriage, covered with what Frank knew were body bags. The smell of diesel fuel, burned flesh, and melting asphalt made his eyes water, and for a moment, he thought he might throw up. Two ladder trucks poured water on a still-smoking crater, whose ragged edge grasped one of the dead horse's forelegs like a shark's mouth. A bomb-sniffing German shepherd sat by its young female handler. Inside the yellow tape, Frank saw a small group of people, who he assumed were FBI agents, along with some of his Charleston PD colleagues. He was sure he knew most of the cops, but they were all but unrecognizable now, their uniforms streaked with dust, their faces black with soot.

He had leaned over to the young officer driving the bike and said, "Let's go. Nothing we can do here." When the motorcycle stopped at the hotel's front door on King Street, Frank bounded into the building and up the stairs.

It had now been a little over sixty minutes since the explosions.

Frank scanned the room for anyone he knew. Twenty or so CPD officers and SLED agents milled around, all seeming to be purposeless, but Frank knew each had, or would shortly be given a mission. Brook Reynolds walked to the podium.

"I need your attention," she said into a microphone. The room quieted. "Across the hall, the Mayor and the Chief of Police are meeting to prepare for a public briefing that will occur in a few minutes. Here is what we know at this point." She read from a sheet of paper.

"Two explosions occurred almost simultaneously. One at the Medical University of South Carolina and one at the Huguenot Church on Queen Street. Our experts believe it was dynamite. The FBI is tracing the source of the explosive material. There were no casualties at the church, and although the steeple has fallen, it appears to have done so because it was weakened by termites prior to the explosion. The blast at the hospital killed two individuals whose identity is pending notification of the families."

Brook Reynolds took a breath. "The blast at MUSC was in front of the laboratory. Two technicians were attacked, but sustained no injuries. Two FBI agents were momentarily incapacitated by blows to the head, but they are not seriously injured and have returned to duty. Surveillance tapes from the scenes show two men entering the hospital and one man entering the church. Here is the first look at the suspects."

A grainy black and white composite image of three faces appeared on a screen behind her. "We have already identified these individuals." A murmur ran through the crowd. Brook held up her hand, and everyone quieted. "They are associated with a criminal group operating out of Horry County which launders money. All three have been arrested before, which is why we were able to match the surveillance tapes to their mugshots. The mayor will ask for help in finding them and will warn the public that these men are presumed to be armed and dangerous."

Brook looked at her watch. "I'm turning the meeting over to Major Munez of SLED. He'll describe the interdiction efforts underway." She left the podium and with two other agents exited the room.

One of Frank's colleagues walked over, nodded to Frank and said, "Hell of a thing."

Frank nodded.

Munez touched the microphone at the podium. "At this moment, teams of special operatives are raiding the last known addresses of the three individuals. Here are the particulars." Munez clicked a handheld control that advanced through three images, each one with a surveillance photograph, name, and address. All of the addresses were in remote areas of Berkley County.

A question came from one of the tables. "Major Munez, are we sure these are the only perpetrators?"

"Yes, but there are other individuals we want to interview."

He put up another picture, this one of an intense man with a monk's haircut. "This man, Imran Sadat, is a person of interest and known associate of the three bombers. He is a suspected member of a crime organization that utilizes illegals to launder money through South Carolina wire transfer locations. We have a team trying to find Sadat."

Someone else asked, "Do you know the motive for these bombings? I mean, these two bombing locations are very different. What links them?"

Frank watched Major Munez for a moment and realized that none of these law enforcement individuals knew about the Task

Force or the potentially contaminated reliquary. What was the major going to tell them?

Frank was surprised that Major Munez held nothing back. He described the computer program from the FIG, the FBI's Information Group, that had determined there was a risk of a biological attack, and the missing Vatican reliquary that had caused an outbreak in Rome. He explained the danger of the missing reliquary. Though he did not describe exactly where, he did say it had been found in Charleston, sent to the MUSC lab for testing, and that test results were not yet complete. He showed the audience a picture of the small box, the same picture shown Thompson just the day before.

When Munez finished no one spoke, so he continued. "We strongly believe that the bombs were planted to cause confusion so that the perpetrators could search for the reliquary. The lab itself had no surveillance equipment, but the employees reported that two men punched the FBI agents just outside the door. The two perpetrators then entered the isolation chamber where the artifact was being tested. They grabbed the object and struck the two individuals working in the chamber. Because the technicians were in protective gear, they were not gravely injured. One even managed to call 911 ten seconds before the bomb exploded. Any questions?"

When no one spoke, Munez added, "One man entered the church and placed the explosive right inside the door, and exited. Nothing seems to have been taken, and that bomb was very small compared to the one at MUSC. It's vital that we find this missing object and the three individuals responsible for the death of two American citizens. This is not considered a terrorism action at this time, but it may yet be classified as such."

The detective beside Frank asked the major, "So what do we do if we find the box? Isn't it dangerous?"

Frank added, "What are we going to tell the public?"

Munez said, "The artifact may be infected with anthrax. If you see it, or you see one of the suspects with the box, do not approach. We will take special precautions to secure it. DHEC is on standby and is prepared. I'm not sure what the mayor will tell the citizens, so for now keep the information about the anthrax danger within this room."

Munez did not talk about the outbreak in 1986, and Frank thought, *why would he?* These men and women had enough to deal with without adding the secretive DOD project to an already unimaginable scenario.

"I have assignments here for all of you," Munez said. "Each of you will be on a team assigned to some aspect in the investigation into the three individuals we've identified." Munez caught sight of Frank and beckoned him over with his left hand.

The detective made his way through the crowded room. When Frank finally got to Munez, the major was reading a note handed to him by a uniformed officer. Munez frowned, leaned over the podium, and asked Frank, "Do you know where Agent Denton is? The FBI just told me that the leak in the Task Force was from Denton's boss, Sergei Molotov."

Georgetown

CHAPTER 66

THERE ARE PARTS of the South Carolina coast that look much like they did over three hundred years ago, begging the question of just why anyone settled there—given the marsh, mosquitoes, alligators, and infertile, sandy soil. Amarintha grinned as she watched the coast drift by, remembering a letter written by a Huguenot refugee in Boston concerning the arrival of two young men from Carolina. She had memorized it for a third grade project on colonial South Carolina and could still recite it.

They have never seen so miserable a country, or an atmosphere so unhealthy. Fevers prevail all the year, from which those who are attacked seldom recover, and if some escape, their complexion becomes tawny, like that of the two who have arrived here, and who are pitiable to behold. Moreover, the heat is so intense as to be almost unendurable, and as to infect the water, consequently producing sickness, as they have no other beverage.

L. K. Clement

It occurred to her that not much had changed. The heat really could be unendurable.

Richard piloted the boat towards the Georgetown marina and into a beautiful inland sea. If you avoided looking left or right where the paper mill and the steel mill stood, you could imagine the delight of the immigrants as they first gazed on this new land, at least before they experienced the "unendurable" heat of a Carolina summer.

"Mom and Ava, you stay near the boat. I'll go in with Thompson and Richard," said Amarintha to Ava and Fannie, as the boat reached the dock. All five of them hopped out onto the pier.

"Ok," said Ava. Fannie grabbed Ava's hand and the two went to the end of the pier that looked out over the harbor.

Amarintha, Richard, and Thompson walked down the pier to the office of the marina. Two old timers stared at the television and did not turn when the door opened. Stuck on the wall with duct tape was a Parts Pup girly calendar from 1965, and maps of the Intracoastal Waterway from Florida to Maine. A glass case under the counter held a variety of fishing paraphernalia.

One of the ancient anglers, with drooping tattoos that had once been on a bicep, finally turned around. "Where you folks from? You heard what happened down in Charleston? The hospital and some other place were bombed."

Amarintha said, "Myrtle Beach," at the exact same time that Thompson said, "Florida."

"No, we haven't heard," said Richard.

The other codger had on a fishing cap and a dirty sleeveless shirt, and said, "Watch this," and pointed to the flat screen TV on the wall that was fighting for airtime with the room's air conditioner wheezing in the corner.

A CNN anchor was speaking about the "Terror in the Holy

City," a moniker quickly slapped on the situation. Creeping at the bottom of the screen was the crawl:

TWO BOMBS EXPLODED IN HISTORIC DOWNTOWN CHARLESTON, SC: ONE AT THE MEDICAL UNIVERSITY OF SOUTH CAROLINA AND ONE AT A CHURCH. NO ONE HAS CLAIMED RESPONSIBILITY. OFFICIALS ARE SECURING THE SCENE. AT LEAST TWO REPORTED DEAD. STAY TUNED FOR MORE INFORMATION.

In the corner of the screen, an aerial shot, presumably from a helicopter, showed two columns of smoke. At the next commercial, one of the two old men turned his attention to Amarintha. "So you from Myrtle Beach? Can you believe this? I'll tell you what I think: it's the Muslims."

Amarintha gave the man a look, left the office, and sat down on a bench just outside the open screen door. She caught bits and pieces of the rant. The old man seemed convinced that Muslim extremists had done the bombing, although what these extremists had against Charleston, he didn't know. In any event, the man with the tattoo speculated that while it would have been natural, and maybe understandable, if Las Vegas had been the target, the idea that Charleston had been bombed was unbelievable.

While part of her felt some gratitude that Thompson had spirited her out of Charleston for what he thought was for her own protection, another part of her regarded his motivation as ridiculous. Thompson couldn't be right. Maybe she was cured, maybe not, but the idea that her recovery could have resulted from contact with something in the reliquary was far-fetched. Even more unbelievable was his belief that this made her a target for some overarching malicious plan.

Why would a crime gang want to capture her? Were these

Russians some kind of religious extremists? Could that be the reason they wanted the reliquary?

Amarintha put her hands to her eyes and leaned over, her elbows on her knees. The memory of what she had felt when her fingers touched the small creamy objects—something between a static electricity shock and a humming vibration—had not left her. Did that mean anything? A logical explanation for what had happened was out there, and one that had nothing to do with the reliquary or its contents. If something in the artifact had triggered an antibody to her cancer, it would not be something that could be bottled and sold.

Amarintha looked down the dock at her mother and daughter who were pointing to a dolphin and laughing. She knew her current bout of good health might be cruelly temporary, and she felt her stomach roil as she watched them.

Thompson and Richard strolled out of the marina office. "I got one of the guys in there to make reservations in his name," said Thompson. "He thinks we're hiding out from our spouses." He grinned and handed Amarintha a piece of paper.

Amarintha stood and said, "And Richard, Fannie and Ava? Are they supposed to be part of the scheme?"

Richard said, "I think those two have had too much beer to worry about the details of our situation."

The five of them walked out of the marina onto the main street of Georgetown. Walking towards a neoclassical house on a side street, now a bed and breakfast, Amarintha noted the oak-covered streets with architecture as wondrous as Charleston's, albeit less of it. As they turned a corner, Sara Strong came running down the sidewalk pell-mell towards Ava. Jack Strong ran behind her. He stopped when he saw Amarintha.

"My mother is alive. She's alive," cried Sara as she hugged Ava.

Both girls were laughing now. Amarintha looked at Jack, who nodded. She asked Sara, "How did you know to come here?"

Ava wiped her eyes and looked at Thompson. "I texted her before Agent Denton took my phone."

Amarintha said, "So, what now?"

"I need to call the FBI. I'll meet the rest of you later."

CHAPTER 67

THOMPSON RETURNED TO Georgetown's main street, looking for a phone booth. He passed a drug store and decided to buy a throwaway instead, realizing that phone booths, in their sparseness, would pinpoint his location as accurately as his personal cell phone would. He bought a cheap phone, left the store and sat down at an ornate bench along the street. He needed to reach Brook Reynolds or Frank Edson, but first he would text his mother.

This is Thompson. I need a picture of you when you were a teenager. Text it to me as soon as possible.

He looked at his watch. Cocktail time. She would respond.

Hello there. I was wondering where you were these days. Is this a new cell? Are you in Lyon?

No, I'm in the United States. I really need that picture. Will call you soon.

Thompson ended the text and punched in Frank's number. The phone rang ten times. He was about to hang up when a voice said, "This is Detective Edson. Who am I speaking with?"

"Don't hang up, Frank. It's Thompson."

"I won't hang up. I need to talk to you," said Frank.

"Listen, I'm sorry about what I did, but there is a leak. I'm sure of it."

"You could have found some other way to make your point, you know, other than slapping my own cuffs on me." Frank stopped, and Thompson realized that the detective wasn't angry. *Thank God,* Thompson thought.

"Your boss, Sergei Molotov, is the leak."

Thompson sat back against the warm back of the bench, stunned. "Frank, how did you find this out? Have you already arrested someone? "

"There were three men involved with the actual placement of the bombs. Two men at the lab and one at the Huguenot Church. We have all three in custody. They're low-levels who haul money to wire service companies all day. The FBI didn't even have to offer them a deal. They walked right into the main police station on Lockwood. According to these guys, the man who hired them sounded like the character Boris in Rocky and Bullwinkle."

"What the hell is Rocky and Bullwinkle?"

"Russian, the man who hired them sounded Russian. They were called around 9:00 this morning and told to come to a North Charleston strip club. A man paid them ten thousand dollars each, gave them the packages and instructed them on how to light the bomb, and told them where to put them. Two of them were to enter the hospital lab, steal the reliquary, and give it to the man who hired them, who would be waiting outside in an SUV. The bomb at the church was supposed to go off before the one at the hospital, diverting attention from the hospital. Instead, it went off after the MUSC one."

"I can't believe they turned themselves in."

Frank snorted. "The two at the hospital got scared because of the isolation suits the techs at MUSC were wearing. They're demanding medical care. The third man showed up a little while later. I guess these three think that life in a United States federal prison is better than dying. Maybe they think they can dig a tunnel and escape like that drug lord in Mexico."

"So, how did this lead to Sergei?"

"The perps told us the man who hired them got a phone call while all of them were in the strip club. The FBI pulled a record of all calls received in the immediate vicinity of the club, and what do you know, your boss's cell phone turns up. Unless you can think of another reason Sergei Molotov would be calling someone at a strip club in Charleston?"

Thompson couldn't believe it. His boss was the damned leak. "So Sergei called the man who paid for these three to plant the bombs? And the man who did the hiring sounded like a Russian?"

"Looks that way. What we don't know is the identity of the man that Sergei called, since the receiving phone in the strip club was a throwaway, but we're proceeding under the assumption that it's Imran Sadat. We've got the three suspects looking at pictures."

"Imran Sadat is Chechen, isn't he? I guess that would sound Russian."

"Absolutely," said Frank. He paused. "The FBI wants you back in the Task Force to help them with Interpol. Agent Reynolds is not prepared to arrest Sergei yet, and she is still arguing with Homeland Security about whether Anton Bunin is dangerous. Homeland doesn't believe the FBI's FIG program is accurate, and says there's no indication that Bunin is planning to attack the U.S. with any kind of weapon."

Thompson didn't think so either, but he said nothing.

"By the way, where are you, and is the Sims family still with you? You know Amarintha Sims could be spreading anthrax as we speak. You need to bring her in."

"Yeah, they are. I still think they are in danger. If Sergei is the leak, and I agree he probably is, then he would have told Bunin who Amarintha Sims is. She's cured, Frank; I know she is. That makes her a target for these crazies. We still can't say for sure what Bunin wants."

Thompson leaned over on the bench and added, "Frank, Jack Strong and his daughter are with me too. Is there any update on what the FBI is going to do to find his wife? He and his daughter both know she's alive."

"No, no update. I'm not sure what Brook's plan will be now. The FBI is going to spend all its time trying to find the missing fourth man and putting him in jail. How far away are you?"

"Nice try, Frank. I'll call you in an hour. Give me time to think."

"You might want to find a way to break the news to Jack that the FBI won't be leaving for Istanbul anytime soon," said Frank.

Istanbul

CHAPTER 68

In Kate's hand was another lipstick case that Zora had brought her. Zora had come in with a tray of tea, and as before, suggested that Kate put on some lipstick.

Kate went into the bathroom and looked at herself. It would take more than lipstick to make her presentable again. Her normally curly dark brown hair, with its now dingy highlights, was lank against her white complexion. Given her haggard face and the enormous dark circles under her eyes, she looked like a meth-addicted owl. Her sweatshirt and jeans hung off her as if she were a scarecrow. She scratched her arms through the sweatshirt and then abruptly stopped, pulling up the sleeve on the left side to stare at her forearm, crisscrossed with red welts. Kate splashed water into her face and willed herself to stay calm.

Retrieval of the note from the tube took much longer than the first time, as her hands shook uncontrollably. This was due to lack of lithium, and she had never craved the equalization that the drug gave her more than she did at this moment. Fumbling, she managed to smooth the small roll of paper.

Bunin is done with you. I have convinced him to drug you and drop you at the Embassy in Istanbul. The drug is already in the tea. Do not swallow. After a few minutes, you should pretend to pass out. Do not wake up until the Embassy brings you inside their building in case Bunin is watching you. Good luck, Dr. Strong.

She staggered back to the main room and flopped down in front of Zora. The older woman nodded, and Kate took a sip of tea, both hands trembling as she brought the cup to her mouth. A monstrous flap of anxiety almost caused her to drop the cup, as she realized that whatever was in the tea was now inside her mouth. The liquid was sickly sweet. Kate gagged, and saw Zora begin to stand up. Kate grabbed a piece of bread, and bringing it to her mouth, managed to soak the bread with the tea in her mouth. Zora sat back down. Kate put the bread aside.

She longed to ask questions of Zora, but had to play the role, a role she was uncomfortably close to, that of a broken, drugged, passed-out woman. Panic was flapping its wings again and her mind raced, even as she felt sleepy. She fell back in the chair and saw Zora's eyes wide above her, the woman's face coming in and out of view.

Zora lifted Kate's head and whispered, "You did swallow some of it, but not much. You will be fine. Just remember to stay like this and act crazy if anyone speaks to you."

Kate tried to speak but couldn't. She saw Zora's face recede and change like a kaleidoscope. Zora disappeared. Her face was replaced by Bunin. He leaned down.

He said, "How much did she take?" His voice sounded like a foghorn.

"Enough," Kate heard Zora say. "Enough, Anton. Let's go."

Kate heard Bunin walk away and speak to someone. Two people, her guards she thought, grabbed her, one under her arms, and one at her feet. They carried her into what she remembered was the elevator, their faces bobbing and occasionally blocking the overhead lights, which flashed their brilliance into her closed eyes.

She felt the elevator move, and when it opened, someone cried out, "What have you done to her?" It was Atay, and she wanted to wave at him, to tell him she was ok, that she understood why he hadn't helped her escape. Kate wanted to talk to him about the splendor of the Byzantine Empire, how the Frankish Crusaders had wrecked the city, stolen its wealth, and raped its women.

She had to tell something else to Atay. Something about a bug, a bug in the reliquaries. Kate wanted to talk to Atay about many things, but she could not and remained dazed and flaccid as the two men placed her in a vehicle and fastened her seat belt. She heard car doors slam.

"Drive," said Bunin. "Take us near the U.S. Embassy in Istanbul, but not within view of their cameras."

Georgetown

CHAPTER 69

ACCORDING TO THE radio news, Sadat's three hired men had turned themselves into the police. The announcer solemnly stated that a fourth man "is being sought as a person of interest." Imran Sadat swung the SUV on to the shoulder of Highway 17 and slammed the brakes. Pounding the wheel, he glanced over at the reliquary tucked inside a leather bag, sitting on the passenger seat of his car, and wondered why in hell Bunin wanted this object.

That Bunin was willing to pay him a hundred grand for what he had thought would be a morning's work had dulled his normal caution. Bunin had not told him the reliquary would be guarded, and had made the deed sound like an easy art theft, an act Sadat had certainly participated in before. The explosions hadn't been intended to hurt anybody, just provide distractions.

He had roared off two seconds before the bomb exploded, managing his exit from the city before the roads had been closed. Not until he was well on his way north on Hwy 17, did he learn from the radio that two tourists and a horse were killed by the dynamite planted at the hospital. Why had his henchmen turned themselves in? They'd be charged with murder for sure, and the prosecutor might ask for the death penalty.

Sadat let off a string of curses. He should have eliminated the men as soon as they retrieved the reliquary, just as he had eliminated Adam Chalk, even though the ramming of Chalk had been an act of rage. He hadn't intended to kill the man, just scare him. Eventually all three would remember the phone call. The Nicaraguans, Panamanians, or whatever nationality they were, would tell the police about the call Imran received while all of them were in the bar.

Why had he answered the call? Thank God he had used a disposable phone, which would slow his identification down for a little while, but eventually the FBI would trace every call made to any phone near the strip club, and would identify Sergei's phone number. The Interpol man would be the link the FBI was looking for, and Sergei would be arrested soon, if he weren't in custody already.

Months ago, Sadat had warned Anton about involving the Interpol agent. He'd been sitting in his Isle of Palms house, leisurely reviewing pictures of items recently unearthed by ISIS in Syria, identifying which buyers would want which objects. Selling these types of artifacts was becoming more difficult, but Sadat's network of museum buyers and wealthy individuals was deep enough that all of the items would eventually find homes. His phone rang.

"Hello, Imran, Bunin here," Anton had said.

"What can I do for you, Anton?"

"I've arranged for another source, someone I think can be very useful to us. He is with Interpol."

For a moment, Sadat had been so shocked, he hadn't replied.

"Have I lost you?"

Sadat had sputtered, "Anton, are you out of your mind? Why would you work with a source there?"

"I have another project. For this one, I am still looking for religious objects, like reliquaries."

"Anton, I thought we agreed that selling items from churches was off limits. 'Stick to the Muslim world,' you said. 'Nobody gives a shit about them.'"

"This is a special project. We will not need buyers. I want the reliquaries for myself."

Imran sneered, "Getting religious?"

"Never mind, Sadat. This man—his name is Sergei Molotov—is working to identify reliquaries that might be available. Did you know that the Vatican does not actually know how many reliquaries they have around the world? Some of them can be obtained for very little effort, at least according to Sergei. Apparently, the Vatican is quite free with information when they are dealing with Interpol. It will be easier for you to meet him than for me to do so. I am on the 'no fly' list." Bunin laughed.

Reluctantly, Sadat had corresponded with Sergei via an Alternative Auctions email account hosted on a Russian server controlled by one of Bunin's companies. The one lead Sergei had passed on about a reliquary in Argentina was worthless, and Sadat had written him off his list of profitable relationships.

Sergei, realizing the low opinion that Sadat had of him, had called Bunin directly to tell him about a reliquary possibly located in Charleston. Bunin called Sadat, presenting the opportunity as a quick way for Sadat to make some money. All he had to do was create a diversion, and steal a reliquary from a hospital. Bunin had asked, "You have people for that, right?" Sadat did. Bunin had given Sadat only three hours to make this event happen, so Sadat called men he had worked with before—men who would not ask questions—and asked them to meet him at a strip club in North Charleston.

Sadat had shown his henchmen a picture of the reliquary that Bunin had texted him. While they were all standing in the strip

bar, the morning's featured attraction, Trixie, walked unsteadily
to the pole in the middle of the bar. When one of the men saw
the image of the reliquary, he had actually crossed himself
before leering at Trixie, who was taking off her sequined bra.
All three men had surreptitiously stared at the stripper while
Sadat gave instructions about planting a small explosion at the
Huguenot Church to go off first, instructions that clearly had
not registered with the men.

Sadat pulled back onto Hwy 17 and glanced at the GPS. He
had no other choice. He'd continue to Myrtle Beach, where
Anton had instructed him to leave the reliquary in a prepaid
box at a UPS Store. Bunin would arrange for him to get out
of the country. The beach town was filled with enterprising
criminals who could create new identification for him.

There was little traffic going north, but he decided he'd divert
left to a side road into Francis Marion Forest and listen to the
radio for any stories that a manhunt was underway before
continuing to Myrtle Beach. He cursed at Anton Bunin as he
drove slowly over the bumpy road into the forest, the branches
and leaves scraping against his car.

At that moment, Sadat heard the whirling sounds of a
helicopter. He pulled the vehicle under a tree, wondering
if he'd been quick enough to avoid being seen. There was no
pretending that the FBI and police would not know who they
were looking for. Why had he used his own car?

He got out of the driver's seat and sat on the ground, looking
up at the sky through the leaves of the live oak. Sadat made a
sound, a cross between a laugh and a scream and remembered
what Samuel had told him.

"You are not a criminal, brother; you are just greedy. Be very
careful or your greed will pull you to the other side. I will not
be able to help you."

Sadat thought that he definitely was on the other side now.

CHAPTER 70

THOMPSON STRODE BACK to the Bed and Breakfast, his head down. Sergei was the leak. He mentally reviewed every conversation, email, and document that he had sent his boss. As he approached the old house, Jack ran down the stairs and grabbed Thompson in a bear hug. "Kate's safe. They found her."

Thompson stepped back. "What? Who found her? How?" *Had the FBI decided to go to Istanbul anyway?* Following Jack up the stairs into the B&B, he watched Sara run to her father, the two of them holding each other. Amarintha and Ava sat on the stairs to the second floor, beaming as well.

Fannie walked into the hall with a tray of coffee and sandwiches, followed by Richard, who was carrying a pitcher of tea. "Let's go into the parlor," Richard said.

The group followed her into a small room with comfortable chairs around a tea table. Fannie put the tray down and sat, as did the others.

"So what happened?" asked Thompson.

Jack rubbed his head. "Detective Edson called me. The embassy in Istanbul found her on the front lawn this morning. Two employees took her to an Istanbul hospital." Jack looked off. "A woman from the embassy is at the hospital, and she will call us when Kate can talk. Thank God, she had some identification on her. She's not physically hurt—just drugged. Sara and I are going back to Charleston as soon as the FBI opens the airport to take a flight to New York and then on to Istanbul."

Thompson leaned over the table. "Let me talk to Detective Edson, and to Brook Reynolds. Someone should go with you."

"Reynolds?" said Jack, frowning. "She tried to arrest me earlier today when I went near the scene at MUSC. She seems to think I'm involved in the bombing. I don't understand it."

Thompson looked down at his hands and then said, "Jack, your wife's kidnapping is connected to the bombing. All three of you need some protection."

Jack stood up suddenly, and Thompson couldn't tell whether he was angry or scared. "Why? Why would Kate need protection now that they've let her go?"

Thompson gazed around the little room at the six people looking at him, waiting for him to answer. Jack sat down and took his daughter's hand.

"Adam Chalk, the dean in Kate's department, persuaded her to go to Istanbul. He was involved with a group called Authentic Auctions that paid academics to provide phony provenances. I was working with the FBI to close it down. As part of my job, I had to investigate Kate, and I cleared her." Thompson looked at Jack. "CPD told me that Kate's disappearance was domestic, so I had no need to look into her absence any further."

Jack's jaw clenched, but he said nothing.

"No one, including me, thought Kate was involved in this ring. Then we got the tip from Interpol. The tip said she was being held by a man named Anton Bunin, the individual who runs Authentic Auctions."

Thompson went on, "At that point, the FBI received information—and I can't tell you how, so don't ask—that Bunin was likely looking for biological material they could use in a weapon."

He waited for questions, but his audience was silent and still. He said, "A reliquary missing from a French convent was thought to have been contaminated with a strain of anthrax, and the FBI traced the reliquary to Charleston."

"Charleston?" Sara said. "How did it get here?"

Thompson gave her a half smile. "If you can believe it, the reliquary was stolen in France by a Huguenot girl in 1685, and brought here then. The thief was an ancestor of Amarintha's."

Before he could go on, Fannie said, "Thirty years ago, my husband worked for the Army in Charleston doing research on bacteria. He wasn't supposed to talk about it, but he did. His team was asked to investigate how long certain bacteria could live. They looked at old bottles, frozen bodies from the Arctic— that type of thing. Somehow he found that reliquary, I don't know how, and he buried it on that lot."

Jack said, "The rest of you already knew this?" He looked at Fannie, Amarintha and Richard. All of them nodded.

Thompson said, "Jack, until we talk to Kate, we won't be able to fill in all the blanks, but it seems likely that Kate was being used by Bunin to identify reliquaries that might be old enough, and might never have been opened, so they could steal them and look for old microbes. Until the FBI finishes their investigation, I think Kate could still be at risk."

"But they let her go," Jack said. "It was this same ring that stole the box from the hospital and who set the bombs, right? They have the reliquary. Why would Kate still be in danger?"

"Three men have turned themselves in, but I still think you and Sara need protection."

Fannie held up a hand. "Amarintha needs protection too. She is the only person we know of that has touched what's inside that reliquary. She touched it and was cured of her cancer."

Sara cried, "Ms. Sims, you're cured?" She looked over at Ava, who sat smiling.

"We don't know that for sure," said Amarintha, who had been sitting in a chair listening. "I need to be tested."

"Look at her, Jack." Fannie said, "She's cured, and whatever was in that reliquary was responsible."

Jack looked from Thompson to Amarintha to Fannie. "I suppose if Bunin knew Amarintha may have been cured by what's in that reliquary, he'd want her too, wouldn't he?"

Amarintha scoffed. "Come on, the facts of the story are already complicated enough. Why add this kind of supposition on top?"

Thompson ignored Amarintha. "Yes, I believe he would," said Thompson. "What is in there can apparently cause disease as well as cure it. It's happened before. The emissary the Vatican sent to Charleston had a document that described the theft of the reliquary and the escape of the Huguenot woman, Marin Postel. I read it. Marin Postel used the contents of the reliquary to heal children at the convent. They had the plague. She escaped with the reliquary and somehow made it to Charleston."

Sara put her head on her father's chest. Jack didn't say anything, but he kissed the top of her head and said, "Don't worry, kid. Your mom is safe at the embassy in Istanbul, and if we need to take a long vacation while the FBI works this out, we will."

Thompson did not want to be the person who burst Jack's happy reunion scenario. Once Kate was retrieved, she would be questioned for days if she were physically able to withstand interrogation. If she arrived in Charleston unable to be interviewed, dark-suited agents would wait patiently in the hospital for her to recover. Jack would not be taking her on a vacation anytime soon.

Fannie said, "It seems strange that the Vatican actually sent someone here to take possession of the reliquary. Do you think they know it might have caused cures?"

"I asked Monsignor Ogier that very question, Fannie," said Thompson, "and he dodged it quite nicely. The Vatican wanted Amarintha in quarantine. The monsignor also wanted to question her himself. That was the other reason we left Charleston. Having the U.S. Government and the Vatican both want you in custody cannot be a good thing."

Thompson's phone rang. "I'll be right back." He walked outside. "Thompson here."

"It's Frank. I guess you heard about Kate Strong from Jack?"

"I did. He and his daughter are prepared to fly to New York, and onto Istanbul."

"Someone from the State Department is going to call him. They already have her on one of their jets. She'll arrive in Charleston around 10:00 p.m." The detective paused. "We also have identified Imran Sadat as the fourth man, the one who paid our perpetrators. The Hispanic men identified him from a photograph. There's an all-points bulletin out on him, but we haven't notified the public yet. We're hoping that with all the cameras on the roads around here, we can find the man. Cameras near the hospital got a clear look at his vehicle—he was in his personal car if you can believe it."

Thompson said, "Sadat was never anything but a white collar, hands-off criminal. I doubt he knew anything about how to do this kind of job. The money must have been phenomenal for him to take such a risk. I assume we'll start seeing his face on television."

"Not yet. We want to try to apprehend him first. Are you ready to come back to Charleston, Agent Denton?"

Thompson didn't know what to say or think. Was he exaggerating the potential danger Amarintha might be in? Finally, he said, "I assume the monsignor is still in Charleston?"

"Funny you should mention him. The technicians had already taken samples from the reliquary before it was taken. Everything was negative. No anthrax found. Even when I told Monsignor Ogier the results, he still insisted that that Amarintha Sims be put into quarantine until he can speak with her. It's very strange."

Thompson said, "And that computer program, the one that predicted a thirty percent chance that Bunin was seeking a biological weapon? What's going on with that?"

Frank snorted. "I don't know. Having an actual crime to investigate kind of negated the discussion around a theoretical one. When Dr. Umstead learned that the reliquary isn't contaminated, he and his team packed up and left. I'm not sure the Task Force has any reason to meet. Of course, the debriefing of Kate Strong might bring up some new information."

Frank stopped. "Agent Reynolds is asking for you to participate in the interview with Strong. You up for that?"

"Yes. But—",

Frank interrupted, "Gotta go, Brook Reynolds is calling me."

CHAPTER 71

F RANK SAT BEHIND the FBI pilot, Brook Reynolds beside
him. The helicopter noise was deafening. Although he
knew he didn't have to yell because of the microphone
built into his headset, he did anyway. "Do Major Munez' people
have a visual on Sadat yet?"

"Not yet," said Brook. "A county cop saw a car matching
Sadat's pull into Francis Marion Forest, but they haven't
pursued him on foot yet. Too many places inside those woods
for an ambush. They're waiting for more resources. You can be
sure Sadat is going to leave the vehicle when he hears this bird,
unless he's ready to turn himself in."

"I'm guessing the FBI will want to take over and charge
him in federal court?" Frank raised his eyebrows at Brook,
reinforcing the question.

"Let's just catch the guy first."

A young female FBI agent in the front beside the pilot scanned
the woods below them with her high-powered binoculars. She
leaned over to the pilot and said something Frank couldn't hear,
and then pointed.

"We've got him!" yelled Brook.

Voices bombarded his ears, and the helicopter began to
hover. Frank leaned over and saw a man trying to run through
a swamp, holding something, looking up at the helicopter.

"We can't land here." Frank could hear the pilot clearly, obviously responding to a question from Brook.

Brook took off her headset and scanned the ground below, clearly frustrated. She leaned over the pilot's shoulder and yelled, "Take us back to Hwy 17 where Major Munez is." She didn't put the headset back on.

A landing zone had been set up for the helicopter in a cleared area next to the highway. SC Highway Patrol and Awendaw Police were diverting traffic away from the intersection where Sadat's car had been found. Brook and Frank left the helicopter and ran over to a large black SUV, where Major Munez of SLED stood with a map spread out on the tailgate.

The major waited until the two of them got close. "Here we are." He pointed to a spot on the map. "I've got people stationed throughout the forest and along the road. We've got a few hours of daylight, and are tightening the circle."

"How do you know he hasn't slipped by your people?" asked Frank.

The major looked up. "Once we got the word he'd pulled off Hwy 17, I started moving people into position. This area is nothing but swamp. Trust me; he will not have been able to get more than a few hundred yards in any direction. He'll be begging us to save him."

Frank snorted.

"Detective Edson, this swamp is full of alligators. Between gators, snakes, mosquitoes and ticks, I promise you, he'll be ready to come along peacefully."

At that moment, a SLED agent with a bullhorn began to yell. "Imran Sadat, you are surrounded. Give yourself up."

The agent began walking slowly into the swamp from the road, yelling the same statement every minute or so.

"Now we wait," said the major.

Frank spent the next thirty minutes pacing the road,

periodically updating the chief of police back in Charleston about their progress. From time to time, he could hear muffled voices communicating on the handheld radios. Brook Reynolds sat in the major's SUV, leaving it only when a late model car pulled up. An FBI agent got out and handed Brook a pair of boots.

There was a shout from one of the SLED agents.

"We think we got him," yelled the major, dashing into the deep underbrush and disappearing almost immediately. After a beat, Frank followed him.

Within a minute, the noise from the road had almost completely disappeared. A new cacophony of sounds was heard from the creatures the police had disturbed. A blue jay cawed and dived towards Frank's head. The mosquitoes began to dig inside of Frank's collar and he slapped them, knowing it was ineffectual. Someone behind him said, "Here use this," and an Awendaw deputy tossed him a can of insect repellent as he shouldered past Frank in rubber knee boots.

Frank leaned against a tree and sprayed himself until the can began to rattle. He looked up and realized he couldn't see anyone else. He stopped, listening. Nothing. He looked down at his black rubber-soled shoes, likely ruined in the sticky mud the swamp had in abundance. Damn. In front of him was a stagnant pond about thirty feet across, a small path to the side showing the likely direction the deputy had gone.

Should he turn back? No way. Frank pushed ten feet further into the black and green maze, and passed a six-foot tall palmetto tree, its fronds thick at the ground. He batted one of the fronds aside and froze, a face on the ground looking up at him. The face was Imran Sadat's and the man was holding a gun.

CHAPTER 72

THOMPSON WALKED BACK into the B&B and found the proprietor setting the table in the long dining room. Thompson nodded at her and then went back into the parlor on the other side of the wide entrance hall. Amarintha, Fannie, and Ava were still there, Fannie asleep on the small couch and Amarintha and her daughter talking in low whispers. His phone pinged.

Thompson pulled his phone out of his pocket and checked his text messages. There was one, from his mother, and it had an attachment. He stood at the door of the parlor and held up his phone to look at the picture in the afternoon light. It was his mother, about sixteen years old. She was smiling, her widow's peak and dimpled chin clearly visible. She was dressed in clothes from the sixties, with straight hair and white knee-high boots, but other than the clothing, she was Ava's twin. He looked back at Ava, who was now gazing at him from the chair she was sitting on.

"What's up, Agent Denton?" she asked. "You look like you saw a ghost." Ava smiled, and he felt as if the picture on his phone had leapt from the electronic to the physical world.

Thompson dropped his phone into his breast pocket. His heart pounded, and his voice squawked when he said, "Amarintha, can you come outside? I need to talk to you."

"Sure, but if you tell me again I'm in danger, I'm going to steal Richard's boat and leave." Amarintha grinned at him as she walked past him outside to the porch.

He followed. "Let's go to the garden."

She nimbly jumped down the stairs. They walked down the winding path towards the garden, where dozens of camellias had been planted over the life of the house. Many were still in bloom. Each one had a metal marker in the ground indicating its botanical name and planting date. Some of the bushes were as large as trees, and the shiny green leaves reflected the setting sun. Thompson could hear crickets and frogs in the nearby marshes beginning their evening serenades. He and Amarintha walked side by side through the green maze of flowering bushes, with every color and form of flower on display. When Thompson finally spied a bench, he motioned to it and said, "Sit down, I've got something to ask you."

Amarintha sat and looked up at him. Her hair and eyebrows were still sparse, but the glow of health was unmistakable, and her face had a more relaxed form, the sharp angles softened somehow by the knowledge that she might be beating her cancer.

"Did you use a sperm donor to conceive Ava?" Thompson said abruptly, staring into her eyes.

She was speechless, her mouth working. Not breaking his gaze, she finally said, "That's none of your damn business. Why would you even ask that?"

Thompson sat down next to her and said again, "Did you use a donor to conceive Ava?"

Amarintha sprang up. "You have no right to ask me such a personal question." She wasn't angry, he realized, just astonished, and a little hurt.

When she turned to go back towards the house, Thompson jumped up and said, "Look at this before you go, please."

He fiddled with his phone, and then handed it to her. Amarintha put her face close to the screen, stared, looked back at Thompson, and brought her other hand to her mouth. "Who is this?" she whispered.

Thompson put both of his hands on her shoulders, waiting until she lifted her face from the phone. "It's my mother," he said.

Amarintha shrugged off his hands and sat back down, still staring at his phone. She looked down at the path. "It's not possible."

Thompson picked a camellia blossom and brought it to his nose. He could not look at her. "It is possible. Ava looks like my mother's twin."

Thompson waited for Amarintha to work it out in her head. "How did your sperm get to Charleston?" she finally asked.

"I was in college. Got mugged, and my buddy and I had to make a donation to get gas money to get back to Raleigh." He looked at her. "Good thing you got me. My buddy grew up to be fat and stupid."

"Well," she said. "I should tell you that I spent a good bit of time reading the descriptions of the donors before settling on you. As I recall, you described yourself as a medium height, dark-haired man of French descent with dark brown eyes, high IQ, physically healthy, and kind. The word "kind" sold me. No other donor used that word."

"But why, Amarintha? Why would a young woman choose to get pregnant from a sperm donor, what were you—twenty-two years old?"

Amarintha was running her finger over the picture of his mother. "I was told when I was ten years old that I might have the gene for early onset Alzheimer's. You know what that is?"

"Jesus, of course I do. Why would anyone tell a ten-year-old that?"

"My father was part of one of the early research studies that identified this form of the disease as inheritable. He would have died from it. Even now, I'm not sure the wreck that killed him was really an accident. He told me I would die young of very severe neurological symptoms."

Severe neurological symptoms, thought Thompson. That certainly summed it up.

"He told me that when I got to be twenty, I should have a baby with someone who likely didn't carry the gene, enjoy being a young mother, the hell with the rest. So I did."

Amarintha rubbed tears from her checks. "Turns out I didn't have the gene. I found that out about five years ago. Can you believe that? All these years I avoided having any relationships. I didn't want anyone to watch me die from such a horrible disease. Guess I'm a lot like my father. There you have it—the reason I marched off and found a donor."

Thompson looked down at Amarintha, and touched her face. She looked up.

She looked down at the phone. "Do you have a picture of her as an adult? Is she healthy, is she, well, sane?"

Thompson laughed. "My mother is the healthiest person I know. She's a teacher, in a French elementary school, almost retired. Very sane, very well balanced. Always bugging me to get married and produce a grandchild."

He looked away. "When I saw Ava this morning for the first time, I just, I just . . ." he stopped, not able to finish the sentence.

"You felt like all new parents feel when they first meet their newborns—only for you, it must have been even more shocking given that your newborn is over five feet tall." She grinned at him, and Thompson felt a rush of feeling roll over him like a gentle wave. Did this woman deal with everything with such equanimity?

She laughed at the expression on his face and came to him, hugging him gently.

"Thompson," she murmured into his shoulder, "I've had twenty years to imagine meeting Ava's biological father. I'm relieved you're so normal. Let me enjoy it before we figure out what to do."

CHAPTER 73

"**I**F YOU YELL, I'll shoot you," said Imran Sadat, as he stood, his eyes never leaving the detective's face. Sadat's light tan face was covered in angry red mosquito bites. His leather loafers were almost unrecognizable, covered with mud, and his white cotton shirt was bloody and filthy. There was a tear at both knees of his pants, and Frank noticed the Sadat only had one sock on, although it looked like a rag. A dirty leather bag lay at his feet.

Frank didn't move, even when what felt like a bird-sized mosquito dug into his back trying to find a repellent-free spot of skin. "I'm Detective Frank Edson of the Charleston Police. You can't get out of here. You're literally surrounded by cops."

Sadat didn't speak for a moment, and then he asked, "How many are out there?"

The men were standing at the edge of the black water swampy pond. The fan-like leaves of the palmetto trees looked like green umbrellas lined up next to the water. The mass was thick enough so that unless someone passed immediately beside them, as the Awendaw deputy had, the two of them would be invisible. He could hear the blue jay, and high-pitched whining he knew was the mosquito army preparing to attack.

"Can I swat the giant mosquito on my back that's sucking me

dry?" If Sadat allowed him to move his hand, he could reach his gun.

"No. Put your gun, your cuffs, and your radio on the ground. Then I want your hands on your head."

Frank complied. Sadat kicked the detective's gun into the impenetrable underbrush.

"Tell me how many officers are out there, and exactly where they are."

The detective took a fractional step backwards, and spoke louder. Somebody would hear it.

"Come on, Sadat. You must have heard on the radio your guys confessed. Walked right into the police station. Surrender, end it."

"You raise your voice again, Detective, and I'll shoot you." Sadat motioned with his gun. "We're going to walk out of here. Now turn around and get back to the road. I'll be right behind you with my gun in your back."

Sadat squinted at him, and at that moment, a monster mosquito, the size of a quarter, alighted on the hand holding the gun. It was a gallinipper, and Frank knew when the bug bit, it would feel like a knife had stabbed Sadat's hand.

Frank mumbled under his breath, "Come on, come on, bite him, bite him."

Sadat let out a yell and dropped his weapon.

Frank dove to the ground, grabbed the gun, and pointed it at Sadat. He sprang up, kicking his feet sideways into the deep brush to locate his own weapon. No luck. Sadat turned and dove into the pond.

"You can't escape this, Sadat," yelled Frank.

The detective waded knee deep into the water, and stopped dead when he saw a ripple on the black surface. An atavistic shudder ran through his entire body. Reptilian eyes blinked. He screamed. "Get out of the water."

Sadat rose from the water, sputtering, green plants stuck to his head.

Frank released the safety on the Beretta, braced his right hand with his left and fired the unfamiliar weapon three times—*pop pop pop.* Sadat stopped, the sour-smelling pond water streaming from his face, and put his hands up, yelling, "I surrender. Stop shooting."

The detective was frantic now, trying to move closer, his feet making sucking sounds as he tried to run through the quicksand-like mud at the bottom of the pond. He pulled the trigger again. The gun clicked. It was out of bullets.

"I'm not shooting at you. Get out of the water!" The detective threw himself backwards out of the stinking pond and clawed his way back to where Sadat had kicked his police-issued Glock. He began frantically beating the brush. He glanced back at the pond. "Goddamn it, Sadat, get out of the water! It's a gator!"

Sadat turned and opened his mouth.

For the rest of his life, Frank would remember the primordial scream that poured out of Sadat's open mouth, a high-pitched unnatural sound, a scream that was abruptly ended by the gargantuan alligator leaping five feet out of the water with its monstrous jaws open. Its mouth slammed shut on Sadat's throat. A spray of blood jetted six feet, spraying Frank's face with the contents of Sadat's jugular vein. Man and alligator disappeared under the water, an immense splash of the five-foot tail the last sight anyone would have of either one.

Frank leaned over and vomited. He wiped his mouth, rubbed Sadat's blood off his face with his sleeve, and crawled over to where his handcuffs and mike lay.

"Detective Frank Edson here. Those gunshots were mine. I found Sadat."

CHAPTER 74

T HOMPSON AND AMARINTHA were still standing close together when his phone rang. It was Frank. Imran Sadat was dead. The reliquary had been found and would be returned to the monsignor. Kate Strong was on her way home, and Frank would be there in a few hours to pick them up.

The detective sounded weary, and his voice was hoarse. Thompson knew better than to ask any questions; the story of how Imran Sadat came to be dead would have to wait.

Getting through dinner without smiling too much was difficult. Jack and Sara were clearly elated, barely able to eat as they waited for Detective Edson to retrieve them and take them to Charleston. Thompson felt an unfamiliar sense of belonging when he looked at Amarintha and Ava sitting opposite him. Fannie and Richard were at the end of the table discussing whether living in Charleston was better or worse than thirty years before, and for the first time, Thompson heard Fannie laugh.

The reliquary was found; Amarintha knew he was Ava's father, and Kate Strong was safe. He ignored the fact that not everything had been neatly wrapped up; that law enforcement still didn't know what Bunin was up to, and that the story of the reliquary was not yet complete.

An hour after dinner, Thompson went to the porch and

waited. Frank finally pulled into the driveway and got out of the police car.

The detective had mud stains on his uniform, and festering bug bites were visible on his forehead. Thompson said, "What happened to you?"

Frank gave Thompson the brief, but gory details of Sadat's death.

"What a horrible way to die," said Thompson.

Their conversation was interrupted by Jack and Sara running down the stairs. "I'll tell you more later. I need to get back to Charleston, as you can see."

Jack walked up to the detective and grasped his arm, shaking his hand. "When does the plane land?"

Frank looked at his watch. "Around ten. Kate will be taken to Trident Hospital in North Charleston." Jack and Sara climbed into the car.

The detective turned to Thompson. "I'd suggest the rest of you stay here tonight. Richard can take the Sims family home on the boat tomorrow, and I'll send a car for you, Thompson, around 6:00 a.m. Everything's almost back to normal downtown, but we still have a good bit of work to do." Frank looked pointedly at Thompson, likely referring to the prep work the team would need to do before questioning Kate Strong.

The detective got back into the car, waved, and drove off.

Thompson sat down in one of the porch rockers. He had an endless list of questions that perplexed him. Why had the Russian let Kate go? What had she been doing for four weeks? He thought he was alone but then heard the creak of a rocker nearby. It was Fannie.

She said, "So I heard on CNN that they've caught the men who did the bombing and found the reliquary. The news is calling it a 'religious object' of some value, mainly because of the red diamond on top of it, and saying that's the motive for the bombing." Fannie scoffed. "I guess we'll never hear about it again now that the Vatican is going to get it back."

Thompson didn't reply.

"Amarintha and Ava are still watching the news in the parlor. I think Richard went to bed."

Both rockers moved, emitting soothing, creaking sounds.

"Thompson, I can tell you care for my daughter." Fannie raised a hand to keep him from replying. "She's one of a kind. Never had a boyfriend. Ever. Her father scared the tar out of her when she was just ten years old telling her she'd die early. I was so mad that he told her about the Alzheimer's, I could hardly look at him. We lived with that ax over our heads for many years, until Amarintha decided to be tested again. She didn't have the gene. Neither does Ava."

Thompson wondered what he was supposed to say and still said nothing.

"I just want to tell you how special she is," Fannie said. "I believe she's cured of her cancer; yes, I do. And if she is, well, now might be the time for the right man to come along."

Before Thompson could utter a word, she said, "Good night," and moved inside. He heard her climb the stairs, her footsteps slow but steady.

Thompson sat on the porch another hour, thinking first of what questions he wanted to ask Kate Strong, and then, as his professional hat began to slip, of questions he wanted to ask Amarintha. Had she ever told Ava her father was a sperm donor? Would she want to tell Ava that he was the donor? Either way, he'd be ok. She'd probably want him to do a DNA test just to make sure. He laughed softly as he realized that he'd essentially do anything Amarintha asked him to do.

When the entire mansion was quiet, he went to his first floor room and took a long shower. Had it actually only been twelve or so hours since the explosion? Thompson flopped into the antique four-poster bed, not noticing the intricate carvings of rice plants on the posts, and instantly fell asleep.

Sometime later, he felt a touch on his shoulder and bolted up. "It's ok," said Amarintha, sitting on the bed. "It's only me." Moonlight spilled into the room, and he could see light reflecting from her body, which he realized, was naked. A robe lay on the foot of the bed.

As she pulled back the covers of his bed and climbed in, she said, "I thought we might practice making babies in the more traditional way." Then she kissed him.

Charleston

CHAPTER 75

SITTING IN TRIDENT Hospital's waiting room, Jack fidgeted. Sara, just as restless, bounced her legs against the chair. Trident Hospital was just outside the area still cordoned off by law enforcement, and still it had taken Detective Edson almost three hours to reach the hospital from the B&B in Georgetown, a trip that should have taken half that time.

Agent Reynolds, now sitting on the other side of the waiting room, talking on her phone, had warned him when they arrived that his reunion with Kate would be short. "We have to debrief her, Mr. Strong. You may speak with her, but only for a moment, and you will not be in her room while we conduct the interview."

He had opened his mouth to protest, but Sara had put her hand on his arm and squeezed. "Daddy, it's ok. The sooner the FBI speaks to her, the sooner we can take her home."

Now they were just waiting. Brook Reynolds stood up, put her phone in her pocket, and walked over. "Kate will be here soon." Jack rubbed his mouth and took his daughter's hand.

They both stared at the doors of the ambulance bay, willing them to bang open. Five minutes later, the doors did just that, and Kate whisked by on a stretcher, along with an IV pole held by a paramedic. Jack got a glimpse of his wife's face—thin and pale, her eyes closed. Double doors down the hall marked "Restricted" banged shut behind the stretcher. Sara clutched him as he stared at the doors.

"The doctor on board the flight said she would be ok," said Agent Reynolds behind them.

Jack wiped his face. "Are they sure?"

"You may as well sit down," Brook said. "No one can see her until they get her settled in a room and examined."

Jack returned to the waiting room, Sara trailing him. Agent Reynolds went back on her phone. After thirty minutes, a doctor came into the waiting room. "Agent Reynolds?" he said to Brook.

"Yes."

"Is this the family?" the doctor said, gesturing to Jack and Sara.

"Yes. May they see her?"

The doctor motioned Jack and Sara to join him in a small room. Brook followed, not giving Jack a chance to exclude her.

"Sit down, please," said the doctor. Jack and Sara pulled chairs close to each other and leaned over the small table. Agent Reynolds sat in another chair behind them.

"I'm Dr. Rushing. I've done a preliminary examination of your wife. We have blood samples being tested, but I'm almost certain that your wife was given some type of hallucinogen fifteen or so hours ago. She is in and out of consciousness. Her vitals are decent, but she is malnourished and has numerous marks on her arms. We have her medical records, and I've had a chance to read her history." He paused.

"I'm assuming that she has not had a dose of lithium for some time. Has she marked her arms before?"

Jack nodded. Sara made a cry and put her hands over her face.

Dr. Rushing looked at Brook. "I understand the importance of the FBI speaking to her, but until we know what she was drugged with, I'm limited as to what treatment I can give. The tests will take another two hours or so."

"I understand, Dr. Rushing," said Brook. "I need to put one of my agents in the room until we can question her."

"Wait a minute," said Jack.

"Mr. Strong, you and Sara can be in the room, but my agent will be there also."

The doctor stood up. "We have her in a private room upstairs. All of you can fit. Room 512."

He left the three of them in the small room. Jack said, "Agent Reynolds, is it really necessary that your agent be in the room? Surely you can wait a few days before you question Kate."

Brook looked at him without speaking. "Sara, get us some drinks, honey," said Jack. Sara scampered out the door, closing it behind him.

"You people never did tell me the whole story, did you?" Jack moved his finger along the cracks in the small wood table. "I knew that two days ago when I met you. You don't think I had anything to do with the bombing anymore, do you?"

"Mr. Strong, I apologize. No, I don't believe you were involved in the bombing, and yes, I did withhold information. Your wife was not kept to do appraisals. She was kept because her kidnapper was likely looking for biological material to make into a weapon."

Jack whipped his head up, a smartass reply on his lips. Brook Reynolds gazed back at him and nodded. "My God. Why would

Kate know anything about that kind of thing? She's a religious scholar, for God's sake."

"That's what we need to find out. I've asked Thompson Denton to participate in the debriefing of your wife—whenever we can carry that out. Do you have any objections to that?"

Jack snorted. "What if I did? Would it matter?" He sighed. "No, better Thompson than people I don't know. Who else will be involved?"

"We will have someone recording the conversation, myself, Agent Denton, and Detective Edson. You and Sara cannot be present. There may also be things that your wife tells *us* that she cannot tell *you*. Please do not put pressure on her to share information with you."

Sara came back in with drinks and crackers and sat down at the table without speaking.

Agent Reynolds stood up and held out her hand. "See you upstairs. I sincerely hope your wife makes a quick recovery."

CHAPTER 76

KATE OPENED HER eyes. Seeing a whiteboard, for a long moment she thought she was in the workroom at the castle, but the writing on the whiteboard was not hers. The writing said something about a nurse and "call, don't fall." She saw the word "Trident" on the board and turned her head towards a window where the light from a street light illuminated a lump on a chair. Someone dressed in white stood by her bed. For a moment, she couldn't focus on anything. She pushed herself up off the bed and croaked, "Where am I?"

She saw movement by the window and said again, louder, "Help me."

Kate fell back on the bed and felt her left arm being held. The lump moved, and she saw Jack spring up from the chair and rush to the bed. A young woman in a suit also stood up, then left the room. *Jack was here?*

"Oh, Kate, oh Kate," he said, kissing her head, and holding her right hand.

"I'm so sorry," Kate cried. Another lump moved, and Sara rushed over. *Sara?*

"Mama, Mama."

"Sara, baby, I'm so sorry," Kate said again, as Sara crouched by her bed.

The three of them cried for some time before the nurse said, still holding her left arm, "You are at Trident Hospital in North Charleston. You've been here about five hours, since around ten last night."

"I'm not in Istanbul?"

"No, honey, you're home," said Jack.

"Oh, my God, you need to get the police here, Jack. Something terrible is going to happen."

CHAPTER 77

AMARINTHA AWOKE IN Thompson's bed. She turned on the light, sat up, and found a note on his pillow, written on the B&B's stationery.

I had to go to Charleston to speak with Kate Strong.

She picked up her phone and noted that it was just after 5:00 a.m. She had felt so safe that she hadn't even awakened when he left. Lying back down, she thought she should go back to her own room before Ava and Fannie got up. She almost laughed, thinking of their faces if they saw her come out of Thompson's room and decided to stay.

Why had her life suddenly turned from grim to glorious? What had she done to deserve it? *Wrong question,* she thought. Shit happened, and whether you deserved it or not had nothing to do with it. She couldn't deny that touching that reliquary had marked a point, a harbinger that announced an uptick in her cancer- centric life. And, finding out that Thompson was Ava's father? The odds of that had to be millions to one.

Years before, she had thought about trying to find out who her sperm donor was. Surreptitious searches on her home computer had slammed that door—donors were protected. Ava had been told when she was a teenager how she had come to be

born, and thought her mother brave for being willing to bear
and raise a child before succumbing to an awful degenerative
disease. Had she been brave?

   She rubbed her fingers and could not stop remembering the
feeling she had when she touched the contents of the artifact.
Thompson said it had been tested and found free of anthrax,
but somehow she had already known that—known that the box
and its contents were not dangerous to her. Why had her father
buried it? How had he gotten it?

   Amarintha lay in bed and allowed images to come into her
head, images she'd been thrusting away as impossible. She,
living in the new house on Church Street. A man, faceless in
earlier musings, but now clearly Thompson, working beside her
in a garden, planting ferns. Ava visiting often, eventually with
grandchildren. Could all this now be possible?

   Who could tell her more about the reliquary? The only
person who had any knowledge of its history was Monsignor
Ogier. Would he speak to her? Just before she drifted back to
sleep, she decided to call him when Richard took them back to
Charleston.

CHAPTER 78

"I T'S OK, HONEY," Kate said to Sara. "I need to do this."
Sara let go of Kate's hand. "Ok, Mom. Dad and I
will be right outside." The two of them left the hospital
room.

Kate was sitting in her hospital bed, still attached to an IV
line. She felt jittery and lethargic at the same time, and willed
her thoughts to focus. The monitor beeped her heart rate and
occasionally the blood pressure cuff on her arm inflated and
deflated with a low whine. She watched two women arrange
some recording equipment, including a video camera.

Jack had initially responded to her insistence that he call the
police by asking her to take a sedative and sleep. She had refused,
telling him that she was afraid that if she waited any longer to
tell what she knew, she would forget what had happened over
the last four weeks. He had finally called a Detective Edson from
Charleston Police. That man, along with a man introduced to
Kate as Thompson Denton from Interpol now sat in chairs at
the foot of her bed. As soon as the detective arrived, she had
started talking, but he had asked her to stop, telling her that
they needed to wait for the FBI. It had taken over an hour for
these four to assemble here, and she felt words piling up inside
her mouth, like horses at the starting gate.

One of the women spoke, "Dr. Strong, I'm Brook Reynolds,

the FBI's Special Agent in Charge for South Carolina. Are you ready to begin?"

"I am. These people are trying to find germs to plant in the Middle East. You've got to stop them." The monitor beeped louder, and Kate fell back. "I'm just so upset. You have to do something."

Agent Reynolds said, "Tell us what happened, beginning with the day you disappeared."

Kate looked at her hands lying on the sheet. "Jack and I had a fight the night before, so when Dr. Atay told me about the new underground city, and how he needed someone to look at the parchments, I just, I just went." It sounded unbelievable to her now that she had gone to work one morning, prepared for a normal day, and had ended up in Istanbul that same night.

"Slow down a bit. Tell me the name of the person you and your boss met with that morning."

Kate told them how the meeting had begun, that there seemed to be urgency to the situation, and that the man from Istanbul had promised her she would be back before spring break. "I didn't think it through. Atay gave me a temporary cell phone. I went home and packed, and then met him and the pilot at the airport." The heart monitor registered an increase in her heart rate and she blurted, "Is it true? Is Adam dead?"

"Yes. We believe that a man named Imran Sadat killed him," said Detective Edson.

"Imran Sadat?" Kate cried. "He and his brother gave me a ride to the College that morning when my bike broke. He murdered Adam? Why?" Kate began to wail, and Jack rushed into the room.

"Can we stop this?" asked her husband.

"I'm all right," said Kate, blowing her nose. "I need to tell them everything."

Jack looked at Kate, nodded, and then left the room, closing the door very softly.

Reynolds prompted her, "Dr. Strong, right now we need to know what you were asked to do once you got to Istanbul."

Kate looked at the woman, who smiled in encouragement. She took a deep breath. "I was asked to look at photographs of parchment pages from a codex hundreds of years old. A codex is a collection of parchment bound like a book. Three of them were found in an underground city in eastern Turkey, in the desert. Everything in this city, not just the parchments, was in tunnels many feet underground, so they were preserved."

The Interpol agent asked, "Did you see the original documents?"

Thompson Denton was his name, she thought, and Jack had told her to trust him.

"No," said Kate. "Just photographs, but I'm certain they were authentic. The lab had everything you need to study photographs. I was expecting to be flown back to Charleston on the third day, and made a preliminary report to Dr. Kemal Atay of my findings that morning."

"Do you have any pictures, any notes from your work?" said the agent.

"No, I don't." She paused, and turned to Agent Reynolds. "Did anyone find Dr. Atay? His family was in danger, too."

"Dr. Atay went to Interpol. The local authorities have him and his family under protection," said the FBI woman. "Please tell us what you found in the documents."

Kate took a deep breath. "After the sack of Constantinople by Europeans in 1204, a Byzantine priest seeded twelve reliquaries with material from bodies. Blood, animal skins, that sort of thing. He sent them to France. Notes on these twelve were marked with the Greek name for false—pseudos—in the parchments. The story was in the palimpsest."

"Would you describe what that is, please."

"It's writing that was done on the parchment originally. A later scribe scraped the parchment, but with special equipment, you can read the original writing. That's what I did."

"You can do that from photographs?"

Kate squirmed. "Well, someone had found the original writing, but it was in code. I deciphered the code."

The Interpol agent murmured, "Incredible."

"And why were you asked to do the translations?" asked Brook Reynolds.

Kate sat up straighter. "This is my expertise, religious artifacts. I also am proficient in the Greek that the Byzantines used in the parchments." Kate unconsciously touched her forearms. "I found out later that Anton Bunin wanted someone who could disappear for a while, someone he could manipulate. He drugged me through the vents with something while I was there, to get me to work day and night." She looked up, a bleak look in her eyes. "And I did."

"The doctors here say you had amphetamines in your system and faint traces of a derivative of LSD," said the detective.

Kate wiped her eyes. "Zora Vulkov kept me from getting the full dose. She told me not to swallow the tea. I suppose that was right before they took me to the embassy. Has anyone found her? She helped me."

The FBI agent said, "The Istanbul authorities say that a plane registered to the New Institute that Anton Bunin runs left for Russia an hour after you were found. We presume that Dr. Vulkov was on board." Agent Reynolds waited and then said, "Let's get back to your findings. What happened at the end of the two days, when you expected to be returned to Charleston?"

"That's when I met Bunin. He told me that I was going to be kept in Istanbul until I identified the exact locations of the reliquaries that were seeded with these disease agents. Atay's people had done some work, but Bunin needed someone with my background to finish it. He chloroformed me then locked me in the castle's basement rooms. I refused to work, but then Atay showed me pictures of Jack and Sara. Atay said Bunin would hurt them if I didn't cooperate."

Kate put her hands over her face, remembering the desolation of her daughter's face in the photographs. "I did the work; I can't really tell you how. Honestly, I don't remember doing all of what I did, but I do know that I identified twelve reliquaries that had been contaminated. Zora Vulkov passed notes to me in lipstick tubes. She explained why Bunin wanted the reliquaries identified."

Kate looked at the FBI agent. "He is trying to create some kind of epidemic in the Middle East. Zora told me that the Russian government was paying Bunin to do this. Is that even possible?"

She saw the four people in her hospital room look at each other. Finally, the detective said, "The Middle East. Are you certain that Bunin wanted to target the Middle East and not somewhere in the United States?"

"That's what Zora told me."

The FBI lady said, "We need to take a break. Please stop the recording." Brook Reynolds motioned to the woman running the equipment to stay in the room, and walked out. The Charleston detective and the Interpol agent followed her.

Kate stared out the window of her hospital room, not certain she had done all she could to stop Anton Bunin.

CHAPTER 79

MONSIGNOR OGIER ROSE from his knees. He sat on his hotel bed and lifted the reliquary from its worn leather bag. An impeccably suited FBI agent had brought it to him an hour before, the young man asking for identification, and then handing him a form to sign. The exchange felt like picking up a prescription, and the monsignor had wanted to laugh at the agent and tell him the leather bag held the most wondrous prescription man had ever known.

It wasn't the most imposing artifact he had ever seen, a rather simple wooden box with a cloisonné figure of a man with long hair. The man had his arms out, hands outstretched. In one hand was an infant, in the other a red flower. If authentic, the red diamond in the middle of the flower was valued at ten million dollars, or so the bankers at the Vatican had told him. He was certain the conservators in Rome would discover that the stone was glass, the diamond long gone, broken apart so that the Huguenot thief could survive. Who could blame her? Marin Postel had been a young woman, what the world called now a teenager, forced to flee her country, everyone she loved dead or gone, her only option to come to Charles Towne.

He brought the reliquary to the small hotel room desk and reached into his briefcase for a leather binder with a lock on its front. Turning the pages, he came to a copy of a document written in 1690. The original was in the Vatican archives, but even in the copy, he could see remnants of the folds, tears, and ink marks that marked the old parchment. The document was a certification of a miracle that had happened at the Convent of Corbie in France in 1685. He had given the FBI a version of this original report—a document created in 1890.

The document answered the question the Interpol agent had asked him—did the Vatican believe the children had been cured? The monsignor had been careful not to lie to the man; in fact, he deeply desired to make the story of the reliquary public, if only to validate the life decisions he had made.

Monsignor Giuseppe Ogier had begun life as Joe, a black bastard brought up by his resentful maternal uncle. Joe's mother had gotten pregnant by a white boy, and the uncle had reluctantly taken the infant when the sister died—the placenta, Joe, and most of her blood blowing out of her like a rocket onto Huger Street. The uncle had hired a wet nurse, named the baby Joe, just Joe, not Joseph, no middle name either, and then thrust the kid onto the nuns at the Catholic school as soon as possible. The nuns nurtured his artistic talents—talents mocked by his uncle, his cousins, his neighbors, and in particular, mocked by the other black boys who regularly pummeled Joe not only for being a bastard, but also for carrying a painter's box.

Sister Jericho, a black teacher from Barbados, had shoved Joe through junior high and high school, and through some machinations that the monsignor knew now had to have been considerable, if not miraculous, Joe received a scholarship to study at the London School of Art. While there, a priest, a visiting curator for the Vatican Museum, had given a lecture on the art of reliquaries and Joe had become obsessed with relics, finally realizing that to study them up close, he would have to become a priest.

So, he did. In later years, when telling the story to his peers, they marveled at the determination and motivation of a young mixed race student to join holy orders. None of them would ever understand. Not one had experienced regular beatings by boys who saw no future for themselves, and who had bombarded their unvoiced despair onto a skinny kid who did not share their bleak outlook. One of those boys, a budding psychopath, had chopped off two fingers from young Joe's left hand with a switchblade, an incident that had shocked the miscreant more than Joe, and thereafter Joe had been left alone.

It helped that Joe had never had any desire for women or men, and the thought of children as sex objects had never occurred to him. When the scandals connected to pedophilic priests erupted, he was so horrified he had almost left the church.

Once these same peers realized that Joe, now Giuseppe, had no political ambition, they had helped him achieve his goal: becoming a curator at the Vatican Museum. There he had been for thirty years, studying relics and the reliquaries that held them. His life was replete with devotion, art, and debates on how best to repair gold that was a millennium old.

Then, while examining an old document from the early 1600s, he saw a drawing of a small reliquary, and recognized it as the object an army captain had tried to sell to him in 1969. The Vatican's inventory showed the object still resident at the Convent of Corbie's church.

"The reliquary isn't in the church," he told the head curator. "I saw it in 1969."

It had taken two years to persuade the bureaucracy that controlled such things to bring the altar to Rome.

He had not been there when the altar was opened and the formal inventory was taken, and once he received word that "Giuseppe's reliquary," as the other curators called it, wasn't in the altar, his story from 1969 was fully believed. He was given open access to the archives to research what had happened to this seemingly insignificant object. Perhaps it would be found, perhaps not, but anytime the Vatican thought one of their irreplaceable artworks had been stolen, Interpol was called. The last location of the reliquary was shared, and Monsignor Ogier began his research.

For ten days, the monsignor scoured the archives to find references to the reliquary, focusing on the most obscure and ancient documents. Just as he had begun to comprehend the story of the small wooden box, the researchers working on the altar became ill, and all of his access to the archives was closed down.

It didn't matter though. He had found what little was there.

The monsignor read the certification again, noting the testimony of a Sister Anne from the Convent of Corbie and of two Huguenot women imprisoned there, who later returned to the Catholic faith. The conclusion of the local bishop was that a miracle had occurred, and that the Holy Spirit moved the Huguenot women to recant their faith and become Catholics. No mention was made of Marin Postel, who certainly had not recanted, and who had been the catalyst for the miracle.

He stood up and went to the desk by the window where the transcript of the interview with Kate Strong lay. He had not been shocked at Anton Bunin's goal. Let him try to spread some ancient disease through the Middle East. Monsignor Ogier had the cure.

He had already taken steps to obtain the original parchments found in the underground city in Cappadocia, as well as the results of Kate Strong's research. The government of Turkey privately supported the Vatican taking possession of the parchments. Dr. Strong's research, incredible though it might be, would go no further, and Turkey would not need to explain to the world how the Byzantines had attempted to sow diseases in France. The Turks' desire to protect an eight-hundred-year-old secret would seem comical to the Americans, whose collective memory rarely survived a single generation. However, Monsignor Ogier knew that if the research were made public, the Islamic hardliners would use it to argue that all traces of the pre-Islamic Byzantine Empire should be destroyed. Icons, portraits, churches, the Theodosian walls, everything connected with the millennium long empire would be destroyed if groups like ISIS had their way.

A rap at his door startled the monsignor. He called out, "One moment, please." He returned the binder to his briefcase and put it and the reliquary in the closet's safe. He straightened his robe and opened the door. A woman stood there, dressed in jeans and loose shirt.

"I hope I am not interrupting you. I'm Amarintha Sims. May I come in?"

He stood still, not believing she was here. He had received a call from this woman the day before asking if he would see her. For some reason, he had not believed she would actually show up. He had been foolish to request that the FBI quarantine the woman, and he felt his face burn as he thought about how ridiculous his request must have sounded.

The monsignor waved his hand to a small table near the desk. Amarintha went to the small table by the window and sat down. "What may I do for you?" he asked. The woman had a radiant glow about her, and she was smiling. She was very thin but did not seem frail.

"I know that the FBI told you that I touched what was inside the reliquary. I want to talk to you about it," she said.

Her directness surprised him. He had been expecting—what had he been expecting? A simpering caricature of a Southern woman? If what he had been told was accurate, this woman no longer had cancer. Was she another miracle that could be attributed to the treasure now in his closet?

"Please sit down." The monsignor motioned to the desk and they both sat in the uncomfortable small chairs that fronted an equally small table.

"What exactly is supposed to be in it? I suppose you know that one of my ancestors stole the reliquary from the convent in 1685. On her behalf, I ask for the Catholic Church's forgiveness." Amarintha was smiling at him broadly now, and he smiled back at her.

"Of course, we forgive her."

His heart was thumping and his mouth was dry as dirt. She sat unmoving, looking at him. He could now feel sweat trickling down his back between his shoulder blades. Before he could stop himself, his hand went to his collar to loosen it. Why would he react so to her? He stood and pulled open the heavy drapes. Could he open the window? He pulled on the glass, unable to open it, and he turned around, not looking directly at her as he spoke.

"Pieces of the True Cross," he said. "That is what our records show."

She frowned. "It felt like seeds to me. They were light-colored, like large grains of rice." She paused. "When I touched them, I felt—I felt something almost electric." She looked back at him, and he was visibly startled when he saw her eyes. One was green, one brown.

He sat back down, heavily. "Are you a believer, Ms. Sims?"

Her gaze did not waver. "A believer in what?" She looked down at her hands and spread them on the table. "I suppose a priest would say I'm an atheist. I don't go to church."

"That is not the criterion to be a believer."

She grinned. "Ok, then I suppose, I am a believer. How

could you study how life begins and evolves and not believe in something? You know that I am a biologist?"

"Yes, I do. I googled you after you called me."

She said, "Would you tell me what exactly what you do for the Vatican and why you were sent to Charleston?"

The monsignor did not reply for a moment. "I am assigned to the Pontifical Academy of Sciences. Our membership includes biologists, physicists, chemists, all manner of academics. I myself am an artist."

He could see the surprise in her eyes. Not many knew of the Academy's existence, or that some priests did indeed have scientific educations. "The academy has its origins in something called the Academy of Lynxes, formed in 1603. Galileo was that academy's first president."

"*That* Galileo? Didn't you guys end up arresting him?"

"Yes, but that house arrest afforded him the opportunity to write his greatest work, *Two New Sciences*. It was his final work and detailed thirty years of his study of physics. We have one of the few originals at the Vatican."

They both were quiet.

"The modern academy includes scientists from all over the world. We study the most intractable issues facing man, including climate change. People of faith should not fear scientific truths. Many Nobel Prize winners have served on the academy, but I am not surprised you had not heard of us."

She tilted her head at him. "Does the academy study relics?"

The monsignor felt a force from her, an indomitable need for truth that radiated from her body. This was indeed the essence of his life's work; his desire for relics to be subject to a level of scientific scrutiny that went beyond what the Shroud of Turin had been subjected to. That poor piece of cloth had been optically examined, dated with radiocarbon methods, chemically analyzed, and its pollen studied by the foremost medical forensic scientists. No, Monsignor Ogier wanted to understand the very essence of the Passion; he wanted to examine the Savior's tears, blood, and sweat held in reliquaries throughout the world.

"No," he said simply. "That is a matter of faith. It cannot be studied scientifically."

She leaned over the table. "Do you know what is in the MUSC report?"

He got up and went to his briefcase, retrieving a document that he brought back to the small table. He put on reading glasses and read aloud:

"The small pearl-like objects, thirty-three in number, are desiccated seeds from a previously unknown variety of *Amaranthus caudatus*. *Cedrus libani* fragments are present. Present also was DNA that appears to be male Homo sapiens. More time is needed to study these findings."

The priest finished reading, put his glasses on the table, and looked at Amarintha. She was gazing out the window and said, "Pieces of a cedar tree, seeds from an amaranth plant, and some genetic material from a man. Nothing in there sounds promising as a cure for cancer, does it?" She turned her head back to him and asked, "I don't suppose you would allow me to take a sample of the material back to the CDC? I wouldn't disclose where it came from."

Monsignor Ogier looked back at her, those incredible eyes steady on his. Should he tell her about meeting her father in 1969? Did she know how the reliquary came to be in the Sims family?

He wanted the examination of the relic to be at the Academy, in Rome, under the auspices of people of faith. The sweat still trickled down his back, but his heart rate had slowed, and he realized he felt calm. Perhaps they could help each other. He would give her one of the seeds.

He stood, but stepped on a loose lace from his shoe, and crashed to the ground, hitting his head on the point of the metal bedframe. He was on his knees, and he could feel his head bleeding.

"Monsignor," Amarintha said as she bent down next to him on the floor. He got up, ignoring her outstretched arms. "Do you want me to call 911?"

"No, let me just look at it," he said. He went to the bathroom and looked in the mirror, and saw he had cut his head over his left eyebrow. It was a nasty gouge, and would likely need stitches. Amarintha appeared behind him in the marble room.

She turned him around and said, "Sit down on that stool and let me wipe the blood away. Then I think we need to call a doctor." He sat down on a stool in the large bathroom, his head aching.

When she touched his head with her fingers, he felt a heat radiating from her fingertips. The pain vanished. The monsignor looked into her eyes and was alarmed to see them, staring and unfocused. Her knees buckled, and she collapsed onto him. With difficulty, he rose from the stool, and lowered her to the floor of the bathroom.

"Ms. Sims, can you hear me?" he asked. He gently tapped her face and then felt her neck for a pulse. It was steady. He tapped her more urgently, but she did not stir.

The monsignor stood, lifted his robe, stepped over her body, and went to the phone. "This is Monsignor Ogier in room 698. I need you to call 911. My guest has collapsed."

He hung up and rushed back to the bathroom, kneeled, put a towel under Amarintha's head, and rubbed her face with his shaking hands. She did not stir. Her pulse was still steady, and she was breathing, but unresponsive to his touch.

An old fear—black man with a white woman—fluttered against his gut. Would anyone think he'd attacked her? He needed to clean himself up. He checked Amarintha's pulse and breathing one more time, tried to wake her again, and when she didn't respond, he stood.

Monsignor Ogier wet a washcloth, and carefully wiped away the blood that had dried on his forehead.

What he saw made him stop breathing. The cut was almost undetectable. He crossed himself, and knelt back down by the woman. He took her hands in his and began to weep as he prayed.

FOUR MONTHS LATER

Rome

CHAPTER 80

MONSIGNOR OGIER FINISHED the oral summary of his report. He was tired and longed to sit down—or better yet, excuse himself. His fatigue was his own fault. He had refused offers of help and had written the report alone. "So," asked someone in the room. "Our Vatican scientists have finished their research? You believe that you have all of the seeds?"

The monsignor looked around the ornate room. Its walls were of polished dark wood, the floor covered in expensive emerald green carpet. His was the only garb of all black, although two attendees did have on dark suits. He wondered who these men were and quickly realized the suited watchers had to be lawyers. He felt like a black crow mistakenly put into a tropical birdcage.

"I have all that were in the Sims' reliquary. I have no way to know whether others exist, or will be found in the future. The ones I have are in a sealed container at the Apostolic Palace."

"What type of plant are the seeds from again?" asked another person.

"A plant called amaranth, which was widely used in ancient times as a cereal. Its name means 'everlasting' in Greek."

There was shuffling of papers, then another question. "If I understand your report, the genes activated by the seeds are connected with color of skin and eyes."

"Yes. Our scientists believe that the expression of these genes is what gives some people the ability to control inflammation in their own, and others' bodies. This can lead to spontaneous reversal of many illnesses. Only those with non-standard melanin levels are affected. People with vitiligo, albinism, or different-colored eyes. Mixed-race individuals could likely also have a response to the material." He coughed. "As the report indicates, the faith of the individual does not seem to be a factor."

"People like you," muttered one of the attendees. The man spoke louder. "You and the scientists are wrong, Monsignor. If a seed from the time of our Lord can cause some people to become healers, it will not be those types of individuals. It will be true believers."

The others shifted in their seats. None of them looked at the speaker. He was an old man, among other old men, dying they said, and none of his colleagues wanted to challenge him.

One of the attendees said, "Perhaps the monsignor could elaborate. You have a theory?"

Monsignor Ogier swayed a little and touched the surface of the gleaming table. "The FBI gave me a summary of the research of Dr. Kate Strong, the American scholar who was kidnapped and kept in Istanbul. The reliquary, according to the Byzantine records that she translated, had pieces of the True Cross. I believe that when the cross was recovered in Jerusalem, by Saint Helena, in the fourth century, seeds of the amaranth plant must have been gathered as well. Somehow the seeds became more than seeds as they lay in the reliquary. Remember, traces of human DNA were found as well."

He closed his eyes and added, "I believe it is our Savior's DNA, from the True Cross."

No one moved or even took a breath.

"We have a chance, using scientific methods, to scientifically prove that our Lord existed, and gave us the gift of life. Not just eternal life, but a better, disease-free life here on earth."

There wasn't a sound in the room. Why weren't they full of joy?

Monsignor Ogier continued, "I found multiple references, both from the Byzantines and our own Church, to the Convent of Corbie's reliquary. The Byzantines knew miracles had occurred in connection with it. They even noted the connection with pigmentation variations." He waved his arms. "The priest sent reliquaries corrupted with disease. The Convent of Corbie reliquary did not have any disease agents put into it, because it was already considered unclean. That's why the priests included it."

The monsignor brought his hands to his eyes. "It's all there in my report."

He put his hands on the table and leaned forward. "Do we have the right to keep these seeds from being studied? What if we can ease humanity's suffering? I come to you with the facts, but," the monsignor raised both hands to encompass the room, "you must make this decision, not I."

Monsignor Ogier sat down, and held his head with his hands. He wanted to cry, to shout, but dared not.

An elderly man at the end of the table sat with his hands on the surface of the grained wood table, hands that had not moved. He said, "Monsignor, you indicate that Amarintha Sims is cured of her cancer. What has happened to her?"

"She is in a coma at the Centers for Disease Control," said the monsignor without lifting his head.

"Let me think, and pray," was the only reply.

The thinking and praying lasted quite some time. No one fidgeted. No one got up.

After twenty minutes, the Pope said, "Destroy the seeds, all of them."

Charleston

CHAPTER 81

AVA TOOK THE key from Jack, and stood weeping in the front yard of Amarintha's finished house. Thompson had his arm around the girl's shoulder, the other arm around Fannie. Sara, Kate, and Richard stood a little ways away, silent, their heads bowed. For four months, he and Jack had done almost nothing but build Amarintha's house. Neither Ava nor Fannie had come downtown during the entire time the two men labored. This was their first sight of the house.

Kate and Sara had chosen wall colors, plants for the garden, and made a hundred other decisions they thought would make this house a home for Ava and Fannie. The kitchen had a pot filler at the gas stove because Thompson had found out that Amarintha liked cooking pasta. Over the stove was a giant exhaust hood, because as Ava had told him, "Mama hates the smell of cooking fish in the house."

There were custom mahogany shelves for all of Amarintha's books in a study that had French windows looking over the garden. Thompson had even bought her an antique sleigh bed after finding out from Fannie that Amarintha had always wanted one. He prayed that one day she, and maybe he, would sleep in it.

When he wasn't working on the house, Thompson spent as much time as he could with the two women at Fannie's farm. At first, all three of them would go to Atlanta to see Amarintha, now at the CDC. After a month, they decided to alternate weeks so she would never be alone.

He didn't know, and didn't want to know, what the FBI was doing to find and stop Anton Bunin. He supposed that if the Russian and Zora Vulkov were located, Brook would call him.

Frank was working to get Thompson a job as a consultant for CPD, but the effort required to learn the vagaries of the American judicial system were beyond him, or so he told Jack. The truth was that Thompson had no energy for law enforcement. When he wasn't at the site, or at Fannie's, he was in Atlanta trying to understand Amarintha's medical condition.

Amarintha had collapsed in the hotel room of Monsignor Ogier, and after the priest called 911, the paramedics took her to Trident Hospital. Fannie, as her next of kin, had been the first person to be notified, and she called Thompson and said, "Something has happened to Amarintha. I know you're Ava's father and so does Ava. Amarintha told us on the boat ride back to Charleston. You're a member of the family now. Come to the hospital."

He had rushed to Trident and found the monsignor, Fannie and Ava huddled in the waiting room of the Intensive Care Unit. "What happened; what's wrong?"

"She came to visit me in my rooms," said Monsignor Ogier. "She wanted to talk about the reliquary. I was going to let her see it again. I fell and cut my head, and she touched me. Then she collapsed."

Thompson had stood there gaping at the man who sat with Fannie and Ava on vinyl couches in a corner of the waiting room. Fannie stood and came over to him, "They're doing tests. So far, the tests show she didn't have a stroke or a heart attack."

The rest of that day and the next were a blur of hospital food, bad coffee, and doctors' reports. Fannie got the head of MUSC's internal medicine, Dr. Frances Kensington, a friend of Amarintha's, involved in the case. After a week of tests, Dr. Kensington had finally recommended a nursing home. Nothing more could be done, she told them. Amarintha's brain scans were normal, as were blood tests, and as the doctor said, "She should be awake. Perhaps it's psychological."

In desperation for a second opinion, Thompson called Dr. Gilstrom of the CDC. Gilstrom, deprived of access to the Vatican priest in Rome, agreed to have Amarintha transferred to Atlanta. There she still was, breathing on her own, but fed by tubes, lying in effigy in a brightly lit room where Gilstrom and his team ministered to her.

There were no secrets between him and Jack, and he, along with Kate, had become close friends. Thompson had spent many hours explaining the sequence of events to Kate, and the motivations of Anton Bunin that led to her kidnapping. She had raged about Adam Chalk for weeks, and according to Jack, refused to go back on her lithium. She would deal with life unmedicated. As she said to Jack, "I endured two weeks of questioning by the FBI without drugs. No need for them now."

The College had promoted Kate, and she was working with Atay to resurrect the project to study the parchments, although no one could find the originals. Atay, in a moment of genius, had copied Kate's work onto a thumb drive. According to Atay, he and Istanbul University were ready for her to come back.

"Oh, Mama," keened Ava. "I wish you could see this."

She couldn't see it, thought Thompson. Not in her comatose state in a room at the CDC.

The house was beige stucco, with white trim and black

shutters—just as Amarintha had requested. Jack had done the fine finish work himself, imbuing his regard into every carefully laid tile, each polished bit of trim, and every painstakingly selected plank of old pine flooring.

Ava took the key and opened the door. Thompson and Ava walked through each room, touching the walls, the stair rails, and even the doorknobs. Fannie followed, and Thompson could hear her sniffling. Jack stood just inside the front door, his hands clasped behind him.

Richard didn't come in. "I have something in the back yard I want to show everybody. Meet me there when they're ready," he said to Kate. He walked back to his own house, his head down.

Ava wiped her eyes and said, "Mr. Strong, it's beautiful. You did just what she wanted." Ava began to sob again. She sank to the floor and brought her hands to her face. Fannie crouched down to hold her, and Sara rushed past her father to join the two Sims women, all of them kneeling on the smooth pine planks. The three of them clutched each other, sounds of crying and murmuring emanating from the huddle. Beyond the living room were French doors that led to a small terrace, and Thompson walked out onto the tiny brick space, attempting not to cry.

Behind him, Kate touched his shoulder and asked, "Will you live here with them?"

"No, not anytime soon," said Thompson, rubbing his face. "My mother will come next week. Ava has an entire extended family that wants to know her. We'll take it slow."

"Is there any hope of Amarintha recovering?" asked Kate.

"I don't know. The CDC is keeping her comfortable. She's in an isolation chamber, hooked up to brain scans. Something is going on in her brain, but no one knows what. Her cancer hasn't come back, but the doctors don't know why she won't wake up." Thompson stopped talking and put his hand over his eyes. "I don't know why she went to see the monsignor, but I believe what he told us—that she collapsed."

Kate put her hand on Thompson's shoulder but said nothing. Jack walked over and the three of them left the terrace, the sight and sounds of Ava's keening becoming fainter.

The landscaper had created the bones of a beautiful garden behind the house. The pink camellias, purple azaleas and white roses were small, but one day they would cover the beds, grow up the brick walls, and encircle the garden with fragrance. A small table sat in the middle of a tabby patio. Blue pansies and white petunias bordered the little square made of seashells pressed into cement.

Ava had insisted that Amarintha would want a gate between her house and Richard's, and that gate creaked as Richard walked from his garden to Amarintha's. He cradled a ceramic pot, a plant sprouting from it. The plant was about a foot tall and was bright with red blooming flowers. Richard carefully placed the pot on a teak table.

Thompson heard the French doors open.

Richard said, "Please, come and see this." Ava, Sara and Fannie joined the group, all of them standing by the table staring at the plant with the red flowers.

Kate whispered, "Oh my God."

"Yes, exactly." Richard said. "This must have germinated from a seed Amarintha dropped when she opened the reliquary. I've been watching it grow by my patio since it sprouted. It bloomed yesterday."

Richard caressed the flower, saying nothing. "I don't know what this means, do you?" He said this to no one in particular.

Ava leaned over and breathed. "It smells wonderful, and look," she said, touching the petals, "it already has seeds."

The End.

ACKNOWLEDGMENTS

THE HARDEST TASK I've ever taken on was writing this book. It's also the most rewarding accomplishment of my life other than my family.

Thank you to Dave Walch who encouraged me to write a novel during a dinner at Ted's Montana Grill in New York City. It's a fitting city in which to begin a writing career.

Writing coach, Maureen Ryan Griffin, read an early manuscript, told me I could write, but that I had lousy punctuation skills. I hope she sees an improvement in both.

Editor Mary Johnston did a masterful job with editing. When we met, she asked me if I could take criticism. I told her I had sold software to New York bankers, and there wasn't anything she could say that I hadn't heard, and with profanity. She performed her job flawlessly with no four-letter words.

Kathy Tuten provided me with a reader's viewpoint, suggesting small changes that made a huge difference in the book.

Thank you to the beta readers who gave so many wonderful suggestions for improving the book.

Family members Katherine Marks, Lisa Rodgers, and Jay Johnson were also early readers, and even though they are related, held nothing back and gave me constructive advice about how to make this book better. Encouraging me every step of the way was my loving mate, Rick Denton, and siblings, Jabos Clement and Sandy Durham. My granddaughters Ava and Sara, and their mother April Johnson, were a three-woman cheering squad. Having a supportive family is invaluable to a writer and I deeply thank you all.

The folks at Gatekeeper Press were fantastic, and guided me every step of the way. Thank you, Rob.

My family does indeed have a Huguenot twig on its tree, Jean Postell (Potel), who escaped France sometime in the 1680s, arriving in what became Charleston, South Carolina. For those of you who are interested in the Huguenot experience, especially in South Carolina, I encourage you to visit the Huguenot Society of South Carolina's website: https://www.huguenotsociety.org

The letter that Amarintha memorized for a third grade project is authentic. The heat in South Carolina can still be unbearable, although with the advent of air conditioning, we modern South Carolinians have become thoroughly spoiled.

Although the characters are fictional, the experiences described in 1685 are accurate. The battles between the Protestants and Catholics during the 16th and 17th centuries are regarded as one of the darkest periods in French history, a period France calls the Wars of Religion. The events were gruesome and the atrocities, on both sides, deadly.

The tales about relics are also true.

The events described in Constantinople connected with the Fourth Crusade are accurate, except for the reliquaries seeded with disease. That part I made up. The book *1453: The Holy War for Constantinople and the Clash of Islam and the West* by Roger Crowley is a deeper look at this city, now Istanbul, and details the events leading up to the fall of Constantinople. It's one of my favorite books, and exposed me to a history I did not know. According to Wikipedia, it was eight hundred years before a Pope apologized for the Fourth Crusade, and in 2004, on the eight hundredth anniversary of the deeds in 1204, Ecumenical Patriarch Bartholomew I formally accepted the apology.

Both the Fourth Crusade and the Wars of Religion are an eerie parallel for what is happening today within Islam.

Human beings seem destined not to learn from history, but to repeat the same play with different actors.

Pray for peace.

CPSIA information can be obtained
at www.ICGtesting.com
Printed in the USA
LVOW13s0034291116
514867LV00026B/627/P